Josiah Bateman

The Life of the Rev. Henry Venn Elliott

Josiah Bateman

The Life of the Rev. Henry Venn Elliott

ISBN/EAN: 9783337332891

Printed in Europe, USA, Canada, Australia, Japan

Cover: Foto ©Raphael Reischuk / pixelio.de

More available books at **www.hansebooks.com**

THE LIFE

OF THE REV.

HENRY VENN ELLIOTT, M.A.

PERPETUAL CURATE OF ST. MARY'S, BRIGHTON;

AND LATE FELLOW OF TRINITY COLLEGE, CAMBRIDGE.

BY

JOSIAH BATEMAN, M.A.

VICAR OF MARGATE, HON. CANON OF CANTERBURY, AND RURAL DEAN;
AUTHOR OF THE "LIFE OF DANIEL WILSON, D.D., BISHOP OF CALCUTTA," ETC.

WITH A PORTRAIT;

AND AN APPENDIX, CONTAINING A SHORT SKETCH OF

THE LIFE OF THE REV. JULIUS ELLIOTT.

THIRD EDITION.

London:

MACMILLAN AND CO.

1872.

NOTE TO THE THIRD EDITION.

The favourable reception of this work, and the sale of many thousand copies, would seem to dissuade from any serious alteration or abridgment. This Third Edition, therefore, though considerably reduced in price, and printed in a somewhat smaller type, is not in any sense an abridgment, but simply a corrected copy of the original work.

———

PREFACE TO THE SECOND EDITION.

In preparing this Edition for the press, a few errors in names, dates, and localities have been corrected; a few sentences which unintentionally gave offence have been omitted; some explanatory notes have been appended and some superfluities banished: but the substance of the work remains the same. If it could have been improved, I should have been glad; and with this end in view, I perused the twenty-six different reviews, more or less elaborate, collected by my publishers. But the wide divergencies of opinion only caused embarrassment, and I was compelled to rest content with feeling gratitude to some of the Reviewers, and learning humility from others.

I almost wish it was allowable to insert comments on the book from private letters written by men eminent in every walk of life; but this would be accounted vanity.

Two exceptions, however, in favour of the two highest authorities of our Church in the Old World and the New, may be permitted. I refer to the late Primate of all England, and the present Metropolitan of Australia.

Archbishop Longley, whose name and memory are dear to the whole Church, having read the book, wrote to me as follows: "I have been very much interested in your 'Life of the Rev. Henry Venn Elliott.' Christian biography ought to be very profitable reading: I find it very humbling." This favourable opinion never varied; and in a brief but interesting account of the last days of his life, written by the Vicar of Addington, who was then in constant attendance upon him, it is stated that "his mental powers remained uninjured, and he was occupied unceasingly in reading devotional books, or in giving instructions about his Charge. His favourite books at this solemn time were Baxter's 'Saint's Rest,' the 'LIFE OF THE REV. HENRY VENN ELLIOTT,' and Mr. W. W. How's 'Pastor in Parochiâ.'" And the same writer adds: "He was very fond of Elliott's Life, and I saw it, and Baxter's 'Saint's Rest,' by his bedside after his death."

Dr. Barker, the Metropolitan of Australia, writes to a friend as follows: "Jan. 29, 1869. I have *so* enjoyed Mr. Elliott's 'Life.' I think there is a beautiful completeness in it, which makes it, to my mind, one of the most interesting biographies I ever read;—the boy—the student—the young clergyman—the beautiful married life—the heavy cloud—through all, the successful labour—those exquisite sermons—and the blessed end! The memoir has given me quite a different feeling about Brighton. I think of it now as CONSECRATED by his Life, and Ministry, and Death." He goes on to mention the joy he felt—alas! that sorrow should now be mingled with that joy—at hearing about Julius Elliott's first sermon, and at receiving the assurance that "he was treading in his father's steps."

The new feature in this Edition bears a touching reference to that " JULIUS ELLIOTT." In the Appendix will be found a brief sketch of his ministerial life, as introductory to his ascent of the Matterhorn, and his fatal slip and early death on the Schreckhorn. This event attracted much public notice at the time, and awakened wide-spread sympathy. The narrative, though brief, will be found, I think, deeply interesting.

I have only, in conclusion, to express a hope that the book itself (with this addition) may retain the public favour it has hitherto enjoyed; and that the good it has done, through God's grace and goodness, may be increased a hundredfold.

VICARAGE, MARGATE.
   Jan. 1870.

PREFACE TO THE FIRST EDITION.

These Memoirs were undertaken at the request of Mr. Elliott's immediate family; and all his papers, collected with great diligence and arranged with loving care, were placed at my disposal. I hesitated, for several reasons, but chiefly because of the pressure of engagements incident to a large and stirring parish. Great love and admiration, however, for the father, and a very sincere desire to please his children, finally prevailed; and the result is before the reader.

I have aimed at keeping myself as much as possible in the background, from a conviction that it is wrong in a biographer to use his subject as a lay-figure on which to hang his own opinions; and that, whilst many may desire to know what Mr. Elliott thought, few will care to know what the author thinks.

It will be perceived, therefore, that Mr. Elliott is the prominent figure in every group, and that the narrative runs on almost in his own words.

Some may perhaps think, as they observe how much the closer type exceeds the wider, that this has been carried too far. But they will find, when they close the book, that they esteem Mr. Elliott all the more, and know him all the better.

For myself, I only claim credit for reducing into order, and condensing into a small space, a very large mass of miscellaneous materials; for portraying honestly an admirable representative of a class passing away, alas! too quickly; and for endeavouring to show how a Minister of God may combine the Christian, the Scholar, and the Gentleman, and serve His Master truly and faithfully, without running to any extremes, countenancing any irregularities, or indulging any eccentricities.

The attempt to please Mr. Elliott's children has been one main object before me; but those who know how exacting is Love, how delicate is Friendship, and how retiring is Modesty, will best appreciate its difficulty. I have from the beginning reserved to myself a certain liberty; but with Liberty comes Responsibility. This, therefore, attaches to me alone, and not to those who trusted me.

I venture, however, to hope that I have not transgressed the proper limits; that the public will feel interested in the work; and, above all, that it may tend to promote, in an humble way, the glory of God and the good of His Church.

VICARAGE, MARGATE.
    May 1868.

CONTENTS.

CHAPTER I.

EARLY LIFE.

CHAPTER II.

COLLEGE LIFE.

CHAPTER III.

FOREIGN TRAVELS.

CHAPTER IV.

HOLY ORDERS.

CHAPTER V.

MARRIED LIFE.

CHAPTER VI.

HOME LIFE AND CORRESPONDENCE.

CHAPTER VII.

LATER YEARS OF LIFE.

CHAPTER VIII.

LAST ILLNESS AND DEATH.

CHAPTER IX.

SUMMARY OF CHARACTER.

LIFE OF HENRY ELLIOTT.

CHAPTER I.

EARLY LIFE.

His Birth and Family—School at Hammersmith—Mr. Jowett as Tutor—Studies—Traits of Character—Early Piety—Letters to Parents—Letters from his Mother—Preparation for College—General Reputation—Leaves Little Dunham.

THERE are men in the Church who need no prefix to their names. They are of all schools, and all callings. There is something loving or commanding in their characters, which wins affection, or inspires confidence. Such, to mention no living names, were John Keble, William Wilberforce, Daniel Wilson, Joshua Watson, and HENRY ELLIOTT.

Henry Venn Elliott was one of a numerous family, distinguished in various ways for their ability. His father, Charles Elliott, Esq., of Grove House, Clapham, and Westfield Lodge, Brighton, was twice married:—first to Sarah Anne, daughter of the Rev. Dr. Sherman, by whom he had five children—Charles, who filled high offices under the East India Company in Bengal, returning to England in 1826, after thirty years' honourable service—William Pearson, also a Bengal Civilian of great promise, who, at the age of twenty-two, was cut off by fever at Sennaar, whilst secretary to Sir Home Popham's Embassy to the Arab States—Sarah Maria, who married Dr. Hugh N. Pearson, Dean of Salisbury—John Sherman, who succeeded to his father's house of business in London—and Eliza, who died an infant.

By his second marriage to Eling, daughter of the Rev. Henry Venn, Fellow of Queen's College, Cambridge, the well-known Vicar of Huddersfield and Rector of Yelling, Mr. Elliott had eight children—Eliza, married to the Rev.

F. R. Spragge, Rector of Combe St. Nicholas, Somerset—
Catherine Jane, married to S. Brasier, Esq.—Charlotte, whom
the Church will ever hold in grateful remembrance for much
charming devotional poetry, and especially for the original
and well-known hymns, beginning :—

> " JUST AS I AM—without one plea,
> But that thy blood was shed for me,
> And that Thou bid'st me come to Thee,
>   O Lamb of God, I come," &c.

> " MY GOD, my Father, while I stray
> Far from my home in life's rough way,
> O teach me from my heart to say,
>   Thy will be done," &c.

Mary Sophia, who displayed great talents, with a well-
stored and highly cultivated mind.   She often acted as
amanuensis to Mr. Wilberforce, and was the bosom friend
of his daughter Barbara.   To her skill in shorthand, and her
gentle persuasions, Wilberforce's "Family Prayers" are
owing.   The bright prospects of her early life, however,
were darkened, as will be related in due season.

Then came Henry Venn, the subject of this memoir—
followed by Edward Bishop, now Incumbent of St. Mark's,
Brighton, and the learned author of the " Horæ Apocalypticæ,"
and other works.   Eleanor, married to the Rev. John Babington, now Hon. Canon of Peterborough, was the last daughter ;
—and Basil Woodd, who was lost at sea in H.M. Ship *Peacock*,
at the age of fifteen, was the youngest son.

It will thus be seen that HENRY VENN ELLIOTT was the
eldest son by the second marriage.   He was born January
17, 1792 ;   and at the age of eight years was placed under
the care of a Mr. Elwell, of Hammersmith.

Mr. Elwell was a good scholar, and turned out many men
of eminence and piety, such as Cecil, Jowett, Langston, Pell
Platt, the two Elliotts, and others.   But the religious
teaching, and the discipline of the school, were harsh and
forbidding.   All was suspicion and espionage.   The pupils
were not trusted, and nothing was left to their honour or high
principles.   One of Henry Elliott's contemporaries, recalling
these early days, says :—

I was myself so disgusted with religion when I left the
   school, that for many years afterwards I never opened
   my Bible, and never said my prayers.

It was well that Henry Elliott had seen religion on its other side. His early dedication to Christ in Holy Baptism; the hallowing influences of a family ordered in the fear of God; the instructions and prayers of a loving, sensible, and most pious mother; all combined to produce those good results which may always be hopefully anticipated: and, blessed himself, he became thus early, as all through life, a blessing to others. A schoolfellow writing to him after an interval of fifty years, says:—

I do not forget that early period when, as an older boy, you exercised a Christian influence on my young mind. There are ties which cannot be broken. The serious regard to religion which you and your brother fostered in me at Mr. Elwell's, has never failed me from that time to this.

And the Rev. S. Langston, of Southborough, whose name has already been mentioned, testifies that in all the years they were together—

He never heard a single word, or saw a single action inconsistent with strict purity and high integrity.

Henry Elliott seems to have been in those days a manly, affectionate, intellectual, imaginative, and somewhat masterful lad; and these qualities, leavened with religion and chastened by affliction, characterised him through life. His frame was robust and his spirits were buoyant. He was a good wrestler, and fond of cricket, skating, and all athletic sports; whilst in his class he was full of emulation, and for seven years stood side by side with a senior fellow-pupil, the one striving to gain, and the other to retain the first place. To this spirit amongst the pupils, rather than to the method of the Master, most of the progress made may be attributed.

In January, 1809, when seventeen years old, Henry Elliott was removed from Mr. Elwell, and placed under the tuition of the Rev. H. Jowett, of Little Dunham, Norfolk. The change seemed very pleasant to the Hammersmith and Clapham lad. His imagination began to play; and since his letters from this date have been preserved, he may well be allowed to speak for himself. He writes to his uncle, the Rev. John Venn, Rector of Clapham, on February 17, 1809, conveying his first impressions, and telling him that he enjoys with the highest zest his studies, walks, and employments. He thus refers to the immediate neighbourhood, and to Castle Acre, four miles distant :—

Passing through several rural lanes retaining vestiges of their summer beauty, and Sporle Wood with its little purling stream and ancient trees, I suddenly came on a commanding view of the village and surrounding country. I beheld with delight the ruins of the castle and abbey, and mounted the hill on which this extensive edifice had once stood. With the enthusiasm of the *antiquarian*, I fancied that here was the council apartment; there, the magazine; in one part the grand saloon; in another, the room set apart for royalty. As I stood on the walls, I fancied the soldiers mounting the scaling-ladders to storm the citadel, and hurled down by the defenders to the .bottom of the precipice.

After apologizing for these fancies, he turns to more serious matter, and describes a course of study which shows that both tutor and pupils were in earnest.

I rise at six for a lecture before breakfast; and with the usual interval for meals, recreation, and devotion, read regularly for eight hours a day. We have read with Mr. Jowett the "Funebres Orationes," and were very much pleased with Lysias and Thucydides. But Plato we did not like so much, except in the latter part. We are now reading Herodotus, and have finished the first book. I do not admire him so much as Mr. Jowett does, for though his simplicity is very pleasing, yet his lies occur so often, and are frequently so manifest, that as I read the history I am always afraid of being deceived, and can hardly give credit to anything he says. In composition, we have to write a copy of verses every week. In one I succeeded; and Mr. Jowett, who is not very bountiful of praise, said there were some purely Virgilian lines. The subject was " Dulce et decorum est pro patriâ mori," in reference to the death of Sir John Moore. I mention this through vanity. We have to write Latin themes, and translate, or re-translate, about thirty lines of Cicero. We read about six chapters of Tacitus and ten pages of Herodotus, and get off by memory about thirty lines of Homer. This is our daily business, so that our time is pretty well employed.

Among Mr. Jowett's pupils were the two Grants (afterwards

Sir Robert and Lord Glenelg), the two Cunninghams, Parry, Babington, Abel Smith, Stephen, Hill, Dicey, Farish, Pell Platt, Gisborne, Brereton, Gorham, Carus, and other men distinguished in after life. The tutor's opinion of the two brothers is thus expressed on February 14, 1809 :—

In nothing do the Elliotts fall short of the high-raised expectations I had formed of them. They are both excellent scholars for their years, and do credit to their late tutor. I feel great confidence in their principles, and trust their example will be a blessing to their fellow-students. Such pupils will of course work me hard.

Henry Elliott stood the work well, but his eyes failed; and we soon after read of the check thus given to his progress :—

Now that I am come into the field—the ripe field of Attic harvest—I have lost my sickle, and am compelled to follow with the gleaners.

Various remedies were tried, with greater or less success; but he remained through life both short-sighted and weak-sighted.

A few extracts from his letters about this time will serve to develop certain traits of character. He writes to his father in March, 1809, and the letter recalls the days of stage-coaches, outside places, hurried meals, and thick great-coats; and manifests a prudent personal economy, and a careful supervision, which did not leave others much choice in the matter :—

With rigid economy I have made the sum given me to answer, but I am afraid I shall not have a shilling left towards the expenses of my journey. I shall therefore have to draw upon you for the sum of four pounds. If it should be a fine night, I propose to travel on the outside to Cambridge, having previously provided for the night air by impenetrable clothing; and Edward, even, will have nothing to fear, being as hard as a flint. Our bed will cost three shillings, and I propose to be in London time enough for an early dinner.

The second extract shows how " the child is father to the man :"—

It would have some weight, if you would write to Bishop (his brother's second name), and caution him in a general way about extravagance with regard to books. Mr. Jowett writes to London for whatever books we desire; and Bishop, delighted with the thought of possessing a good library, sometimes takes advantage of this liberty."

Here we have clearly enough the "elder brother," and the "book-collector;" and who that has seen the groaning shelves of the author of the "Horæ Apocalypticæ" will not smile at this first quiet instalment?

In the next we have an affectionate description of his tutor, Mr. Jowett; and if a tinge of presumption is discernible, it may be pardoned in those early days. It was all worked out in after-life; and a real, not a fancied character, is being placed before the reader.

There are many men who would dazzle more than Mr. Jowett, but few would gain such unqualified esteem after intimate acquaintance. His parts are not brilliant so much as solid; although the vigour of his fancy may now be somewhat abated at the age of more than fifty, yet his strong judgment, rendered still stronger by experience, is at least unimpaired, if not increased. A close acquaintance with a person of such talents will be ever esteemed a blessing by those who know how to value it; but when those talents are accompanied by a simple and unaffected piety, producing as its fruit an exemplary conduct and irreproachable conversation, is not the blessing next to invaluable? May the merciful God direct me to walk in his steps, and in due time to experience that unruffled peace which shines in my endeared tutor!

The overflow of a full intellectual mind will be discerned in the next letter. His anticipation of the pleasure of the vacation was mingled with regret at the contemplated absence of his sister Mary. He says:—

I shall not like to forego the pleasure of your society. Perhaps you would take some delight in mutual study, in reading Virgil and Cicero, and in making verses, both Latin and English, and in a thousand employments, exquisite to those who have a taste for knowledge. During the whole half-year I have been employed in classical learning, and, as I wish to obtain more general knowledge, I intend to devote the vacation principally to this purpose. I think of beginning Hume's "History of England," for I am really very little acquainted with the history of my own country, and am perhaps culpably deficient. I expect to find it more difficult than the Roman to be remembered; as I think the characters brought on the English stage, though undoubtedly worthy of a record, are yet less conspicuous than those first-rate heroes of Rome who serve as guides upon the way. You begin with Romulus and Numa, which afford you light of themselves enough to bring you as far as the first Brutus, after the expulsion of the Tarquins. In the meanwhile, as you pass on, you observe, though not with the minutest attention, the five intermediate kings, till Brutus forces himself irresistibly upon your sight, and carries you on to Cincinnatus, who in his turn brings you to Coriolanus; Coriolanus to Camillus; and he to Fabricius, who bears a distinguished part in the Pyrrhic war. After this the bearings are so glaring and conspicuous, that you cannot miss your way, and are carried in safety to the Augustan age; and then the scene varies, and the minor heroes come on without any order. At one time five or six rise together; then a dark interval succeeds, in which you are guided only by scattered and glimmering tapers (if you will allow me to use the metaphor) in comparison to the bright sunshine before. Then you are in continual danger of losing your way, and are obliged (as in the case of English History with myself) to learn off the names of the emperors, in order to have any regular-view of the subject."

Surely this is much beyond the common style of a brother of eighteen to a sister of nineteen years of age, yet the buoyancy and brightness it indicates were quite natural. His sister Eleanor, referring to this time and a little later, bears testimony to that effect. She says:—

I must preface all I write by saying that, as a girl, my brother was my *beau idéal* of everything that a young man ought to be, and the standard by which I judged others. When I left school, and when he was at home for his vacations, the kind brotherly interest he took in the completion of my education, I can never forget. The usual routine of school had left much to do in the way of mental cultivation, and this beloved brother endeavoured to supply the deficiency by prescribing a course of reading in which he himself became the Examiner, writing out questions to be answered in a certain number of hours, and pleasing himself by giving me marks according to the accuracy of the answers. I have some of these very papers now in my possession, in his own handwriting. Mitford's " Greece," Paley's " Evidences," Blair's " Lectures," were amongst the volumes he chose. Surely it was not a common thing for a young student thus to devote time and thought to a younger sister. Those who scarcely knew him before crushing sorrow had nearly broken his heart, can hardly conceive the sparkling, gladdening influence he spread around us all in the years of his early youth and manhood. He was the life of all; and, amidst all his gaiety and lightness of spirit, there was a classic elegance in his jokes and fun, that told of a mind richly stored, and full of resources at all times.

A letter written Oct. 29, 1809, will give a little variety, and exhibit another phase of his mind.

"My journey to London," he says, "was pleasant enough, except that I had no companion to converse with. Two gentlemen, who sat close to me on the coach, conversed during the whole time on religious subjects, in a style which the world would call Methodical. However, as they did not address themselves to the whole company, I maintained the character of the author of the ' Antidote to the Miseries of Human Life;' that is, a continued taciturnity. The next morning, being Sunday, we went to hear Dr. Buchanan, at Welbeck Chapel. The subject was the ' Mosaic Jubilee,' which was to be followed by two other discourses, one on the Wednesday, for the ' King's Jubilee,' and the other last Sunday, on the ' Heavenly Jubilee.' On Wednesday, we walked to London from Clapham, and in the evening went to see the illuminations, which, in the principal streets, were numerous and splendid. As I had seen nothing of the kind before, I was highly delighted with the novelty and brilliancy that surrounded me. With John and Bishop I went down Bond Street, St. James's Street, Pall Mall, Charing Cross, and as far as the Admiralty; but, as they did not wish to see any more, I parted from them, and took a *solitary* walk through the crowded Strand and Fleet Street, and on as far as the India House, where the mob was so great that I endeavoured in vain to penetrate it. Thus enjoying the *pleasures of solitude*, I strove, with a mind undisturbed by the noise and jostling,

to penetrate or imagine the various motives for this great
display. They were the greatest at the Bank and the
India House; the Bank displaying 18,000 lights, and the
India House 8,000. But the India House surpassed everything, from the concentration of the lights in a smaller
compass and better form. I got home about eight o'clock
in the morning, and enjoyed a *very* sound sleep. On Friday
we were again at Little Dunham, with a new pupil."

This new pupil, and some changes amongst the others
occurring at this time, seem to have had a sinister effect. It
serves, however, to display Henry Elliott's firm and conscientious character. He was not one to yield, as so many do,
to bad influences, but was ready to grapple with and resist them.

"What I principally object to," he says, "are their topics of
conversation, which, though common to young men, are
not what I have been used to, or what I can endure to
hear. If these things are not left off, by one especially, I
intend speaking to him very freely on the subject."

Nor did this shrinking from "evil communications" arise
merely from a refined and delicate mind. It had a better and
a surer foundation; it was based upon religious principle.
The "life of God" in his soul, though not matured, had been
maintained; and much of the lowliness and meekness of a
child of God was combined with a diligent use of all the
means of grace. His daily study of Holy Scripture with a
fellow-student is thus described.

I read with S—— a small portion of the Bible in the morning
or evening, frequently both. As we read, we both offer
what remarks may occur to us; but as he has not had the
advantages of a religious education, that part principally
devolves upon me. Mr. Jowett has lent me a Bible, and
may God give me grace to understand its invaluable contents. Though I have some knowledge of the doctrinal
parts, I find my heart an unkindly soil to receive the
practical and spiritual parts; so that I perpetually go to
them, not because it is my delight, but because it is my
duty. I cannot exclaim with David, "My soul breaketh for
the very longing desire it hath always unto thy judgments;" but I can pray with him, "Open Thou mine eyes,
that I may see wondrous things out of Thy law."

To his father he writes, in 1809:—

It has been of late my daily and nightly, and sometimes

fervent prayer, that the Holy Ghost might pour His light upon my benighted soul, and open my eyes to my real state; that He would show me the evil of sin, and my need of Jesus; and impress upon my mind the great inconsistency of my conduct as professing to follow the commands of God. I have sought for true repentance, as necessarily preceding a holy life; and if I obtain this through the infinite mercy that is extended towards us in Christ Jesus, then I shall account my salvation nearer than when I appeared to believe.

And again to his mother, in the same year:—

I do love God, but not as I ought. My affections would rather fix themselves on anything than Him, and ambition and vanity have much too large a share of my heart, which ought to be His alone. My faith is very weak, sometimes at the lowest ebb; and then again it revives a little, through the merciful interposition of that Redeemer of whom it was said, "A bruised reed He will not break, and smoking flax He will not quench." In this arduous contest I have need of every assistance; and as the fervent prayer of the righteous availeth much, I entreat you, my dear mother, never to forget me at the throne of grace, and to pray that I may be enabled to lay everything at the foot of the cross, and to esteem "all things but loss for the excellency of the knowledge of Christ Jesus my Lord." I think He is still with me, still hath not left me, and has given me something of that peace of mind which infinitely exceeds the pleasures of the voluptuary, or all this world can bestow.

In the following year, June, 1810, he looks a little backward and forward, and gives expression to his views as touching the ministry of the Church, and the influence of his mother on his mind.

"The country is not so delightful," he says to his mother, "but that I can conceive something nearer to perfection. Indulging the fond imagination (perhaps never to be realized) that I shall be a faithful pastor of the Church of God, my mind stretches forward to the blissful anticipation of future scenes. I sometimes think it may come to pass that I shall enjoy the beauties of nature in some retired, perhaps romantic, little village, with a beloved mother; and that *the strokes drawn on my tender mind by her parental care* shall one day be renewed and retraced, to remain for ever."

Meanwhile that mother was watching him with the tenderest care and deepest interest. Her letters to him were singularly gentle and wise. Cautions were mingled with "comfortable words," and love illuminated all. She refers with regret, on one occasion, to some satirical remarks which he had made. They were unusual, and she fears that, if indulged, they may become habitual.

"For sixteen years," she concludes, "the watchful eye of a parent has distinguished you, Harry, by the appellations of 'mild' and 'gentle.' You are by nature peculiarly fitted to be a 'Son of Consolation.'"

She says in another letter :—

I need not remark, for well you know, what my intercourse with you has been. The endearments of infancy and childhood were almost unclouded; the anxious fears of a mother's heart were dispelled by hope ever brightening, and at length succeeded by the purest joy. And when adult age expanded the mental powers, and the smile of heaven dawned on the attainments of human science, how grateful, how happy was I, admitted to engraft the name of a tender friend on that of a parent, possessing your confidence, and sharing every pleasure you enjoyed. Such has been the unusual blessing of my lot.

And again :—

I have felt your filial affection my joy and treasure. I have only feared for your health and eyes. I thank you for speaking so faithfully as in your last letter. If in this instance you appear in an untried character, that of a counsellor, it has only been to prove that under the benign influence of the grace of God you will be, in *what is to come*, what you have already been in the past. Your dear father thinks of you with that pride and delight which I love to see and to share.

And again :—

The God of your fathers has designs of mercy for you. He has taught you to pray, and then heard your prayers. He shows you some glimpses of His beauty, and favours you with some taste of His sweetness. You see and acknowledge your own weakness and utter inability to persevere in the right way without a power that is from above. I offer up my thanksgivings and prayers on your account. Be not agitated with desponding fears. Although you cannot say at present that you have "already attained," yet be found in the path of duty, and in the use of the means of grace, and all will be well.

And once more :—

You, I trust, my Harry, have made a faithful surrender of yourself, and every power you possess, to God. You desire to be employed in the service of the sanctuary; and having attained all the ends of earthly learning, to lay them at the feet of your great Master. This being your noble aim, regard all the rest as a means, not as an end.

The same notes of love and joy are touched in a letter to her husband.

What happy parents are we, that Henry's success in academical pursuits is the least and lowest part of his praise!

An event which occurred at this time at little Dunham, tended to deepen these serious impressions. He tells it himself :—

This house is now the house of mourning. Mrs. Jowett died last night, and has left Mr. Jowett a widower, and seven children motherless. Her mind was almost always wandering in delirium, but in lucid intervals, what dropped from her was very satisfactory.

All the servants are weeping bitterly, and the whole village is mourning, and saying that Little Dunham never sustained so great a loss. I remember with pleasure that I never had an unpleasant word with Mrs. Jowett, or one that I would wish to retract.

The lesson this mournful dispensation of Providence teaches us is obvious, but important. Vanity is inscribed on everything mortal. We may be called away, though surrounded with friends and pleasures. We must appear before the bar of a just and omniscient God!

When hearts thus wounded had been somewhat healed, studies were resumed, and with more ardour in Henry Elliott's case, because Cambridge now loomed large before him. The prospect brought one serious matter to an issue.

"I understand," he says, "that the freshmen at Trinity are required very early after their admission to attend the Holy Sacrament—a custom surely in many cases highly profane. Mr. Jowett, when he informed me of this circumstance, very kindly advised me to receive it here, where I should have more leisure for reflection and preparation. He is of opinion that if a person can truly say that he desires to be 'Christ's' (and if that wish be true, it will undoubtedly influence him in everything), he is a qualified communicant. Tell me what you think on this important subject. It is my daily prayer that I may not receive it unworthily; and, from its retirement, I should like Little Dunham for a place to begin."

He made good use of his remaining time for study, and opened his mind upon the subject both to his father and mother. To his father he says:—

As the time for commencing my career at the University approaches, so does my fear and anxiety increase. I feel that great responsibility attaches to me. I think that when a young man begins the world, it is of great importance that he should set out well; for we generally contract at the period of from eighteen to twenty-one the most prominent features of manhood and old age. I hope for myself that I shall not entirely disappoint your expectations; but, on the other hand, I am sadly afraid you expect too much.

To his mother he says:—

I am afraid I shall never like the mathematics. When a young man has passed his time constantly in classics, and has been paying his devoirs respectively to interesting Clio, to pleasing Euterpe, to dignified and pathetic Melpomene, to simple Thalia, to light and jokesome Terpsichore, to amorous Erato, to moving Polyhymnia, to beautiful and sublime Calliope, he finds it difficult to reconcile himself to the stern and more manly features of Urania, however attractive in her name. I hope, however, her good sense will by degrees overcome my prejudices. We begin Euclid to-morrow with Mr. Jowett, and I dread a discovery of my dulness. I have crossed over the "Pons Asinorum" alone, and have advanced along the first book. In mathematics, quickness is an indispensable requisite, and that, as you have often told me, I have not.

The time was short. At the end of June, he received his list of subjects from Mr. Hudson, the then tutor on his side of Trinity College, and he expresses his pleasure that they came before the dog-days! The subjects were the Prometheus Vinctus of Æschylus,. the three Orations of Demosthenes, the second and third Georgics, the first six books of Euclid, and first parts of Algebra and Plane Trignometry.

"This," he says, "the arena in which I am to contend with about seventy competitors, is spacious enough to admit of the display of all the ability I shall be able to muster between this and the time of action."

It would be easy to enter into further details, and thus fill up the interstices of his character, and show how he visited the poor, read with them, and sent their children to school; how he used his influence always for good; how honourably he dealt with his allowances; how wisely he chose his associates; how ready he was to impart knowledge; how sisters loved, and friends leant on him. But it is not necessary. Enough has been said to give a good idea of his early life, and to inspire interest, it may be hoped, in his future course. That he left Little Dunham with an unsullied character, one final extract from the reminiscences of a fellow-pupil will suffice to prove.

There was much amongst our companions that was base and vile; and had I been left only to the influence of such, I tremble to think what might have been the consequences. But I had a tower of strength in Henry and Edward Elliott. Henry stood pre-eminent for everything that was good, morally, intellectually, and physically. I had often occasion to admire his manly, lofty spirit, which, supported by high Christian principle, great ability, and no small share of personal prowess, exercised a powerful control over the licentious and profane amongst us.

And now this scene of life may be allowed to pass away like some dissolving view. The ruined castle and abbey grow indistinct; the village church and rural lanes,

"Where the blue-bell and gowan lurk lowly unseen,"

fade out of sight; the little river winding through the valley becomes a wreath of mist; the groups of students mingle and disappear, and when Henry Elliott is seen again, he is in his rooms at Trinity College, Cambridge.

CHAPTER II.

COLLEGE LIFE.

Goes into Residence at Trinity—First Impressions—First Check—First Friends—Dr. Jowett—Bickersteth—Contest for Senior Wranglership— Elected Scholar—College Examination—Long Vacation at Ampton— Formation of Cambridge Auxiliary Bible Society—Successes and Failures—Sunday-schools—Opponents and Respondents—Rev. Henry Venn—Visit to Yelling—Rev. John Venn's Death-bed—Takes his Degree—Gains his Fellowship—Chorus to his Sisters—Audit ale to his Father.

IT is desirable that every reader of this chapter should admit a few axioms, such as the following :—that there is no life like University life; no University like Cambridge; no college like Trinity; no learning like classics and mathematics; no place like the lecture-room; no honour like a good degree; no world outside the undergraduate world! These axioms admitted, the chapter will be found lively and pleasant enough.

In the month of September, 1810, Henry Elliott left Little Dunham, and in October, accompanied by his father, he entered into residence at Cambridge. His first impressions are conveyed in a letter to his mother, dated October 26.

My dear father has been very kind. But he is gone; and my uncle is going this morning, and then I shall be left alone, launched in my little skiff into the wide ocean of the world. My dear mother, pray that I may not be desolate; that He, who taketh up the orphan, may take also under His Almighty protection the child that is separated from his home, and cover him with "the shadow of His wings." Indeed, it is a momentous period, and will have a material influence on my future life. Mr. Simeon has been exceedingly kind. Almost his first words to me were, "Now, Mr. Elliott, remember that these rooms are always open to you. I owe much more to your dear grandfather (the Rev. H. Venn, of Yelling) than I shall ever be able to repay by attention to his grandchildren." I was prepared to expect something of distance, but I found nothing of the kind. . . . I quite love Professor Farish; he has so much simplicity, benevolence, candour, and condescension, that I no longer wonder at the intimate friendship that subsists between him and my uncle. Few men, I think,

have the dispositions of their minds more easily portrayed
on their countenances. . . . My modesty in Hall was not
sufficient to prevent me from making a hearty meal, and a
leg of mutton which was near me felt my courage, and
bore ostensible marks of it. . . . My rooms are very comfortable. The people of the house are civil, and ready to
oblige.

During the first term he experienced a severe check in the
failure of his eyesight once more. It was like the string for
the soaring bird.

"I go into the lecture-room," he says, "my heart burning
for distinction, and witness the success of another. I go
into chapel, where the declamations are delivered, and
hear the prelude to manly eloquence. I am athirst for
the same fountain, and when I look into the Cambridge
Calendar, the very nomenclature of honours fans the latent
flame. By this dispensation, may I lose all ambition
except in heavenly attainments, and learn the vanity of
earthly things, and the value of that knowledge which
teaches humility!"

His first friends were Fraser, Bickersteth, Brereton, and
Babington. Of the latter, who more than fifty years after
stood at his dying bed as his brother-in-law, and received
almost his last farewell, he says :—

He is a man of great suavity of manner, ability, and piety.
He was a pupil of Mr. Kempthorne, and, as might have
been expected, has advanced far before me in mathematics,
and I don't know but that he is my superior in classics.

Puckle, and Whish of Emmanuel, he also mentions, and
speaks about pleasant wine parties and antiquated tea parties.
Notwithstanding their antiquity, however, he was twice
invited to tea by Dr. Jowett,[1] and spent the evening in a
manner which may excite a smile from some, and a note of
admiration from others.

"I enjoyed," he says, "both times a mental feast. I would
premise that Dr. Jowett is esteemed the most elegant
Latin scholar in the University. He was so good as to
read a comedy of Terence with me during the two evenings,

---

[1] Dr. Jowett was Regius Professor of Law, and Fellow of Trinity Hall :
a man of high repute; a great lover of sacred music; a friend of Simeon,
Milner, Farish, Wilberforce, and of all good men and good things.

and this we alternately translated into English. Now I had never read a play of Terence in my life, and as I was called on to exhibit my knowledge quite unexpectedly, and both times without preparation, I was somewhat at a loss, and now and then blundered. Yet the pleasure I derived from hearing Dr. Jowett construe, far outbalanced my fear and shame."

Instead of remaining up for the vacation, he was compelled by the state of his eyes to return to his home at Clapham, where he spent his time in desultory studies, and was placed under the care of a skilful oculist. The mischief was found to be in the eyelids, and was attributed to overwork. Partially benefited, he returned to Cambridge for the Lent Term, when friends gathered round and read to him and with him.

"Besides my kind friend Babington," he says, "I have now another efficient friend in Francis Cunningham. He reads to me my lecture in Demosthenes, and I hope the benefit is not entirely on one side, for as he works at it beforehand, our mutual mistakes are corrected, and two are profited by the same exercise. To-day I heard of some Greek Iambic verses which I put into Mr. Monk's[1] hands. He conferred on them the honour of his approbation."

He unveils the secrets of the lecture-room in the same letter. One of his fellow-pupils of Little Dunham is the hero, or rather the subject:—

Poor ——! he was put on to-day to construe. The amœbean dialogue ran thus: "Mr. ——, will you go on, if you please?" "I have not read it, sir." Pause. "Have you read any of it?" "No, sir." "Do you mean to read any of it?" "Yes, sir." "Then you had better begin now." Oh, Dunham! how dark will thy groves be, and how deeply wilt thou blush in thy inmost recesses when thou art made conscious of this transaction!

Yesterday Bickersteth was ordained in our chapel by the Bishop of Bristol, our Master, and in about a month he goes to Acton, in Suffolk. With Bickersteth God will be, in whatever situation of life he finally settles. He has more than once occurred to my mind, when, in St. Mary's,

---

[1] Mr. Monk was Classical Lecturer at Trinity; afterwards Tutor, Dean of Peterborough, and Bishop of Gloucester and Bristol.

the preacher exhorts his hearers to pray that "there never may be wanting a supply of fit men to serve God in Church and State."

He soon enters into all the excitement of the examination for honours, and his remarks will interest University men, who love to look back to those early days, when hope was young and aspirations fervent. The almond-tree now flourishes, but there was a time when it blossomed. Henry Elliott is speaking of the examination for the year 1811, and says:—

The contest between French[1] and Dicey was very hard. After the examination of Monday, Tuesday, Wednesday, and Thursday, Dicey was about twenty-seven marks ahead. On Friday they were bracketed together, and Barnes,[2] who was appointed to examine them, said that he *could* make either of them Senior Wrangler; meaning that he saw through their strong and weak points, and that, by giving questions on the subjects in which either excelled, he could assign the victory. Well, after fighting in close contest the whole day, Dicey was only about his twenty-seven marks still ahead; for Barnes gave complete satisfaction by the impartiality of his examination. Now sometimes the Senior Wrangler has been 400 or 500 marks above the second, and a man may get fifty or more for a single proposition or problem. Smith's prize did not alter the face of the matter, for Dicey was first, and French second. I should have mentioned that poor French, about six weeks before he went into the Senate House, lost his father and a sister, so that his attention was naturally drawn off. The Senior Wrangler for next year is said to be either Neale of St. John's, or Jordan of Trinity; nay, report has gone so far as to mark out the Senior Wrangler of my year! Starkie of St. John's, says that "his father and brother were both Senior Wranglers, and he swears he will."

In April, 1811, Henry Elliott, through the favour of Mr. Preston, a Fellow of Trinity, moved into excellent rooms in Neville's Court:—"Sitting-room eighteen feet square, bedroom ten by six!" About the same time he sat for a Trinity Scholarship. His eyes suffered, but he succeeded.

"I thank you," he says to his father, on April 29, "for your

---

[1] Afterwards Master of Jesus.
[2] Third Wrangler; Fellow and Tutor of Queen's.

kind congratulations on my success, which indeed you have
thought too highly of; for it is, after all, no remarkable
honour.   I inclose you my two letters, the one announcing
myself as a candidate, the other of thanks for the favourable decision.   They will amuse Bishop, and perhaps
Mr. Pearson will peruse them with interest and indulgence
on my account."

In June he writes to his friend Babington an account of
his college examination :—

Our examination closed at 8·30 on Friday night, and from
three o'clock till that hour I was writing as fast as my
fingers could move, save a few intervals of transition from
question to question, not unlike the time occupied in
changing horses on a journey. We had two papers, one on
the Olynthiacs and the other on the Georgics. On the
whole I satisfied myself with my performance; but my
Olynthiac paper was the better of the two. In the morning we had Euclid, and question papers—ten questions, of
which four were "deductions." Some I did right, some
wrong. When correcting one, and getting it right, papers
were called for. $\phi\epsilon\nu, \phi\epsilon\nu.$ It is a great happiness that it
is over. I expect the Classes out on Tuesday, and I shall
go up to town directly that occurrence takes place.[1]

The long vacation was spent at Ampton, near Bury, in
Suffolk, where he read with Mr. Cotterill,[2] who had lately
been presented to the living by Lord Calthorpe.   There were
about six pupils;—two in the vicarage, two in the village,
and two (of whom Henry Elliot was one) in Lord Calthorpe's
house. It was all in the hands of workmen; but two rooms
which were finished sufficed for himself and a son of Sir
Horace Mann. Here he seems to have enjoyed himself
greatly; and here for the first time, by alluding to a young
lady "to whom he had not seen a parallel in respect of piety,
elegance of manners, and the cultivation of a fine mind," he
shows that he was becoming susceptible of such influences.
The lady, however, soon married, and passed out of sight,
and he resumed his former habits and customary expressions :—

"Oh that you could be with me," he says to his mother, "and

---

[1] He was in the First Class.
[2] Father of the Bishop of Grahamstown, now Bishop of Edinburgh.

enjoy the lovely prospect which is constantly mine, of Lord Calthorpe's Park! I should then admire more than I do the woods, the water, the flowers, and all that contributes to my satisfaction."

In July he writes to his sister Mary:—

As yet, I have not been able to acquire a relish for mathematics. But in a short time I shall be able to give you my opinion on Paley's " Evidences," for I have begun them. Now and then I find a little time for Latin and Greek. I cannot converse in Latin, but when I read it, it is equally intelligible with English, and Greek is not very far behind. All composition but letter-writing lies dormant. We have a great deal of interesting conversation at our family meetings, and sometimes downright argumentative battles. On these occasions we split into sides, marshal our forces, attack one another wherever we find a weak point, and generally come to the conclusion of the Abyssinian prince, in which nothing is concluded. However, we gain much by viewing the strength that may be mustered on the opposite sides; and as from our small numbers all of us who take any part in the contest are πρόμαχοι, we infallibly clash. I assure you, your sex does not lose its representation when represented by Mrs. Cotterill. Possessed of immense information (for I think she has read nearly every good English book that you would mention), she plants it well, and not unfrequently sweeps the field with chain-shot.[1] Pray remember that I am an egotist, and have talked so much about myself only in hope of a similar and equal return from you.

In the following October term at Cambridge, he seems to have taken an active part in the formation of the Auxiliary Bible Society there. The idea originated with the young men, who, full of zeal, were not aware of the formidable obstacles to be encountered at that period. The circumstances deserve a sketch. The consternation of the seniors when the idea became known, the opposition of Dr. Marsh, the absence of Dr. Milner, the pensive silence of Professor Farish, the fears, tears, prayers, and persuasions of Mr. Simeon, the apparently fruitless efforts of Mr. Wilberforce,

---

[1] Mrs. Hannah More used to say of Mrs. Cotterill, that she could never fathom her mind.

the contemplated postponement of the meeting *sine die*—all followed eventually by the presidency of the Duke of Gloucester as Chancellor, by the Chairmanship of Lord Hardwicke, by the adherence of the Bishop of Bristol and the Dukes of Bedford and Rutland, by the presence and bold advocacy of Dr. Milner and Professor Farish, by the winning address of Dr. Steinkopff, and the brilliant speech of Mr. Owen :—all this affords a striking contrast, and, as detailed at length in the " Life of Charles Simeon " by Canon Carus, need not be repeated here. It will suffice to say that the " H. E." referred to in that memoir is the Henry Elliot of this biography. It was an episode in his college course, and caused some interruption to his studies.

Apart from lectures, his chief reading this term was for the University Scholarship, in which he failed, as he did also in the following year. Three weeks also were spent in the preparation of his English declamation in chapel, for which he gained the second prize : Vice-Chancellor Kindersley gaining the first, and Mr. Ingle the third. The prizes for the Latin declamations fell to Sumner (since Bishop of Winchester), and Musgrave (the present Archdeacon of Craven and Vicar of Halifax). The remainder of the college year was given mainly to mathematics :—

"Last year at our annual examination," he says, " I succeeded solely by dint of my classical learning. I was conscious that I was inferior—very inferior—in mathematics, to some of my compeers ; indeed one of the Examiners told me so. At Mr. Cotterill's I did not read mathematics as I ought to have done, and I condemn myself for not paying enough attention to the pursuit, which was the express object of my visit. I am deplorably behindhand. Our next college examination consists of nothing classical ; and I am maintaining an obstinate struggle with my aversion to the study, and forcing myself to it. In less than three weeks I shall leave Cambridge, and the moment I have done with these complex figures that surround me on all sides, I will clear the table and indulge my natural thoughts.

"Mr. Bickersteth is shortly to be united to a Miss L——, of Kirby, an excellent person. The affair was transacted in two posts,—the first carrying the offer, the second bringing back the acceptance."

Having passed the second year's college examination, and a special note having been attached to his name, " particularly distinguished in St. Luke," he went for a time to Westfield Lodge, Brighton, where his family were then residing, and on June 12, 1812, he writes to his friend Babington :—

Home is a sad place for study! Here am I, who, by Slegg's account, ought to read through the whole of Dealtry's Fluxions during the short interval I am with my friends, have scarcely advanced into the third chapter! The weather is so bright and delightful, the downs and the sea so inviting, the pleasure of my friends'. society so great, that the mathematics—which you know were never a very favourite study with me—have assumed an aspect unusually disagreeable. My manner of passing the day is tolerably uniform. I rise about six; breakfast and prayers are included between eight and nine. From ten to one I study. At one I either ride out with my father on horseback, or accompany my mother in the carriage, or walk out with the party. We dine at four, and the rest of the day is given up to the family. I don't regret the time thus spent, for I feel anxious to be with my father, and to amuse him. I consider it a duty to strive to be the comfort and solace, so far as I may, of his declining years. Old age has many evils accompanying it, and in my father's case these are not forgotten in literary pursuits. To a Christian it must be interesting, as he approaches the confines of life and death, to view at once the insufficiency of this world, and the perfect bliss of which, a few years gone and a few more troubles past, he will be a partaker for ever. I trust to these feelings my father is not a stranger, and I find pleasure in making myself a partner in his pursuits and recreations.

He then refers to the approaching marriage of his sister Eliza, and adds, touching himself:—

I feel more and more that acquaintance with young ladies is delicate and dangerous. We cannot be too much on our guard, both on our account and theirs, and there is nothing in which we have to pray more for God's assistance and direction. Once, like a moth, I was willing to fly about the flame, and to please myself with its brightness, but I never suspected that its brightness might dazzle, and its flame burn. Henceforth, I believe, I shall not differ in judgment from you.

In August, 1812, he returned to Ampton, to spend part of a second vacation with Mr. Cotterill. He seems to have read hard. Ten strokes on the clock was the last sound he heard at night, and four the first in the morning. He felt he was gaining ground in mathematics, though to it he was "sacrificing all the desires of a classical taste, and medicining his mind by nauseous study." He became much interested in the Sunday-school, and on parting with his class in October, addressed them very feelingly. All were melted into tears.

"I blessed God," he says, "that something did seem to have been done; and I prayed that it would please Him of His infinite mercy to grant that the seed sown in the hearts of these innocents might spring up to everlasting life."

In November he was again in Cambridge, commencing his third year, and still employing his leisure hours on Sunday in communicating religious instruction to the young. Indeed, for a considerable part of his undergraduateship, he was accustomed to spend that day with a friend, then curate of Waterbeach, five miles from Cambridge, and to teach in his Sunday-schools.

The details which follow, written to his mother in February, 1813, may almost be classed amongst the "Vestiges of Creation," yet they may be interesting to antiquaries.

I shall have my hands full till March 16. In the third year of an undergraduate's residence he has to dispute publicly in the Schools, once as respondent, when he defends two mathematical and one moral subject against the abilities of three antagonists. He has, moreover, to lay aside the character of defendant, and appear as first, second, and third opponent. On Friday I mounted the rostrum as third opponent; and though I did not excel in the mathematical argument, yet in the moral I was complimented with "strenuè disputâsti." Nothing is spoken but Latin, and the respondent's battle often lasts three hours.

"My dear friend Snow," he adds, "has had another severe attack of illness, in which it has been my privilege to watch for hours by his pillow, and to minister to him. He is now better, and grateful to all who attended him. This will tend to cement our friendship."

On the 6th of March he writes to his sister:—

On the 4th of this month I rose to deliver my declamation in Trinity Chapel. It was in English, and on the following subject:—" Was Charles I. justified in not acceding to the propositions of Parliament immediately before the Civil War?" My antagonist was a man of sense, but extremely violent and republican in his political principles, and quite at home in his defence of Parliament. He has delayed taking his M.A. degree two terms on purpose that he might not lose his chance for an English declamation prize. Therefore I conclude (for my trepidation would scarcely allow me to listen) that his dissertation was able and elo-· quent. He has been so polite as to send me an invitation to dinner, but I doubt if I shall go, for I have my suspicions about certain lords who are his intimates. As for my own declamation, I am so tired and disgusted with it that I shall say nothing of its qualities. You will hear it by-and-by. Classics and my declamation have left me many degrees behind my competitors, and behind lectures also; and now I must woo the Muse with downright constancy, and make up my deficiency in love by the most assiduous attention to the old rigid dame whom I hate with all my heart.

The more I reflect and turn my eye inwards upon the nature of my mind, I am convinced it was meant to contemplate other scenes, and to find an enjoyment in them which I will defy a profound mathematician to comprehend. Yet these rigid studies, which I pursue from a sense of duty, will be of service to a mind like mine, given too much to castle-building, and the imaginary pursuits and occupations of my friends.

You ask me what is the most frequent train of my thoughts. I answer, HOME—whenever I am not studying and in company. Home is the companion of my solitude when I seek a refuge from lectures, and preparation for lectures. I do not think there was ever a being loved his home more than I do. I have so much treasure there, that my heart must needs be there also.

My friends here are all well—Babington, Cunningham, Snow, Brereton, Bevan, Lyon, Gisborne, the two Manns, the two Wilsons, Sperling, Dornford, Puckle, Carr, White, Whish, Neale, Grey, &c. But of all these, Babington and Gisborne are more my brothers than my friends, tho others more my friends than my brothers.

He thus comments on his position in another letter, written at this time :—

I feel quite happy now that the SCHOOLS are fairly overpast. Indeed, when I look round on all sides, and find myself surrounded with comforts I have not deserved, and friends good and holy beyond my expectation, I feel grateful to God for the disposition of my life. It is worth coming to Cambridge, if it were only to see the reality of a Christian life as exhibited in one or another of my friends. May God grant that I may be more like them in everything. We are expecting John Cunningham and Daniel Wilson down to preach the Church Missionary sermons.

All readers of religious biography will be more or less familiar with the " Life and Letters of the Rev. Henry Venn," who having laboured for upwards of twelve years in the large and important parish of Huddersfield, in Yorkshire, retired in the year 1771 to Yelling, in Huntingdonshire, where in the year 1797 his sun set without a cloud. So elated was he, ever and anon, at the prospect of death, that it proved a stimulus to life. Upon one occasion he himself remarked some fatal appearances, saying : " Surely these are good symptoms ; " to which Mr. Pearson, his medical attendant, replied, " Sir, in this state of joyous excitement you cannot die !"[1] He was one of that fine body of Evangelical clergymen, full of earnestness, piety, love to Christ, unwearied labours, good sense, and good works, who pleased God, and helped to raise the Church from the torpor of the last century. One son he had, who became Rector of Clapham, and the associate of the Wilberforces, the Grants, the Thorntons, and the rest of that band of worthies.

Both these exemplary members of two past generations are now brought before us for a moment by the pen of Henry Elliott, the grandson and nephew of the third generation.

From Cambridge, during the year 1813, he makes a pilgrimage to Yelling, and describes what he saw and felt, in a letter to his mother :—

I set out for Yelling in a gig with Francis Cunningham.

[1] To Henry Elliott himself Mr. Pearson said, " Sir, the joy of dying kept him alive."

The day was fine. The sun threw his cheerful beams on the dark foliage which concealed the village from our view, and all was still and peaceful. As we descended the hill, and then passed through the cottages to the little inn, I looked at each tree and shrub and footpath as the inanimate creation which had witnessed the domestic life of those whom I love. "These," thought I, "saw the infant years of my dearest mother, and these were the witnesses of her earliest joys, and amidst these she was brought up." My heart was full when we reached the village; and after ordering a rustic dinner, we walked out to see whether we could meet with any one who had known you, and had loved the inhabitants of the parsonage. We found two old men of the names of Curzon and Gale (I think). The former was blind. He talked with feeling of my revered grandfather, and inquired after you and Miss Jane with affection. With Gale we went to the church, but it was almost in ruins, and the steeple which once pointed heavenwards had been taken down by Mr. J——'s orders. "Sir," said Gale, "he was obliged to have a man who was a stranger to do it, for he could not get one in the parish to do it for him."[1] Amidst the ruins of these steeple-stones (for nothing had been cleared away) I saw the inscription which told me that my grandmother lay buried under my feet. The church walls were overgrown, as well as the churchyard, with weeds and nettles, and the inside presented a picture that asked in piercing accents—"Could this have been the loved and frequented House of God not twenty years ago?"

"Desolate was the dwelling of Morna."

I stood in the desk and pulpit, and afterwards sat down

---

[1] The publication of the details contained in this letter has led to an explanation by one of the surviving members of the then Rector's family, which will be deemed quite satisfactory, and is willingly inserted. It appears that the steeple referred to was in a ruinous and unsafe condition, from having been struck by lightning. The Rector deemed it necessary to take it down, but, unfortunately, he omitted to apply for a Faculty before doing so, and consequently the whole expense, both of the removal and rebuilding, fell eventually on himself. Whether the parishioners differed with him in opinion does not appear; but they absolutely refused to render any pecuniary assistance, and it was whilst this matter was in controversy that Mr. Elliott visited Yelling. Hence the state of things he found existing, and hence the old man's story—dwelling on results but omitting causes—as given in the text.

in the clergyman's seat, that I might think that I had been where, but a little time past, so many saints of God had presented themselves. From the churchyard we went to the parsonage, viewed the little row of trees planted by my grandfather, the barn in which he worked, and the palings turned by " Master John," as Gale said. " For," he added, " Mr. Venn never cared to refuse his son anything that he set his heart upon."

Fortunately Mr. J—— and his wife were absent, and the door of the rectory opened with a silver key. We went through the parlour, and drawing-room over it, the bed-rooms, the kitchen where the people used to come to evening prayers, and all parts of the house. It is not pretty unless viewed in its associations, and then it is at once peopled with men of God, and full of heavenly splendour, life, and joy. The garden and gates are all altered. Time, too, has done much to deface the moral beauty once exhibited here. We were shocked to hear the voice of the blasphemer, and Mr. Cunningham rebuked him. We met with another pious woman who owed everything to my grandfather, and received her first impressions of religion under his ministry;—and then we returned to Cambridge with feelings you can more readily imagine than I describe. Such was my visit to Yelling.

Almost contemporaneously with this touching visit to the last abode of the father, he stood at the death-bed of the son —that " Master John " already spoken of:—

" It was a little after nine o'clock," he says. " The room was dark, and nobody was with him. On feeling my way to his bedside I met his hand, stretched out with his usual affection to greet me. 'Thank you, my dear Henry,' he said, 'for coming to see me. God bless you for all your kindness to me.' I felt that all favour was from him, and all acknowledgments due from me; and I said, ' My dear uncle, I cannot bear that you should thank me. I ought to thank you ; and I hope I do feel grateful for all your counsel and kindness, and the paternal affection you have ever shown me.' 'You know, Henry,' he answered, ' it was always my desire to have you for my curate at Clapham ; and whilst I continued in health, I looked forward to this ;'—and then he sketched a scene which is never to be realized. 'I should have taken the greatest part of the duty myself, and then I should have freely communicated with you, and given you advice about your plans and sermons, and I should have had no reserve with you.   But,' he said, after a long pause for breath, 'God sees fit to take me from this life, and His will be done. Here He has dealt very graciously with me.   He has given me, even in a temporal sense, everything I could desire—a comfortable income—the kindest friends—the most dutiful and affectionate of families; and now I leave these things, and have a journey to perform.   I feel that I must soon enter Jordan, and in the passage I shall put off this corruptible, this body of infirmity and hindrance, and enter, through Jesus my forerunner, into the promised land!   Henry, when you return to college, do not suffer your pursuits to draw away your heart from God!   And when my own dear boy is there, watch over him, guide him, and admonish him in the Lord.   I believe you are seeking the favour of God; only persevere, and you shall have it.'   After another pause for breath, he continued: 'And now, my dear Henry, I shall see you no more in the flesh, but I would fain hope and believe that I shall meet you again—it will be in heaven—to part no more—to be for ever with the Lamb!'

"'It is a great comfort,' I replied, 'to me, my dear uncle, that though I may not see you again here, I leave you in the hands of your God, whom you have served so faithfully.'

"'Oh no, don't say so, Henry,' he replied. 'I have served Him very unfaithfully, and very imperfectly.   My trust is in His great mercy, and in the blood of Christ, which cleanseth from all sin.   No,' he continued, 'if I were to choose my own epitaph, I would have engraven on my tomb that passage from the Ephesians' (iii. 8, 9), quoting the Greek, ἐμοὶ τῷ ἐλαχιστοτέρῳ, κ. τ. λ.

"'Henry, you are going to take Holy Orders, as I have done. While you are in health, and before sickness comes, let it be your sole and earnest business to preach the Gospel, to teach, exhort, reprove. . . . Put your fellow-creatures in mind of heavenly things, and direct their eyes to the Saviour of the world.   And that these things may suitably affect even yourself, meditate often on death, judgment, and eternity.   You will know when you come to a death-bed how little everything else appears. Oh, Henry, pray! pray! pray! Be ceaseless and importunate in prayer and in using the means of grace. You have but one thing to do; do it with all your might. I have not breath to go on.' And then he bade me farewell, kissed me, and gave me his blessing, saying, 'May God Almighty be with you, and strengthen and comfort you. Amen, Amen.'

" I fell upon his neck again, and kissed him, sorrowing most of all for that he said, 'Ye shall see my face no more.' "

The Rev. John Venn, of Clapham, died in July, 1813: and thus the threads of three generations were entwined together for a time. Henry Elliott stood at the grave of his grandfather, and sat by the dying bed of his uncle; and now he too is gone, and the place which once knew him knows him no more. And thus before long will the pen fall from the hand of the writer, and the book from the hand of the reader. May we then be hidden in the clift of the Rock! May we "die the death of the righteous, and our last end be like his! "

But we must return from meditative, into active life. The last long vacation was spent by Henry Elliott at Cambridge in hard reading. He was called in October to vacate his rooms in Neville's Court; but being entitled to rooms as a Trinity Scholar, it caused him but little inconvenience, and not half so much anxiety as the prospect of his examination.

In a letter inscribed " Mater amata," he says :—

A thousand thanks for your letter. It was sweeter to me than the sweetest strains of ancient poetry that beguile my solitary hours. I am now reading very hard, and with far more doubt and anxiety than I either ought or wish to feel. I assure you I think the matter very uncertain.

With these lowered expectations (the best auguries of success), he entered the Senate House in January, 1814, for his final examination, and came out fourteenth wrangler !

When it is remembered that this is the man who was seen slowly passing over the " pons asinorum " at the end of 1810, and who was heard mourning over the premature vacation of

1811, because he had hoped to read the first six books of Euclid before going up to Cambridge, the result speaks volumes for his mental power and indomitable perseverance. Mathematics were not to his taste—nay, he positively disliked them. He had at one time, when he found practically how indispensable they were to success at Cambridge, entertained the idea of migrating to Oxford; but his mother and his wise friends dissuaded him. His mother, with all the spirit of one who was a daughter and a descendant of Cambridge men and clergymen in an uninterrupted line for a hundred years, says to him in one of her letters: "Oxford shall not have you, if I can help it." Doubtless it was perceived how important close reasoning and mental discipline must be to one who was somewhat given to indulge day-dreams, and whose imagination was always fond of play.

He listened to advice; he did violence to his inclinations; and he had his reward. None of his forty-nine mathematical competitors could have come up to Cambridge less mathematically trained than he, and yet he outstripped all but thirteen in the race.

But now his classics came into action; and a few weeks after the Mathematical Tripos, he went in for the Gold Medal. There was then no Classical Tripos. The contention was for the gold medals, which were then and are still given every year, to the two best classics who have taken mathematical honours. Millett of Trinity now gained the first, and Henry Elliott the second. He himself describes the result of the examination in a letter to his mother, dated March 16, 1814:—

You will join with me in thanking Almighty God for crowning me with success. This morning I was elected second Medallist. Mr. Millett, who is one below me on the Tripos, and a friend of Mr. Dealtry's, has the first medal. The candidates were six in number, being those amongst the Wranglers and Senior Optimes of this year who thought they had any chance of success. Pray for me that I may be thankful, and that whatever influence or respectability may attach to my character from this event may be devoted to Him to whom it is due. I understand that at the Commencement I shall be presented with a gold medal of the value of fifteen guineas. On Thursday I have to declaim in Latin in the Schools; this is an exercise attached to the medal. On Friday (D.V.) I hope to visit you all.

A recapitulation of some of these matters, and a relation of others, is pleasantly made by Archdeacon Musgrave, his contemporary and friend. The reader will appreciate the details :—

"I believe," he says, "that throughout Elliott's whole time in college he never allowed anything to break in upon the sacredness of the Sunday, as a day devoted to religious study, when not occupied in religious worship or teaching. Elliott, Babington, the two Wilsons, and others—and, in a minor degree, myself—were the originators of a very wonderful meeting of the Bible Society. I well recollect, too, our taking a public part in another meeting, for, I believe, the Church Missionary Society,—the only time, probably, when we either of us appeared on the stage at the theatre in Barnwell.

"Well, we passed through the remainder of our undergraduateship together as friends, took our degree the same day, and both sat for the Chancellor's Medals. Six went in for them—Millett and Elliott, the successful candidates; Kindersley (Vice-Chancellor), Walker (late Head Master of Leeds School), Pearson (Fellow and Tutor of Emmanuel, and Christian Advocate), and myself. The most perfect good feeling prevailed at the time, and was never for one moment interrupted afterwards; all acquiescing with entire good faith in the adjudication of the prizes. I believe I was the first to communicate to them both the intelligence of their success."

Professor Sedgwick adds his valuable testimony as follows :—

Though full of the buoyant spirits which too often have led young men into words and deeds of folly, he never seemed to forget his principles. His conversation and his life were so pure that his moral influence, after I had the happiness of knowing him, was always in a good direction, restraining from evil, and urging on what was good and truly valuable to a young student. And his high spirits and genial temper gave a charm to his life which made me at once to love him as a friend and to honour him (though considerably younger than myself) as if he had been my senior, a kind of elder brother.

The edifice of University honours had better be crowned at once, and the chapter closed, though the progress of nearly two years must be thus anticipated. Having obtained the college prize of ten pounds, as a B.A., for the best essay on the character and conduct of King William III., in October, 1815, Henry Elliott went in for his Fellowship. It is rarely gained the first year, and there was no exception in his case.

"You left me," he says to his friend Babington, "in the middle of my examination on Tuesday morning. The following day produced a stiff passage from Thucydides, which I had not seen, to be translated into English prose, and a Greek chorus into English verse; also, in the afternoon, a miscellaneous question paper. On Wednesday the examination closed with a paper on metaphysics. 1 sat up the whole night to refresh my little stock; and the trial, and my strength and spirits, came to the same absolute termination together. On Thursday I went to town, and on Saturday returned to Cambridge. On October 1, Amos, J. Romilly, Scholefield, and Kindersley were elected Fellows. Hudson informs me that the examiners were well pleased with our year,[1] which had trod on the heels of the other, and would have secured, it is conjectured, two of the Fellowships, if the papers of the candidates had furnished the only criterion. Kindersley was the first of both years. Hudson tells me that I stood second, if not first, of the unsuccessful ones, and that he considered me certain of a Fellowship, if only there should be two vacancies next year."

Mr. Hudson, the tutor, was right. On October 1, 1816, Henry Elliott writes to Mr. Babington :—

I have great reason to be thankful that this morning has crowned all my literary hopes with the highest honour to which I ever aspired. I was elected Fellow at nine o'clock. Walker and Musgrave are both elected with me. Five of our year, viz., Croft and Lodge, besides ourselves, decidedly excelled the year below us, including Waddington! Indeed,

---

[1] All the above, save Kindersley, late Vice-Chancellor, were of the year before, and most distinguished men :—Amos, the eminent barrister; Romilly, Registrar of the University; and Scholefield, Regius Professor of Greek.

the examiners have complimented us very highly. The Vice-Master said he never knew a more satisfactory admission, except that, Croft and Lodge having acquitted themselves so well, it was a "heart-rending" thing that there were not five Fellowships vacant.[1] I did very ill in my mathematics, but my classics, metaphysics, and history righted the poor vessel.

He adds further particulars in a letter to his mother of October 4 :—

I have just heard one of the most pleasing testimonies that have been given to the manner in which we have acquitted ourselves. It is the custom to meet over-night at the Master's (Bishop Mansell) lodge, and there and then to settle who shall be elected the next morning. Sometimes, of course, the matter is long and vigorously disputed. On this occasion one of the examiners told Musgrave that the whole business was settled in seven minutes—as short a time as it was possible to inspect the necessary college books, and ask the votes. No other names were mentioned except ours, and not a doubtful word was said respecting character or circumstances. The examination was too decisive to admit of these being taken into consideration. For my sister's amusement I subjoin a translation I wrote of a Greek chorus in Sophocles. It was a race by my Muse against time, and the exercise was written, and the fair copy made, in one hour and, three-quarters exactly.

"STROPHE.

"Stranger! thy wandering steps have led
  Where white Colonus rears his head;
  Where best thine ear may list the gale
  That vibrates in the night-bird's wail;
  Where best thine eye may view the scene,
  That, mantled round with thicket green
    And foliage dark of ivy,
  And laurel branches clust'ring high,
  Impervious to the curious eye,
    Is vocal with her minstrelsy.
  This screen—in vain the sun essays
  To pierce it with his noontide rays;
  Here peace and solemn stillness reign,
  And Bacchus with his festal train
    Here celebrates his revelry.

---

[1] Croft was afterwards elected Fellow of Christ's; and Lodge, Fellow of Magdalene, and Librarian of the University.

"ANTI-STROPHE.

"Here, fed by Heaven's perennial dew,
 The crocus blooms, of golden hue:
And here the flower that bears thy name,
Narcissus! still supports its fame:
For this the chaplets bright among,
On tutelary statues hung,
    The first and chief was seen:
Here fountains play and meads around
    Echo the ever-wakeful sound.
Cēphīsus, too, meandering
O'er the broad plain, profusion scatters,
And downwards rolls his limpid waters;
But chief, amidst our guardian powers,
Shine, dancing in our native bowers,
The Muses and the Muses' Queen." [1]

Whilst this chorus was sent to his sisters, seven dozen of Trinity audit ale were sent to his father, as the "first-fruits of his Fellowship;" and in the letter announcing it, his brother Edward inserts a paragraph:—"We have been walking round the Trinity Fellows' garden. (N.B. Henry likes to walk there!!!) Good night!"

CHAPTER III.

FOREIGN TRAVELS.

Effects of College Life and Honours—Offers made to him—Relaxation—Dr. Chalmers—Mr. Snow and his influence—Curacies of Harrow, Preston, and Godstone—Letters—Morbid state of Mind—Preparation for leaving England—Leaves England—Switzerland—Great St. Bernard—Testimony of Mr. Moncrieff—Venus de' Medici—Rome—Naples, Pompeii—St. Peter's—Mariolatry—Joined by his brother Edward—Greece—Asia Minor—Jerusalem—Traditions—Samaria—Nazareth—Bedouin Arabs—Perils by Land and by Water—Collections—Return to England.

COLLEGE life, entwined with University honours, is an ordeal through which few pass unhurt. Both soul and body feel the strain. Character may be maintained, but religion suffers. The fruit may still be good, but the bloom is gone. Henry Elliott felt and mourned over this, and it led him to pause long before he took the next step in life.

[1] Note by Henry Elliott—

"Me quoque vatem
Dicunt pastores: sed non ego credulus illis."—VIRGIL.

He had scarcely left the Senate House, after receiving his degree of B.A., when Professor Monk sent for him, and in the name of Dr. Butler, Head Master of Harrow, offered him an Assistant Mastership in that distinguished public school. It would have been worth 500*l.* per annum; and he thought of his many brothers and sisters, and greatly wished to be able to dispense with his father's continued and liberal allowance. But, on the other hand, he dreaded the temptations inseparable from such a post, and felt too young to take the stand that would be expected from him. He feared, also, that the duties required from him would interfere with his reading for the Fellowship, which was then his primary object. After taking counsel, therefore, with a few choice friends, he declined the offer.

Another was made to him about the same time, rather more out of the usual course, viz., the Professorship of Theology and Classics in Hayti. This was offered by a black gentleman, a Mr. Saunders, introduced to him by the Hon. C. Shore. The terms were 800*l.* per annum, and a prospective offer of the bishopric, intended to be founded for the island in connexion with the Church of England. He smiled and declined it, and finally resolved to read at Cambridge for his Fellowship; to take pupils; to spend his long vacations in choice country spots; and, besides enjoying the intimacy of his own family, to cultivate the society of such friends as Hannah More, the Wilberforces, the Hoares, and the Trevelyans.

This plan was carried out, and he alludes in some of his letters to a summer spent at Chepstow, and to a Bible meeting at which, under Mrs. Hannah More's auspices, he took part.

"I spoke," he says, "for twenty minutes without hesitation, and then I suddenly lost all my ideas for a time, and had my senses only recalled by the compassionate cheers of my audience. You will say I must have had a face of brass to speak before Mrs. Hannah More. But so it was, that her countenance and her manner whilst I was speaking were, to me, the most animating cordial. I was more struck with the wonderful sweetness, benevolence, and charity of her character, than by any brilliancy of talent."

His brother Edward had now joined him at Trinity College, and during term time he was glad to assist his studies. It was said at the time, of the brothers, that "their lamp went not out all the night." The one read early, the other late; so that while one was extinguishing the lamp, the other was lighting it. They jointly entertained Dr. Chalmers on his visit to Cambridge.

"We have had the honour and pleasure," Henry Elliott says, "of having Dr. Chalmers with us. Edward and I were almost his sole hosts. All his fire and genius are subdued in private, and you would never detect his latent talents, unless now and then by an observation of peculiar sagacity. His humility is most striking. Generally he is silent and reserved. He was extremely well pleased with Cambridge, much more than with Oxford. He gazed on Newton's statue, and examined Newton's MSS. with all the interest of a genuine disciple."

Several visits were paid at this time to his friend Snow, who was now in Holy Orders as Curate of Winterborne Stoke. Mr. Snow had a strong character and a grave, commanding presence, and he exercised great influence over Henry Elliott. A journal of every day, and almost every hour, during a week's visit, makes this sufficiently manifest. Henry Elliott was mourning over a cold heart, and affections estranged from God. He had written to his sister, some time back, and thus describes his spiritual state:—

I am afraid that my steps in religion have been retrograding since I began to read severely. Indeed, severe study is a very unfavourable soil for religion, though at the time it appeared to be my duty. I grieve to find myself so little consulting the glory of my Redeemer. The questions that occur in fixing the minutiæ of my words and actions are not "Will this bring honour to the Cross of Christ, which I profess to have taken up?"—"Will such a turn of the conversation show my love to Him?"—"Will such an action be as it becometh His disciple?"—but they all seem to point to the polar star of self; all concentrate in securing honour and affection for self; and SELF seems to sit on the throne of God.

In such a state, all I can do is to cast myself upon the Saviour, who refuses not the vilest, and to cry unto Him for a new heart and a contrite spirit. I hope that the greater opportunities I now enjoy, and the longer time to use them, will, by the influence of the blessed Spirit, make me dif-

ferent from what I am. Pray for me, my dearest sister; for
the present time is a time of darkness with me and of trouble.

It was with a hope that his darkness might be turned to
day that he sought his friend Snow, and he seems to have
derived benefit from their mutual fellowship and prayers.
The benefit, however, was not unmixed. Mr. Snow's views
were very extreme. He was scrupulous and impulsive, and
before long fell into error, and (though but for a time) seceded
from the Church. It was feared that Henry Elliott might
have been caught by the ebb-tide, but these fears proved
groundless. Further inquiry—which was naturally forced
upon him at such a crisis—as to the foundations of the Church,
her constitution and her services, only led to a firmer conviction that she was built upon a Rock, and stood "the pillar
and ground of the Truth." Several letters, now to be introduced, will abundantly demonstrate this. They refer primarily
to the curacies of Harrow, Preston, and Godstone, which
were pressed upon him by Mr. Cunningham, Mr. R. Carus-
Wilson, and Archdeacon Hoare, but are interesting in a
secondary sense, as exhibiting traits of character, and eluci-
dating this brief and unsettled period of his life.

The first is to Mr. (afterwards Archdeacon) Hoare, at Bland-
ford, and is dated December, 1814 :—

I thank you for your advice on non-essential doctrines. I am
endeavouring to follow it; and I especially pray that I may,
as much as possible, receive my teaching on these points
only from God's Holy Spirit. I have been on the brink of
embracing certain notions, from my great reverence for the
surpassing piety of certain individuals who held them. I
particularly allude to our dear friend Snow. I received on
Sunday a letter of two sheets and a half on the subject, in
which he discusses it with great earnestness.

The next is to Mr. Babington, and is dated June, 1815 :—

I can readily conceive the surprise and grief which you have
experienced upon hearing the report you mention, by the
anxiety I suffered myself, and the tears I shed when Snow
first announced to me his intention to leave our Church.
I was brought up to reverence the Church; and almost as
soon as I could lisp, I remember my mother used to teach
me some of our prayers, and instructed me in the nature of
our Service. What I admired, perhaps from prejudice,

I have since learnt to love and to venerate from the deepest conviction of its excellence. When I was in the North, the case of W. W—— led me to examine very accurately the character of our services, and the constitution of our religious ceremonies and Church government; and though I confess that the Church of England does not appear to me altogether perfect, I despair of ever seeing anything like it on this side heaven. My danger is rather on the side of excessive admiration. For I often think, when I reflect on the peculiar Providence which caused our Liturgy to devolve on prelates so different (save one) from the present race of bishops, that a peculiar portion of the Divine Spirit rested on those who composed our formularies, and shed a degree of inspiration upon the volume. I have always gone to church expecting to derive greater benefits from the prayers than the sermon, and have always lamented the wanderings and coldness of my heart at the one time more than at the other.

Having thus satisfied you that the report which has given you so much concern is utterly without foundation, I will next mention the only ground upon which I can conceive it to have originated. You know Mr. Cunningham has wished me to be his curate, and with the kindest affection has pressed the point in very many letters to me. Now, after much and painful examination of the state of my own heart last winter, I found that I could not with a safe conscience take Orders. My evidences were trembling and doubtful, and I thought that, in a Minister's case, his hopes should be bright and his evidences unclouded. I wrote to Mr. Cunningham to say so, and on that ground declined his curacy. Nor is it at all unlikely that from his mention of the circumstance, some may have construed my suspension of taking Orders into a resolution not to take Orders at all; and then, very easily and naturally, a resolution not to take Orders in the present crisis, and considering my connexion with Snow, would be converted into disaffection with the Church—though it is only *dissatisfaction with myself.*

Pray make Cambridge in your way to Peterborough, and I will then show you a correspondence with Snow, that will convince you I neither incline to his example in leaving the Church, nor to the opinions which have caused his secession.

The third letter, written to W. Carus-Wilson, Esq., of

Casterton Hall, Westmoreland, with immediate reference to the Preston curacy, enters more fully into the whole subject, and exhausts it. It is dated December 13th, 1816.

I confess I shrink from entering on a sphere requiring, as it seems to me, a high and exalted measure of Christian grace. Until November last, it appears, I think, to have been my duty to pursue my college studies, in obedience to the particular wishes of my dear parents. I am now released from this mode of life; and in preparing to enter upon another, even the holy office of the ministry, it is my steadfast desire and continual prayer that I may not rashly assume its awful functions. Outwardly, my dear sir, all may appear correct and decent (and I am sure I would thank God that I am preserved from bringing any manifest reproach upon my profession); while inwardly the contest may be very dubious, and even worse than dubious. I would not deny the goodness of God in inclining my will, above all things, to be reunited to Him, through our adorable Redeemer; but I must own that I think greater and clearer evidence necessary that I am really a child of God, than any I can now discern in my own heart. On this particular subject I had some sweet and consoling reflections in a letter from William (the Rev. W. Carus-Wilson, his college friend). But it is not that I expect victory to be complete over my manifold corruptions. I only want to see decisive proof that the victory will be ultimately mine, or rather my Lord's. I do hope to experience in a far more lively manner the " powers of the world to come " eclipsing the pleasures and deceitful glories of this present world;—to see in my own case this body of sin and corruption putting on, or beginning to put on, incorruption. I trust these views do not proceed from any sinful backwardness to occupy a difficult and perilous station. If I know my own mind, I would not refuse any post to which Providence might call me. But while I hope that I should not, like Jonah, flee from the presence of the Lord, I should very much fear to rush into it. And the same feelings which would lead me with joy to any sphere, however difficult, assigned me by God, would also lead me to tremble at taking the easiest assigned me by myself. My plan therefore is, in the first instance, to seek for some obscure and retired village, where there shall be little food for vanity, and much opportunity for a more intimate acquaintance with my own heart, and with Him who came into the world to change it, and to sprinkle it with His own cleansing blood for the remission of sins that are passed.

The ideal retirement referred to in the last paragraph of this letter was not realized, and it was well that it was not. Both mind and body had evidently been overtaxed, and nothing but lapse of time, entire rest, and change of scene, could restore their healthy tone. Henry Elliott's deference to the voice of conscience in the matter of Holy Orders is admirable, and well would it be for our Church if all who enter its sacred precincts and take its vows upon them had as deep a sense of the responsibility they incur, and the qualifications they require, as he had. But it was not on this point alone that the future looked dark, and that he felt inclined to take a morbid view of things. His correspondence, which used to be loving and affectionate, had become somewhat harsh and exacting. His friends complained, and he replied with floods of tears, and many apologies. Even his own home, the very centre of all his heart's affections, did not charm him as heretofore. Once and again he joined the family circle, and once and again he left it unhappy and dissatisfied. It was the voice of wisdom and common sense, then, which bade him give up the idea of the retired village, and seek health and restoration, clearness of sight, vigour of mind, and future usefulness, in foreign travel and new scenes. Half the mischiefs of the present day result from the fostering of scruples, the indulgence of morbid fancies, the feeling of our own pulses, and the looking exclusively on our "own things" instead of *also* on the "things of others."

The reader will be glad, then, to see Henry Elliott preparing to exchange the combination-room of Trinity, the intellectual gladiatorship, the Fellows' garden, the brooding walk, the period of indecision and inaction, for the society of the monks of Great St. Bernard, the free mountain-air, and the glorious panorama of the Alps.

In July, 1817, he set out on his tour, accompanied by the late R. Scott Moncrieff, and John (the present Sir John) Kennaway. He crossed the Channel to Ostend, spending two nights in the passage. He passed through Antwerp, admiring the cathedral. the docks, and the pictures.   He lingered at Brussels, visiting the field of Waterloo, plucking a bean-stalk from one of the greenest knolls, gathering some flower-seeds from a garden at Hougoumont. and cutting a walking-stick from Picton's tree.   In a *calèche*, purchased for the onward journey," he visited Namur, Liége, Aix-la-Chapelle, and Cologne.   He then skirted the banks of the Rhine, wondering at the lovely scenery, gathering up and sending home to his sisters the legendary tales attached to the many castle-crowned heights, and coming into contact with several interesting and eccentric characters.   Amongst these last he names Madame la Baronue de Krüdener as having excited a good deal of attention.

" She imagines," he says, " that she has a Divine mission ; and, as she exercises this privilege from the windows of her auberge wherever she goes, the novelty of a woman's preaching, in spite of an Apostle's express interdict, has excited much hostility.   My own opinion is that she is not perfectly in her right mind. . . . Her figure is of the middle size, but very thin ; her countenance is sallow and melancholy, her eyes striking and wild, her action impassioned, and her visionary fancies are mixed with so much religious truth that I can well conceive, to a mind not well poised with judgment, they might present an air of inspiration."

They had a long interview with her, and then passed on to Schaffhausen, Constance, and Zurich, as pedestrians.   From Zurich they walked six leagues to Zug, and four more by the lake to Art, ending the day by ascending the Righi.

" Our great object," he says, " was to reach the summit of the Righi in time to see the sunset.   By doing four hours' work in three, we succeeded. and ten minutes before sunset we gazed on a scene which well repaid us for our fatigue.   In the west the full orb of day descended in cloudless glory, aud wrapped the horizon in a glowing blush: whilst along the south. untouched by the rays of the sun, but perfectly clear, lay outstretched before us the whole range of the Alps and glaciers, cold and cheerless.   The contrast was magnificent.

" The next morning we left our beds' to witness the rising of the same orb, whose setting we had seen so favourably on the preceding evening.   We fixed our eyes on the same cold and cheerless mountains, and in a moment their summits were touched successively by the first rays, and by their illumination announced that the lord of creation was risen. After the lapse of a few seconds the sun rose full and majestic above our horizon also, and for a moment I was half persuaded to be a Persian. In a short time afterwards he shone on all the valleys, lakes, mists, and clouds, which were far below our feet, and seemed indeed to 'rejoice like a giant to run his course.' As for the Hotel on the Righi, the accommodations were sufficiently miserable; and, to tell the truth, many a time would I have been glad to change my bed for our coachman's over the stable, or to compound for anything clean and unmolested."

Lucerne, Meyringen, the falls of the Giesbach and Staubbach (where the water after descending nine hundred perpendicular feet generally becomes mist), the lakes of Thun and Brientz and Lausanne, were all visited, and then from Martigny the ascent was made to the Great St. Bernard.

Details of what has since become an every-day route would fatigue the reader; a pause is only made at the Hospice, and a letter inserted at some length, because it forms a link with what has gone before, marks a break in his journey between Switzerland and Italy, affords a fair specimen of his style, and is in itself full of interesting matter. It would be a loss to the reader to omit such a letter:—

I left England because I had the choice of spending a year either at home, or in visits to different friends, or in seeing the manners and scenery of other countries. I thought the last plan likely to produce the greatest share of knowledge; and—if one may compare the fruits of such a barren soil as I have ever found my heart—not the least of religion. And even at this moment, on cool reflection, I cannot say I see cause to change my opinion. Henry Sperling, whom I met a fortnight ago, told me he found travelling the best preparation for Orders. But then I have very little right to quote such a precedent.

His story is interesting and melancholy—without a home, without a guide, without a servant, without a friend or companion, he travels on foot from place to place. His little Bible, which is always in his hand, is his guide, his friend, his company. This seems to me the essence of religion. He said to me that ever since he had adopted this mode of life, he thought the months had never passed so happily. If his strength should be confirmed, he will return to England, I doubt not, a bright lamp in the sanctuary of our country. For my part, though I fall very far short of such attainments, I can truly say that I have enjoyed something occasionally of the sweet peace of religion, and some glimpses of that gracious Presence which surrounds me wherever I roam.

Occasionally I wander in advance of my companions, and in the sublime oratory of nature I sit me down on some rude stone, and with my little Greek Testament endeavour to trace the footsteps of Him who passed through His own creation for our sakes, without a home, and as one destitute and forsaken.

My Sundays, which are perhaps the days you would expect to be counted as the greatest loss of religious exercises, have generally passed more happily, and I would trust more profitably, than those I latterly spent in England; only, as we have seldom any public means of worship, and I have no book but my Greek Testament, I feel the want of some variety of employment, and in the afternoon, not unfrequently I take up my pen to address some of my dear friends at home. I have often pleased myself with the idea that, though separated by seas and mountains, we have been engaged at the same time in the worship of the same God and Saviour; your "two or three" being indeed many, ours within the literal number concerned in the promise of the Lord's presence. If I had time I could interest you with some of our Sundays, but now I must turn to other subjects.

Monday.—On Saturday we set out from Martigny, and walked to St. Bernard. The first part of the valley is very exquisite, the last five leagues not at all so—and in the situation of the monastery itself there is nothing beautiful and but little which is sublime.

It was dusk when a châlet was shown me, where a traveller had been murdered six weeks before, and, as Scott and I walked round the rocks (Kennaway being in the rear on a mule and with the muleteer), I confess it startled us to hear a loud shrill whistle very near us, but from whom we could not discern. On our arrival we were cordially greeted by the monks; a chamber was appointed us; and after a little repose we all met for supper. It is the plan of this singular institution to receive all strangers and travellers free of expense: if they are needy, they clothe them; if they are hungry, they feed them; if they desire it, a lodging is provided for them as long as they wish to remain. No one is refused; and the time has been when they have received and fed two hundred persons in one night. Indeed, at all seasons, as the pass of St. Bernard is the speediest into Italy, their profession of hospitality is no sinecure.

There are about twelve of their famous dogs, who all came forward to salute us on our arrival, and you will readily believe they received no small share of caresses. In the Museum of Berne we were shown one of these dogs, stuffed, who had saved twenty lives. From M. Barras I learnt a curious instance of their sagacity.

The Italian courier last winter passed from Aosta to the Grand St. Bernard on a very inclement afternoon, and they endeavoured to persuade him to abandon all thoughts of going forward. The courier was resolute to proceed. The monks then sent out two servants with him to direct him on his way. As these did not return, another servant, with three of the dogs, was despatched in search of them. It was remarkable that the dogs refused to go, giving every sign of reluctance—which was the more singular, as the dogs selected were the best of the whole number, most willing in general to exert themselves. However, life was at stake, and the dogs were forced. That night none of them returned. Some days afterwards they and the servants were discovered buried under an avalanche half a league from the convent, and all dead. Commonly, when the dogs show themselves unwilling to go out, it is taken for granted that extreme danger is on the road, and the hand of death abroad.

As we had walked about twenty-five miles, and all ascent, the day before, we thought ourselves sufficiently praiseworthy in rising a little before seven, and attending the breakfast table before eight, when the same party met us as at supper. After breakfast I attended their morning service, for I can always join in the Psalms, and in many of their prayers, and you would be surprised to find in their ritual the originals of the finest pieces of our own worship. For those which are addressed to the Virgin

Mary I substitute others; and when the Host is elevated, instead of kneeling, or prostrating, or crossing myself, I always stand upright, to signify my dissent. A short prayer that particularly pleased me in the St. Bernard Offices I translate for your perusal. It is a Latin Hymn to the Holy Ghost:—

Come, Holy Spirit, and send from heaven a ray of Thy light. Come, Thou Father of the poor! Thou Giver of gifts! Thou Light of the world! The blessed Comforter! The sweet Guest of the soul, and its sweet refreshment! Thou our repose in labour! Our coolness in heat! Our comfort in affliction! Our most blessed Spirit! Fulfil the hearts of Thy faithful! Without Thy influence there is nothing in man which is not weakness and guilt. Oh! cleanse that which is sordid; bedew that which is dried up; heal that which is wounded; bend that which is stubborn; cherish in Thy bosom that which is cold; guide that which is wandering; and grant unto Thy servants, putting their trust in Thee, the merit of Thy righteousness; grant them final salvation; grant them everlasting joy! O Lord, hear my prayer, and let my cry come unto Thee.

I was so much delighted with this and some other prayers in their offertory, that I asked permission to copy it. The monks insisted that I should keep the book as a souvenir of St. Bernard, and you will probably one day see its old rugged appearance. I cannot deny myself the pleasure of sending you one other translation:—

O blessed Lord Jesus Christ! I pray that Thy most Holy Name may be the last word that my mouth shall ever utter. O gracious Jesus! I pray that Thy most sacred body may be my last refreshment, and the sustenance which I shall enjoy and feed upon for ever. O gracious Lord! I pray that my last sigh may be the last pain I shall endure to all eternity. O gracious Lord! I pray that Thy most blessed face may be the first object which my soul shall behold when it is released from this mortal body. O gracious Lord! I pray that Thou Thyself be my Guide and my Companion from this land of exile to my eternal home and country. Amen.

You may, perhaps, with me, trace a Catholic tinge in these

effusions, yet it is such Catholicism as would never have occasioned a Protestant's separation. *O si sic omnia!*

But to continue my narrative. After dinner one of the Chanoines came to me, and asked if I would like to walk out to see the view of Mont Blanc from a neighbouring eminence. Accordingly we set out, and with some difficulty reached the summit of Chennilet; and thence, on a ridge in many places not a yard wide, and on either side looking down a precipice of dreadful depth, we gazed on a panorama sublime beyond all description. Mont Blanc, with the whole range of the Savoy Alps, seemed but a few miles distant; behind us were the Alps of the Canton of Berne, and on every side we were encompassed by peaks and glaciers. Our height was nine thousand feet above the sea, and we saw distinctly the whole scene spread out before us—a scene which is far above the habitation of man, and to which our views from the Righi and Grimsel were mere nothings. We really looked down upon the surface of the Alps. They were mostly below us, and some few more aspiring mountains had a very grand effect on the ground of the clear blue vault of heaven.

I shall never forget the scene; and the terror of our situation, requiring a cool, steady head, gave additional interest to the singular landscape.

In descending, we were in some danger. Scott Moncrieff and a Mr. Lyon, in entering on a large, steep surface of frozen snow, lost their footing and slid down from the top to the bottom. They had each snow-pikes, which from time to time they fixed in the snow, and so retarded their descent, and kept their heads from going down the foremost part of their body. They both gave themselves up for lost; and Scott told me (when a fortunate rise in the snow afforded them an opportunity of stopping themselves) that he was beginning to lose his senses from the great velocity acquired. If this had once been the case, they would have gone down head foremost upon pointed rocks, and would in all probability have been dashed to pieces.

This accident was owing to their neglect of the monk's advice, who called to them to take care. Taught by their example, I was more cautious. First the monk sat down, then I behind him, with my legs stretched out close to him. We both had pikes, and as we descended, when we

found our velocity too great, we fixed more deeply in the
frozen snow our pike-heads, which we always trailed under
our arms, and which in this way operated as a drag-chain
on a wheel. With this precaution we slid down, rapidly
indeed, but with pleasure and safety; only the inclined
plane on which we passed was of course extremely cold,
especially as I had nothing on but jean trousers! We were
about three hours ascending and descending.

After our return to the convent I passed some hours alone in
my chamber, but I was suddenly startled from my meditations by the entrance of Mons. Barras, *le Clavandier*. He
told me in a few words that an Englishman had set out by
himself long after us to reach the same point—that he had
lost his way amidst the precipices, and was in a place
where he could neither ascend nor descend, nor stir a foot
—that by loud cries and by elevating his handkerchief
and waving it, he had endeavoured to make his situation
known. His handkerchief was at last descried by a Capu-
chin, and instantly, as I was told, two monks went up like
lightning, and servants with them.

As this Englishman was my friend, John Kennaway, my first
impulse was to run to his aid. I was sitting in slippers,
and I instantly begged to have my shoes. Mons. Barras
tried to persuade me to remain at ease, for that night
would come on in half an hour, and I could not possibly be
of any service. But, as I persisted, he pretended they
should be sent, and left me. I must say it was the only
intimation of my wishes in that house which did not meet
with the most prompt compliance; and in this case the
neglect was intentional, to prevent my running into danger.
I was obliged to go into the offices below, and get my shoes
myself.

When I went out I found a crowd of people at the door, some
observing the distant precipices with telescopes, others
calculating the chance of escape, and the greater part offering conjectures as to what was doing by the people who
had already arrived at the place of action. They all
instantly opposed my going up, saying that nine persons
had already ascended with ropes and lanthorns; that the
monks who set out first had reached a spot above the
precipice within hearing of the unfortunate prisoner, and
had apprised him of the necessary steps to be taken; and
that, as I was ignorant of the way, I might lose myself and

distract their attention, or, if I arrived, embarrass their
efforts; so that, on the whole, I gave up the idea of
climbing the rock myself.

Three hours passed without intelligence; the lanthorns had
been seen to move; and to shrill whistles and sounds made
through a speaking trumpet, no response was made. We
concluded that our friend was extricated, and that the
party were making the circuit of the rocks on their return.

At last the poor fellow arrived himself; his clothes torn to
pieces, and the skin at the end of the fingers of one hand
completely torn off. The account given was as follows:—
He had lost his way, and thought if he could reach one
summit, he should then proceed in safety. With this view
he made considerable efforts to climb the precipice. He
slipped once ten feet downwards, and stopped, as if by
miracle, within a few inches of a rock, over which if he had
passed he would infallibly have been dashed to pieces.
His bâton, which slipped with him, went down five
hundred feet perpendicular! Not warned by this escape
he still continued his exertions, till he found himself in a
place where he could neither move backwards nor forwards,
neither stand upright nor sit down. His two feet were
planted in two little hollows about the size of the palm of
your hand; his back was supported against the rock in a
position half reclining.

If his heels had slipped from these hollows, he would have
fallen down a precipice and been killed on the spot. If
his legs had yielded through fatigue, the effect would have
been the same. A steep perpendicular rock above forbade
all hopes of ascending higher.

In this position his arms only were at liberty, and these he
used to wave his handkerchief, seconding the chance of
observation by loud cries. He was fully aware of the near
approach of night, and though he had no fear of dizziness
in his giddy situation (for he had a remarkably steady
head) he said that, if he had not been seen, fatigue would
have disabled him from keeping his station, and he must
have dropped down to certain death.

Thus circumstanced, and thus reflecting, he saw with indescribable joy that his distress was observed, and he was
perfectly amazed at the promptitude and agility with
which the monks ascended to the steep above his head.
Here, after directions given and received, two young men,

chamois hunters, famed for their dexterity, went down to the bottom of the rock; one was unable to ascend, the other succeeded, and resting on a neighbouring ledge contrived to fix a rope about his body. With this, he was drawn up to the top by the monks above, and then they all came down leisurely together.

Thus most providentially was he rescued from the jaws of death; for if this accident had happened an hour later, his situation would not have been observed. If it had occurred on the other side of the Hospice, the rocks would have shut him out from view. If he had been on the Grimsel or Scheideck, or on any other mountain but St. Bernard, he would have perished from the ignorance or inactivity of the people.

But no words can do justice to the prompt and rapid assistance, to the admirable dexterity and judgment, or to the unaffected kindness which these interesting ecclesiastics rendered to our poor countryman on this occasion. They all told me it was a dreadful place, and the events of that evening will be the theme of St. Bernard to many a future traveller. There can be no doubt that they saved his life.

I took leave of the Capuchins and of Mons. Barras with sincere regret, and in the Swiss mode of salutation. To the latter I could not help saying, when we parted, " J'espère, Monsieur, que nous nous rencontrerons dans un endroit encore plus haut que celui-ci." He replied, " Je l'espère, Monsieur, moi-même, de tout mon cœur !"

This letter, interesting in itself, and a specimen of many for which space cannot be found, serves to show the general bearing of the writer, his courtesy, his intelligence, and the secret of his popularity with all who knew him. His late friend and companion, Mr. Moncrieff, who left him about this time and returned to Edinburgh, bore testimony to him after the lapse of fifty years, as follows :—

It is not likely that I could recount any of our adventures which you do not already know. This, however, I may say, that nothing occurred which could in the smallest degree diminish the opinion I had previously formed of your father's noble character as a true Christian gentleman, actuated at all times by the highest principle, of great talents and attainments, of a manly spirit, and of sincere piety.

E

Henry Elliott, in company with his rescued friend Kennaway, now descended the Italian side of the Great St. Bernard. They soon found themselves at Turin, whence they proceeded to Milan, Genoa, Pisa, Florence, Rome, and Naples, returning again to Rome for the Holy Week. At Florence he tantalizes his sisters by telling them how he was captivated by the sight of the fairest form he had ever seen. Never had he imagined a face so lovely and form so faultless as now met his eyes. As acquaintance ripened he did his best to improve it. His intercourse was almost daily, and his admiration increased at every interview. Personally, he had nothing to complain of; no one seemed preferred to himself: there were many admirers, but none more favoured. No harsh word was ever spoken to him, no door ever closed against him; and yet he could make no impression. The smile remained upon the face, but there seemed no heart within. His grew warm, but hers remained cold, hard, and impenetrable as marble. At length he tore himself away, with a vision of beauty which he should never lose and yet never possess.

The sympathising reader may find the clue to this tender episode, when, in the Tribune of the Uffizi at Florence, he stands before the "Venus de' Medici."

At Rome he was "infinitely delighted, and infinitely grieved:"—

"Tears have rushed into my eyes," he says, "at the sight of the Forum, the Capitol, the gorgeous palaces, the solemn temples fast hastening to decay. I have stood where, a little more than 1800 years ago, I might have listened to the eloquence of Cicero, and beheld the majesty of the Roman Senate. I have passed under the triumphal arches of Constantine and Titus, and seen the candlestick of the Jewish Temple sculptured in bas-relief on walls by which, to this day, the Jews refuse to pass. I have walked up the 'clivus capitolinus,' and paced the pavement of the great hall of all the Cæsars. These mighty remains, and the fond and melancholy recollections which still hang around the Seven Hills, and haunt their ruins, might well render a soul not absolutely lost to all feeling, sad and pensive.

"But it is not merely the decay of all that was once glorious and renowned which has filled my measure of grief. It is the knowledge and view of the decay of the immortal part—the degeneracy of mind—the grave of noble sentiment and virtuous conduct over which I mourn. There is no Caius Marius sitting amongst these ruins. In the room of the most dignified and high-minded people on the face of the globe, you have now a nation—the dregs of Europe—absorbed in mercenary and selfish feeling. The Swiss glory in not being Italians. If you suspect their fair dealing and show your doubts, they say, 'Vous n'êtes pas encore, Monsieur, en Italie.' Then when you cross the Alps, they tell you at Turin, by way of eminence, 'Je suis Sarde.' At Florence, 'Soyez tranquille, Monsieur, je ne suis pas Romain.' A person with whom I had dealings cautioned me against putting any faith in these people here, concluding by saying both of Romans and Neapolitans, 'Ces deux nations! elles sont la canaille de tout le monde.' Such are the successors of Fabricius, Cato, the Scipios, the Lælii, the Brutuses. It makes my heart ache with grief. I shall not attempt description; for no magic can make a reader a spectator. For this reason I shall not say much on what we have seen of the antiquities of Rome, and I shall even venture to omit the glorious church of St. Peter's, the Transfiguration, and the frescoes of Raphael; but not because they have not absorbed my attention and exalted my admiration; for St. Peter's will still be the finest (incomparably the finest) church I have ever seen, and the Transfiguration by Raphael the finest picture in the world. Let me, however, tell you how and where we spent our Christmas Eve and Christmas Day. On Christmas Eve we went, at nine o'clock, to the Quirinal, or the Pope's private chapel, to attend the vespers, and witness the celebration of mass. About four-and-twenty cardinals were present in their robes, and the priests who officiated were most richly dressed. The music was vocal, and the service very long, and the dignitaries who attended gave it an air of importance and solemnity; otherwise it was not remarkable. From the Quirinal we repaired to the church of San Luigi Francese, where the great altar was one blaze of light, and every part and corner of the chapel were crowded to excess. The service consisted chiefly in chanting, with a fine organ accompanying. It began exactly at twelve at night, the hour when, according to the Catholic doctrine, our Saviour was born. We next visited the great church of the Capuchins, which was equally crowded, though with a lower class of worshippers. It was a very striking sight to see the Host elevated in this church. Before its elevation, a little bell rang as is usual. A deep and awful pause ensued ; every head was bent in the lowest prostration; the assistant priests all knelt at a distance round the altar, and at the moment when the consecrated wafer was raised on high, every Catholic made the sign of the cross, and his lips moved to the words of whispered prayer. The reverence and awe evinced, bring to mind Moses putting off his shoes, for the place where he stood was holy ground. I never saw any ceremony equal to this for the solemnity of its manner, and its impression on a whole congregation. The organ of the Capuchins was very sweet.

" From thence we went to the church of Santa Maria Maggiore. Here was the great festival. The matins for the day were performed to a congregation still more numerous, and in a church far more magnificent than those we had already visited. It was a noble sight to see the immense nave and the aisles completely filled (for in Catholic churches all is open space, and the distinction and wretched appearance of wooden pews is unknown). Santa Maria Maggiore is a remarkably long church, and through the perspective of the columns and their intersections, the unnumbered multitude was seen assembled to welcome the morning of the ever-blessed Nativity. In the Borghese Chapel the English only were admitted. Indeed, throughout Italy, they are treated with every sort of public distinction, and their convenience during the evening and morning of Christmas night was particularly consulted.

" In this chapel it was a beautiful sight to see two hundred priests, each with his torch in his hand, and in white robes, enter in procession, eight of them bearing a rich shrine with a waxen figure of a child reclining on its top, and containing within the famous relics of Santa Maria Maggiore, namely, a piece of the manger, and a part of the swaddling clothes—at least, so they say.

" Then, too, between three and four, just the hours when the angels are thought to have appeared to the shepherds, the organ, with all its usual choir, struck up, ' Gloria in excelsis Deo !' The anthem, taken with the time of its performance, and also the sight of the immense crowd of worshippers, who even at this unseasonable hour met to celebrate their religious rites, and to welcome in the morning of man's salvation, was to me the finest part of the observance.

"In the morning at nine, the Pope and cardinals met in the same church of Santa Maria Maggiore, and mass was celebrated with the utmost pomp by the Pope himself. Altogether the ceremonies disappointed me. St. Peter's was not illuminated, and the offices performed there were of an inferior order. It was the recollection of the subject, and the exact time when the several parts took place in the great scene of the Incarnation of our Lord, and the view of countless numbers, all wakeful, and assembled to worship 'the child Jesus,' which formed the grand part of my impression."

Having witnessed the ceremony of a lady taking the veil— "a sad and melancholy scene"—he left Rome by the Appia Via, and passed through the place that was once the "Appii Forum and the three taverns" of St. Paul, travelling with all speed to avoid the robbers, and reaching Naples on January 15, 1818 :—

"What a lovely scene," he says, "is the Bay of Naples! Altogether it seems a place which, by its society and its own intrinsic beauty, promises to yield us more pleasure than any town we have visited."

He stayed there six weeks, and entered a good deal into society.

"Of the foreigners," he says, "I see most of the Archbishop of Tarentum. His house is open every evening, and after one introduction to his conversazione, you go whenever you please without further ceremony. At his house I meet the best society in Naples. About seven o'clock we read for an hour. The book is commonly the 'Lives of the Popes,' just now published by the French Academy—very entertaining, and so frank in speaking of the defects and private conduct of the Pontifical gentlemen, that they have very wisely prohibited it. After an hour's reading, more persons come, and a general conversation ensues. The evening closes with cards. When they are introduced I take my hat. The Archbishop himself unites the manners of a courtier to the science of a prelate. He is a very able man, and his information on all subjects is prodigious. He has introduced me to the Marchese Bario, a great collector of books and pictures, and to the Chevalier Sementiri, a professor of chemistry. The Count Solaro della Margherita, a Turinese, and his friend Azillio, have also pleased us much.

"Of the English we have seen but little, except of Lord Calthorpe and Sir J. C. Hippesley; but, to put you in possession of our proceedings, I will sketch the journal of the last few days:—

"*Monday Feb* 9.—Visited the Grotto del Cane, a small cave where there is so noxious a vapour that nothing can live in it. We saw a dog undergo apparently the agonies of death, but when taken out into the pure air he revived immediately; thus the poor dog dies three or four times a day. In the evening we went to the Archbishop of Tarentum and to Lord Calthorpe.

"*Tuesday, Feb.* 10.—Visited Pompeii. A spectacle unique, and to me in the highest degree interesting. We were engaged to Lady Bute in the evening.

"*Wednesday.*—Made calls for Kennaway's approaching departure. Dined with Sir H. Lushington; a very agreeable party. I learned much of the manner of travelling in Sicily.

"*Thursday.*—Ascended Vesuvius, over burning ground, and lava still smoking. The sight was awful.

"*Friday.*—Kennaway parted from me to return to Rome and England. I said to myself, 'Now I am alone in the wide world;' but, unexpectedly, Henry Sperling arrived, and dissipated my ideas of solitude. The evening I spent at the Archbishop's.

"*Saturday.*—Made calls in the morning, and searched the booksellers' shops for some particular editions of several works. Dined with Lord Calthorpe.

"*Sunday.*—Went to service at Sir H. Lushington's and heard an excellent sermon from Mr. Alford, from the text, 'Adam, where art thou?' Where was I? The question presented itself in more shapes than one.

"*Monday.*—Sat down to write this letter. If you write directly, write to me here. If not, to Corfu."

His idea of Naples and his description of Pompeii deserve,

however, a longer notice than can be gained from the above. The following extracts will interest the reader. He will not forget the lapse of time since they were written, and may indulge the hope that the harsher features of the description are now softened :—

At Naples, and indeed in the major part of Italy, there is a considerable facility in the manner of making acquaintances. After being presented, and invited once to a house, you may go nearly as often as you like. If they have public nights, you go after the first time without a second invitation. But this same system of general society, which makes acquaintance so easy, renders friendship and intimacy difficult. They receive every one to a certain extent, and therefore very few are admitted beyond the line and limit of this extent. They very rarely give dinner parties, excepting the ambassadors and ministers. They see company of an evening with very little expense, as only a few glasses of lemonade, or iced-punch, or ice, are handed round to those who take them.

They are excessively fond of theatres, and their boxes are more usual and licensed places for receiving visits than even their own homes. Occasionally they invite to their boxes, and towards the conclusion of the entertainment the servants bring in a hot supper.

Their meals are a cup of coffee without milk and saturated with sugar, before they rise, and nothing else. At two they dine, and immediately after dinner coffee is taken as in the morning; and at nine or ten they repeat their dinners—at least, their supper and dinner are not widely different. The great bond of society is intrigue, and a sort of adjutant consideration is gambling. Hearing that the Princess Belmonte gave two public nights, where a great deal of Italian society was to be met with, I procured an introduction to her; but as I found a regular faro-table established in her house, and that the amusement was gambling, I have not repeated my visit.

The Redolto, which is very near the Opera, is, in the same way, a continual attraction. Four licensed gambling-tables go on all night, I know a little of an Englishman who won 500*l.* in an evening, and a Frenchman who lost about the same sum at a sitting.

The system of intrigue and immorality which is so lamentably universal, has its rise in two causes that I can discern, and perhaps others that I cannot discern. In Italy the whole fortune of a family is entailed on the eldest son ; the younger sons do not marry, and follow the law or the army as their profession, and a life of gallantry as it is called.   The other is the plan on which the marriages are made.   It very often happens that the only knowledge a gentleman has of a lady is the view of her at a balcony, or in the theatre, or, if his good fortune favour him, he has danced once or twice with her at a ball. On the first visit the matter is concluded, and it would be the highest disgrace on his part, and the deepest affront to the family whose alliance he seeks, after the visit of introduction, to recede.   Caroline Ungaro is at this moment demanded in marriage by a Knight of Malta, to whom she has never spoken, and who has not seen her since two years ago at the theatre.   The poor knight has travelled to get rid of his passion in vain.   He is a man of honour and a gentleman.   She refused him at once ; and, as I am very much in the confidence of the family, I took the liberty of reasoning with her on the subject, and combating her only ground of objection,—" Je l'ai vu deux années passées.   Il ne me plaisait pas."   I said, " But pray see the gentleman ; you know nothing of his character, his manners, his abilities ; the constancy and ardour of his affection may at least obtain this favour."   " Ah ! Monsieur Henri, alors vous ne savez pas qu'après que ce monsieur sera présenté, tout est arrangé, et qu'il n'est pas possible de faire une retraite."

Such is the system ; and the consequence is, that such *fanciful* marriages often see the end of the love which contracted them in two or three days.   With a perfect indifference to each other, the lady receives the attentions of another, and the gentleman imitates the manners of the unmarried younger son, and seeks his pleasure somewhere else.   Thus the manner of their marriages furnishes the mutual dissatisfaction of man and wife; and the denial of portions to younger sons, a sufficient number of unprincipled young men to take advantage of it.

The next extract relates his visit to Pompeii :—

You know that it is a Roman town buried under the ashes shot forth in one of the eruptions of Mount Vesuvius, A.D. 79, and distant about fourteen miles from Naples.   This eruption, which was so fatal to the inhabitants of the

first century, is the highest benefit to the traveller of
the nineteenth; for, by excluding the air, and secreting the
city from the ravages of time, and the wanton pillage
of successive revolutions, what we have of Pompeii is
as fresh and as perfect as if the town had been just sacked
by an army, or desolated by a fire.

The houses and temples, indeed, are all unroofed: and the
moveables that either the lapse of time could decay under
ground, or the fire of the hot cinders consume, or the
industry of the inhabitants previously remove—these are
gone; but still the spectacle is unique. You enter a
Roman town; you walk through their streets; you see
their houses, and the various domestic arrangements made
in them; you view the pavement positively worn by the
wheels of their carriages; you are present, as it were,
to a generation passed away, mixing for a moment in their
feelings, their habitations, their manner of life, their ornaments, and their amusements; you walk through their
gardens, as laid out by themselves; you are shown shops
where vessels of oil and wine were served to casual cus-
tomers, with the very marks of the glasses on the marble
slabs; you tread on their mosaic floors, and enter into their
bed-rooms, where the walls in some parts preserve the
frescoes as if they had not been executed a month.

In other towns you see isolated ruins, or a large assemblage
of ruins, with the bustle of modern life superseding and
forbidding all possibility of deception as to who you are
and where you are standing. But in Pompeii, as you walk
with your guide through the solitary streets, yourselves the
only spectators, or perhaps passing a party like yourselves,
employed in viewing the ruined city, I should think meanly
of the man who did not find himself forcibly hurried back
to days long since gone by, and who should not reflect with
melancholy self-application on the speed of time, and the
mighty revolutions which take place in all that is great or
stable in man's estimation.

The circumference of Pompeii is calculated at about three
miles. At present only about three streets have been
opened, one of them leading directly to the Forum. It
is not subterranean; you walk in the open air, beginning
with the street of the Tombs. There you see the names
and ages registered without, as in a modern churchyard,
and the urns containing the ashes of the dead ranged

in little recesses within. These monuments have the appearance of being almost fresh from the chisel; one raised by a father to his darling boy, aged twelve years, particularly interested me. The tombs are on each side the street; and as they terminate, you enter the gate of the city, and see the sort of watch-box where the sentinel performed his duty of guard.

One of the first houses on the right as you enter, commanding an enchanting view of the bay, belonged to a friend of Cicero. They show you a door where the skeletons of two men were discovered, one with a vessel full of jewels and articles of value, which he was conveying away; the other with a lamp in one hand and a bundle of keys in the other. They are supposed to be a master and his slave, in whom the desire of saving their property overpowered the sense of danger; for the mountain gave such timely notice of its intentions that all the inhabitants escaped excepting a few invalids, from whom age or sickness had taken the power of moving.

Leaving that part of the city which is excavated, we pursued our way over vineyards and olive-grounds, beneath which the rest of the town still continues buried, till we reached the Amphitheatre. This is equally perfect with the other theatres, and by simple inspection I understood at once all the difficulties and hard names respecting the arrangements of the gladiatorial spectacles—the orchestra, the curia, the vometoria, the procenium, which I had in vain puzzled over in Juvenal, and Virgil, and Ovid. If a few boards were laid down, you might exhibit, with the greatest ease, at this moment, games of gladiators and wild beasts. The very dens of the animals are entire, with the little troughs of water provided for them, and the openings by which they entered the arena.

He returned to Rome in time to witness the ceremonies of the Holy Week. The following description is from a letter written to Mrs. Williams of Tiddenham. It will interest the reader as a beautiful bit of word-painting :—

The finest parts of the ceremonies were, first of all, the famous Miserere of Allegri in the Sistine Chapel, towards the conclusion of a service. The lights were all put out, one by one; and after a solemn pause, the Pope and cardinals bowing their heads to the earth, four voices, without instrument of any kind, chanted a lamentation so touching and aërial that it melted every heart, and would well suit the requiem of a dying Redeemer.

The second, a very remarkable and imposing part of the offices of the week, is the benediction of the people from the gallery of St. Peter's on Easter Sunday. Unnumbered crowds filled the spacious court which leads to the Basilica; and the very roofs of the Colonnade, and the windows and roofs of distant houses, were all thronged. The Pope then came forward and raised his aged hands over the people, and, making the sign of the Cross, gave them all his benediction. The effect was impaired by only about half the people kneeling.

I have only now to mention the internal and the external illumination of St. Peter's. The first was performed as soon as it was dark by the suspension of a single cross just before the great baldaquin, or tabernacle of the high altar, which stands under the magnificent cupola. The cross is hung with lamps on both sides. It was night, and the immense aisle and transepts and side aisles were full to excess. Nothing could be finer than the long lines of light which the cross darted along the pillars and recesses, glancing on the moving mass collected together, while it stood itself in the centre of the cathedral, fixed and simple in its beautiful lustre.

In particular we remarked the grand tomb of Clement XIII., where he is sculptured with a hand outstretched. The tomb is behind one of the four massive pillars which support the dome. The light of the cross, glancing by one of these immense supports, struck on half the monument, and it seemed as if the dead Pope was rising with astonishment, his hand outstretched and his face bent on the illumination which had roused him from the sleep of death and disturbed the repose of his ashes. Indeed it was a noble sight.

But above all I never saw any spectacle so uncommon, and so exquisite, as the first illumination of the exterior. The lamps followed exactly the form of the building, tracing in fire the architecture and outline of it, without any blaze or glare, so that at a distance it looked like an enchanted castle, and such as wandering knights have encountered in fairy-land. All Rome was abroad to see. Exactly as the clock struck eight, before the third stroke, all was changed, and the illumination became a mixture of lamps and torches. It was not so beautiful as the first, because it was not so simple, but the change was effected with magical celerity, by men trained to the business. This external illumination was added to the usual ceremonies, for it is appropriated to St. Peter's day. The compliment was paid to the King of Spain and the Hereditary Prince of Bavaria, who were both at Rome.

He adds in another letter:—

These were the finest parts in the " Function," as it is called; but they were attended with so much that was merely personal and trivial—so pitiful in its meaning, and wearisome in its length:—they were accompanied with so much fatigue and bustle, and crowding—that the week was anything but holy, and I believe every one rejoiced when it was over.

He shrank from the Mariolatry—which has since culminated in the Immaculate Conception—and other flagrant errors involved in these imposing ceremonies, and often, during his sojourn in Italy, entered into discussion with the Romish priests and dignitaries with whom he came in contact in the churches, or to whom he was introduced in general society. One specimen will suffice:—

I was conversing with two Italian ladies, when the priest came in, and began to speak on religious topics. They told him that they had been conversing with me on the same subject, and that I did not worship the Virgin Mary nor believe in the authority of the Pope. Supposing I was ignorant of the language, he blamed them for doing this in any case, and told them it was absolutely necessary to know the character of a person before they ventured even to speak on the subject of religion. But when they assured him that I was " very religious," and a believer in Scripture, his countenance brightened, and he proceeded to question me. He seemed to think there was very little difference between Turk, infidel, and heretic. " Do you believe the Scriptures?" "Yes, with my whole heart." "Do you believe that Jesus Christ was very God and very man?" " Yes, with my whole heart; it is the foundation of all my religion." " Va benissimo!" and he drew his chair nearer to me, and seemed to open his eyes and perceive that he was not looking upon a monster. "We shall then be able to go on clearly," he said. "You believe in the perfect purity of Jesus Christ?" "Yes." "Now a perfect effect cannot come from an imperfect cause or origin?" "Undoubtedly not." "It therefore follows that, as Jesus Christ was spotless, His mother, the Virgin Mary should also be spotless, and without the taint of original sin." Here it became my turn to speak. I had the choice of two arguments. I could say, in reference to a perfect effect requiring a perfect cause, that the Holy or Great God was the cause, and the Virgin Mary only the instrument. But I preferred another argument which struck me at the moment, and I said, "Your reasoning proves too much; for if the Virgin Mary be without the taint of original sin, then by the same argument of cause and effect, her parents were without the taint of original sin, and in the same way the parents of her parents, and so on up to Adam and Eve. Original sin is therefore entirely destroyed." To this, after some time, he replied that "God could, by a singular exercise of His power and privilege, give to the Virgin Mary that purity which was denied to the rest of mankind." And without allowing me to urge that the miracle (for miraculous it must be somewhere) might just as well take place respecting the birth of our Lord in the flesh as respecting the Virgin Mary, he proceeded to other circuitous proofs, alleging that what could not be proved directly, must be proved indirectly. In the midst of his scholastic puzzle respecting reasoning *à priori* and *à posteriori* we were interrupted by company, and the priest took leave of me cordially, and begging my acquaintance, which I shall be happy to give him.

At Rome, his brother Edward joined him. He had been successful in his college course, and had obtained a Trinity fellowship at the first examination. Henry Elliott was delighted; and his congratulatory letter, written from Milan on October 31, 1817, proves that foreign travel had weakened none of his home affections. Thus the letter runs :—

My dearest Brother and Brother-fellow.

In the course of my wanderings I have experienced many moments of exquisite pleasure, but I do not remember to have felt any thrill of joy so sudden and so lively as that which ran from my heart through all my veins when I started at the news of your success. Grave and taciturn and sober as my general character may be, I forgot gravity, taciturnity, and sobriety, and literally leapt for joy, clapping my hands and exciting the astonishment of the passengers. I believe they took me for an improvisatore for the moment. In truth, my dear, dear Edward, you have given me the highest joy by your splendid success. I delight to think that now we may fairly be considered on a par : and if God has been pleased to gladden the hearts of our beloved parents with any honours of mine heretofore, the balance is now even, and your contingent, by one mighty article, fully made up.

The brothers were now together, and together they returned to Naples. Then crossing the country to Avellino and Bari, and passing through Cannæ, the site of Hannibal's victory, they sailed to Corfu, and set out on a tour through Greece. Henry Elliott declares his object to be an earnest desire of seeing Greece, as a source of much useful thought and investigation, combined with a curiosity not perfectly content with seeing nothing but what the crowd of English who, up to the present time, had been his companions, could see as well as himself.

In the straits of Corfu, on May 2, 1818, he writes :—

I rose this morning at four o'clock, and watched the sun as he ascended behind the hills which were once the limits of Pyrrhus' kingdom, and shone upon those countries with rays as bright, and on hills as verdant as formerly ; but the spirit which animated the body is dead, and Greece is but the tomb of its ancient glory. I visit it *as a tomb*, with feelings of deepest reverence for the mighty dead, and pity for the fallen living.

At Corfu, they were courteously entertained by Sir Thomas Maitland, the Governor of the Ionian Islands, and received letters of introduction, among others, to Ali Pasha, by whom they were received and fêted in Oriental style. They passed over Mount Pindus (the fabled abode of Apollo and the Muses), through the Plains of Thessaly, along the vale of Tempè, and so on to the foot of Olympus and Ossa :—

"We looked earnestly," he says, "at the mountains so ennobled by the old poets, and the valley which they loved and regarded as a model of perfect beauty. There they

were; their features the same, even their names but little
varied. Nature was still unaltered; her smile as sweet,
and her beauty as engaging as ever. But the kings, the
heroes, the statesmen, the poets, the historians—how
changed indeed is the scene! Really, I sometimes lament
over Greece as I would lament at the tomb of a friend.
All that we have seen hitherto is like a moving panorama,
crowded with the bustle and hurry of active life; but in
Greece, silence and solitude brood over the mighty dead,
and your sympathy and pity seem in some measure, as it
were, to compensate for the wrongs of time and the woful
change of masters."

Whilst expressing these feelings, he was passing over to
Constantinople, a city to which, he says, "even Naples must
yield the palm." Here they stayed more than a month, and
were much indebted to the hospitality of Sir Robert Liston,
the English ambassador, where they met all the limited
society of the place, enjoyed divers *fêtes champêtres*, and made
many excursions—often breakfasting in Europe, taking coffee
in Asia, and returning to Europe for dinner. He describes
one excursion, which may suffice as a specimen of others, to
Nicæa, or Isnik, as it is now called:—

"This is the place," he says, "famous for the first Christian
Council over which Constantine presided, and where Arius
was condemned. It was the residence of Pliny and Catul-
lus, the delight of the emperors, and the rival of Constantinople. It is now a miserable village; seventy houses, of
which fifty-eight are Turkish, stand where once seventy
thousand stood, and by their appearance denote that arts
and sciences have long taken their flight. One solitary
Greek priest, or pappas (as he is called in this country)
performs service in the only Christian church which remains. He possessed, himself, a copy of the Gospels in
Greek; and in the same language there was in the church
the ritual of the Greek service, containing portions of the
New Testament, divided according to the seasons of the
year. This was all that was to be found in Nice of
the Bible. The old Testament not at all; the New not
entire. The priest was the only person that could read;
yet this was the place where learning flourished, and
doctors met to discuss the hard questions of theology, and
assembled councils decided the faith of the world! . . . In

every mosque I saw traces of God's temples—pillars, arches, pavements, many of great beauty, which had once another use than to serve the purposes of the false prophet. As I paced the aisles of a decayed mosque, once a Christian church, I asked a solitary Turk, reposing there during the heat of noon, and whose cough had startled me like a voice from the dead, what he knew of the place. 'Effendi,' said he, 'it is an old, old building, not the work of our nation.' Near the south gate of the walls, which still remain in all their massive and sullen grandeur, are the ruins of the Council Hall, with the throne of Constantine and the Patriarch."

These excursions ended, the brothers left Constantinople, and travelled chiefly on horseback (Henry Elliott suffering his moustache to grow, in order to look the more like a Turk), in company with Lord Balgonie (Réaumur's thermometer averaging 37° at noon), to Smyrna. Finding H.M.'s ship the *Spey* at Smyrna, and receiving a courteous invitation from Captain White, they set sail for Athens, and arrived on September 20.

In a letter dated October 12, 1818, he says·—

"You can conceive but you cannot know, how lovely Athens is, even in its ruins. The Parthenon, the Erechtheum, the Propylæa, though decayed by time, and pillaged by Alaric and Lord Elgin, still consecrate the Acropolis, as it were, the residence of divinity. Every step of ground is marked by some mighty hero buried there—some building, the very model of architecture and standard of proportion, existing in greater or less perfection—some action sung by the poets of Greece and re-echoed by the world. . . . And the natural scenery I shall never, never see equalled—seas running into all the varieties of bays and gulfs, forming promontories, and headlands, and the long sweep of receding shores. These views combine the beauty of lake and the magnificence of ocean, with islands gemmed on its laughing surface, and united to a sky which is ever blue and ever brilliant. I used to think that I had little natural enthusiasm, but now I believe I have still some smouldering embers, which only wait a fanning wind to burst into a blaze."

The brothers made Athens their head-quarters for nearly five months, travelling over the Morea, and visiting all the spots most celebrated in Grecian history, both sacred and profane. These tours were made pleasanter by the company of other English travellers who joined in them. Lady Ruthven (who, Henry Elliott says, was called " the Queen of Athens " by all the population of the lower class there, so that in his walks he was accustomed to ask the peasants whether " the Queen " had passed that way, as the surest method of obtaining the information he desired), after a lapse of nearly fifty years, recalls, and has recorded, the pleasant reminiscences of these days :—

Most interesting were the months we spent together in Greece; and all our excursions to Marathon and other famous places were rendered doubly delightful by Mr. Elliott's charming conversation. He was a fine Greek scholar, he soon acquired the Romaic, and, as you know, wrote an essay about the difference of the pronunciation of the ancient and modern Greek. We made excursions together near Athens, and one of the marbles we dug up together is now at Cambridge. I lost a favourite maid at Athens, and he wrote a beautiful epitaph for her tomb, which is now in the temple of Theseus, where she was buried. We were also for weeks together at Janina, during the last period of Ali Pasha's rule, and had fêtes from his sons, when Mr. Elliott interpreted all the fine things they said to us.

In the month of February, 1819, they tore themselves away from Athens, and Athenian friends :—

" After so long a residence," he says, " I loved it as a place *far more* than any other to which the course of my travelling has brought me. I have been so happy there sometimes, and so sad at others, that when I looked back at it for the last view of its temples and walks and Acropolis I could not help bursting into tears. It was on the sacred way to Eleusis, just where the road ascends Mount Corydalus, and turns to the secluded convent of Daphne. There I saw Athens for the last time. I shall never see anything like it, nor do I wish it. I may add, that I shall never part with kinder friends than we found there in the Ruthvens and others."

In the following month (March 1, 1819) the brothers themselves parted. From Athens they had bent their steps northward, visiting Thebes, Delphos, and Thermopylæ. A small

vessel, or caïque, had been engaged at Trichari, on the Gulf of
Volo, and now lay waiting off the opposite coast of Eubœa.
They crossed over, and sitting on a grassy mound, read Psalm
cxxi. : " I will lift up mine eyes unto the hills, from whence
cometh my help—"   Then the land breeze springing up,
Edward prepared to return to England, whilst Henry embarked and set sail for Palestine.

The little caïque went beating about the Ægean Sea,
making but slow progress towards Smyrna, the desired haven.
The Greek sailors were so timid that, if the wind was fair and
fresh and he urged them to hoist sail, they said, " A caïque
cannot support the sea ;" if it was calm, " We cannot row all
day ;" if it was evening, " We shall be benighted ;" if it
threatened to rain, " The weather is spoiled :" so that, what
with the rain, the night, the sea, and the wind, his dread
of delay was fully realised.   On March 5, he landed at the
small island of Scopelo, and writes home thus :—

After four nights, in which I slept in a sort of place or hole
   in the caïque, just long enough for me, but so low that I
   cannot *sit* upright, I was glad to sleep on shore. I was
   taken in by a Greek woman, who is a widow, and has
   three daughters, two of them pretty, one of them remarkably
   so. She marvelled much at my solitary condition, told me
   if I would remain in Scopelo they would choose me the
   prettiest bride of the town, and give me one of the beautiful
   gardens of orange-trees which surround it ; and when I still
   continued inexorable she asked, whether I had father or
   mother? and won my heart afterwards by adding, " Ah, they
   are now saying, ' Where is our dear child ?   Is he safe ?
   Is he well ?'" and at their supper they drank to your
   health and to our meeting. This was so little expected on
   my part that I began to be melancholy, I suppose, for the
   captain (such he is called by courtesy, having three sailors
   under him) said to me, " Effendi, don't be so thoughtful.
   God is good." He used the same words to me when I
   parted with Campbell and Edward, when my heart was
   very full. A little Greek boy, five years of age, full of
   spirit and intelligence, as the Greeks usually are, took a
   fancy for my foreign garb, and begged me either to stay in
   Scopelo or to take him with me. The captain and his
   mate, Evangeli, were sitting by the child at supper, and
   told him *they* would remain with him. " No, gentlemen,

said the little fellow, accompanying his words with expressive action; "eat and drink as much as you please at our table, but then good-bye to you; the English Effendi stays here without you."

On March 18th he arrived at Mitylene, and on the 26th at Smyrna. But this chapter must not linger, as he did, in Asia Minor; neither must the reader be invited to visit, as he did, the interesting remains of Smyrna, Ephesus, Samos, Miletus, Halicarnassus, and Cyprus.

An exception may be made in favour of Ephesus, once the wonder of the world, twice visited by an Apostle, addressed in words of inspiration, and warned by the Lord Himself— "Repent, and do the first works; or else I will come unto thee quickly, and will remove thy candlestick out of its place" (Rev. ii. 5):—

"I walked out," he says, on the 8th of April, "to see this ancient and celebrated city, and found myself among ruins where not a human being was to be seen. The stork had built her nest on the top of the ruined arches or towers, and by the monotonous tapping of her bill recalled the idea of existence. I was tired with the silence after a while, and in a ruined mosque of magnificent workmanship and dimensions I fired a pistol to make at least an echo, and break the desolation of the scene. A number of wild birds flew from their roosting-places with shrill cries, and after wheeling in a circle returned to their nests among the ruins. I found scattered everywhere columns and monuments of exquisite beauty, and bas-reliefs of the oldest date; but all was still, silent, and solitary. I was much struck with the response of my guide, when finding him ignorant of the history of Ephesus, I endeavoured to explain to him how and why the 'candlestick' had been removed out of its place. 'Effendi,' he said, 'do you not know that at Ainsuluk' (such is the local name) 'the houses cannot multiply, nor the number of inhabitants increase? If they build more than the present number of sixteen, in a little while they return to it again. If in one or two years the number of the children is increased, some mortality is sure to follow, and cut down the surplus. This was once our own place, and here the Turks cannot multiply. Such as it is, so it remains, and so is the will of God (πόσον ἐνι τόσσον θέλει εἶναι· ἔτι θέλει ὁ Θέος).' Just as I have related, the Greek made his remarks. I neither sought nor expected them, but they seem to me very striking."

Before the narrative passes on, some of Henry Elliott's remarks whilst *in transitu* may be deemed worthy of note, as conveying his sentiments as to the past and his anticipations as to the future. Two extracts will make these plain:—

Since I left England it has fallen to my lot to mix a good deal with the higher class of English society; and there is something pleasing in the ease and kindness with which I have been received. But it is painful to see that the intercourse has not been of a more directly religious character. In most cases they have had reason to suspect, if not to know, my principles; but as the system of travelling society is constituted, there is no place found for a religious man, as a religious man. The Calthorpes, when in Italy, abstained from society on principle. They passed through the country, saw its spectacles, its statues, its paintings; but of Italian society they knew nothing, because they did not enter into it. To me the door was not thrown so wide open, because I cannot boast of a title, or large property; but I found it ajar. I judged differently from them, and entered. In entering, I saw many things that I would not have seen, and heard much that I would have rejoiced not to hear. But if my intention in travelling was to see, not merely things, but men and manners, there was no alternative. I must have done as I did. Whether this speculation has been injurious to me, is a question as yet unsolved.

This is the backward look. Looking forward, he says:—

To me, the object of my highest ambition, and the proposed limit of my travels, Palestine, is in some measure " the Land of Promise." . . . I cannot refuse myself the gratification of visiting a scene in comparison with which all other lands lose the name of interest, and dwindle into trifles or amusement. To walk in Gethsemane, and to pace the shore of the Sea of Tiberias, to see Bethlehem and Bethany, and Mount Hermon, and Zion, and Libanus—at the very idea my blood flows in a swifter current, and my imagination kindles with a brighter flame. At the same time it seems to me that the information I am in quest of will fully justify my route, even in the near prospect of a sacred pro-

fession; and it will be my fault if my two years abroad
do not yield a more abundant harvest than any other of
my life.

On Whit Sunday, May 30, 1819, Henry Elliott reached
Jerusalem.

"I entered," he says, in a kind of daily journal, "by the gate
called, even now, the 'Gate of Bethlehem.'   The Turks
gazed at me, and the Arabs—an odious race—knit their
brows in token of malice against my dress and country.
I alighted at the Franciscan convent of Our Saviour, and
was welcomed kindly by the Father and the Priesthood of
the Society.   It was at three in the afternoon that I arrived,
for I was very anxious to be present during a part of the
day of Pentecost.   But I was so exhausted by the heat of
the sun that I was unfit for anything.

"In Jerusalem the very stones would cry out against the
man who should not humble himself before God, with such
an example of the Divine judgments in his sight.   If my
memory be correct, the first desire that I breathed before
God was for His mercy to His poor people, and the restoration of their fallen city.   For indeed it is a scene that
might draw tears from a stone.

" *Thursday.*—'Ben venuto alla Terra Santa' was the salutation
of the Fathers to me.   They are Cordeliers of the Order of
St. Francis.   The President is a Maltese, and the Society
consists of about forty fathers—men, as far as I can judge,
of a simple and unoffending life, drawn hither by the fame
of the place where our Saviour lived and died, and suffering
among a strange people every species of indignity and
wrong.   One and another of them generally come to my room
to pass an hour with me, and to tell me some story of
Turkish insolence or extortion.

" *Saturday.*—I have now seen nearly all.   I have made the
circuit of the city.   I have walked about Zion, and seen
her bulwarks and told her towers; and what shall I say?
They have shown me the three stations at which our Lord
fell under the weight of the cross; the house of Veronica
in the place where she presented a handkerchief to wipe His
face, and which was returned to her with a likeness mira-
culously imprinted; the place where the daughters of
Jerusalem met Him; the street by which the Virgin Mary
joined her Son on His way to Calvary; the rock on which

His diciples slept during our Saviour's passion, and the grotto where He prayed in agony.

"They have pointed out the house of Caiaphas, the terrace where David walked, and the pool in which Bathsheba washed herself. They have discovered the sepulchre of the Virgin, and the tombs of unnumbered saints; the house of Anna, and the site of the palace of the rich man before whose doors Lazarus lay full of sores.

"In short, all—all is known, as if by revelation, and nothing remains for doubt or conjecture! Cunning men have made the piety of the pilgrims an occasion of the grossest frauds.

"When I found myself thus bewildered in the maze of falsified tradition, I allowed my guides to show me every object of their veneration, and, by dint of being told all, believed nothing.

"Having completed the round, I took Josephus into my counsel, and examined when and why the Catholic Church adopted its opinion respecting the site of Mount Calvary, and Mount Zion, and the place of the Holy Sepulchre.

"I applied also to the Jewish Rabbis; and as they have ever continued to cling to this seat of their empire, and from generation to generation have kept their opinions unchanged, I attached much weight to their local appellations. I thought the more highly of their information, because it seemed to me to agree uniformly with what was clearly deducible from Josephus and other ancient authors.

"From the Jews I learnt that they agree in opinion with the Catholics and Greeks respecting the site of the Temple, Mount Zion, the Mount of Olives, the Brook Kedron, the sepulchres of their kings, the Pool of Siloam, the sepulchre of Zacharias, the villages of Bethany and Bethlehem, and various other particulars of minor importance. With regard to the Holy Sepulchre and Mount Calvary, it is little to be doubted that they were well known to the Christians in Jerusalem at the time of its destruction by Titus, A.D. 75.

"Having with much difficulty brought myself to believe that the present Church of the Holy Sepulchre is really on Mount Calvary, I entered into it one afternoon, and remained there all night. The morning that followed ushered in Trinity Sunday. The fathers who are here immured, come in by rotation, and remain two months, at the expiration of which time they are free to go or stay, as they please.

"Their religious services are very rigid; for besides the care of the church and the numerous chapels, and their services in the day, they rise half an hour before midnight, and again at three, after midnight, for their vespers and matins, which are as long as our morning services. I rose to them both, chanting with them the psalms appointed; went with them to the several 'holy places;' and then, while the organ played, I retired apart to the Sepulchre, and as the sound ran through the vaulted roof, now in full measure, and now fainter and fainter, it was luxury to listen, and to abandon myself to the softening influence of the music and the place.

"At that Sepulchre the silver lamps are ever burning un-quenchably; and day and night, as the hours roll on, the Latins, the Greeks, and the Armenians succeed each other without intermission, offering incense, and honour, and worship to the 'Lamb that was slain;' and ever, though in different tongues, prayers and praises and hallelujahs ascend without ceasing from Mount Calvary. May God grant that forms so interesting by local connexion may not lose their power, or be bereft of all their sacredness, by the superstitions with which they have been mingled.

"The present church was built by the Greeks twelve years since, who obtained the licence from Constantinople, in pre-ference to the Christians of other professions, by a bribe of some thousands of pounds. They have built the church on its former ground, and have divided it into three parts. The part where the Tomb is, over which is a magnificent dome, with two galleries running round its base, belongs to the Latins. The right to celebrate Divine service within the Sepulchre is common to all. The body and largest part, and the fairest, is appropriated to the Greeks; and the lowest part to the Armenians. But, notwith-standing this arrangement, their quarrels are most indecent, especially at the season of the Holy Week. They are not ashamed to come even to blows; and the Turkish soldiers have been obliged to interfere to separate the Christian combatants in the temple of the 'Prince of Peace.'

"Father Francis gave me a ground plan of the church, show-ing the different holy places, which it must be confessed are most conveniently near each other. It would seem as if the Roman soldiers and the terrified disciples had all united in so strict an economy of space, that they had an eye to the church hereafter to be founded, and took care that no remarkable event should exceed in distance the limits of a handsome edifice. Hence it arose that the place where our Lord was scourged, where the crosses were erected, where the garments were divided by the soldiers, where our Saviour was buried, where He appeared in the garden to Mary Magdalene, and several other localities of note, are all comprised within the body of the church; and, by a marvellous foresight, the sanctity of the Temple was augmented and the trouble of the pilgrim abridged.

"But, irony apart, how infinitely superior would have been the simple mount of Calvary, and the Tomb wherein the Son of man was laid, uncased in marble and unenclosed by walls!

"I now ride out of the gates early in the morning; and when I have escaped from the mummery and absurdity and imposture to which my well-meaning hosts the friars are, unwittingly, accessories, I gaze on the scene around me, and rejoice that the power of man cannot turn the mountains into churches, or the valleys into sepulchres of saints.

"These mountains are all marked by ancient tombs, hewn in their side. They themselves rise on every side of the city, and, by the steep and rugged ravines they interpose, they form the defence and bulwark of Jerusalem. I recollect that 'as the hills stand about Jerusalem, so the Lord is round about His people from henceforth even for evermore.' And then I think that He continually surrounds my beloved parents, and I offer a prayer that, though little deserving such mercy, I too, their child, may not be excluded from His shadowing wing; and then, though the way is long, and the difficulties many, and the journey solitary, I take courage, and expectation lights my eye with the idea that soon we shall meet and bless the Lord together."

JERUSALEM, *June* 5, 1819.

On Thursday morning, at six o'clock, I set out on horseback, accompanied by a Janissary, for Bethlehem. I had a young man, a well-informed guide, with me, and my servant Vasali. We rode out of the city by the Gate of Bethlehem. At a little distance from it were sitting by the wayside some lepers, to whom it was not permitted to enter the

city. Without offering to approach us, they begged our
alms.

We crossed the ravine immediately under the walls of
Jerusalem, and, ascending the opposite hill, we rode over
its top, which is level and rocky, till we arrived in half an
hour at the Greek convent dedicated to St. Elias; and my
guide showed me the sepulchre of Rachel and the Pool of
Solomon.

An hour's ride brought us to Bethlehem. It has vines and
olive and fig trees in abundance, especially on the slopes
of the hills, where are shown us the fields where the
shepherds kept their flocks by night, and heard the anthems
of the angelic host. We were kindly welcomed by the
Superior and my friend Father Francis, who had left
Jerusalem the preceding evening. I found a hospitable
roof and an abundant table, where the Lord of Glory had
nothing but a stable for His birthplace and a manger for
His cradle.

Father Francis accompanied me to the several consecrated
scenes. First and chief, we descended by a narrow stair-
case, dimly lighted, to the chapel erected where the infant
Jesus was born. It was a dark and subterranean grotto,
said to comprise the stable where the Holy Family lodged.
It is lighted by large lamps of solid silver, which, as they
hung above our heads, threw a religious glimmering
around us. They hang in a single row along the middle
of the ceiling, reaching the exact place where they assert
the Saviour was born. Fourteen other silver lamps shed
their splendour in a half-crescent, or circle, on the spot
where "the star of the East" had before shed its guiding
ray. These lamps are some Latin, others Greek, and others
Armenian; the different bodies of Christians obstinately
disputing the right of adorning these sacred places.

Having visited other points of interest, he says :—

In the afternoon we returned to Jerusalem, and retraced our
former road near the tomb of Rachel. At a well by the
wayside, I found, according to the patriarchal times, the
flocks and herds of the shepherds gathered to be watered.
The Arabs let down their pitchers, and filled the stone
troughs for the women. The men were not, indeed, like
Jacob, nor were the women "beautiful and well-favoured,"
yet it was interesting to see even a humble imitation of

the patriarch's courtesy, so near the sepulchre of her to whom the courtesy was offered.

It was early the next morning when I left Jerusalem by St. Stephen's Gate to visit some part of its immediate environs. I passed down the side of a deep ravine, and narrowly escaped an injury by the hurling of a large stone at me by a party of Arabs seated and smoking near the gate. At the bottom of the ravine I crossed a dry and rocky bed, through which, in winter, a brook runs with violence from the mountains on the north-east.

On the other side, at the foot of the mountain, a small plot of ground was distinguished by some olive trees of an extreme age. Here I stood for some time, and contemplated in silent reverence the sacred scene. Here, too, Mary, I thought of you, and your hymn, which you copied for me into my little travelling-book in manuscript. For that channel was the channel of the brook Kedron, and that garden of olives was Gethsemane!

My guide carried me next to the sepulchre of the Virgin, a deep and subterraneous grotto, formed into a church with infinite labour. From this tomb of the Virgin, I proceeded to ascend the mountain immediately above Gethsemane. It was the Mount of Olives, where David and a few of his faithful adherents went up, barefooted and weeping; and where a greater than David sat and wept over the city that rejected and crucified Him.

I called to mind that this mountain was His nightly resort, when He came up to the feast of the Passover: and on its summit a small octagonal chapel (now converted into a mosque) marks the spot which tradition has assigned for His ascent into heaven. Be this or not the accurate scene of that great event, it is certain that from this mountain— a favourite resort during His sojourn among men—the Lord of Glory took His flight to heaven, and left His last adieux with His disciples.

I have sat here several times looking on this city—now how changed! The revolutions of man, the fate of empires, and the history of the world cannot preach so loud or so awful a lesson as the view of Jerusalem from the side of Mount Olivet. In this Mount of Olives they showed me, near the Garden of Gethsemane, a flat part of the rock where the three disciples slept, and a grotto in which, at the same time, our Lord underwent that bitter part of His suffering which is called by way of emphasis "His Agony." They have taken upon them to fix the very spot where the Lord's Prayer was dictated to the disciples; and because in the side of the hill there is a curious cavern with twelve niches, they have assigned it to the twelve Apostles, and gilded the story by asserting that they there composed the Creed which bears their name.

Such pious frauds—at all times indefensible—become doubly guilty here; for really they have so occupied the ground of holy history by their pretensions to the knowledge of each precise spot and petty detail, that a man's feelings and associations have not fair play. These painful revelations defile the remains of the city of God more grossly than the sackage of Titus, or the impiety of the infidels; and Jerusalem has suffered more from its friends than its enemies.

Nazareth, June 10, 1819.

I have arrived at this village of blessed name and memory, in peace and safety. It was rather a perilous stage. The different tribes and villages through which I passed, amuse themselves, when they have no better employment, with making war on the Turkish Governor, or each other. Happily, it is harvest time, and the necessity of getting in the fruits of the land has led to general peace and occupation. I was in no way molested: even the usual *caphur* or tax, extorted from the passenger, was abandoned. For my part I put a bold face on the undertaking. I say a bold face, because every one said it was foolish and dangerous to go without a guard from the Government, and with no one but a servant and a lad and the two owners of our mules.

I had reasons for declining a guard. I had already assumed my Mameluke dress and long pistols; and passed with the Arabs as travelling with the authority and commission of a public person.

In order to make but one night upon the road, we set off early in the morning and travelled the whole day till dark. The heat was excessive, and, notwithstanding an umbrella, my face has been peeled by the sun. The turban, though it shelters the head better, gives very little shade to the face.

I parted with the fathers of St. Salvador with real affection, and I left them all with a regret that I think was mutual.

Passing through the Gate of Damascus, we left on our right the Sepulchre of the Kings, and traversed a desert, sterile, and rocky ground, till, in three hours, we arrived at Beer. Beer is a pleasant village, blessed with an abundant fountain, at which the Arab women were washing their clothes. It was the retreat of Jotham, when he fled from Abimelech; and the Christians, who are determined to give a story to every place, say that the Virgin rested here when she returned to Jerusalem to seek the child Jesus.

We continued our journey by rough and precipitous roads, and in five and a half hours passed by Gibeah of Saul, and saw a ruin on an elevation which passes for the place where Saul encamped, when God gave to Israel that remarkable victory over the Philistines. Our road from Beer was in the direction of their flight, and the valley of Ajalon at no great distance. We passed on by a valley thickly planted with beautiful fig-trees; and as the sun had now passed the meridian, and beat on my poor head and body with intense heat, I was glad to find a seat and a shade under a high rock, from which trickled down a clear but scanty stream.

Some ruins of a village and monastery marked the place; and opposite the rock which gave us its most welcome shadow another cliff reared itself abruptly, so as to form a sort of strait or pass in the valley. Here we ate our frugal dinner, and rested for two hours. The place was remarkable; and as the traveller is often obliged to proceed for hours in this country without finding a tree or rock to shelter him from the sun or dew, it could not fail to be a favourite resting-place with those who were journeying in this direction. I made these observations before I knew that this spot was supposed to be Jacob's "Bethel," when he took of the stones of the place and put them for his pillow, and in the visions of the night saw the angels ascending and descending from heaven.

To Naplosa it is twelve hours. The two last were through a delightful and broad valley, very distinct from the narrow ravines which form the valleys in Judæa. We left two Arab villages, famed for their irregularities and rebellions, a little to the left, and turning short round we passed between the mountains Gerizim and Ebal, and when their shadows had covered the plain, crossed the olive grounds, and entered the gates of the city.

It is large, ugly, and very populous. The Arabs were sitting smoking in the bazaars (which were dimly lighted), and enjoying the cool of the evening. I found a lodging in the open porch of a solitary Greek church; and though I was very, very weary, before I closed my eyes I read the story of Abimeloch, and the exquisite narrative of our Lord's conversation with the woman of Samaria; for Naplosa was once called Shechem, and afterwards Sychar; and "Jacob's well was there."

After a short excursion on the following day to see this well, on my return I sent for the priest and principal person of the Samaritans. They both of them came to me. They were tall men, of the same cast of countenance—the face very long, the nose prominent, the eyes sunken, and the forehead high, with black hair. Their physiognomy was so peculiar, so distinct from the physiognomy of the Arabs and Jews, and yet not less marked and decisive, that I should have been glad to have seen more specimens of their race. It is certain that they are the descendants of the ancient Samaritans; preserving, unmixed with other nations, their families, and pure from innovation and interpolation, the creed of their forefathers. I learnt from them that in Naplosa their number amounted to two hundred. When I inquired in what particulars they differed from the Hebrews in their religion, they answered that "they differed very materially: first and most, that they held that mountain" (pointing to Gerizim) "to be the spot from which, by God's appointment, prayers and sacrifices ascended to heaven with peculiar acceptance: that the Jews, on the contrary, maintained that in Jerusalem was the Sanctuary of God: and that, moreover, their Scriptures differed in many places."

I was anxious to buy a copy of their Scriptures, but they refused to sell them. It struck me as a remarkable circumstance that I should hear in this city, from the mouth of a Samaritan, the very point of difference between them and the Jews which, in the same place, eighteen hundred years ago, formed the first subject of inquiry of the Samaritan woman, when she perceived that the Lord was a prophet. "Our fathers worshipped in this mountain: and ye say that in Jerusalem is the place where men ought to worship." If I am not mistaken, it is the only passage of Scripture which adverts to this point of controversy between the Jews and Samaritans.

I arrived at Nazareth fitter for an hospital than for the inquiries and research of a traveller. The sleep and freshness of the night, however, in some measure restored me; and in the morning .... I felt myself able, at least, to visit what was remarkable in the village of Nazareth. I will mention some particulars briefly of the Luoghi Santi, or Holy Places, as they are termed. The Church of the Convent is so built as to comprise a grotto, seven or eight steps below its level; this is said to be the residence in which the Virgin received the Annunciation of the angel Gabriel. I was next shown the workshop of Joseph, and the synagogue (a small, dark, stony Greek church) in which Jesus was accustomed to teach on the Sabbath day, and where He opened the book of Esaias at that passage, "The Spirit of the Lord is upon me" (St. Luke iv. 18). I was also taken to the house where our Saviour used to eat bread with His disciples; and as a proof of the identity of the room, in the middle of it is shown a large circular table of rock, like a vast cylinder, round which twelve persons might stand to eat, but certainly they could not adopt the usual manner of reclining. They showed me also the chapel of the Annunciation, the house of Joseph, the synagogue and cœnaculum of our Lord. They will even carry the imposture to so degrading a detail as to exhibit the kitchen in which the blessed Virgin cooked her dinner.

I feel the strongest dislike to the juggling and dishonesty of those who first propagated such deceits, who baptized and consecrated, as scenes of the most sacred events, places in the highest degree absurd, and who were guilty of supposing that religion could be served by the fraud of pretended revelations.

To me it is enough that Nazareth still bears the name it bore two thousand years ago; and I love to think that to those hills the "Lord of Life" retired as His oratories, and that the plains and valleys near it were those in which He passed His spotless life, and delivered His divine instructions. However, there are still two places endeared to the Christian, not by the falsified traditions of the Catholics, but by the immutable marks of nature: the first is the fountain called " La Fontana della Madonna ;" and undoubtedly, as that is the only spring of water in the village, we may conclude that its pure and copious streams furnished to the Holy Family the beverage of their simple table: the second is the precipice to which the men of the city led Jesus to cast him down headlong. It is at some distance from the present village. I followed a bridle-way along a deep dry ravine, which in the winter becomes a watercourse to conduct the mountain torrent on its way to the plains of Megiddo, and the river Kishon. The path became so difficult and rocky that I was obliged to dismount and walk on alone. On either side of the ravine, bare mountains raised their rugged forms about me, and brought to my recollection the passes of romantic Switzerland. Just where the dell issues in the great plain, the hills turn off to the right and left in steep precipices; and under the face of the perpendicular rock a rude altar intimates to the pilgrim the spot where the Lord of Glory suffered one of the many indignities of His life from an evil and perverse generation.

Nazareth itself is a poor village, standing on elevated ground in the hollow of several hills, which form a part of the fine chain of mountains bounding the plain of Esdraelon on the north. Its population amounts to about three thousand. They are almost all Christians, and the major part Roman Catholics. When the Host was elevated on the day of " Corpus Domini," I remarked that the women, to testify their grief, beat violently on their breasts. It is the usage of the country now, as it was in the days of our Saviour.

Early the following morning, while the dew was yet fresh on the ground, I rode out of the village, and passed along the glens which are at its foot, to ascend Mount Tabor. Tabor stands insulated at the north-east extremity of the plain of Esdraelon. It rises to a great height, and appears in the bee-hive form, just as Raphael has painted it in his immortal picture of the Transfiguration, which you know passes for the finest specimen of the art.

The view from this elevation is as grand as nature and as interesting as Scripture can make it. Towards the west, looking over the golden landscape presented by the pastures and fields of the plain of Esdraelon (a landscape just now gay in its summer dress, and rich with its harvest and harvesters mingled together), the eye meets Mount Carmel

and the Mediterranean; on the east, Mount Hermon, and
the Sea of Galilee; on the south, the high places of Bethel,
and the fatal mountains of Gilboa; and on the north, a
tract of bold hills running westward towards the sea, and
eastward to Libanus and Anti-libanus. The snow-clad
ridges of these two mighty chains complete the magnificence
of the landscape.

Below, in the plain, Debora, bearing still the name of the pro-
phetess, and Cana of Galilee, and Endor, and the course of
the river Kishon, and the fields of Dothan where Joseph
found his brethren, form resting-points, where the mind
relieves the eye, and connects the beauty of nature and the
grandeur of the prospect with the history of the people of
God, His judgments and His tender mercies.

I remained here a considerable time, for it was impossible to
be altogether insensible to the impression it made. Tabor
is generally supposed to be the "Mount of Transfiguration,"
and with so much greater probability, as there is no other
single high mountain near Nazareth.

In Nazareth I bought several silver medals. The peasants
find them after heavy rains, on the sides and amidst the
ruins of Mount Tabor. In Jerusalem, too, I selected a few
copper coins: one of these latter has the legend "Gaza,"
and really belongs to the city the gates of which Samson
carried on his shoulders; though my faith did not extend
so far as that of the seller, who wished to persuade me that
the coin was coeval with the hero!

As Arabic is the only language spoken in Palestine, all my
communications with the people were through the medium
of an interpreter. This circumstance has constituted a
very decided difference between my tours in Greece and
Palestine. In the former I could converse with any peasant
I met, and inform myself of his feelings, prejudices, and
manners without mistake. In Greece, therefore, though
abroad, I felt at home. In Syria, on the contrary, I am a
perfect stranger, and I feel so. The country is also too
dangerous and barbarous to admit of solitary rides and
walks, and those meditations of a "sweet and bitter fancy"
which love what is lonely and tranquil.

The Arabic all seems to come from the throat, and the people
in their common discourse vociferate so that you would
suppose they were always in a passion. They are very
swarthy, their eyes clear and flashing, the nose prominent,

the forehead high, and the contour of the face oval. The majority of them live in tents, as the posterity of Ishmael. They are called Bedouins, and own no subjection save to their chief. These Bedouins are the Arabs who bring the race of horses to such high perfection; and to speak the truth, I could enter into the joy they feel in their horses, when I mounted on one of these spirited and beautiful creatures, and galloped along the level desert with a speed which seemed to scorn the ground.

And now I am come to the close of our day's journey—remarkable not only for the recollections I have noticed, but also, to me, remarkable as the first day of my return homewards. I could not help thinking of Jacob's journey, and his affecting covenant with God:—"If God will be with me, and will keep me in this way that I go, and will give me bread to eat, and raiment to put on, so that I come again to my father's house in peace; then shall the Lord be my God." (Genesis xxviii. 20, 21.)

I was afraid to vow; I have found my heart so deceitful; but I strove to pray to the same effect:—for, indeed, I have of late become often melancholy and have thought with something like dread of my solitary condition, my long distance from all who love me, and the perils of the sun, the land, and the sea. If I should never return to you (as I trust in God I shall in peace), may we meet where Jacob has terminated a longer journey than that from Beersheba to Haran, and where, without a pilgrimage of more than two thousand miles, we may all, through the unspeakable mercy of Jesus of Nazareth, visit the heavenly Zion, and become citizens of the new Jerusalem.

Although he thus turned his face homeward, yet there was still before him much travelling "by land and by water;" and it was more than a year (August 1820) before he reached what he calls the "cold and foggy triangle." His movements were not unattended with risk; for the Archipelago abounded with corsairs, and more than once he had to rouse and encourage the seamen to load the guns and prepare to fight. He complains of always having contrary winds, and the little caïque in which, after parting with his brother, he had crossed to Smyrna, instead of making the passage in three days, was tossed about, as we have seen, for some weeks. Palestine, also, was much more lawless then than now. He once owed his life to a false but timely word of his attendant. In one of the rocky passes in Palestine he saw a Turk abusing a poor peasant and endangering his life. He rushed to the rescue, brandishing his sabre ; but would have been soon cut down himself had not his guide exclaimed, "Hold! are you ignorant that this is the physician of the Pasha of Damascus?"

The perils to which he was exposed, were well known to his family at home, and they were in a constant state of anxiety, more or less.

During one period of his absence, owing to some irregularity of the mails, his family were for a long while without communications of any kind; and so great was their alarm that the idea of going into mourning for him was entertained. They still remember the joy which overspread the household when a heap of letters at once arrived ; and his brother sprang upstairs waving them in his hand, and exclaiming, "Hal's alive! Hal's alive!"

Very soon after his arrival in the Holy Land he had been obliged to lay aside the European dress altogether, as hateful to the inhabitants, and exposing him to daily and hourly insult.

"You would not know me," he says, in a letter to the Rev. Joseph Pratt of Peterborough. "Fancy me with moustaches, well grown and long, with a turban on my head, and my whole costume that of a Mameluke, with a sword and two immense pistols stuck in the shawl which I wear as a girdle. I passed for a Turk with the natives; and my dress being scarlet, which is the colour of distinction in Egypt, a whole party of Arabs squatting on their mats and smoking their chibouques, would get up and make me a profound reverence. I used to receive it with the utmost *nonchalance*, as my unquestioned due. A friend of mine went a step further, and let his beard grow for four months. Yet I escaped in the dangerous and inhospitable land of Syria without an injury, while he came off very narrowly with his life, and was happy in having no more than his jaw broken by the blow of a club tipped with iron."

So much for Palestine. In the return journey, all the gaps he had before left were filled up. He revisited all his favourite spots in Greece, and tarried long in Italy, Sicily, and Venice.

His last letter is written from Basle, dated July 14, 1820,

and addressed to his father. He thanks him for the liberal remittances he had received, which, besides enabling him to enjoy the pleasures of the tourist. had enriched him with many valuable treasures. He had been eager throughout in purchasing medals and rare coins. Lord Ruthven wrote to him to say that he had left a very bad name behind him in Italy and Greece, in that he had given the most extravagant prices for such rarities, and so raised the market that people did not know now how much to ask. And his friend the Archbishop of Tarentum, who had entered *con amore* into his numismatic researches at Naples, wrote to him two years afterwards as follows:—" Datemi le nuove delle vostre numis-matiche occupazioni. O caro Elliott! si sono vendute due moneta di oro Tarantine inedite *di un preggio raro!* " He spent, moreover, about 200*l.* on choice editions of the classics. He purchased many beautiful cameos as presents to his family, and was the bearer of the real attar of roses, and other choice perfumes, dear to ladies.

" To-day is Saturday," he says. " On Monday I hope to set off for Paris, and to reach it in six days. It is my intention, with your permission, to remain there a week, and then set off to join you. I am running my journey very fine, for I have only twenty louis to carry me to Paris. I have tried in vain to sell my *calèche* at Florence.

" When I was there I sent off four boxes of alabaster: two (whichever you prefer) I beg you and my mother to accept as a testimony (such as a gift can be) of the love and duty I have ever borne you, during my absence of three years. It wants but three days to complete the three years. If, as I trust in God, we meet in peace, we shall indeed have true reason to bless the Omnipresent mercy that has watched over the absent and the present. May the union, which can only be by Him, be also in Him! "

On July 21, 1820, he reached Paris, and on August 9th he was once more at home.

CHAPTER IV.

HOLY ORDERS.

Joy at his Return—Visits to Friends—Sir Walter Scott—University Pursuits—Father of his College—Curacy of Ampton—Ordination—Pupils—St. Mary's, Brighton—Priory of St. John, Wilton—Offer of Sandon—Consecration of St. Mary's—Extracts from Sermon-book—Offer of Winsham—Family affection—Letters—His Father's death—Tablet to his memory.

WHILST abroad, Henry Elliott had spoken of England as the "cold and foggy triangle;" but when he returned home, it was as "the ark to the dove." Words failed to express his feelings of delight. On August 10, 1820, he wrote to his friend John Babington:—

As a brother returned, I beg to send you the assurance of a love which never went away. I am at least an Englishman all over. I love my country's landscapes, its manners, its looks, its education, its government, its men, its women, its table. I love the whole system of its society, and its religion, a thousand times more than I ever loved any country in my life. So much for the creed and confession of my national partiality.

Nor were the greetings which he received less warm. His friend the Rev. William Carus-Wilson (and his words were echoed by many others) says, Aug. 12 :—

I cannot describe the sensation with which I heard of your return from your travels. Be assured, my dearest Elliott, if there is a person whom I love and value it is yourself; and if there is a friend to whom I owe a debt of gratitude, it is you.

After surrendering himself to all the charms of home for a time, and recovering from his fatigue, he made many visits to his widening circle of friends: some new, and the pleasing result of travel; some old and long-tried. One or two incidents occurring during a visit to Scotland, are remembered by his friend Scott Moncrieff :—

He went to spend a Sunday at Glasgow that he might hear Dr. Chalmers. He was disappointed, for the Doctor did not preach. But he seemed to think himself no loser, when a young man stood up in the pulpit, whose appearance was particularly striking—" with the front of Jove

himself," he said : and who gave them a sermon of surpassing power and eloquence. The young man was Edward
Irving.

Another visit was to Yair, a lovely place on the banks of
the Tweed. Here his professed skill in judging of a man's
character by his handwriting was tested. Several specimens
were put before him, but one particularly attracted his
notice. There was no word to indicate the writer, and the
handwriting he had certainly never seen. After due examination, he described what he supposed would be the
characteristics of the writer. One trait was mentioned after
another, all of which were pronounced correct : and at last
he wound up by saying that he could fancy the writer to be
just such a man as Benjamin Franklin. The writer was
Benjamin Franklin himself!

Whilst sojourning at Edinburgh, he was introduced to
Sir Walter Scott, and gives a graphic account of the inter-
view. At dinner he sat between Sir Walter Scott and
Mrs. Lockhart :—

> Sir Walter said nothing very remarkable. His conversation
> was rather that of good information and good-nature, than
> of a style embellished by sallies of wit, or bursts of imagi-
> nation. But when he got to anecdote, he told several
> stories with great point, and hit shrewdly and with nicety
> the mark at which anecdote aims. He told how Wilkes,
> on a public occasion, when a man's stories, more prolix
> than high seasoned, were excused because he had got to
> his *dotage*, said : "Sir, I tell you that he is past *dotage*, and
> has got to *anecdotage*." I do not hold with John Wilkes so
> far as it applies to Sir Walter Scott, and I am sure that
> the next new novel will pass muster as a proof of his sanity
> and vigour of mind. Its title I prognosticate will be 'The
> Pirate.'

After dinner we sang the Jacobite song—

> "Here's health to the king, boys!
> Ye ken wha I mean, boys!"

> Mrs. Lockhart played the accompaniment on the harp,
> which she touched with much, though singular, enthusiasm
> and taste. All the rest of us joined hands in the chorus.
> My friend declared that I was in the precise condition of
> Waverley—a poor, unsuspecting Englishman, drawn in to

make deep protestations against the House of Hanover, without my will or knowledge. Abbotsford is a strange, ill-adjusted pile, built at much expense, half castle, half abbey, with all the awkward passages, small rooms, and little light, in which our ancestors studied safety rather than convenience.

These visits ended, Henry Elliott settled down at Cambridge. His moustaches disappeared; his turban shrunk into a college cap; his Mameluke scarlet dress was exchanged for a Master of Arts' black gown; and his sword was beaten into a steel pen.

In compliance with the wishes of his family, he began diligently to collect all his letters from abroad, and to prepare them for the press. Great progress was made, and several large manuscript books were filled, from which these pages have been enriched; but the plan was never completed, nor the printer set to work.

The pursuits of the University seemed more congenial to him, and into all plans for its improvement he entered with great zest. In March, 1821, he writes as follows to his brother :—

To-day we had to vote on French's new scheme of an examination in some Greek and Latin classic, a Gospel, and Paley's " Evidences." It is to take place at the end of the fifth term ; and the men who pass are to be divided into only two classes. It is, in fact, the Oxford Little-go. I like the principle of a Little-go; but this I think objectionable, so that I shall give it a negative. But I believe it will surely pass.

Into the intellectual society of his college he entered with unfeigned delight, being well prepared by thorough knowledge, refined taste, and long travel, to bear his part in the mental arena. Who would not envy his daily and hourly intercourse with men like Monk, Clarke, Evans. Scholefield, Peacock, Whewell, Romilly, and Sedgwick—all Fellows of his own college?

He consented occasionally to take a private pupil, under exceptional circumstances, as the following extract, given in proof of the conscientious performance of his duty, will show :—

Lord —— has passed with a facility that I did not look for,

into all the idleness and dissipation of Cambridge. He came to me twice during the term. Four more' times will nearly complete the other two terms, and then with an easy conscience I am to receive my hundred guineas per annum. In truth, six hours well paid! There has been no distance or aversion between us. Many serious expostulations I have had with him, and many fair promises has he given. If the next term should be a fac-simile of the past, I shall write at once, and throw up my office. If the umbra of a tutor is necessary to a nobleman, and his quarterly bills are deemed imperfect without the items of such a charge, there are men in the University on whose conscience the office will sit more easily than on mine.
The Hon. G. R. —— is in every respect the opposite of Lord ——; and I have with him all the satisfaction that a man can feel in the daily conviction of his usefulness to another.

He was Sub-Lecturer also in his College, and one of the Examiners, year by year. He attended several courses of University lectures, especially those on Geology and Chemistry.

He acted also as Father of his College, as the phrase runs, presenting the "οἱ πολλοί" and "Ten-year Men" for their degree, after having helped them, by his advice and partial instruction, to obtain it. He often indulged in a good-natured smile on such occasions. Thus, in December 1822, he writes :—

I have been very busy in my paternal office. Alas! this office of whipper-in to the idle pack of "οἱ πολλοί" is no sinecure. One man, whom three years and one term of University life have not yet transmitted in safety over the Pontine marshes" (*alias* the *Pons asinorum* before alluded to, *alias* the Asses' bridge, *alias* the Fifth Proposition of Euclid), told me with great candour and openness, the other day, that he must own he could never bring his mind to an attachment to the mathematics!
Again, in March 1823, he says :—
This morning my paternal duty again led me to a Divinity Act kept by poor W——, a rude, unlettered man of ten years' standing, proceeding to his B.D. His Northumberland dialect set off the false quantities he made in high relief. Greek he could hardly spell or read, and the arguments of his opponents were Arabic to his head. However,

he had been rightly drilled to remember that if he denied the conclusion of his adversary, "Nego consequentiam" was the Latin for such denial. The Opponents produced their arguments:—at the end of the first syllogism, "Nego consequentiam" he called out; at the end of the second, "Nego consequentiam" was again heard.

"Probes aliter," said the presiding Doctor to the Opponent, after trying in vain to make the respondent understand the argument.

The Opponent submitted. "Probo aliter" ("I prove it in another way"), he said to the Northumbrian; and forthwith another syllogism appeared in its threefold form. At the end of the first part, "Nego consequentiam" again was ready. At the end of the second, the same. At the end of the third, the same. It was useless going further; and Mr. W—— goes down to Newcastle, and rides henceforth in his carriage (for he keeps one) a "B.D.;" and talks big, no doubt, of the Act he kept under the Bishop on "Justification by Faith alone,' and the "Credibility of the Resurrection!" There is something disgraceful in this by-way of admission to academical rank and honour; though truly the "Nego Consequentiam" of this morning in the Divinity Schools got quite the better of my gravity.

The fee to the Father of the College in those days seems to have been a guinea from each undergraduate Son who was presented and passed.

· Henry Elliott took an active part in the election contests of the University, and was a canvasser for Lord Hervey in the election of 1822. He cultivated close friendship with the good, and never concealed his principles, nor shrunk from the reproach of Christ. Mr. Simeon, calling on his mother in 1822, brought tears into her eyes by saying: "Your sons are my joy!" His influence was thrown into the right scale; and he was always accounted a religious man. He remained a firm friend to the Bible Society, attending the annual meetings, and aiming to increase the number of its friends. He was also forward in introducing other kindred societies into Cambridge. His Sunday evenings during term were passed in company with young men, earnest and right-minded; when the sermon of some able Divine would be read and discussed, with a view to present edification, and a future preparation for the Ministry.

But all this while, though charmed with his literary pursuits and University friends, and desirous of doing as much
good as in him lay, he was not content. This was not to him
the great end of life. He was, after all, living "to himself,"
and not "unto Him" who died for us, and rose again. His
original purpose of giving himself up to the "ministry of the
Word," though delayed, was never altered. His mind
seems never to have faltered, and no other profession
was ever mentioned. It had been his earliest aspiration
and his constant aim; and it now became the turning-point
of life.

His desires also were quickened by a visit to his brother
Edward, who had already taken Holy Orders. The even
tenor of the life he saw, and the pleasant duties, so efficiently
performed by the young curate, hastened his own decision.
After some hesitation as to the place he should select, he
finally decided to take the Curacy of Ampton, where, in 1811
and 1812, he had been a student under Mr. Cotterill.

In speaking of the place, July 22, 1823, he says :—

I feel doubtful whether in accepting Ampton Curacy I have
not too much considered many worldly motives: such as
my attachment to Lord Calthorpe; the pleasure I take in
such society as he collects around him; the neighbourhood
of Lord Hervey; the summer solitude, which is just what
I should desire. I feel as if it were serving the Lord on
easy terms. Let me have your constant remembrances as
a friend who will not forget me at the Throne of Grace.
What encourages my doubtful mind is, that I pray, and I
trust sincerely, that I may occupy that station which is
best suited for the service of my Master—if I may call Him
my Master, to whom I have been so unfaithful and un-
feeling.

"I am not to go to Ampton," he adds in another letter,
"till January. I am to live in Lord Calthorpe's house
about six months, during five of which he will be absent;
and then to take possession of the parsonage, now occupied.
It is thus that the pegs and cords that have fixed my tent
to the side of Alma Mater (and a kind mother, I must
say, I have found her) are at last on the point of being
loosened and taken up. May the God who accompanied
the Patriarchs in their goings, bless the place where I
shall again fix ' this tabernacle,' and be with me in my

removal, till the frail provisions of the traveller are over, and he is at rest and at home."

As the time of his ordination drew near, a deep seriousness, and sense of the importance of the step he was about to take, pressed upon his mind. In a letter dated October 27, 1823, to his friend Babington, he says :—

The chief object of this letter is to tell you that next Sunday, November 2d, if there should not occur any unforeseen impediment, I am to receive Holy Orders from the Bishop of Ely. I need not, on the most solemn occasion that can occur in my life, commend myself to my own dear friend's earnest recollection and prayers. Put up in your congregation the Ember-week prayer; and let it be the subject of your petition for me, that God would grant me an honest and merciful admission to His Holy Temple; and that, without falsehood or hypocrisy, I may be enabled out of a good conscience to make answer to the awful questions that will be put to me. From the high— and I find just—account I received of Francis Cunning-ham's parochial example, by a promise of real antiquity that I would pay him a visit, and by the thought that I should be undisturbed, I have been spending the last few days at Pakefield.

He was encouraged by a few affectionate lines from Mr. Wilberforce, on October 21, 1823 :—

I have been not more uncivil to you (and incivility to you almost deserves a worse name) than I have been unjust to myself in delaying so long to answer your friendly letter. . . . Believe me, my dear Sir, the somewhat nervous state of mind you experience in that solemn act of devoting yourself for life to the service of God in the ministry, does not indicate your being less fit for that sacred designation. May it please God to bless you with abundant usefulness; and then you will occupy the most honourable station in human society! I trust I can truly say that there is none I so much covet for those who are nearest and dearest to me.

Henry Elliott was ordained deacon by Dr. Sparke, Bishop of Ely, at Ely, on Sunday, November 2, 1823, and priest by Dr. Bathurst, Bishop of Norwich, at Norwich, on Trinity Sunday, June 13, 1824. On this last occasion there were

eighty-four candidates; and it will not surprise the reader
that the examining chaplain, Dr. Valpy, placed Henry
Elliott first, and was pleased to say that it was the best
examination he had ever superintended. In consequence,
he was appointed to preach the Ordination Sermon in the
following year. He did so; and at the request of the
Bishop it was printed.

His maiden ministration was on Sunday, November 9,
1823, when he read prayers twice at Ampton, reserving his
first sermon for Yelling; when he preached from the text
"I am the God of Abraham, and the God of Isaac, and the
God of Jacob. God is not the God of the dead, but of the
living." (Matt. xxii. 32.) His mother and one of his sisters
were present.

Thus Elisha took up the mantle of Elijah; and the
grandson began where the revered grandfather had ended
his testimony.

Ampton did not suit him. It was not likely that it
would. Even now the population only amounts to 130;
and in the year 1824 it would be still fewer. It might be
pleasant enough to live in the Hall, but the Curacy was
not yet really vacant. A clergyman occupied the parsonage
and performed the duties. Henry Elliott, therefore, being
for the time disengaged, and knowing that the Curate
in charge of Fakenham Parva, some miles distant, and
belonging to the Duke of Grafton, was in delicate health,
offered his gratuitous services, which were accepted.

After the lapse of a few months, however, this arrangement was altered, and he moved to Ampton Parsonage, and
took charge of the parish. All that was to be done he did,
and did well. He established a week-day lecture, he increased the schools, and preached with great animation and
good effect. "No congregation," he said, "was more interesting than a large, rustic, attentive church-full of
villagers." "In preaching to them," he adds, "I sometimes
forget myself, and think indeed of my solemn commission,
and the issues of life and death attaching to it. I
have found many cases of the 'listening ear,' but few as yet
of 'the converted heart.'"

But the change was great, and the sphere contracted: and
in order to cheer his solitude, to help out his income,[1] and to

[1] His receipts for this year from his Fellowship were but 125*l.*, and out

employ his time, he took one or two pupils, increased after a while to three or four. He tells his friend Scott Moncrieff of these things in a letter written from Ampton Hall, March 2, 1824:—

I am, as you know, now ordained to the holy office of the ministry; and preparatory to my taking charge of Ampton and Honington in August, I have taken the duty of a small parish at no great distance, called Fakenham.

My ministry has begun under as favourable circumstances as I could have expected, considering how unqualified in some of the most important parts of my duty I am, and how great a mercy it is that I have engaged in this service without (I hope, at least, without) a violation of my conscience.

The great diminution of our Fellowships has also obliged me to add the office of "Tutor" to that of "Pastor," and I have begun with two pupils, one the son of Mr. S. Hoare, the banker, the other a son of Lord Harrowby. With each of these lads I receive 300*l.* a year; so that, by a strange perversion, the main profession of life brings me about 100*l.* per annum, and the corollary six times that sum.

One of his later pupils (the Rev. C. B. Pearson, son of the former Dean of Salisbury, now Rector of Knebworth) recalls these days, and describes Henry Elliott graphically as a tutor:—

I went to him as a pupil to prepare for Oxford, having left Eton possibly with some conceit of Etonian scholarship, which led me to form a rather disparaging expectation of Mr. Elliott's knowledge of classics, and especially of composition. I knew he was highly distinguished at Cambridge, and a Fellow of Trinity, but I imagined his fame rested rather on mathematics than classics. I speedily discovered my mistake, however, and found not only that the superior accuracy of his scholarship enabled him to detect numerous deficiencies in my own, but that the elegance of his mind, and his wide acquaintance with Greek and Latin authors, set him in his right place as a master of composition. He read carefully with us many of the best classical writers, and I can safely say I learnt

---

of these he had to pay thirty guineas towards building the new court of Trinity.

more in one year with him than I had ever gained before,
or since, in the same time.

It was a real pleasure to study with him. He worked with
us, as if it was quite as important a matter to himself as
to us. He slurred over no difficulties, and the varied
information with which his mind was stored was all at
our command. He was in every sense an accomplished
man of letters. He delighted in history, ancient and
modern, and occasionally he would give us a modern
subject for discussion and debate, in which, after hearing
both sides, he used to sum up the arguments with much
skill, and often with considerable eloquence.[1]

In hours of recreation he was equally agreeable. He was
strong and active, and joined in our amusements; would
run, leap, and wrestle with us; or, in bad weather,
challenge us to indoor games.

Mr. Elliott lived simply, and the Parsonage and *ménage* were
small; but he was extremely particular about manners,
dress, and attention to hours, and resented any want of
refinement, or disorder. The parish was very small, and
the people all of the agricultural class. I have no recollection of the sermons we heard, beyond an impression that
they were very simple and affectionate, and suited to the
few rustic folk who were present. I remember that he
made us take turns to read the lessons in a great old-
fashioned desk, and that the music was supplied by a
barrel-organ in a gallery, which Lord Calthorpe's butler
used to grind, and with which he was jealous of our
attempting to meddle.

Another pupil, the son of the late Sir Benjamin Hobhouse,
between whom and himself there existed the greatest possible
affection, bears similar testimony.

" At a distance of two and forty years," he says, " I retain
few particulars of my late tutor and friend, whom to know
was to admire, to esteem, and to love. It was in the year

---

[1] It is a little amusing to find the late Prime Minister, Lord Aberdeen,
referring to these things, and writing: "I think your exercises of extempore discussion on some popular topic of the day well calculated to give
an interest to these political matters. At the same time I am a little
jealous of interference with what I consider my peculiar province. Might
not interesting subjects of discussion be found a little removed from the
actual politics of the day?"

1825 that I became his pupil, and it was truly a happy period of life which I passed under his domestic roof. He was of opinion that eight hours a day was a fair portion of time to devote to study: not that more was impossible, but that the fruit would be disproportionate to the labour, and the effects perhaps injurious to the health; and under this arrangement we steadily worked, with no small pleasure and advantage. . . .

" Out of church, his ability in extempore comments upon Scripture was perfectly equal to that which marked his pulpit-teaching; and the memory of those brief but cogent and luminous expositions, delivered in private, often recurs to me with sincere gratification. His travels in the East had supplied him with a copious fund of Biblical illustration, upon which he would draw in a familiar way, as pleasing as compendious, and always commanding the attention of even the least erudite hearers.

" To crown other merits, his temper was superior to every trial, and never gave way under whatsoever vexation. As no man is perfect, it may be supposed that I have given one side only of his character; but, in truth, I am at a loss to name an imperfection."

This is the testimony of pupils as regards their tutor. Numberless letters are yet preserved, and might be quoted, to show the interest felt by that tutor in his pupils. He watched their course long after they left him, and never ceased to lift up the warning voice, or to speak the encouraging word, as occasion required. He sometimes said that he had no liking for pupilizing; but this was in moments of weariness only. It had become habitual to him, and did not cease till his marriage.

He did not, however, stay long at Ampton. His health flickered, his voice failed, and after a service of nearly two years, that is, in October 1825, he resigned the cure, and returned to Cambridge. He writes to his friend Babington on November 4th :—

I came into college partly to repose from overwork, partly to keep certain exercises necessary to my being made one of the college preachers, which both gives priority in college preferment, and enables a man to hold property, or a living from external patronage, without vacating his Fellowship.

It requires about two months to complete the exercises. I had not come up a day (and it is not a week since I came) before the head lectureship became unexpectedly vacant, and was at my option. It is worth 200*l.* a year, and only requires residence till the end of May, at which time I hope to bid adieu to college entirely. After much deliberation, and the unanimous advice of friends, I accepted it. Residence is the only drawback; for it is the least burdensome office in college, and best paid. I feel the post here responsible and dangerous. Pray for me.

He settled to his work, officiated gratuitously as curate of Long Stanton, was frequently in London, took part in the stirring controversy regarding the circulation of the Apocrypha by the Bible Society: and it seemed very likely that his course would run upon the much-frequented road of a residence in college, a useful academical life, and in due time some piece of college preferment. But "man proposes, and God disposes." There was a niche prepared in the Temple, and before long Henry Elliott was called to fill it— the proper man in the proper place.

His family had for many years been accustomed to resort to Brighton, and sojourn in Westfield Lodge upon the West Cliff. The reader acquainted with the locality, and aware how many noble squares and streets now stretch beyond, and hold out the hand to Hove, will smile to hear how in those days (about 1811 or 1812) there were but three houses further west, that the Lodge lay open to every wind, and that the field to which it owed its name was " sprinkled with young lambs." Here, finally, the family settled, removing altogether from Clapham, and upon Brighton thenceforth their interest was concentrated.

At this time it was contemplated to erect in St. James' Street, Brighton, a proprietary chapel to be called St. Mary's, on ground given by the Earl of Egremont upon three conditions:—that the appointed minister should be a Dr. Everard, that a good and sufficient pew should be assigned to his lordship's household, and that 240 free sittings should be appropriated to the poor.

On what conditions Dr. Everard ceded his rights, and how far the chapel had advanced when he did so, are points not now accurately known. But with the cognizance and approbation, no doubt, of the Earl of Egremont and the vicar of

Brighton, the privilege and property were both transferred to Mr. Elliott's father, and on August 17, 1826, possession was taken, and a contract entered into to complete the building for the sum of 2,000*l.* The whole cost eventually amounted to nearly 10,000*l.*; and Mr. Elliott senior, having presented it to his son when consecrated, left it to him as part of his inheritance after his death.

This chapel is now well known to every visitor at Brighton. It presents no special ecclesiastical appearance. The exterior is Grecian, with a well-proportioned but somewhat heavy Doric portico. The interior has the seats and galleries of fifty years back, and there is a small chancel, with pulpit and desk on either side. Invalids find fitting pews; and every arrangement is made for the convenience and comfort of the congregation; but the real attraction has ever been that crowded congregation itself, listening with rapt attention to their beloved minister!

For here, in due time, Henry Elliott found his appropriate sphere of duty, and here he laboured without change for eight-and-thirty years. He truly called it "the most solemn crisis of his life;" and if the reader compares the past records of that life with what is yet to come, he will observe how circumstances develope character, and how, when the tree finds its congenial soil, the fruit becomes not only good, but golden—rich, ripe, sweet and abundant.

Nearly a year elapsed before the arrangements were completed and the building finished, as the following extract from a letter written at this time shows :—

March 29, 1826.—After much deliberation and reluctance I have consented to be appointed to a proprietary chapel at Brighton (which, when finished, will be called St. Mary's). The urgent desires of my parents and family; my own wish to be placed near them; the importance of the sphere, the necessity or at least the propriety of my being engaged soon in some fixed clerical duty:—all these considerations induced me to accept the offer. I believe I shall go there in July. Hitherto I have been in the ministry a simple parish priest, and profitable and sweet have I found the occupation. But life hastens on, and my friends have thought that I ought to labour in a post where education and theological knowledge have a fuller influence.

There was one short episode in his ministerial course this
year, but it had no bearing on the subject now under discussion.   On the presentation of the Dean of Salisbury he was
appointed to the Mastership or Priory of St. John's, Wilton,
near Salisbury.   It was almost a sinecure.   He found the
small private chapel attached to the hospital in ruins, and
spent several hundred pounds in restoring it; and when the
perpetual curacy of Burcombe fell vacant, to which as Prior
he had the presentation, he made an addition to the stipend
of the Incumbent, on the understanding that there should
be two services on Sundays at Burcombe, instead of one
fortnightly, as had previously been the custom; and that
there should also be a service at the chapel for the benefit of
the " brothers and sisters."

Mr. Elliott resigned the Priory in 1832.   It had no influence
on his general career, and certainly added nothing to his
emoluments.   He used to say in after life, however, that it
was the only piece of preferment he ever had from the
Church.

St. Mary's Chapel was fully before him at this time.   On
July 24, 1826, he says :—

I had expected before now to have settled down to ministerial
duty at this place, in the Proprietary Chapel purchased for
me by my father.   But the bankruptcy of the builder, the
carelessness of the lawyer, and the roguery of the vendor,
have interposed much difficulty and delay, and I must see
the business safe on its way to a further stage towards
completion, before I can properly leave it.   In the meantime I have charge of three pupils for the summer.   I
intend in the present state of my affairs to carry them
over to Rouen, to hire a house in the suburbs for two or
three months, and there to set up housekeeping.   I beg you
to give me letters of introduction at Rouen, which may
facilitate our plans, or open to us any sources of valuable
society or information.

It was not, however, till September that he could leave
England; his three months dwindled, therefore, to about six
weeks.   Even these were not spent idly.   He officiated each
Sunday after the first, and administered Holy Communion to
the small company assembled.   Amongst them was Monsieur
R——, a member of the French Protestant Church, who
burst out into an encomium on our Service; then heard pro-

bably for the first time. A Sunday-school was also organised under his auspices, and arrangements were made by which the English service might become permanent.

Henry Elliott returned home in November, and was met at once with an offer from Lord Harrowby of the Vicarage of Sandon, in Staffordshire; but, being pledged to the chapel, and unable conscientiously to undertake both duties, he gratefully declined it :—

"If I had not been so far engaged in St. Mary's, I should probably," he says to his friend Babington, "have come nearly into your neighbourhood. Lord Harrowby wrote to me a fortnight ago to offer me the living of Sandon, in Staffordshire, and in a manner such as greatly to enhance the kindness of the proposal; but it would have involved residence, and I declined."

In January 1827, his chapel was ready for consecration. The first entry in a series of sermon-books, kept journal-wise for many years, as a record of Sunday services, and certainly never intended to see the light, runs thus :—

St. Mary's Chapel was opened for divine worship by the consecration of the Bishop of Chichester, on Thursday, January 18, 1827; I, as the first chaplain, preached the consecration sermon from the text, "This is none other but the house of God, and this is the gate of heaven" (Gen. xxviii. 17). The chapel was quite full. I was requested by the Bishop to print the sermon, and I had his permission to inscribe it to him; but I judged it better not to print it. Mr. Wagner, the Vicar, read prayers.

The deed of endowment and consecration is then appended, with a list of the "ornaments" and "communion plate."

No district was legally assigned to St. Mary's, though very efficient schools were opened, and district visitors appointed; but it was looked on as a Chapel of Ease, owing allegiance, and paying tribute (from the sacramental alms) to the Mother Church and the Vicar of Brighton. No pressure of duty seemed to require that he should at once give up pupils; partly, therefore, from unwillingness to refuse the numerous applications made to him ("overflowed by applications of this nature," is his expression), and partly to increase his income, which, as derived from the pew-rents of his chapel, was always precarious, and at first very small, he took a

house in Cannon Place, and continued to receive pupils till
the year 1832. Amongst these were the Duke of Abercorn
and his brother, the stepsons, and Lord Haddo the eldest
son, of the Earl of Aberdeen (the late Prime Minister),
Sir Edward F. Buxton, Robert Williams, Gurney Hoare,
Percy Burrell, Edward Hoare, Bertie Matthew, and Henry
Goulburn.[1]

The first Sunday after the consecration of St. Mary's, the
services were divided between himself and his brother
Edward. The texts were, Acts vii. 32, and Isaiah lvii. 15. At
the first administration of Holy Communion the number of
communicants was fifty-two, and the amount of the alms
4l. 5s. 6d. Mr. Elliott adds, "I was sorry to see no pence."

Extracts from the sermon-books just referred to, some
family letters, and a few movements hither and thither, will
fill up the interval between this period and the year 1833,
which marks an epoch in his life. The mingling together in
the extracts of the names of men once so united as to minister
in the same church, enter the same pulpit, and preach essen-
tially the same truths, but since so widely and so fatally
diverging, is sadly observable. It points to the rapid changes
of a watering-place; tells of a wide circle of friends; and
reveals a Church harassed by unhappy divisions. The
nameless little touches of criticism shown in these extracts,
and never intended for publicity, are only inserted as characteristic of the gentle critic. Changes and losses by death

---

[1] Henry Goulburn, mentioned above, was the son of the Right Hon.
Henry Goulburn, Chancellor of the Exchequer, and Member for the
University of Cambridge. His career was short but very brilliant. He
took his degree in 1835, and was first in the Classical Tripos, Senior
Medallist, and second Smith's prizeman. He was elected a Fellow of
Trinity College, at his first sitting. His appearance was most attractive.
Joshua Watson said, that as he stood in the chapel of Trinity College,
waiting his turn for receiving the Holy Communion, it was impossible to
take the eyes off his face.

An eminent lawyer said of him to Mr. Elliott, "There is nothing to
prevent his walking straight up to the woolsack." To which the reply
was given, "One thing there is—his health." He was as eminent for his
piety as for his intellectual powers and attainments. It was told Mr. Elliott
that Goulburn was killing himself by reading twelve hours a day at
Cambridge. "Do they give him credit for reading twelve hours a day?"
was the response:—"No; he never studies after nine o'clock. At nine he
shuts up all books, and reads his Bible." This regard and esteem was
mutual; and when honours fell thick upon the pupil, he wrote to the
tutor saying, "I owe them all to you." Mr. Elliott selected him as god-
father to one of his sons.

may thus be introduced also without impeding the course of
the narrative.

April, 1827.—I hope I and my chapel prosper. The congregation has increased beyond my utmost expectations: and
their deep attention is enough to raise any one to some
sense of the solemn duties which a pastor has to fulfil.

July 15.—No help. Sermon in the morning, John iii. 20, 21.
In the afternoon, I preached Mr. Rolleston's sermon on the
" Pure in heart."

July 29.—Mr. Wagner read prayers and preached, Mr. Peacock
assisting. Collection for Parochial National Schools,
30*l.* 10*s.*; the highest in all the churches and chapels
here.

August 5.—Sacrament: communicants fifty-six. In the afternoon, I read the first Homily (both parts) on Holy Scripture.

September 2.—Dr. Wordsworth, Master of Trinity College,
Cambridge, assisted me in the morning. Congregation
overflowing. In the afternoon, read Mr. Spragge's sermon
on the " Syro-Phœnician Woman."

September 9.—Sermon in the morning, an adaptation of Bishop
Stillingfleet.[1]

November 18.—Sermons for Church Missionary Society. Morning (exchanged with me), Rev. R. Anderson. Evening,
Rev. John Cunningham.

November 25.—No help; took leave of my congregation for
four Sundays, having been appointed by Dr. Wordsworth,
one of the Select Preachers at St. Mary's, Cambridge.

It was on this occasion the writer of this memoir, then an
undergraduate, first saw and heard Mr. Elliott. He was very
popular at Cambridge; and the galleries of old St. Mary's
used to be crowded when he preached. His manner was
simple and unaffected, his voice very sweet and musical; his
action gentle and becoming; his style attractive, interesting,
imaginative, and descriptive; his doctrine evangelical and
varied, and his mind so evidently serious and earnest as to
produce on the minds of others a corresponding impression.
Several of the series of sermons thus preached before the
University have been printed, as will in due course be
mentioned

---

[1] It will be seen that he did not hesitate occasionally, when pressed, to
preach or adapt sermons not his own.

Christmas Day 1827.—Communicants, 157.   Collection, 14*l.* 5*s.* Thanks be to God.

March 16, 1828.—Charles Musgrave, vicar of Halifax, having come to see me, preached twice for me, excellent sermons, to the satisfaction of all my congregation—Isaiah xxviii. 16, and 2 Cor. vii. 10.

April 27.—No help.   The last two months, of March and April, periods of discouragement.   Congregations thinner than the departure of visitors would account for.   Sermons more serious, and attention not less.

Whit Sunday, 1828.—Morning and afternoon same text—" the Manifestation of the Spirit."   Dr. Maltby assisted me in the Communion, and read prayers in the afternoon.

June 15.—Mr. Melvill, of Peterhouse, preached very impressively on Psalm xcvii. 12.

July 27.—I read prayers.   The Rev. J. H. Newman, fellow and tutor of Oriel, preached on Isaiah liii. 2.   A capital congregation.

August 10.—Mr. Basil Woodd in the morning; Mr. J. Pratt in the afternoon.

August 17.—Robert Wilberforce read prayers.   The Rev. J. P—— preached on 2 Cor. iv. 18.   The sermon wanted the rich filling up of the Gospel.

September 14.—A poor servant girl put 3*l.* into the offertory collection, interpreting literally, " they forsook all and followed Him."

September 28.—The Rev. —— preached a sermon altogether extempore, having found when he descended from the reading-desk that his sermon-case was empty.   As might be expected, it was a poor performance ; but, may the Lord bless it.

October 5.—I did the whole two duties with the assistance of the Rev. Charles Simeon.

January 18, 1829.—I was absent at Ampton.   The Rev. J. H. Newman took my whole duty.

January 25.—Glad to be back with my flock.

March.—During this month I was absent at Cambridge as Select Preacher a second time, and preached five sermons on —1. God not the author of temptation ; 2. On conviction of sin ;   3. On the simplicity of Christ's Gospel as a remedy for sin ;   4. On temptation ;   5. On Satan the tempter and Christ the interceder.   I was heard by full congregations with much attention, especially by some of the leading

M. A.'s and professors, such as Rose, Whewell, Romilly,
Peacock, Henslow, Thackery, &c.

June.—Rev. —— preached. "Tenuissimus."

August 16.—I returned after five Sundays' absence, during
which my dear brother fully supplied my place.

August 23.—Preached an old sermon on bad connections;
from Ahab and Jezebel's example.

April 18, 1830.—At five o'clock this day Mrs. Lee, a member
of my flock, died. At two o'clock, I administered the
Holy Sacrament to her. On Easter Day she had received
it in church. I believe she died in the Lord. The same
evening administered it to Miss R——, who is near her
end. Much peace in believing. I never saw a sweeter
example of Christian resignation.

In reference to these ministrations to his sister, Lord M——
writes: "He has conferred obligations on many persons, but
on none greater than on me. I shall never forget his
affectionate kindness."

May 1, *Saturday.*—Sir. T. Blomefield and I called on the
Vicar with the remonstrance against "the Band," in the
form of a petition to him to apply for its discontinuance on
Sundays. The petition was transmitted to the commanding
officer of the 4th Light Dragoons.

June 6.—No band all May. Now played again, but on the
Chain Pier, not on the Steyne. This requires payment,
and a person must go out of his way to encourage it. It is
more their own sin than that of the town, though may
God remove even this.

June 27.—Rev. Hastings Robinson read, and I preached on
the King's death—Eccles. iii. 20.

October 17.—I read, and the Rev. Charles Simeon (dear and
excellent old man!) preached an admirable sermon from
1 Cor. i. 30. He was fifty minutes: rather low, but very
distinct.

December 15.—Miss R—— died, I trust with an "abundant
entrance ministered unto her." She was an example of
the longest and most patient sufferings I have known.
I visited her for nearly three years.

March 6, 1831.—Rev. John Sargent, Rev. H. Alford, and
Rev. W. H. Seymour assisted me.

June 26.—Sermons for Irish famine at Mayo, Ireland. Collection 114*l.* Glory be to God, who opened the hearts of my flock!

July 10.—Rev. —— preached; metaphysical nonsense.

The living of Winsham, in Somersetshire, was offered to him in the August of this year, in the kindest manner, by Dr. Ryder, the then Bishop of Lichfield and Coventry. Mr. Elliott would not have been unwilling to have held it as a resting-place from Brighton, putting a curate into the vicarage-house; but the Plurality Act forbade, and Brighton was too important a place to be resigned.

September. — Archdeacon Pakenham, Archdeacon Spooner, Gerrard Noel, Professor Farish, Mr. Guest, and Mr. Joyce of Hitcham, all assisted me in various ways this month.

September 5.—I spit blood. "Work while it is day; the night cometh."

October 10.—Rev. Mr. Dodsworth preached: introduced the Oxford Baptismal Regeneration controversy.

November 13.—Baptist Noel preached most impressively in the morning. In the afternoon I preached on Family Prayer; and, in consequence, had twenty applications from families to set up family prayer in their houses. Full congregations.

December.—Rev. Daniel Wilson came here this month for the Newfoundland Society. He attended my Cholera Meetings.

January, 1832.— Rev. —— preached. An illustration of Cowper's clerical coxcomb.

January 29.—Lost my voice, and could not preach. It returned but slowly.

March.—Collection for Widows and Orphans; amount 51*l.* 8*s.* It consisted of notes, 10*l.*; gold, 14*l.* 10*s.*; half-crowns, 11*l.* 15*s.*; shillings, 11*l.* 14*s.*; sixpences, 3*l.* 6*s.* 6*d.*; pence, 2*s.* 6*d.*

April 22. *Easter Day.*—Large congregation. Rev. W. G. Lyall, Professor Pusey, and Rev. J. Thorpe assisted at Holy Communion.

In all these varied ministrations, Mr. Elliott's family participated. His parents constantly waited on his ministry, and were edified. The tie of affection was unbroken, and mingled with it there was a little of that sweet formality which arises from a combination of respect and love. Though living so near, Henry Elliott still wrote letters to them on birthdays and holidays. When they visited him at his house, dear old-fashioned courtesy was always maintained. He never failed, as long as she lived, to select his mother from amongst his company, apologizing with a smile to his chief guests, as, with her tall, thin, and graceful figure leaning on his arm, he led the way to the dining-room. A New Year's letter to both parents follows :—

Many be the blessings of the New Year! If they be as many as the kindnesses of my dear parents to me, the year will teem with blessings. In retrospect, I thank them; in prospect, I bless them, and anticipate for them a nearer view of the felicities of that world to which they must be now, in the course of human probability, fast approaching. May those heavenly joys be dearer and dearer to us, and our hold and grasp upon them (the hold of precious faith) be firmer and firmer—as mariners quit the plank to lay fast hold of the vessel in which all their treasures are embarked! How dear heaven must be to the Christian of ripe and full age, who has seen each year deposit in that garner some of his choicest fruits and fairest flowers, so that he may say, " I have much more there than here!"

I wish to all the beloved members of Westfield Lodge a happy and holy New Year; to my two dear sisters, to my honoured and aged parents; and I hope to repeat these wishes in person on Thursday.

A letter to his mother on his birthday follows :—

January 17, 1832.

When at this morning's early dawn I recollected the anniversary of my birth, and thought of that Angel of the Covenant who had led me and fed me these forty years in the wilderness—when I thought of my many deviations from the right way, and my poor and scanty return for all the mercy and goodness which has attended my every step, I could not but mourn before my great and unwearied Benefactor, I could not but bless His name, who yet hides not His face from me, but continues me in His holy service, accepts my ministry, honours me with a place and name amongst His people, and preserves in my heart a growing attachment to His name, His cause, His service. An act of contrition, the first and meetest offering of the day, is followed by one no less demanded, that of thankfulness and

praise; the one strictly private, the other encouraged and
assisted by a meeting of those allied in blood, in long-
endeared communion, and who on this occasion feel with
me, and for me, as no others can. To see, and to be with
my parents on this day, therefore, well agrees with my
feelings and theirs, and at the usual hour it is my intention
to present myself at the social meal to receive the blessings
of my parents and to communicate the pleasure I feel to
every one.

In May 1832, he attended a meeting of the Bible Society,
which circumstances connected with the Apocryphal or
Trinitarian controversy rendered very interesting :—

LONDON, May 3, 1832.

I attended the Bible Society on Wednesday. The room was
magnificently full. The Bishop of Chester, the Bishop of
Calcutta, and the Bishop of Lichfield spoke very delight-
fully, and J. W. Cunningham very cleverly. But the gem
of the enjoyment was Gerrard Noel's recantation. His
feeling voice, candid apology, and lowly spirit of meekness
touched every heart, and he was received with enthusiastic
cheering.
This morning, I went to breakfast with Daniel Wilson, the
new Bishop of Calcutta, at Islington, and dined with a
party of twenty at the Buxtons'. To-morrow I breakfast
with the Bishop of Lichfield, and dine with the Hoares at
Hampstead :—a farewell party to meet the Bishop of Calcutta. He shed tears—eloquent tears—at both meetings—
the Church Missionary Society and Bible Society. . . . I
should have returned home on Friday, but I stay to see
him for the last time, before he leaves for Calcutta.

Mr. Elliott's holiday this year was spent in France, his
choice being determined by the hope of benefiting a friend,
who was then very unwell, and soon after died.
In July 1832, he wrote to his mother :—

Yesterday we passed an interesting Sunday. Mons. R——
preached on the text—" Except your righteousness shall
exceed the righteousness of the Scribes and Pharisees," &c.
I was concerned to hear from these words a dry moral
essay, destitute of all the peculiar principles which the
Gospel offers for the construction of the ' better righteousness.' Not a word of the " new creation " in Christ Jesus.

Our piety was to be sincere, disinterested, and humble: which the piety of the Pharisees was not. Just at the end we were told that, if our sincere, disinterested, and humble piety had any frailty or imperfection, Jesus Christ would intercede for us, and procure our pardon. Alas! that in a land like this, of gross darkness, the Protestant Lamp should burn so doubtfully and dimly.

The English service immediately followed. A son of Sir Sydney Smith read prayers, and I preached. If Mons. R—— omitted Faith, I certainly insisted on it; though I hope I fully brought up Good Works closely in the rear. There were about 150 English present, and all most attentive. One lady came up after service, with tears in her eyes, to thank me.

I begin now to think much of a month of separation from you and my beloved father, whom I constantly in my prayers commend to our heavenly Father. I hope that this year, which emancipates me from pupils, will enable me to devote more time to those to whom I owe, under God, not only my being here, but all hope of well-being hereafter. Rest then, my beloved parents, assured that I ever think of you with tenderness and gratitude; and that I find such thoughts increase when I have liberty to think as I please.

He returned home early in August, and says:—

I resumed my place at St. Mary's, read prayers and preached on "The Lord is my shepherd," with a preface concerning my absence. My joy is greater in returning to my post; for I could not have thought my flock was so much attached to me, if my absence had not called forth sufficient proofs to convince even a sceptical heart. On Monday is the confirmation.

And again on the 13th:—

I thank the Lord who has brought me again in peace to *my Father's house* and my *home* and *ministry*. May I testify my sense of His mercy by discharging with less unfaithfulness every duty involved in those large words! Yesterday we had a capital congregation. I preached in the morning on the Epistle for the day, and in the evening on " vows and covenants." After the evening service I called to the altar those who were about to be confirmed, and gave them a charge. To make up for lost time I meet them every day at one o'clock, alternately at the chapel and at my own house.

The time was now at hand when the first great breach in the family occurred, and when its head was to be removed. The circumstances are briefly narrated by Mr. Elliott in his journal. No letters relating to it are preserved. He says : —

On Monday night, October 15, 1832, soon after eleven o'clock, my beloved father departed this life, in the faith and peace of the Lord Jesus. Only six hours' illness preceded, and for only two was danger suspected. He fell asleep without a sigh. Two friends had called on him at four o'clock, before the pain came on; and the conversation, they said, was quite in a heavenly strain. On Sunday (the previous day) he was at St. Mary's, and spoke of his own unworthiness of the honour of building a temple to the Lord, and of the goodness of God to him. All fear of death was taken away; he had not only a good hope, but "a crown of rejoicing" laid up for him. This was said when no one had a suspicion of approaching death. He breathed forth his soul so gently that we who stood by—Kate, Mary, our sweet mother, and I—knew not the precise moment of his departure. "Blessed are the dead which die in the Lord."

A deep black border surrounds this memorandum in the sermon-book. A list of the pall-bearers and mourners is appended. The Rev. Robert Anderson preached the funeral sermon from the words, "To whom much is forgiven, the same loveth much :" making kind and honourable mention of the departed. The Rev. B. Guest preached in the afternoon from "He being dead, yet speaketh." Henry Elliott adds :—

I attended both services, and sat in the very place where my father sat the Sunday before. I felt calm and collected at all parts, but when the Fifth Commandment was read, and the hymn sung : the effect then was unexpected. May the Lord give me grace to make proof of my ministry! Hitherto I have done nothing.

A tablet to the memory of Charles Elliott, as founder of the Chapel of St. Mary's, was erected in the chancel bearing the following inscription :—

To the Memory of

CHARLES ELLIOTT, Esq.,

The Founder of this Chapel, which was consecrated and opened in January
1827,

This stone is dutifully placed by its First Minister, his own son,
Henry Venn Elliott.

Close to this spot he worshipped on the Lord's Day, Oct. 14, 1832,

The next day in the Courts above.

He was a man of prayer, and his life was the path of the just,

Which shineth more and more unto the perfect day.

But his whole hope of salvation was in the mercy of God in Christ Jesus
our Lord.

With what carefulness and propriety he reared this temporal edifice

All around declares.

With what earnestness he looked for the House not made with hands,

Praying always

That its inhabitants might be gathered and prepared within these walls,

Is best told in a letter found with the inscription underneath :—

" TO BE OPENED AFTER MY DEATH.

" Many and most fervent have been my prayers for a blessing on your
ministry in St. Mary's Chapel. I bless God that He put it into my heart
to build a Temple for His worship and service. May it be a holy Temple
to the Lord for generations to come, and many be born there, who shall be
your crown of rejoicing in the day of the Lord Jesus.

" The Lord fulfil all thy petitions."

BORN JUNE 12, 1751.   DIED OCT. 15, 1832.

CHAPTER V.

MARRIED LIFE.

Anticipations—Realities—John Marshall, Esq.—Miss Julia—Narrative Letters—Hallsteads—Successful issue—Development of character—Poetry—Songs without words—Nonsense—Cloudland—Autumn—Sorrowful anniversary—Marriage—Mountain-top—Settlement at Brighton—Hymn-book—Single Sermons—St. Mary's Hall—Laying Foundation-stone—Opening day—Thorns and Prickles—Birth of his Son—Ode to Harry — To Alfred — Bath — Cambridge — London — Letters — The Lakes—Mrs. Pusey—Dr. Steinkopff—Dr. Shirley—Framfield—Mrs. Elliott's illness and death—Consolatory letters—Submissive letters—His Mother's death—Sisters' deaths—Harry's death—Living for Eternity.

ONE generation goeth, and another cometh. Sunshine follows clouds; smiles chase tears. Heaviness may endure for a night, but joy cometh in the morning.

A few years back Henry Elliott, when writing from Ampton Hall to his friend Babington, and referring to several marriages then on the *tapis*, went on to say :—

> For my own part, I am really delighted. Who can tell whether the " knot baccalaurean " being now at last united, I may not come in for a share of the relaxed influence of the spell? Who can say whether I shall not soon cease to be a mere hearer of other men's marriages?—" semper ego auditor tantium." Really I must now look about me. Boswell and Hankinson are married this year; Sperling, too. Walker and Musgrave, only a fortnight ago, paraded in married state in the streets and colleges of Cambridge, before my very eyes—nay, in my very rooms! Has Cupid's quiver nothing then, for me?

Again, on May 22, 1826, he writes to another friend from Cambridge, and says :—

> I should rejoice in witnessing your welfare and happiness in your new estate. There. by the way, you stole a complete march upon me; not only in deserting the long occupied rank of bachelorship, and thereby increasing the stigma that begins to fasten upon me and others who still move in that unenviable corps, but also in never advertising me of your intentions. So that it was pretty nearly a month after the event that I heard my friend was married.

He was now about to wipe off " the stigma," and his

married life, supplemented with a few other events, will furnish the contents of this chapter.

During the winter of 1827-8, John Marshall, Esq., of Hallsteads, Ulleswater, had visited Brighton to recruit his strength after a severe attack of illness. His family accompanied him, and they repeated their visit during several consecutive years, always attending Divine Service at St. Mary's. They thus formed a portion of Mr. Elliott's flock. In public, he preached to them as to all others, such doctrines as he believed to be not only true, but most practical, most consoling, and most elevating; and they received the word at his mouth. In private, hearing that one member of the family was unwell, he, as in duty bound, visited her. All this was with him a simple performance of ministerial duty as an "ambassador for Christ."

The young ladies being left alone on one occasion, he introduced his sisters to them, and this led naturally to some personal and friendly intercourse. The result was that gradually a predilection for one of the sisters, Miss Julia Marshall, deepened into a true and firm affection. Until the summer of 1833, however, he kept silence. The death of his honoured father in the previous year had made him possessor of a handsome competence; and some singular coincidences were rightly interpreted as auguries of success and indications of God's good providence. Hope then sprang up, and Love, like Jordan in the time of harvest, overflowed all its banks. He took courage, and ventured, on July 10th, to address a letter to Mr. Marshall, asking for his daughter's hand, as for "a jewel, which, though unworthy in himself, he would wear most delicately, and treasure as his life."

The answer speedily arrived, and was so far favourable as that he was invited down, and in a few days was on his journey to the North.

Thirty years after, the writer heard the narrative of these events from Mr. Elliott's lips. The household had been dismissed, the lamp burnt dim, the fire had gone out, while he told of this episode in earlier and happier life, and of his long journey to the North to tell his love and win his wife. He was travelling through the night outside the coach; his anticipations were alternately hopeful and sad; his thoughts were mingled with prayers; he asked God to give him some "token for good," some sign of His favour, some removal of his anxiety, some approval of his purpose :—when suddenly, the Sun arose, and shone upon him " with healing in his beams." He received it with gratitude as a pledge of success ; and when reminded with "frigid philosophy," that the sun would equally have risen had his suit been unsuccessful, he acknowledged it, but said that he spoke of the effect wrought on his own mind. It was to him like a vision brightening his prospects, and bidding him be of good cheer : and, whilst telling the result, his pulse beat and his eye kindled, as if again at the starting-point of life.

But soon the voice lowered, and the lips quivered, as he told of the light extinguished, and the bright hopes dimmed, and the long solitary journey of life since passed, and of God's wise discipline, and the lessons he had had to learn, and the anticipations of future reunion in the " house not made with hands, eternal in the heavens :"— and then words failed, tears flowed, and friends parted.

There is something so tender in his love, so bright in his short day of happiness, so touching in its close, that the reader may be gratified with more copious details than are usually given. The first extract may be made from a letter to his sister Mary, dated July 17, 1833 :

I have made my proposals to Julia Marshall, and am accepted by the parents, if Julia consents. She will see me, and then decide. It was a bold step I took. But my mind was so agitated, since hope sprang up, that I have never had a day's quiet, or a night's usual rest, since. I believe I am following the Lord's gracious guiding. If ever I committed my way to Him, it was in this instance. He only knows how it will end. It has altogether been a wonderful story. If the door had not seemed to me to open from God, I should not have ventured to seek an entrance. But when His hand, as I thought, opened, I should have been wanting to His own gifts if I had not entered. The opinion I have of Julia I cannot express. I have one critical difficulty to pass through ; but God, who has helped me hitherto, can, and I trust will, help me through that. I am sure I shall have your sympathy and prayers.

The next extract describes his arrival at Hallsteads. It is written to his mother, and dated July 29, 1833 :—

At last I am at this house, romantic as any spot in England,

and brought here by a course of events equally romantic.
But at this moment my fears predominate, lest it should
be the will of God that all this bright and warm sunshine
should be overcast.

I reached Penrith by the mail on Saturday, and came to
breakfast here yesterday. There was a natural restraint in
my reception; but it wore off a little in the course of the
day. I am conscious myself of an excessive timidity, and
a constraint in my manners, which I strive in vain to
overcome. A few hours will determine much more precisely the current of hope or fear. May the God of all
mercy guide me, and bless me in this momentous crisis of
my life! I have earnestly committed my way to Him.

The reason you did not find the place in the map is, that the
grounds are small; only about a hundred and twenty
acres. The house is just what it should be for the size of
the grounds. It is a most beautiful place, and contains
just as much of space and opulence as to be consistent
with the highest ideas of comfort. The lovely lake
washes the margin of the grounds, which are laid out with
perfect taste.

On July 31st, his letter to his sister Ellen is full of joy, in
which every reader will sympathise :—

"Rejoice with me," he says: "Julia has accepted me. A
few hours after I wrote my dejected letter to my beloved
mother, I had a walk for two hours with my Julia, and,
instead of keeping me in long suspense and probation, she
generously plighted her precious heart in exchange for
mine. How joyful was I! And my heart at this moment
overflows with thankfulness to God, who has led me by
the right way to the right person. Yesterday I should
have written, but a party was formed for ascending Helvellyn; and as soon as possible after breakfast we assembled, set off at eleven, reached Patterdale at twelve,
mounted the great upheaved barrier in high spirits,—but
none so high as mine,—crossed such ridges and precipices
as the ascent up Ben Lomond cannot in the least equal,
got our luncheon, surveyed the sea in three different
directions, and then came down to dine at six o'clock. In
these degenerate days, think of the health and activity of
four young ladies in walking for eight hours up and down
Helvellyn! The happiness of possessing such a treasure

as my Julia seems too great for me. God grant that I may not experience any terrible reverse. Julia sends a daughter's and a sister's love. God bless her for the words! Again he writes from Hallsteads, on August 7, 1833 :—

Deeply as I loved Julia, and highly as I valued her, I find every day fresh and fresh reason to bless God, who has provided for me such a treasure. And her sentiments are so just, so holy, so pure, so gentle; all her behaviour is so modest and winning; her heart so confiding and affectionate; her manner so delicate and ladylike; her mind so richly furnished, and so finely constituted in its original powers; that I find in her nothing to be changed, and everything to be loved. She is, I do assure you, an exquisite creature; advanced from the rudiments in which she appeared at Brighton, to a mature perfection, not only of Christian character, but also of manners and influence, which prove her to be most richly qualified to adorn the station which is to be hers, and to superintend all the female departments of my church. I am, I confess, in danger of making an idol of her; but I pray, day by day, that my love and *perpetual complacency* in her, in all she says, in all she does, in all she appears, may be submitted and consecrated to the Lord. He gave me this most precious gift, and I strive to carry it to Him, and to beseech Him that I may really possess it as His gift, as a bond of deeper gratitude and love to the Giver, and as a rich talent to be used in His service. Already we have begun some religious work, and every morning we read the Scriptures together. Bless the Lord, O my soul, and let all that is within me bless His Holy Name!

It may be well to remember, however, that nothing has yet been laid before the reader to justify these high encomiums, and to make him feel, with Mr. Elliott, that the sweet lady of his choice deserved, and more than deserved, them all.

The full development of her character,[1] as one of the matronage of England's Church, has yet to come; but as a

---

[1] This developed character has been thus beautifully and poetically drawn by Aubrey de Vere :—

> " To all her gentle ways was bound
>   A grace from woodland memories caught;
> Her voice retain'd that touching sound
> (Pathos, not plaintive, though profound)
>   Contented rills first taught.

chosen bride she may at once brighten these pages. Poetry
affords the best insight into the mind : poetry, therefore,
in the present case, shall open the lattice ; and the reader,
looking in, will see thought, imagination, purity, tenderness,
religion, all tinted, like an opal or an angel's wing, with
love, joy, and peace.

Some of her compositions have appeared in various publications—in Sir Roundell Palmer's "Book of Praise;" in
the "Sheltering Vine;" and in the "St Mary's Hymn
Book." But the following specimens, now gay, now grave,
selected from many others, have been hitherto confined to her
own circle. Surely they will suffice to win the reader's
admiration, and to excite his interest in all that follows!

The first poem to be inserted has an additional importance
from the fact that Mendelssohn said, when it was read to
him, "Many have tried before to express what they fancied
I meant to convey in that music, 'Songs without Words,' but
no one has ever before succeeded in putting into words the
thoughts and feelings which were in my own mind, so nearly
as this poem does."

SONGS WITHOUT WORDS.

Sing no words to-night;
　But play that air for me,
While I in calm delight
　Sit musing silently:

That soft low murm'ring air,
　With its solemn wave-like swell;
There are hidden meanings there
　Which words may never tell.

The heart has secret cells,
　And mines of ore unwrought,
Where many a treasure dwells
　Of never utter'd thought.

"Amid the stress of toilsome life
　She, for ethereal stillness framed,
Advanced, 'mid scenes for others rife
With vulgar troubles, care and strife,
　Uncrippled and unmaim'd.

"In clamorous streets and crowded mews
　Her face its cloudless candour kept;
Her heart, like flowers refreshed by dews,
The mountain's moontide mists diffuse,
　In endless sabbath slept."

Sweet the poet's song,
    Clothed in its finish'd grace,
When the numbers roll along
    With proud and measured pace;

But it seem'd more sweet to him
    When it floated on his ear,
Like warbled echoes dim
    From a spirit-haunted sphere.

Fair may be the form
    Shaped by the painter's hand,
When in breathing beauty warm
    We see the image stand;

But to him it seem'd more fair
    When it gleamed upon his eye,
A radiant thing of air,
    Which he worship'd silently.

Nought may ever be
    So beautiful, so blest,
As the first virgin sanctity
    Of feelings unexpress'd.

We read them in the gaze
    Of some belovèd eye,
Where the spirit's sunbeam plays,
    And we watch it gleam and die.

But their charms we may not tell;
    They are sullied by a breath;
They are like a fairy spell
    Which in utterance perisheth.

Then sing no words to-night,
    Or sing them with thine eyes,
While I in mute delight
    Shape my own phantasies.

NONSENSE.

"Good nonsense is an exquisite thing."—MARRIAGE.

Nonsense! thou delicious thing,
    Thought and feeling's effervescence,
Like the bubbles from a spring,
    In their sparkling evanescence;
Thou, the child of sport and play,
When the brain keeps holiday,
When old Gravity and Reason
Are dismissed as out of season,
And Imagination seizes
The dominion while she pleases :—
Though to praise thee can't be right,
Yet, Nonsense! thou are exquisite!

When for long and weary hours
  We have sat, with patient faces,
Tasking our exhausted powers
  To utter wise old common-places;
Hearing, and repeating too,
Things unquestionably true,
Maxims which there's no denying,
Facts to which there's no replying;
Then how often have we said,
With tired brain and aching head,
"Sense may be all true and right,
But, Nonsense! thou art exquisite!"

When we close the fireside round,
  When young hearts with joy are brimming,
While gay laughing voices sound,
  And eyes with dewy mirth are swimming,
In the free and fearless sense
Of friendship's fullest confidence,
Pleasant then, without a check.
To lay the reins on Fancy's neck,
And let her wild caprices vary
Through many a frolicsome vagary,
Exclaiming still in gay delight,
"O, Nonsense! thou art exquisite!"

A LEGEND OF CLOUDLAND.

The bright things and the beautiful that I have seen to-day,
As gazing up into the sky in mute delight I lay!
The wonderful, the glorious things! Oh, had I but the pow'r
To tell a thousandth part of all I saw in one bright hour!

Long time 'twas but a dazzling dream of vague magnificence,
Whose ever-shifting glories mock'd my weak, bewildered sense;
But then the vision grew more clear before my stedfast eye,
And I saw a long procession pass in solemn splendour by.

They were the spirits of the blest, but just from earth set free,
And methought that still they wore a shroud of dim mortality;
Not yet all glorified they seem'd, but they floated tow'rds the light,
And every moment as they soar'd wax'd brighter and more bright.

Silent and slow they moved along, with calm and even pace;
Soft viewless airs were wafting them to their blest resting-place:
But one among the train I mark'd who linger'd on her track,
And I marvell'd much what tie had pow'r to hold that spirit back.

And then I saw a babe whose head lay nestling on her breast;
His dimpled arm about her neck caressingly was prest,
His rosy lip was seeking hers, his clear blue eye the while
Seem'd waiting but a look from her to flash into a smile.

One gush of passionate tenderness, one pang of natural grief,
Cross'd o'er that mother's lovely face, but ah! their sway was brief;
Soon radiant grew her upraised brow, her meek eyes fill'd with prayer—
"O Father, train my child for heaven, and I shall meet him there!"

And still they rose a countless throng, in solemn slow array;
And still my heart went with them all upon their heavenward way:
But then I mark'd another there, bound by some unseen ties,
Who hover d long upon the brink, as though she could not rise.

There was one who held her down to earth, and on her garment knelt,
In whose sad eyes an untold depth of speechless anguish dwelt;
" And canst thou, wilt thou leave me thus, mine own beloved one !
And must I seek my widow'd home thus desolate and lone ?"

She veil'd her mantle round her head ; she did not, could not speak;
For ah, how strong is human love ! the human heart how weak !
But with cla-p'd hands, all fervently for strength she seem d to pray,
And fainter grew that passionate grasp, and she soar'd from earth away.

They floated on—they floated on—that bright and shadowy train ;
Their skirts of fleecy splendour swept the blue ethereal plain :
And now another band advanced from some far region blest,
Around whom breathed soft airs of peace—an atmosphere of rest.

Methought as messengers they came, to guide, with wings of love,
These younger sisters from the earth to their blest home above ;
Holy and pure, as angels' are, were their resplendent eyes,
And full of heaven's own light they smiled a welcome to the skies.

I saw them meet, I saw them kneel, wrapt in a long embrace,
And as they knelt, a glory fell on each uplifted face ;
Awhile, as from excess of joy, they paused with folded wings ;
The silence of their rapture told unutterable things.[1]

Then onward, onward still they moved towards the glorious sun,
They drank his rays until they grew like light to look upon ;
And methought that could I follow them with firm unshrinking eye,
I soon should see heav'n's golden gates receive them all on high.

But ah, in vain I sought to pierce the dazzling depths of light,
For a dimness and a darkness came across my aching sight,
And all those bright and beauteous things pass'd from me like a dream ;
I was again on earth ; and oh, how dark this earth did seem !

AUTUMN.

(October, 1840.)

O'er the rich and mellow dyes
 Of the foliage fading,
O'er the grey and quiet skies
 Hill and valley shading,

Pensively a spirit broods,
 Nature's pulses stilling,
Breathing through her solitudes,
 Her recesses filling.

---

[1] Quoted by Hankinson in his " Ministry of Angels," and acknowledged in a note.

Like the faint and quivering smile
On the cheek of sadness,
Misty lights gleam out awhile,
With uncertain gladness:

Like to eyes of farewell, all
The loved past recalling,
Fill'd with tears that do not fall,
But are nigh to falling:

Even thus doth Nature gaze
On her children dying;
Not a murmer doth she raise,
Nor a breath of sighing,

Nor one long, low dirge-like wail
Through the valley swelling,
Sad with memory's farewell tale,
And of parting telling.

With a calm that is not gloom,
Softly, meekly, tender,
Doth she to the quiet tomb
Her progeny surrender.

Less like mourners o'er the dead,
Bow'd in silent weeping,
Than like mother o'er the bed
Of her infant sleeping.

Shall we not a wisdom learn
From her silent preaching;
And with eyes attent discern
What her looks are teaching?

See we not herein how Faith
Leaves her loved ones sleeping?
Yielding them, ah! not to death,
But to Heaven's own keeping.

But we must now return to sober prose, and take up the
dropped thread.

Time passed on, and the month of October found Henry
Elliott again in the North, with his wedding-day approaching.
But a sorrowful anniversary intervened. On October 15th,
in the previous year, his father had died. He paused, and
remained in deep retirement at a place called Shap, occupying
the day in self-examination and humiliation before God, and in
writing a long and loving letter to his surviving parent.
The sad day and the filial duty ended, he passed on to
Hallsteads. From thence, after a short stay, he visited
Casterton, and was present at the consecration of the church
erected by his friend the Rev. W. Carus-Wilson, in close
proximity to his Clergy Daughters' School. Both church,

school, and sermons are described very fully and graphically ; and he says—

I would rather have built this school and church than Blenheim or Burleigh. So Dr. Watts said, he would rather have written Baxter's "Call to the Unconverted," than Milton's "Paradise Lost."

The seed of his own St. Mary's Hall, at Brighton, seems to put forth a first shoot, when he says :—

I offered up a little prayer that the Brighton School might receive a similar blessing when I saw, in going over all the rooms and offices of this Clergy Daughters' School, at Casterton, how perfectly everything was arranged, and with what looking up to God it was begun. God is not like to Isaac, unable to bless twice. We may pray in another mind than the mind of Esau, "Bless me, even me also, O my Father!"

The Bishop of Chester's sermon (Dr. Sumner, afterwards Archbishop of Canterbury), and a sentence from that preached by Chancellor Raikes, of Chester, are worth preserving. The Bishop's text was, "And in this house I will give peace." He described the different kinds of peace—the peace of ignorance, of superstition, of self-righteousness, of indifference ; and then the true "peace of God which passeth all understanding." The Chancellor's sermon was a reconciliation of St. Paul and St. James in the matter of justification by faith, from the text, "Faith without works is dead." "A tree is a tree," he said, "though it be dead. So of faith."

A short interval occurred, and then the day was fixed. He writes to his mother, October 20, 1833 :—

Our wedding-day is fixed for the 31st. We go to Patterdale in the first instance, and after a week, to Silverdale, where we shall stop for a fortnight ; and at the beginning of December we propose to move south, first to the John Marshalls, then to Tuxford, and so on by degrees to your dearest self. Julia is all that you can desire your daughter to be ; only a little too timid as the day draws on, and a little too grave.

It came to pass, even as arranged ; and from Silverdale, on November 13, he writes to convey to his mother the particulars of his happy marriage. It was as quiet as possible, owing to the sudden illness of a near relative; and the wedding-dress—let ladies sympathise—arrived too late :—

" Little recked I," he says, " whether my love was in colours, or in bridal white. Was it not enough that she became mine ? She says that in pronouncing the marriage vows my voice was clear and most decided, and overstepped in its haste the slow dictation of Mr. Askew. Her own behaviour was calm and collected, very modest, and very simple. We did not return to Hallsteads. When she was in the carriage going to Patterdale, she turned to me, and with eyes suffused with tears, said, ' Well ! now I am trusted entirely with you.' How eloquent were those few words to me ! How are they written for ever in my soul ! My thanksgivings abounded. I felt that all uncertainty and difficulties were past, and that God had piloted my bark into a peaceful and beautiful haven. And now a fortnight's married life only makes me feel the assurance of- a full and settled judgment, that God has dealt with me most wonderfully and most graciously."

But the bride herself has only as yet spoken in poetry. A few of her own words in prose, written to her sister in December 1833, will tell of the arrival of the wedding party at Westfield Lodge, Brighton, and of her own feelings on the occasion :—

When I entered this place, and felt my heart beat painfully, as I drew nearer and nearer to a scene so endeared, so consecrated, thoughts of you, my beloved sister, mingled tender sadness with the thrill of expectation : and when we had at last reached this dear house, and Mrs. Elliott had welcomed me with a mother's blessing ; when the turmoil of joy was a little over, and I found myself seated once more in the dear familiar room, and feeling myself entirely at home, thoroughly one in heart and affection with them all, do you think, my beloved one, my heart did not turn to you ? Oh, could you but have been there ! Could you but have knelt by me, whilst Henry's voice, pouring out to God the fulness of a glad and grateful heart, seemed to consecrate our joy ! Surely none was ever so blessed as I !

As the traveller with toilsome steps and winding path ascends the mountain, lingering at times, and again pressing onwards with renewed strength, now shuddering at the deep ravine, and now admiring the lovely prospects, till, led safely by his guide, he reaches the summit, and rests for a while, before on the other side the descent begins, so is it now with Henry Elliott. He is on the mountain top— a happy man. The sunshine was never so bright, the air was never so fresh, the prospects were never so beautiful as now.

In a short time, little feet ran to and fro, and little voices broke the silence, answering to the real or pet names of Harry, Alfred, Efie, Blanche, and Julius. But before this last name was well pronounced, "a cloud overshadowed them," and they "feared as they entered into the cloud."

All this, now figurative, will become plain as we proceed. Mr. Elliott's life turns at the point we have reached. But before the descent begins, let us linger with him, and observe his married life, and Church work, while his mind is still all buoyancy, and his body all vigour.

He has now one to speak for him and of him: and the young wife's journal-like words are very sweet, and deserve quotation:—

January 1834.—Henry gave us a very impressive sermon on "Redeeming the time." Redeeming the time; buying it back from the base uses to which it had been put; redeeming it as precious in the sight of God; giving it to Him, as having an absolute right to us and all ours. The time—general and particular times; opportunities, the flowers and blossoms of time; the time of youth, of health, of sickness, and of affliction when God has a message to the soul—all are to be especially redeemed. I cannot tell it you. But it seemed to stir up my soul. We went to the school (H. and I) between services, and did not come home. Though rather busy and bustling, we are very happy, and our *tête-à-tête* meals and quiet evenings are quite delightful. We have prayers in the morning at 8.30. I read part of a chapter with the Commentary, and dearest Henry prays. When we have breakfasted, then we often read. We have been reading Isaiah. But there are many interruptions. Generally, one or two poor people come. Henry sees them, and inquires into their cases. Then arrangements have to be made, and things looked after in the house.[1] The stables are damp, and the carriage is getting spoiled, and the rain comes in here and there, and so on. Yesterday we were busy arranging forests of books, which are not yet quite finished. We dine at two, if rainy, and at five, if fine. The evenings always seem very short. Saturday (happy Saturdays!) we are sure to be quiet. I have lately often written for Henry, to save his eyes. The hours slide on imperceptibly, for you know one must have a little time for conversation. Prayers at 9.45.

March.—We had an interesting lecture on Wednesday, on the text, "Charity seeketh not her own." Henry combated various false notions respecting the nature of selfishness, and attacked Shaftesbury's idea that virtue becomes mercenary when it looks for any reward; with various other errors of modern philosophy. I confess I was disposed to think it a little too metaphysical: but dear Henry has had several testimonies to its usefulness from various persons, who said he had exactly answered the arguments they continually heard urged against religion.

May.—Our two last pastoral evenings have been very interesting, and it was such a joy to have our beloved mother once more amongst us, and seeming to add a greater blessing by her presence. The subject was St. Peter's address to Cornelius—more argumentative than usual, touching on the Divinity of Christ, and the proofs of His resurrection—but very interesting, and with one sweet part where Henry spoke of Christ's coming as our Judge, and the expectation with which a Christian looks forward to this coming;—it is not a stranger he expects, nor a stern and awful judge, but One whom he has long known as his nearest and tenderest friend, with whom he has held sweet communion, to whom he has poured out his heart, dear to him as the bridegroom to the bride, intimately united with Him as the vine with the branches, as the head with the members.

June.—We had a very interesting pastoral meeting yesterday. The subject, 1 Peter ii. 1—8; a full and rich subject.

---

[1] Their first house was at 33 Brunswick Terrace, changed in the autumn of 1835 to 31 Brunswick Square, where Henry Elliott remained till the last. "May the good Lord make it His own house, even a Bethel," he writes, when superintending the removal.

The hindrances in our minds which prevented our growth in grace from the reading of the Scriptures; the great Corner-stone, the everlasting security of the soul that rests on Him as its foundation; the different reasons for which men stumble at it; the duty of being built on Him, not only for eternal salvation, but for daily strength, light, comfort; the nature of spiritual sacrifices; the way in which every action may become a spiritual sacrifice—all this was dwelt on with much fullness.

July.—The last pastoral subject was on St. Peter's confession of Christ. I think it was the most beautiful Henry has ever given—the description of what the Saviour is to the believer. Is there not enough in Him to break the heart if hard, to melt it if cold, if touched by God to sympathise with it, if depressed to raise it, if sorrowing and desolate to fill it with heavenly consolation?

July.—I can hardly help repeating in every letter how happy Henry makes me. But, indeed, when day after day brings out fresh cause for love, it is difficult not to express that love. Often I have such a sense of extreme happiness that it fills my eyes with tears. If I am sad or anxious, he enters into every feeling; he prays with me, and I feel comforted and strengthened. His tenderness seems to grow every day, and every day I feel more and more the blessing of that entire union of feeling, that perfect confidence, that intimate repose of affection which is granted me with him. I think that a human heart could hardly hold more happiness than mine did on Friday evening, when Henry returned home; and on Saturday I could not but weep with joy to feel how gracious God was in giving me such love.

To her husband himself she writes in December 1834 :—

I must tell you about Lord C——. He listened to your sermon (the Vine and the branches) with the most riveted and earnest attention. The perspiration stood in large drops on his forehead. He said afterwards, " I never heard such a sermon; and every word seemed meant for me!" The next day, his man of business was with him. He said to Lady C——, " Whatever was the sermon Lord C—— heard on Sunday? He can talk of nothing else." I tell you this, dearest, because it is so remarkable and encouraging. Mrs. S—— also delighted me by speaking of the extreme interest her children take in your sermons, and the animation with which they came last Sunday to tell her what they had heard.

Cheered and encouraged by such loving sympathy, Henry Elliott entered heart and soul into his ministerial work. His church was crowded, his labours were abundantly blessed, the number of communicants continually increased, and he was immersed in a sea of occupation, which knew no greater variation than that of a high or low tide. He suffered as all men suffer who thus labour; and more than once was laid aside by serious illness, which, however, rest and change removed.

He now brought out his Hymn-book, the compilation of which had afforded him pleasant occupation during his wedding tour. It has passed through many editions, and is still largely used. Up to the present time. thirty-two thousand of the full edition have been sold, and fifty-eight thousand of the abridged edition, containing only those hymns which were adapted for public worship. A few were his own composition, and some were from the pen of Mrs. Elliott. It came out during the episcopate of Bishop Otter, who gave the book the advantage of his full and deliberate approbation.

"I applied to him," Mr. Elliott says, "to allow me to dedicate the book to him. He kept it till, as he said, he had read it *all through*, and then sent it back with his entire approval."

He printed also several single sermons which had been preached on public funeral occasions, particularly one on the death of the Rev. Henry Mortlock, which was enlarged into a Memoir, and reached a second edition. It met with general acceptance, and amongst the records preserved is a letter from Lord Howe, in which he says:—

Her Majesty Queen Adelaide commands me to assure you that she has just perused the little Memoir with unfeigned pleasure, and she trusts not without profit; for a more interesting narrative of the too short career of an excellent humble-minded Christian could not have been compiled. The Queen charges me to convey her best thanks.

This year (1834) was rendered memorable by the laying of

the foundation stone of St. Mary's Hall, an establishment
which became henceforth one great object of his life, and
will hand down his name to posterity as a wise and unwearied
benefactor to the Church.

To those who travel through the length and breadth of
our land, treading its quiet valleys, ascending its swelling
hills, skirting its seaside retreats, penetrating its " black
country," and wandering about its immense cities, there is
one object .always attractive, whether in its costly grandeur
or in its primitive simplicity, viz., the parish church; and
next to the parish church, the parsonage. There is generally
something distinctive about it. It looks like the abode
of peace, and the centre of union and resort to all. There
the rich man finds his almoner and counsellor; and there
the poor man takes his sorrows. There charity is dispensed,
and studies are pursued; and from thence, as from a well
of water, supplies are drawn for sacred services and Church
ordinances. Externally nothing seems more fair and bright.
But penetrate within, and how many anxieties may often-
times be discerned! The increasing family, the narrow
income, the pressing duties of the father, the failing health
of the mother: with no prospect of advancement, no provision
for the future, no employment for the sons, no opening for the
daughters—this is indeed the reverse side. And many a
sufferer, when looking upon the pictured representation of
his church and parsonage, nestling so sweetly amongst the
trees, and reflecting so accurately the sunshine and the shade,
is disposed sorrowfully to turn the picture to the wall. Many
illustrations of these things present themselves even to a
cursory observer:—

A clergyman, with wife and child, is living in apparent
respectability in a northern township. He is a gentleman,
and has had all the discipline and advantages of college life.
His wife is a lady. His house and its arrangements are
pleasant to look upon. There is the paddock and the pony,
and perhaps the little antiquated carriage. The church
is well attended; the people well cared for; the schools well
built and filled. On the surface all is smooth.

But inquire within! The income is 92*l.* The house is not
the parsonage (for there is none), but it is rented at 28*l.* per
annum. The pony earns his food by drawing coals. The
private property has been spent at college, and in preparation

for Holy Orders. Upon little more than 60*l.* per annum the family must live, dispense charity, keep up a respectable appearance, mingle with society, and carry the son through college! How can these things be?

Another clergyman, very similarly located, has a larger family, and a larger income. That is, there is a wife, a son, and four daughters, and an income of 130*l.* per annum. They minister to six thousand people, and are fitted for any society. But then—they keep no servants, and have meat only three times a week!

A clergyman, the father of two children, is a confirmed invalid, and has been so for sixteen years. Many a time has he risen from his sick bed to minister in the church, and has then returned to bed again; his family fearing he would die under the exertion. Expenses necessarily arise, debts accumulate, and at length a sale is forced, and the furniture all parted with. The only refuge of the family is *the church* (for all these tales are true), and there they remain till some temporary accommodation is procured elsewhere. The father shortly after dies; and leaves three shillings and sixpence in the house!

Such cases might be multiplied to any extent. They were known to Henry Elliott, and pressed upon his tenderest feelings. At Casterton Hall, in the North, in communication with his friend the Rev. W. Carus-Wilson, he had seen and admired the successful working of the Clergy Daughters' School, and he now steadfastly purposed to set on foot a similar institution for the South. A prospectus was issued in 1832, enumerating the peculiar advantages offered by Brighton—the sea-air, the sea-bathing, the healthy breezes on the Downs, the facilities for obtaining good masters on easy terms, the concession which he was ready to make of free sittings in his chapel, and the reasonable expectation that the schools would elicit the aid and sympathy of visitors. His scheme contemplated the admission of 100 girls, as a " nursery for governesses for the higher and middle classes." Each pupil was to pay 20*l.* per annum, and for this they would be educated, boarded, and partly clothed. French and the elementary parts of music were included under this term of education; but drawing and the finishing parts of music were to be accounted extras, and paid for accordingly.

This proposal met with a liberal response, and donations

amounting to 2,330*l.* appeared in the "Report" of the following year. An acre of valuable land was given, in the first instance, by the Marquis of Bristol. The institution was received under royal patronage; the Duchess of Gloucester earnestly supporting it. Plans for the building were gratuitously furnished by George Basevi, Esq., and on April 21, 1834, the foundation stone, as already mentioned, was laid. The simple ceremonial is described by Mr. Elliott himself, as follows:

May 2, 1834.

Last week we laid the first stone of the "CLERGY SCHOOL," without pomp, or procession, or previous notice; for the message came hastily that all was ready. Lady Augusta Seymour, as Lord Bristol's daughter, laid the first stone. Miss Wardell was carried there. Mr. Lawrence Peel, as one of the trustees, attended; and Lady Jane, as his wife, and as one of the largest contributors, accompanied him. Their children were also there, as Mr. Peel wished them to see "the beginning of a work from which much good, we trust, will spring up, which they, and not we, shall live to behold." A few friends were there, and the contractor with his family; but no one else besides the workmen. They all took off their caps, and I read from the Prayer-book a few collects. Psalm cxxvii. followed; and that was all; and then we returned to our respective homes. This quiet committal of the work to God suits my views better than a festival. If we live to see it completed, then we may rejoice together.

God spared him, and he saw it completed and opened on the 1st of August, 1836. The original cost, including the estimated value of the land, and the encircling walls, was 4,250*l.*, but great alterations and improvements were afterwards made. A new wing was added; ground was bought for a playground and kitchen garden; the pleasure-grounds were laid out in terraces and rockeries and flower beds by Sir J. Nasmyth and Mr. Basevi; a greenhouse and summer-house were erected; servants' dormitories and a hospital suite of rooms were provided; some building land all round was purchased to prevent supervision, and eventually to provide a small endowment. So that the outlay from first to last, including the value of the land, and the purchase of the furniture, exceeded 12,000*l.*, and finally approached 16,000*l.*

The house, as it now stands, is three stories high, and in the Elizabethan style. It contains accommodation for seventeen governesses, one hundred young ladies, a housekeeper, and sixteen servants. There are a library and refectory; a sitting-room for the lady superintendent, and a board room for the trustees; a school-room, three class-rooms, eight music-rooms (the number of pianos being sixteen), three invalid rooms, and eight dormitories. There are also a detached room for calisthenic exercises, cloisters for wet weather, and a fives court.

A small endowment from rents amounting to about 35*l.*, a reserve fund left to accumulate for the future, the payments from the pupils, and a fluctuating sum raised annually by donations, collections, and subscriptions: all these just suffice to support the establishment, and enable the trustees to train and educate for governesses the daughters of the poor and pious clergy of the Church of England. Nine hundred and eighty-one have from the beginning received the benefits of the Institution. Every diocese in the kingdom, and out of the kingdom, has sent its candidates. In the report of its fifteenth year, it was stated that twenty-seven daughters of missionaries had been received; and the institution still continues its most beneficent operations with unabated vigour.

It is easy thus to speak of results, and point to the successful issue of a well-devised plan of usefulness, begun in humility, consecrated by prayer, carried on in dependence upon God, and crowned with His blessing. But it is impossible to describe the complicated and often harassing details. The building did not start up at once as by the magic wand of any one large donor, but rose gradually by the accumulated offerings of many. Objections of all kinds had to be met, and obstacles of all kinds had to be removed, Mr. Elliott had to win adherents, to enlist helpers, and to elicit charity. All virtually depended upon him; and had he faltered, all would have failed.

Again and again he declares how little, when he began, he knew what responsibilities and burthens the work would entail upon him. Writing in 1859, to Dr. Esdaile the founder of a somewhat similar institution in Scotland, who visited Brighton in order to avail himself of Mr. Elliott's information and experience, he says :—

The Lord hid from me the expenses and difficulties of the

work. If I had known them, I should not have ventured upon it. On the other hand, He did not leave me in difficulties, but raised up friends, patrons, and gifts beyond what I had, even in my most sanguine mood, calculated upon, and this from the beginning."

Again, in addressing his congregation at St. Mary's, he says :—

Unless I had possessed the standing of the minister of St. Mary's and a few years' experience of the liberality of its members I should never have begun, as I did in 1831, to revolve in my own mind this enterprise, and to make myself responsible for it. I should not even have had sufficient faith to begin it then, and to become responsible for the expenses of it, if I had foreseen their amount, and the difficulties of the whole undertaking. Good men and wise men prophesied that it would be "a splendid failure." It might be wanted, they said, for the North of England, and for clergymen of St. Bees, but the South neither needed it, nor would accept it. An ample experience has falsified these predictions. I know that it is deeply needed. I know that it is thankfully accepted from Berwick-on-Tweed to the Land's End. I know that, so far from being a splendid failure, God, in His mercy to me, and to those who have honoured me in this great work with their confidence, has made it, within its limits, a great blessing.

Mr. Elliott himself gave largely—how largely no man knows. Ostensibly his subscriptions and donations, exclusive of gifts of land, furniture, and books, amounted to 2,500*l*; but anonymously he gave much more. He left, moreover, to the institution a legacy of one thousand pounds, land valued at 2,500*l*., and one thousand books out of his library. This liberality went far, first to the completion, and next to the stability of the design :—but it was his trust in God, his prayerful spirit, his steadfast purpose, his lavish expenditure of time, his attention to details, his unwearied labours, his great forbearance, his wonderful perseverance, which under God's blessing insured the result, and led to the quiet, simple, devout, and successful opening, which Mrs. Elliott, his helpmeet in this and every other good work, shall herself describe :—

August 1, 1836.

On Saturday we received our superintendent or organiser,

Miss Tomkinson, who is to reduce our chaos into order; and our first pupil, Mary B——, the daughter of old friends of Henry's, who have had great losses of fortune, and are now living in much penury. You cannot think what a strange sensation it gave me to see them in our house, the first governess and the first pupil of St. Mary's Hall! Now it begins to assume the form of reality. Before it was a vision, a future and still future thing, ever talked of, but never realised.

You ask if we open to-day? Henry went up at 9.30 this morning (Miss Tomkinson remaining with me and cutting out linen). He intends us to go up at 4.0 and find all things ready. Miss Tomkinson says they went into the Casterton School when scarcely a room had a door to it; so we shall be better off than they. Many are, I trust, helping us with their prayers this day. . . . We cannot conceal from ourselves that there is much in present circumstances, and that there has been much lately, which is depressing—I will say mortifying and humiliating—to natural feelings. Our mode of opening is not what would have gratified any feeling of self-complacency, and we know there are many ready to make the most of our failures and discouragements. But what then? Surely this is (is it not?) that our motives may be thereby purified, and our eye made more single. "Not unto us, not unto us, O Lord, but unto Thy Name give the glory," was yesterday's text; and none could have been more appropriate.

Tuesday.—How much has passed since I wrote the above! I am in despair to think how little I can tell; but I must give a slight sketch. Henry returned at four o'clock, said things were moving on, and thought it possible to get in that night, but he feared exposing Miss Tomkinson to discomfort. She, however, was not discouraged, but expressed a wish to go. We, therefore, swallowed a little dinner as quickly as might be, loaded a fly with linen and provisions, and went up. You may think how our hearts beat. Oh! if you could but have seen us, and been with us, in the pretty little mullion-windowed room over the entrance. It looked so pleasant; a bright fire, the floor carpeted, the table spread with tea, happy faces round it, our hearts full of a thousand mingled emotions! It was

the beginning of the accomplishment of hopes so long
cherished, the dawn of a day that should go on in increasing brightness. We looked around and saw in the beautiful
building which sheltered us, and in these its first inhabitants, tokens of His favour, who had thus far prospered
our handiwork; and praise mingled with prayer, hope
with retrospection. The earnest longing after God's presence; the one desire, " Abide with us, and make this Thy
dwelling-place," swallowed up all else. It is indeed an
evening to be much remembered by us. Dearest Henry's
prayer of dedication; the joy, hope, thankfulness, and
confidence which inspired his every look; the novel and
romantic interest of that large uninhabited house, with
the evening darkening over it; our walk home as we left
it, and saw the moon, just past the full, rising over the sea;
the still heavens above us, peopled with their innumerable
worlds of brightness, and looking down as if to guard
and bless us—all this forms a picture not to be soon
erased.

Twelve pupils were at once received into the school thus
opened. The number was increased at the Christmas of that
first year to twenty-five, and in the second year to fifty; in
successive years to sixty, seventy, eighty, and ninety; and
on August 1, 1841, the full number of one hundred was
received within the walls, and this number has been (with
very few brief exceptions) maintained ever since; the applications for admission having been far in excess of the ability
to receive them. Will not every reader of this book be
henceforth a much-needed contributor?

The internal arrangements for the comfort and religious
instruction of the pupils were matters of serious consideration
with Mr. Elliott: for although there was a Board of Trustees,
yet they were appointed by him on the understanding, which
he fully carried out, that he was not to be interfered with in
the management of the Institution. All concerned were too
glad to leave it in his hands; and till the close of his life
everything was ordered by him. Hence *endless trouble*, but
admirable results.

The trouble may be imagined from the fact that one huge
packet of letters connected with the Institution is docketed
" Thorns and Prickles," and very appropriately so; for it
contains long correspondence with incompetent governesses,

unreasonable parents, curious visitors, and defaulting sub-scribers. It makes Mr. Elliott responsible for sick children who had never put themselves upon the invalid list; for yeast which would not raise the bread; for butcher's meat which had fallen below the required standard; and, though very rarely, for the misbehaviour of pupils and servants!

It shows, moreover, that sometimes his motives were misconstrued, and his good evil spoken of. It tells of a report, circulated at one time, that he was *paid* for his chaplaincy; and the smile which curled his lip when he heard of it, is not yet forgotten. Then, again, when he had himself given the greenhouse to the Hall, because the gardener complained that he could not keep his geraniums alive through the winter, it was said, "Oh, St. Mary's Hall must be very rich to afford a conservatory!"

All reproaches, in fact, fell upon Mr. Elliott, and were borne by him with admirable equanimity. He weighed the good against the evil, and was content. Complaints were examined into with the utmost impartiality, and all that appeared wrong was, as far as possible, set right. But let any Clergyman, in charge of a large congregation in a crowded watering-place, conceive of labours such as these, voluntarily continued and constantly increasing for thirty years, he will then be able to estimate aright Mr. Elliott's "Thorns and Prickles." And no better proof of his "endless trouble" can be adduced, than the fact that the duties which he performed single-handed, have since his death been shared between three.

But, on the other hand, the results were admirable. Unity was preserved; power and responsibility were combined; one authority was recognised; and Mr. Elliott trod the passages of the house as a master. He was the father and head of a family whom he loved, and whose temporal and eternal welfare he earnestly desired. Religious instruction was communicated without one jarring note. Every fortnight he gave a divinity lecture; and how many times in a week his carriage stopped at the Hall gates is beyond enumeration. Even when duty called him elsewhere, he generally drove "round by the Hall"—the Hall being at one extremity of Brighton, and his house at the other!

The burthen did not press upon him so heavily in the early days of the Institution, because it was shared by his wife; who took part in the examinations, and assisted in the correspondence; and whose influence was "gentle and irresistible."

One thing which frequently detained him for hours was this:—when he thought he had finished his work, and was leaving the Hall, a lady would suddenly emerge from some ambush: "Might she have some conversation with him?" Sometimes it was more than one. And when he had left the house, and thought he was free, he would often be held captive in the garden for a longer or shorter time. Even the children were sometimes "naughty on purpose," hoping to attract Mr. Elliott's notice, and to have a private interview with him.

The recollections by a former governess will be read with interest. She says:—

When I went to St. Mary's Hall, what first struck me in Mr. Elliott was, the charm of his voice. I heard him talking to one of the children; and help and sympathy spoke at once in those rare tones. The fact evident to everyone, was the delight he took in the Hall. His thoughts were continually reverting to it, in plans for its increased usefulness or happiness. His work there seemed always recreation and enjoyment. He came to it as a labour of love; and not unfrequently the sunshine of his gladness cast its radiance on others, and made all around bright. Very pleasant it was to see him with quick elastic tread mounting the steps leading from the terraces to the Hall door, sometimes indeed running, as if worry and weariness were things unknown, and speaking cheerily to any he met in passing to the superintendent's room; or to catch a glimpse of him, as, with kindling eye and beaming expression, he stood for a minute at the entrance to the dining-room during one of the meals—perhaps a friend or two with him, to whom, with a sort of fatherly pride, he seemed introducing his large family. Or on some festive day, when there was tea in the open air, very pleasant it was to see him join in the general joy, and take his place at one of the tables; interesting and instructing all within range of his voice, with incidents of foreign travel, or anecdotes of early days.

There was an unmistakable air of authority in Mr. Elliott, as he walked up the large school-room, accompanied often by his friends and the benefactors of the Institution, on

the afternoon of the divinity lecture. The whole school
was then ranged before him in graduated ranks, the
governesses at the sides, the servants in the rear. After
a short introductory prayer, the lecture began. There was
a great variety in them. If a sermon preached on the
preceding Sunday had been thought difficult, he would
recapitulate and explain. Or he would take for exposition
some of the beautiful Scripture biographies. At another
time, having left a Scripture prophecy, or its fulfilment,
with the pupils for study, he would examine them on it,
gathering up the results with additional information
derived from classical or ancient works. Or if a great
fault had been brought under his notice, he would take a
subject applicable to it. In all these varieties, the patient
sympathy of the father was mingled with the varied learning, doctrinal teaching, and practical lessons of the tutor
and pastor.

Mr. Elliott had great administrative powers. The order,
method, punctuality, and strict discipline maintained in
the Hall was almost military in its character. He was
generous by nature. He loved the beautiful and the true;
and his aim was to make St. Mary's Hall perfect, so far at
least as human infirmity would allow. Time, to him so
precious, he gave lavishly. Labour he counted pleasure.
And besides numberless incidental expenses and presents,
supplied by his purse, he gave at this time 100*l*. per annum
to its funds. He spared no trouble in little things. He
had planted trees in the grounds of various kinds successively, but none prospered. Giving up the attempt, he
turned to the flower garden. The gardener had not been
successful, and Mr. Elliott brought Sir J. Nasmyth, who
was skilled in landscape gardening, to lay out the grounds.
I remember how interested he was in carrying out the plans
suggested. The rockeries were not then so bright as now.
He asked me to write out a list of wild flowers and rock
plants suited to a chalk soil; and one afternoon two large
packages came, and were opened in the recreation hour,
much to the delight of the children. Thus large-hearted
and energetic, with a temper so genial that it ever seemed
longing to bring all into one bond of Christian union, who
can forget his constant use of the Collect for All Saints'
Day? With talents so manifold and so well balanced, and
combined with His blessing without whom " nothing is

strong, nothing is holy," is it wonderful that Mr. Elliott was successful in no measured degree, or that he gained the unbounded love of the fresh young hearts, so tenderly cared for, so variously and generously helped?

The feeling was not transitory. Amongst those who have long since entered on life's sterner duties and conflicts, it still remains undiminished. Could it be otherwise? It was like a parent's tenderness and care, impossible to forget.

One of the surviving pupils of the opening day on August 1, 1836, writes as follows :—

Mr. Elliott had the power of attaching the young to him with the strongest ties, and I believe in those early days of St. Mary's Hall, there was not a girl who was not most deeply attached to him. A smile or a word from him was dwelt upon for days. On the occasion of the dreadful storm of November 1836, he came to the Hall as soon as he was made aware of the danger we had been in, and read the 46th Psalm; and after an earnest prayer and thanksgiving to God for our own preservation, he talked for more than half an hour in a most soothing and impressive manner, and then, with a merry laugh, saying he should turn carpenter, he began most energetically to assist in taking down beds, and bringing them into the dining-room, which was turned into a sleeping apartment for some months. We valued his lectures very much; though sometimes we were a little in awe of him.

But during the three years I was there, it was of Mrs. Elliott we saw the most. She used to take our class once a week, either to study poetry, of which she was so fond—and well I remember how beautifully she used to read it—or else occasionally the Bible, or some book such as Abercrombie on the "Intellectual Powers." . . . We used to look forward to her coming with much delight.

The next extract from the letter of a St. Mary's Hall pupil refers to a somewhat later period :—

" I went to St. Mary's Hall," she says, "just after losing my dear father, and I arrived in Brighton with a heavy heart. Mr. Elliott had invited me to stay for a day or two at his house before entering the Hall, and I remember the affectionate kindness with which he met me. From that day, for six and a half years, he was a second father to me.

"He used often to have several of the pupils to tea with him in Brunswick Square, and after tea he gave himself entirely up to their amusement. I fancy I see him now, playing games with the younger ones; and when the party consisted of elder ones, he would read or show us curiosities or pictures. Those evenings I shall never forget.

"A great part of his time was spent at the Hall. I always knew his step, and felt happy when he was near. He would give me his blessing, and I felt that it came from his loving heart. He was full of love; and his sympathy with any one in joy and sorrow was tender, and always ready. Many a trial has been solaced by his dear words of comfort. He never spared himself, but laid himself out for good. In the midst of his parochial duties, which he faithfully performed, he never forgot 'his children,' as he affectionately called us, at St. Mary's Hall. I remember he used to say, that if St. Paul could write those words, 'that which cometh upon me daily, the care of all the churches,' he could say, 'that which cometh upon me daily, the care of St. Mary's Hall.' And truly his work there was nobly done. His delight was to make us happy. At the end of each half-year, he used to meet and address us before parting, and then bid each one 'Goodbye' individually. He used to give a parting gift to those who were about to leave permanently. I shall never forget my parting interview with him. He gave me a Bible, with his love and blessing, commending me to God in prayer. I felt, when he died, as if my second father was gone. He proved himself a true and precious friend to me."

"Take heed that ye despise not one of these little ones," said our blessed Lord (St. Matt. xviii. 10). To fill a niche, and have the memory enshrined in young hearts like these, is a privilege assigned to few. Mr. Elliott was a special exception. Such testimonies as those given above might be multiplied thirty-fold; but it needs not. Let Mr. Elliott's own words conclude this narrative of St. Mary's Hall, which will only call occasionally for notice in subsequent pages. They form the conclusion of the last sermon he preached on its behalf:—

And now that I am old, and must soon give up my account,
    I shall give it up with joy as to the work which St. Mary's
Hall has been privileged to perform. And may the Lord,

in that day of His coming, answer for me, blotting out my many short-comings and wrong-doings, and granting to me the beatitude of His kingdom, for the merits and atoning blood of our Lord and Master, Jesus Christ.   Amen.

We now turn and retrace for a short space the narrative of his married life, mingling it with interesting extracts of letters from himself and his wife.

On August 28, 1834, his eldest son, Henry Venn, always called "Harry," was born. He was the first of five children —three sons and two daughters—to whom allusion has already been made. The entry in his sermon-book is expressive of deep gratitude: "May he be," he says, "as Samuel, given to the Lord and accepted by Him."

"I gave thanks to-day," he says to his mother, "for God's great and undeserved mercies to me, my wife, and my child—which seemed to make many hearts vibrate; and many dear friends came into the vestry afterwards to congratulate me. May the spirit of his mother, and his grandmother, and her revered and noble father, be abundantly poured forth on the child."

A touching interest attaches to this, his first-born son. It is impossible to conceive of a more lovely face and figure. A portrait in water-colours of mother and child is still treasured in the house. He stands in the foreground, full of life, and bright as a cherub by Murillo. Golden locks curl round a countenance full of beauty, mirth, and intellect. He looks out of the picture, whilst the eyes of the young mother, graceful and reclining, are fixed on him expressively, as if the words which follow were playing in her imagination, and ready for her pen:

TO HARRY.

(AUGUST, 1837.)

My bright one, my gladsome one, my sunny-hearted child,
Sport round me in thy mirth, with thy frolic gambols wild;
Thou music and thou sunshine of thy mother's ear and heart,
Let me look on thee, and feel how fair a thing thou art!

Yes, pause amid thy gladness, and stand before me now,
Stand with thy bright hair waving like a halo round thy brow;
The airy spirit of delight breathes in that eye of thine—
I look on thee and wonder, and scarce can think thee mine.

Where learnedst thou the music of those ringing notes of glee?
Those tones of fairy mirthfulness were never caught from me;
And if ever smiles like thine across my face might play,
The memory of such a time from my soul hath passed away.

Methinks the breeze that fann'd thee with light and pleasant wing,
That play'd amid thy golden curls, and waved each glossy ring,
Hath whisper'd in thine ear with its soft and flute-like tone,
And breathed into thy speech a cadence like its own.

Methinks the birds thou lov'st to watch skimming by on pinions fleet,
Or the flowers, for thee meet comrades, so fresh, so fair, so sweet,—
Methinks that thou hast caught from them a motion and a grace,
Which prompts each speaking feature, and lightens o'er thy face.

I look on thee, my bright one, then I turn away my sight,—
Thou art still before my closèd lids, a vision of delight;
And then the tears are in my eyes, a quick and sudden gush
Of nameless, dim forebodings, which seem the heart to crush.

But ah, I will not listen to the inward voice of fears,
Nor gaze upon the future through a misty vale of tears;
But mine shall be the faith and hope of one to whom 'tis given
To look upon her little one as consecrate to Heaven.

A pale and tender bud we brought thee to the shrine
Of Him who bade young children come, with voice of love divine;
And by faith we saw thee laid upon thy Saviour's breast,
We heard His words of blessing, and felt that thou wert blest.

And now, when thy close-folded leaves are opening one by one
Like dew-impearlèd blossoms beneath the morning sun,
Shall we doubt that He who heareth prayer will bless thee with His
      love,
And nurture thee with dews of heaven and sunbeams from above? .

Oh, early be it thine to know thy Shepherd's staff and rod,
And early may the God of grace vouchsafe to be thy God!
God of thy joy and gladness, of life's sweet morning hour,
Of thy heart's first springing tenderness, of thy mind's first opening
      power.

Then sport around me still, with thy gambols free and wild,
With all thy uncheck'd mirthfulness my sunny-hearted child,
And every glad and joyous charm to thy radiant childhood given,
Be, like the scents of morning, borne like incense up to heaven.

Mr. Elliott's church and congregation now demand some
notice; and the interchange of thought between his wife
and himself during their occasional separations will be
available. The following letter has more than a passing
interest. It suggests truths which many clergymen have
yet to learn:

"I hope," he says, "that —— will have the common delicacy
  and propriety not to preach to my flock, as if studiously,

all the points on which we differ. This he did the last
time; and instead of there being (as there ought to have
br-en) a feeling for me, there was only a feeling for himself,
as if I acted harshly in not expressing an approbation
which I did not feel. I do not deny the doctrine of ' final
perseverance,' but I cannot assert it in the pulpit because
of the conflicting texts of Scripture. I do not deny that
Christ will ' come personally before the Millennium to
reign on earth;' but I will not assert it, because not yet
assured of its truth. Why should my people be taught
what perhaps I may be afterwards obliged to unteach?
I do not doubt that ——, and others like-minded, are my
superiors in the Divine life. I have always allowed this,
and said this; but I should not therefore be justified before
God in permitting them to teach my people doctrines which
I believe to be uncertain at the very least, as the un-
questionable verities of God's word. I cannot compliment
away my responsibility."

The wife of one of his friends died in June 1835, and he
makes the following striking remarks upon the occasion :—

Tuesday night she died. I was up the whole night in his
house, and had to announce to him the departure of his
wife. She was a quiet, gentle creature ; affectionate, and,
towards man, in all her behaviour remarkably blameless ;
much afraid of any loud profession. but exhibiting satisfactory proofs that she was a child of God.

Her husband was almost distracted ; but in the agony of his
mind, God made a few words spoken by a clerical friend
who was present to act like oil on the troubled waters.
One thing the bereaved husband said, which I think remarkable :—" I never knew before the value of a minister
of God! I could say to myself what was said to me ; but
I perceive God will make the blessing flow in an appointed
channel, and puts power on His ministers. Those few
words saved me from going out of my mind."

A characteristic note accompanies this letter :—

Dr. Wolff was here last week, and left a very general impression in his favour—a strong one in my mind, to say nothing
of a sudden kiss in my face in the midst of a conversazione.

A few words from his wife, after her return from a short

visit to the north, will convey a vivid picture of his engagements at the close of this year :—

Without being very effectively busy, we have been so thoroughly unsettled, and the days so full of interruption, that I have had little leisure or strength to spare. The pressure of constant society, constant excitement, constant demands of one kind or another, is at times felt in an overwhelming degree. This I most deeply feel. Some trial, some difficulty or perplexity of circumstances, something contradictory to the natural taste, is very needful in a lot like mine, to temper a cup of otherwise unmingled sweetness.

Just lately we have been feeling the pressure and annoyance of many cares. However, all is now getting settled, and it is a great blessing that dearest Henry is so well—decidedly stronger, though he has been so overwhelmed with fatigue and hurry, and though still the weakness of the throat warns him that he cannot do all he would. His church has never been so full; crowded in the mornings to overflowing, and full also in the afternoon. He says he thinks God is trying him now with prosperity as regards his congregation : and he feels this to be a call for more watchfulness and prayer. Oh, the joy it was to me to be in that dear St. Mary's once more! I almost feel as Miss H—— said the other day, "One longs to die there, and never leave it to return to this busy week-day world."

My Harry will smile at you now, with his little roguish face. His lips have learnt to say "Papa." You would love to see him laying his little head confidingly on his shoulder and clinging to him when any one would take him away.

In December 1835, his second son, Charles Alfred, was born. It completed the father's joy, and called forth another sweet burst of poetry from the happy and grateful mother, addressed to her sister Ellen :—

ON ALFRED'S BIRTH.

(December 17, 1835.)

Mine own sweet sister, while I lie
A happy prisoner here,
Ee'n as though present to my eye
I feel thee ever near.

Methinks thou look'st upon me now—
  Thine own sweet smile I trace,
The patience of thy placid brow,
  Thy meek and gentle grace.

Methinks I see thy soft eyes fill
  With tears of tender joy,
Beholding me serene and still
  Beside my baby boy.

Thou see'st me gaze with happy eyes
  Upon his balmy rest,
While cradled in my arms he lies,
  And pillow'd on my breast.

I feel the clasp of his small hand
  Around my finger twine;
By his soft breath my cheek is fann'd,
  His heart beats close to mine.

The silent consciousness of bliss,
  Joy's deep and full repose,
With which in such an hour as this
  The thankful heart o'erflows:

And all the glad fond thoughts that rusn
  Into a mother's mind;
The prayer, the praise, which long to gush,
  But seem no words to find:

The quiet tears that oft will steal,
  Past mercies to recall—
Belovèd one! full well I feel
  Thou know'st, thou shar'st them all.

For, like two lutes attunèd by art
  In concert fine and true,
No string can vibrate in my heart
  But thine is trembling too.

In February 1836, Mr. Elliott accompanied his mother and sisters to Bath and Clifton. In a letter to his wife he says :—

I had to go and secure seats at Mr. Tottenham's chapel for them. We heard him with much delight in the morning : in the evening I went to Mr. Jay's with Eleanor, and returned from the *élite* of Dissent, thankful to God for His mercy in assigning my place in our Church, and thankful above all for the Liturgy. Mr. Jay, in his prayer, balancing between praying and preaching, fell into the irreverence of appearing almost to inform God as he would inform his congregation. The singing was the only thing I envied ; but he pays professional people. I called upon him by my mother's special desire. Kiss my boys.

London and Cambridge were visited, and the last stirred
his spirit like a war-horse, who " paweth in the valley, and
rejoiceth in his strength."   In the month of April he says :—

I have seen Simeon (who had received 600*l.* that morning
from different persons for his purchases of Corporation
livings), Farish, Sedgwick, Whewell, and Carus, besides
others whose names are less familiar to you, of the standard
trees of these academic groves.   I was impressed, as I
always am, with the high tide of intellect in Cambridge.
I never see anything like it elsewhere.   The perpetual
and vigorous speculations of the mind are as rapid and as
eager as the experiments of trade and labour in their present
effervescence.

Every book, near or remote, profound or shallow, from
Germany or France or America, it matters not : grave or
amusing, it also matters not ; scientific, literary, or theological,—has its readers, and its masters, who have taken
the honey, and criticised the structure, and exposed the
refuse. . . . . It is a dangerous place ; and I would not live
in it, even if I were not married.   For I think that I
always see that science and literature and theology may
enter the mind, walk about it, and dwell in it, without any
holy influence.

There is not the "fourth" walking with them, whose form
is "like unto the Son of God."   Their very correctness of
demeanour, and enforcement of discipline, has a new fear—
that of making men satisfied with the "form of godliness,"
without the power.   I saw but little of the revival of
religion spoken of.   But that must be sought for among
the young men.   I was glad, on the whole, to leave.   To-
morrow I go to town.

April 9.

Lord Abercorn received me most kindly, and invited
Christopher Wordsworth, Dr. Longley (since Archbishop
of Canterbury), and Mr. Cunningham, to meet me.   The
first came; the others were engaged.   Lord Aberdeen,
Lord Haddo, and a few more, were the company.   Lord
Abercorn came up to my bed-room last night, and sat for
a long hour; in the course of which I found room for a
few better words.   It is a splendid house, and newly
furnished; but yet it makes me sad.   Oh, for a surer
portion, an inheritance above, that fadeth not away!

A few months later (October 1836) he was again in Cambridge, and had a last interview with Mr. Simeon, who died on November 13th.

October 19, 1836.

I went this morning to see dear old Simeon, lying very ill in his bed. All visits are declined, as he is too weak to see any one. But on my card being presented, he desired me to be admitted, and I prayed with him. As he lay almost motionless in his bed, he whispered forth this remarkable answer to an observation of mine, " Well, dear sir, I trust that in this trying hour your soul reposes in confidence on the faithfulness of God in Christ Jesus?" He replied very slowly, and in a whisper, pausing between the words, " I have no doubt of my acceptance, nor of God's having ordered from the beginning all that relates to me. His wisdom is infinite; His goodness unbounded; and as to the issue, I am without a doubt, without a fear, and without a wish !"

I hope to see him again to-morrow. He said, " I consider myself very near my end."

In April 1837 he was again appointed Select Preacher at Cambridge, and delivered four sermons in the University Church: two on the " Name of God;" one on the " Man of Sorrows;" and one on the " Pure in heart;" besides preaching in the chapel of Trinity College.

" The College," he writes, " is in one of its periodical excitements—the Easter election of scholars. So this afternoon, astonished at finding myself at leisure, and one of the examiners being ill, I sat down to examine for him a huge bundle of Greek prose translations, and finished them before tea. So, they say, an old mail-coach horse meeting accidentally a quaternion driven along the road, from mere sympathy and habit set off and performed the stage by their side, as he had been wont."

His wife joined him at Cambridge.

" Truly," he writes, " I am proud of my wife. We have seen only a few things, and mean to proceed at leisure, which is the only way to see things well. But Oxford had her first and romantic visit at the age of seventeen, when she wished she could have gone to college, and entered the lists of literature. Dear creature! she has entered better lists than those. We shall be obliged to see very little of each other in quiet, our friends are so hospitable. We have already five dinner invitations, all from Fellows of Trinity. So that I live still amongst my own people."

Previously to this visit of his wife, he had been reviewing his position at Brighton in a very striking manner in a short letter to her.

April, 1837.

I am sure few have to bear the weight of that cross, which consists of duties multiplying and rapidly succeeding each other, till fulfilment becomes impossible, and life is a series of arrears. This is my cross. And I feel it not only in accusations of conscience for not improving time more carefully, but also in the restriction of all outpouring of the heart. Things affecting dear friends and their fortunes, books and their instruction, sermon writing and its responsibility, visits of civility, visits of the ministry, accounts and settlement of secular property, relatives and their children, the doubts and difficulties of my congregation, St. Mary's Hall and its superintendence, my feeble and straitened hours of devotion,—all pass in such a crowd and pressure, that there is no quiet time for the mind to seek a resting-place. It is indeed an ἐπισύστασις, an "insurrectionary confederacy of things," often introducing a hopelessness of spirits, which is bitter to the soul. Let pass one half-hour, and you cannot overtake the duties of the whole day. They pass on. They look at you with reproachful eye, and then vanish away.

His wife confirms these words in briefer terms.

The lot of dearest Henry is one tempered with very different ingredients: many comforts, many joys, many temptations to elation of spirit, but also many crosses, many misunderstandings, many misjudgments, and, above all, the continual pressure of a burden too great for his strength. As S—— says, "There are only *twenty-three* hours in the day at Brighton, and only *fifty* minutes in an hour!"

In the spring of the year 1837 he had a Confirmation, and began to show the effects of over-work. His eyesight failed, and his throat had more than once greatly suffered, even to spitting of blood, and inability to perform any duty. He was now also much troubled by temporary deafness, arising from an abscess formed in the ear.

"My present amendment," he says, " is, I trust, indicative of perfect recovery. But it is well to be reminded of the tenure of all our best things here. A little danger teaches us the inestimable value of our senses. The eye, ever ranging over the various pictures before it, carries with its use a perpetual consciousness of delight: the ear hears perhaps little to give it positive delight, for music and musical tones of voice are not very common; but suspend the sense, or paralyse it, and every moment you are conscious of much loss and dismemberment: destroy the sense, and the soul shuts up its opening petals, folds into darkness what would rejoice in the light, becomes solitary because shy of giving inconvenience to others, or conscious of crippled faculties to amuse and instruct. Berridge said, you know, when his eyes were dim, 'God has long had my heart, and now He is welcome to my eyes.' And Eli said in a worse case, 'It is the Lord; let Him do what seemeth Him good.'"

Missionary work, as we shall soon see, was dear to him. He had already appealed successfully to his congregation for the erection of a church in Tinnevelly, to be called "Brighton St. Mary's;" and now, in 1839, when good tidings had reached England from Daniel Wilson, Bishop of Calcutta, with reference to the conversions in Krishnagur, he read the Bishop's Indian letter at length from the pulpit, instead of a sermon, and called a meeting of his congregation in the ensuing week, which resulted in an extra subscription, amounting to 150*l.* In this year the Rev. Henry W. Fox, of Durham, one of the most devoted and self-denying men of modern days, offered himself to the Church Missionary Society; and in the year 1841, he went out, in company with the Rev. Robert Noble, a man like-minded with himself, as a Missionary to the Teloogoos, in Southern India. "The crisis of their decision," Mr. Elliot says, "was at Brighton, and in the midst of Brighton associations." And in the last letter, written on board ship by Mr. Fox himself to Mr. Elliott, he says :—

On you I look as my Missionary Father, for your kind counsel and assistance to me in the year 1839 was, under God, the great means of enabling me to take this course, for which I each day find fresh reason to thank you.[1]

---

[1] See preface, which was written by Mr. Elliott, to the Memoir of the Rev. H. W. Fox.

In 1840, St. Mary's Chapel was shut up for alterations and repairs, and it afforded a respite to Mr. Elliott, who, with all his family, retired to the Lake country. Their enjoyment of it was heightened by previous anxiety touching their little girl, of which Mrs. Elliott says :—

The trial is almost greater to Henry than to me; he is so very fond of the child, and I think he almost takes too apprehensive a view.

He himself says :—

My darling little one is taken dangerously ill with fever. . . . A sword went through my heart all this week.

The child was spared, and journeyed with them to the Lakes, and sweet pictures of domestic life follow.

" It is so great a delight," she says, " to see Henry's enjoyment both of the beauty and the quiet of Patterdale. He has already arranged his papers about him, and is really studying the sermons, and considering how best he can comply with the request to prepare them for publication; but a heap of letters, to be continually answered, keeps him back sadly. Both the little boys are full of health and glee, and almost in an ecstasy at the beauty of the flowers, and the freedom of rambling and scrambling up hillsides, and by the banks of a stream, and through a garden which to them seems almost endless. As for baby, she is the most joyous little creature; her smile meets one like sunshine."

" We have been on an excursion," he says himself, July 29, 1840, " to Coniston, Windermere, and Keswick. The weather was delightful. Keswick Lake we saw, with as great variety as three days could bring, in great perfection; and, to prevent all being given to pleasure, I had the happiness of preaching the everlasting Gospel in Crossthwaite Church. In our way from Ambleside to Keswick we called at Mr. Wordsworth's, and got our luncheon there. Kind and hospitable they always are, with their slender means and large hearts.

" All the little town of Keswick was alive and gay in its preparation to receive good Queen Adelaide. Late in the evening we returned to our deep seclusion; but behold! who should be at the little inn at Patterdale but the whole royal suite—Her Majesty, and her sister the Duchess of

Saxe Weimar, Lords Denbigh and Howe, &c. So in the
morning we took our boys down to the inn to see Her
Majesty, and to offer, each one, a little bouquet of flowers.
I asked leave of Lord Howe, whom I knew; so they were
introduced to Her Majesty, who graciously shook hands
with them, and received Harry's nosegay. Alfred was shy,
and never presented his. She asked me their ages, and
then accepted the offer of the boat we had placed at the
disposal of the party to see the lake. This is the first
royal visit to Patterdale."

In August he himself returned to Brighton, leaving his
family behind, and not only plunged into the usual chaos of
clerical duty, but into house painting and repairs. A few
extracts from his letters may be inserted. The first will
excite a smile, the other will be read with interest. After
having once dismissed the painters, he found that another
room was left undone, and would soon require doing, and he
says :—

August, 1840.

I confess that I did not wish for the trouble and invasion
and smell of paint again in the house; but, according to
Professor Sedgwick's courageous resolution in addressing
himself to the *toasted cheese*, after a feast-day dinner at
Trinity College Hall, I, too, mustered courage, and said
as he did—" Well, one indigestion will do for all."

September 2.

I rejoice at your account of Harry's birthday. May they
enjoy many such ! But as for my own birthday, I think I
shall never enjoy another. So much of life past, and so
little done for eternity ! So that it comes to me with a
great oppression of heart.
Your letters lighten the weary overladen days, and gladden
the cheerful ones. I would have you know how much I
value them, but I would not have them cost you fatigue.
Yesterday I was very busy all the morning, and then
dined at two o'clock, after many kind invitations, with
Dr. Pusey, and had four hours of close and interesting
conversation with him   I asked him point-blank the
question, " Do you think you have increased the unity of
the Church by your publications and your movements?"
And he answered just as I expected : " No, not at present;
but perhaps, ultimately, it may be so." There was great

kindness; for after three hours, he walked the fourth with
me.   There is always, I think, a haziness and mistiness
about his views; not as you see on Helvellyn from your
lofty position the tenants of the upper air, but as from the
low and misty valley.   We talked much of the Apocrypha,
which he thinks had a half inspiration.   Towards the end
I spoke to him fully and freely on what I thought would
support an immortal soul in dying, namely, "The righteousness of Christ," "The Lord our Righteousness."

I met afterwards, at tea, a remarkably sweet person, with
her husband. who are members of my congregation.   They
asked me the critical question, "What is the precise
difference between you and Dr. Pusey?"   Taken off-hand,
I said, "Dr. Pusey would get his religion from the Church,
and I mine from the Bible."   I told Pusey this, and he did
not dispute the fairness of it.

September 15.

Dr. Steinkopff is at my mother's; a man of seraphic spirit.
The day before yesterday, Eliza observed, after breakfast
was begun, "I believe we did not say grace;" on which
the good man stood up, and with his foreign accent and
beaming countenance lifted up his eyes and said, "Lord,
pardon Thy servants, who can begin to enjoy any of Thy
mercies without first thanking Thee.   Bless the Lord, O
our souls, and forget not all His benefits!"

He was twice in St. Mary's on Sunday, when I preached
two sermons, on "Hezekiah in adversity," and "Hezekiah
in prosperity."   I think I never saw the church fuller.
God grant me grace to take a lesson from the harvest, and
to improve the sunshine!

September 28.

I had a few lurking thoughts of spending two Sundays away
from home, as there is a prospect of a supply of clerical
help.   But yesterday brought me to a sense of my duty.
It is such a harvest-time for ministers, the town being
very full, that no labourer who loves his work ought to
be away from the fields.

Dr. Steinkopff left this afternoon, and has left a holy and
heavenly impression behind him.   At the anniversary of
the Bible Society I again spoke.   May God accept it as
a little service I was very loth to offer!   Lord Chichester,
Mr. Nottidge, and Mr. Munro spoke very well: so that on

the whole it was quite a Church thing. What a pity and a shame it would be if a society had circulated twelve millions of copies of the Scriptures, in sixty or seventy different languages in which they never existed before, and the Church had remained negligent all the while of her responsibility!

He tells the Rev. H. Hoare, who had inquired as to his method of performing family prayers:

I do not know what book it was we used at Uckfield. We are in the habit here of reading the abridged commentary of Scott and Henry, with Thornton's Prayers and Kennaway's Prayers; but oftener, I think, I pray with my family without book, and I alter or add as I please, both in the commentary and the prayer, at all times.

Later in life, however, and for many years, the Psalms were read every morning at family prayers; and none privileged to be present can forget the peculiarly reverent and joyful expression of his countenance whilst standing in his place and reading the alternate verses.

He tells his wife what is his notion of true repentance:—

October 5.

Yesterday was a beautiful Sunday. We had overflowing congregations, and one of the largest Sacraments I remember; a little more than two hundred communicated. I took for my subject that touching passage of Jeremiah xxxi. 18, "Ephraim bemoaning himself." I treated repentance as being a perpetual and growing thing in the Christian mind, instead of a state to be passed through and then left. My precious mother is a little better. She attended the long service, and was none the worse.

October 10.

I shall soon now exchange sentences for smiles, and the limited communication of letters for the full and unchecked interchange of the heart; and the delight of reading thy thoughts, dearest, in thy handwriting, for the delight of reading them in thy dear eyes! I often think the heavenly state will have yet fuller and gladder means of communication. But "eye to eye" and "face to face" is the best we have here.

The year 1841 opened brightly. In the spring, his family was all around him, and his wife speaks of "the crowded church, the large communions, and the acceptance of my husband's labours." In the summer, two months were passed at Framfield, which, being only sixteen miles from Brighton, admitted of constant intercourse, varied only by the calls of duty, such as are described in the following letters. In July, he writes to Mrs. Elliott, and describes a visit to his friend Henry Blunt, of Chelsea and Streatham. There is a reference also to the contemplated marriage of his wife's sister, Cordelia Marshall, to Dr. Whewell, the Master of Trinity College, Cambridge :—

July 13, 1841.

I found that dear Blunt had only arrived at Streatham on Thursday. He was full of spirit and affection, but looking very ill. I fear still "Hæret lateri lethalis arundo." I heard his old cough. He is earnestly bent on setting in order his great house—the parish of Streatham. He brought all the way from Rome for me a mosaic of the Forum, and gave it me with words full of affection. I preached at his church a Church Missionary sermon, "She hath done what she could;" resting much on New Zealand. He praised it beyond its merits, and God gave a liberal spirit, so that 55*l.* was collected, which they say is very good for Streatham.

The Laboucheres received me with the greatest kindness. They regretted you were not with me. Every one who has seen only a little of you, loves you, my own beloved; but those love you best, who have seen you most.

July 19.

Yesterday we had a delightful village Sunday. I went with Mr. Shirley (afterwards Bishop of Sodor and Man) to his hamlet church of Osmaston, and formed one of his hearers. He preached on the nature of conversion, a plain —very plain—searching, and excellent sermon, which sent me home to ask my own conscience the question, "Have I ever been converted?" In the afternoon I preached to his flock at Shirley, in his dismantled church, with one side down and open to the air. The fact of a clergyman holding service in a state of things which would so well have excused his labours, was a loud testimony to his care for their souls.

In this visit I have had great delight. Old friendships
require renewals, and five or six years is the utmost length
to which we should let them run, if we mean to keep them
up. In heaven there will be none ot these long silences
and forgetful intervals.

But the following journal-like letters, written by Mrs.
Elliott, will best describe these happy holidays at Framfield.
They will soon be found to possess a tender and touching
significance, apart from the sweet words themselves :—

July 1841.—Here we are, in the delicious country—the soft
sweet air, the green leaves, the rustling wind, the tinkling
sheep-bell, the voice of birds, the breath of roses, the scent
of hay-fields, all around us, and the sense of indescribable
repose! Oh, it is delicious! How you would have liked to
see our enjoyment to-day—a complete holiday! Strolling
out the moment after breakfast, gathering flowers in our
small but pleasant garden, looking out on the distance at
downs and woods, with pleasant lands between. The
downs have been so beautiful to-day with their change of
light and shade.
Then we found our way to a common, lying high, with a
pleasant view all round. Harry had a chase after fox-gloves,
honeysuckles, and ragged-robins.
We have no clock, so dinner chose to come before one o'clock;
then we transferred our after-dinner play to the garden.
Harry was up in the medlar tree, and acted King Charles,
while Papa and Alfred sought for him. Then we sent the
children to walk on the common, and Henry and I sat
under the trees, and mused upon the happy flies poised in
air, and circling in mazy dance about us; talked of
'Il Penseroso' and 'Lycidas;' came in, rested, and read;
and still it is scarcely four o'clock. How long the days
are in the country! Alas! Henry goes away to-morrow;
home, to vote for the county; Saturday to Streatham, to
preach; Monday to Mr. Babington's; Thursday to Shirley;
and home the next week. However, I believe it will do
him good, as his journeys will not be hurried.
July 29.—Henry has just been giving the children such
a holiday! He has got a swing put up in a tree, which is a
supreme delight. It is a delicious thing to see their enjoyment in the country, to be associated with them, to watch
and promote their delight. Yesterday evening we had an

exquisite little walk. It had been very windy all day, and threatening rain; heavy showers came on in the afternoon, but a little before six it cleared, and we all went forth—papa, mamma, and the three elder ones. The wind had sunk to sleep, the clouds all scattered away; the air was so balmy, the calls of the birds so sweet! Papa and the little boys ran on and played, while I planted my camp-stool, and sat gazing on the sky, my little girl beside me, gathering flowers.

Henry's days with me here are worth many elsewhere, in the opportunity of quiet intercourse, and the enjoyment of walks, drives, and reading. It is no little delight and benefit that he can be so much with the children, and exercise that influence which is most powerful in hours of play and leisure. I feel so thankful for his help and guidance in regard to the children, and for his peculiar qualifications for their education.

Over this fair scene, and these thankful anticipations, there comes now the "overshadowing cloud;" and the echo of the Master's words is heard, "What I do, thou knowest not now; but thou shalt know hereafter."

> "When Heaven sends sorrow,
> Warnings go first,
> Lest it should burst
> With too much might,
> On souls too bright
> To fear the morrow."

Mr. Elliott returned to Brighton for a short time, and these words followed him:—

"FRAMFIELD, *August* 21, 1841.

I longed to write to you last night after you were gone, only I thought I should write too mournfully. I cannot tell why I should have felt this parting so painfully sad, since I trust it will be but short; but so it is that a weight of lead seemed on my heart. If I did not know how vain are presentiments, at least in my case, I should almost dread that some unknown evil was hanging over us. But this ought not to be a Christian's feelings, and I have sought and found comfort in commending you to the God whose you are, and whom you serve: and very sweet is the feeling that while united in Him we need fear no parting.

August 30. . . . Farewell my own beloved. My thoughts were much at St. Mary's yesterday. How glad shall I be to be there again ! God ever bless and keep you, and bring you in safety to your fond wife.

J. A. E.

Upon this foreboding, but loving letter, the following words are written by him to whom it was addressed, as a sad and prayerful comment :—

These are her last written words to me. May God, even her God, fulfil all her desires, and especially this last, that I may be brought in safety to her—where she is—even with Christ Jesus. Amen.

On September 4, Mr. Elliott brought back his family to Brighton, and on October 24th his fifth child, Julius Marshall, was born. There had been no real cause for apprehension. When he had been asked after his wife's health some weeks before, he replied that all was well. "Only one thing," he added, "makes me tremble—she is so perfect. God knows her faults, but I do not."

On the day of the child's birth he had gone to Westfield Lodge, full of exultant joy :—

"I am the happiest man," he exclaimed, "in the kingdom. I have a unique mother, and a unique wife ! How true are the words—

'Make you His service your delight,
He'll make your wants His care.'"

Yet, alas ! the fly-leaf of his family Bible tells how soon this joy was turned into overwhelming sorrow. Mr. Elliott writes in it as follows :—

This union, most dear, most blessed, most entire, begun, continued, and ended in God, it pleased the All-wise Ruler to dissolve in a heart-rending manner, on November 3, 1841, by *Scarlet Fever*, supervening on childbirth, and introduced, it is supposed, by the medical man who attended her, and who came straight from a house full of it in its most malignant form ! On Tuesday night, October 26th the fever made its fierce onset, and on Wednesday, November 3rd, about 8 o'clock in the morning, she "died in the Lord." She was a woman of incomparable loveliness, the desire of my eyes, the pride of my condition, the joy of my heart. Losing her, my life is a blank to me and eternity alone precious. But He who took her was the same who gave, and He took her to Himself.

Into the distressing details of an illness thus communicated and thus fatally terminated,[1] it is impossible to enter. Strong in affection and fearless of consequences, her sister, Lady Monteagle, and her sister-in-law, Mrs. Spragge, attended her throughout it with unremitting care and love. The fever ran its terrible course unchecked for seven days. It was attended for the most part with delirium or prostration, so that the sufferer was like one whose senses are wrapt from earth; but in her extreme feebleness she was heard to murmur—

> " Weaker than a bruised reed,
> Help I every moment need."

Her husband's prayers and tears she was scarcely conscious of, but with great reluctance suffered him ever to leave her side. " They don't know," she had said, " what good it does to me to see you." At length, unceasing restlessness subsided into mental unconsciousness, which finally terminated in death.

A most affecting letter was found some little time after her death, in her desk, addressed to her husband; which, omitting one or two personal allusions, runs as follows :—

Sunday, October 24, 1841.

My DEAREST, DEAREST LOVE,

I would fain write something more to you, to be given to you, if it should please God to take me from you. Yet what shall I say? My heart is too full to say what it would. I cannot tell you of the love I feel—the fond, the grateful love. I will only say that if I should be taken, remember that I do not cease to bless God for what you have been to me, my guide to spiritual blessings, my best earthly treasure, given to me by God to lead me to Him : and united to me, as I trust, in Him, with a union death cannot sever.

To Him I commend you and our darlings. Tell them, should I go, that it was my prayer, my hope, my one desire that they might be children of God. You will bring

---

[1] Mr. Elliott forgave what might have been considered by others an unpardonable, though of course unintentional, offence in a medical man. " Tell Mr. ——," he said, " that I do not look at second causes."

them up for Him. I had meant to have written to my
parents again, but have deferred it too long. Tell them I
fondly and gratefully remember all their love. . . . I desire,
whenever the time comes to call me home, to be found
"in Christ." If I touch but the "hem of His garment, I
shall be whole." Farewell, best beloved. God bless you,
and be your God, your all in all.

Your ever fond Wife,

JULIA A. ELLIOTT.

Comment upon words such as these—which came like the
"writing from Elijah" in the old time (2 Chron. xxi. 12)—
and intrusion into a grief so sacred and profound, would be
impertinent. Mr. Elliott was crushed, broken down, and for
a short time very ill. His aged mother was unable to look
up, and felt the blow almost too heavy for her enfeebled
frame. When first she saw the babe (baptized Julius), she
looked at him fixedly, and then, bursting into an hysterical
passion of tears, said: "Sweet, precious little orphan! Oh,
may the blessed God be to thee Father, Mother, Friend,
Guide, Refuge! May He bless thee for ever and ever!
Amen." Yet she rose to duty with her natural energy. She
shut herself up with her son, and exerted herself to support
him—reading, conversing, and finding comfort herself in
comforting him. He himself was silent and unmurmuring.
He had an eye open to His remaining mercies, but it was a
tearful eye. He searched the Scriptures, was much in
prayer, communed with his own heart, and endeavoured to
learn why the stroke was sent, and, above all, desired to
have it sanctified. He remained for a fortnight in close
retirement at his mother's house, and then returned to his
own. Nor was he bereft of the solace of friends. Sympathy
was deeply stirred; but amongst its manifestations none
were more striking than in two letters, written by Sir James
Stephen and Dr. Pusey. The former is abbreviated, but the
latter is given at length. It may comfort others as it did
Mr. Elliott.

Sir J. Stephen says:—

That God may sustain you, that He may Himself interpret
to you the sense of this mysterious dispensation, and that
He may enable you to resume with calmness the duties of
your sacred office, and to discharge them with a zeal and a

success continually increasing, until He shall at length reunite you to her whom you have lost, are wishes which have been during these melancholy days continually in my mind, and which have not seldom formed themselves into prayers. . . . The day will come, nor is it very remote, when your heart will cease to ache as it now does, —when the habit of thinking of her as enjoying the holiness and the peace of heaven, yet really, though silently and invisibly, the companion of your solitary path on earth,—when the tranquilizing sense of trust in God continually acquiring strength even amidst the darkness in which you move,—when your increased power of ministering to the consolation of your fellow-sufferers,—when parental affections, flowing in a deeper because a more confined channel than before,—when your own nearer approach to the world where she is waiting to receive you,—will together diffuse over your mind a peace more unbroken, and even a cheerfulness more abiding, than you knew even at those moments when you hung with fondest delight over the treasure from which, for a little while, you are separated.

May the peace and the love and the blessing of God be with you and your children! I have never said to you before, and but for this sad occasion I should never have said it to you, that there are few men whose friendship I value more than yours, or whose happiness is dearer to me.

Dr. Pusey says :—

My dear Brother in sorrow,—You have often taught that "through much tribulation we must enter into the kingdom of heaven;" you have often preached the Cross of Christ; I pray God to give you grace to abide tranquilly under its shadow: dark though it be, He can make it gladlier than any light; He can make it a joy to us to go on our way weeping, if so be for this night of heaviness we may the more look and hope for the joy which cometh in the morning which has no evening.

Fear not, my dear friend, to sorrow; we cannot sorrow too much, so that it be a resigned sorrow; it would not heal if it did not wound deeply; there would be no resignation if it were not grievous to be borne: it is the penalty of sin to us, though to them the gate of Paradise; we may sorrow, so that we offer up all—our sorrows, our anticipations, our past, ourselves, to Him.

It is indeed an awful thing to have all life so changed at once; all earthly joy gone; every joy for the future tinged with sorrow: it is awful, lest we fall short, as heretofore, of what was meant for us by it. It is a solemn, sacred change; we ourselves are no longer the same, since what was part of ourselves, one with us, is gone; no human love seems to come closest to our hearts since that which is nearest is out of sight. But be not downcast—at longest "the time is short;" and, though you are stronger than myself, a few years passed and we shall no more think what billows we have past, but only whether they have brought us nearer home.

I do, indeed, grieve for you. If I may speak on so sacred a subject, never, since my own was withdrawn, have I seen one who seemed to me so to realise the Christian wife as yours, or in whom I felt so strangely sympathising an interest. All joy must seem to one now like a dream; but it was deeply beautiful to see yours, so gentle, teachable, mild, holy. And now that, too, is gone.

Sorrow is a strange mystery, a great one, for to His saints it is part of the mystery of the Cross. And so what would be nothing but punishment in itself becomes God's chiefest gift, and the sorrows He sends are deeper blessings than His joys. One often sees persons who seem to one to want nothing to perfect them but some heavy affliction. I know not what your lot has been—you seemed always buoyant; but since it has come, it must be what is best for your soul, and that the more since it is so very heavy. It makes one's heart ache to think of it, and your five little ones. But fear not; do not look onward, but upward where she is. Time will seem very slow at first, but after a while it will begin again its rapid whirl, which is carrying us so fast to the eternal shore. And then, if these sore, stunning blows have deepened our penitence, set us on a stricter way, made us gird up our loins and prepare ourselves for His coming, humbled us in the dust, and made us glad to lie there, and see that we are dust and ashes and worse, decayed by sin, whatever men may think of us, how shall we see them to have been " very love!"

God give you grace, my dear friend, in this your day, to see why this visitation comes; and may He who dwelleth in the contrite heart replace in you what He has taken, by the indwelling of his own love.   God give you His peace.

With humble sympathy,

Your very faithful Friend,

E. B. PUSEY.

Pardon my having written so much; but my heart was full, and I could not but write.

Under the peculiar circumstances of the case, but few were invited to be present at the funeral, which took place in the family vault at Hove.   But it was stated in the public prints of the day, " that the many weeping widows, and the poor of St. Mary's Chapel, who surrounded the grave, testified their sorrow for a loss, which only those who were acquainted with her many virtues could appreciate."

The funeral service was performed by the Rev. E. B. Elliott, and the following inscription, abbreviated from one originally composed, still bears witness to the love which gathered round her in life, and to her sure and certain hope in death.

Underneath this stone

Is interred the body of

JULIA ANNE,

The tenderly beloved wife of the

REV. HENRY VENN ELLIOTT,

In sure and certain hope that

The Lord Jesus Christ, in whom she believed,

Shall raise it up at His coming

In the likeness of His glorious body.

She died

November 3, 1841.

" What I do thou knowest not now;

But thou shalt know hereafter."

The reader will desire, however, that Mr. Elliott should now speak for himself.   The following is among his first utterances, and is addressed to his wife's sister :—

November 15, 1841.

I thank you, dearest S——, for all your kind words and all

your dear, affectionate intentions. They are very dear to me. Alas! however, my grief can admit only of one Comforter; my loss, of only one Repairer. I am striving hard to cast myself on His "all-sufficiency." But I, too, know full well the terror that has only touched you, that perhaps for my sins, and for my want of improvement of the blessed example and society granted me for eight years, God has removed from me the delight and repose of my soul. But in her illness, I did so pour out this grief before God; I did so supplicate Him that for this cause at least He would not take her from me, that I do hope it was more in love than in wrath that He has made me desolate. Alas, how desolate! I know not the man who could suffer such a loss. I know not the home that could be the experiment of so fearful a change. Pilgrim and stranger, henceforth, is written on my condition. Let me then prepare my heart, or rather may He, whose is its preparation, estrange me from all things earthly, and transfer my desires to the kingdom where Christ is, and where she is with Christ in rest.

Yesterday I went twice to St. Mary's. It was as much as I could bear. Edward preached a very beautiful sermon on John xvii. 20, 22, "That they all may be one," calling us to look to a nearer and dearer union than any we have had here. Mr. Goode, of Clapham, preached in the afternoon:—"All these died in faith, not having received the promises." (Heb. xi. 13.)

Next Sunday Mr. Baptist Noel preaches the two annual sermons for the Church Missionary Society, and the Sunday after, if the Lord will, I hope to speak to my dear and sympathising flock. The great mass was in mourning, I heard.

I beg to thank your dear papa for his remembrance of me. May God comfort him and all of us, first sanctifying the affliction to us. I desire to remember that if it has no sanctification, comfort would only be an unhealthy opiate. I hope he will come, and you too. What am I to do with my babes? God can and will take care of them.

One more letter, written a short time after to the late Lady Charlotte Baillie Hamilton, may be inserted; and then the narrative must needs pass on.

January 13, 1842.

I feel deeply indebted to you for the kindest sympathy that Christian friendship can offer in affliction so bitter as mine. It has pleased God to take from me the delight of my eyes, and the repose of my soul, and to make what I used to think as happy a home as could be found, homeless! I know not the man who could lose more than I have lost; but I will not and I do not repine, nor impute to my heavenly Father any needless severity. Only I sometimes think, since the anguish of the stroke has been so extreme, that there must be in me some great deficiency, which I daily play that I may discover and correct. But the sum of my disconsolate thoughts always comes to this; that God alone can heal the wound which God has inflicted. He alone can make up to me by His presence, His smile, His love, my unutterable bereavement.

You, dear Lady Charlotte, knew and loved her. And I find now that I am more than ever united to those who loved her. They knew a little, what I knew best, how rare and exquisite a specimen she was of all that is most lovely and attractive in nature and in grace. But I must not go on, for I find the gushes of passionate remembrance too much for me. I have indeed been laid in the very dust; but God can be to me more even than my beloved was to me, by imparting to my broken spirit more of His presence, His smile, and His love.

I bless His holy name that I can justify Him in all that He has done; and I feel ashamed of my tears and my despondency, when I think of her incomparable gain. Does not St. Paul say that, "to depart and be with Christ is far better," and is there not in His presence the "*fulness of joy*," into which I have not a shadow of a doubt that my beloved has entered? How selfish, then, is my sorrow! And how weak my faith .when I look at my motherless little ones, and remember with a pang that they will never even know their incomparable loss, never even know what a mother she was to them!

But God can put greater grace into lower channels; and He is not restrained to any particular method or line of blessing. Besides, the time is very short; then we shall go to her who cannot return to us.

Dear Lady Charlotte, I desire to thank you and dear Mr. and Mrs. Scott with a grateful heart for sharing so well my grief, and remembering me in your prayers. If one member suffer, all the members suffer with it. I have had large experience of this truth in my deep affliction. Oh, may God requite to the hearts that have bled with mine, their compassion; and may you and they find mercy in their hour of need!

Hitherto I have spoken and preached of affliction as one who had put his lips to the margin: but now God has made me drink the bitter cup to the dregs. Pray for me!

Give my kindest love to your dear daughter and son. God bless you all, and may you not require His discipline that I have needed.

Ever most affectionately and gratefully yours,

H. V. ELLIOTT.

P.S.—Your most kind and touching bounty to St. Mary's Hall—how can I thank you enough for it! It has greatly moved me. So God raises up generous friends who will not let the work die. May He grant to you, dear Lady Charlotte, a full and rich recompense in that kingdom, where the services rendered to Christ's little ones shall not pass unnoticed or unrewarded. Amen.

You will be glad to hear that I have regained, in a good measure, the health I had lost. I could not sleep, and then my nerves began to fail, but now I get sleep by hyoscyamus or henbane.

My beloved mother is very suffering; slowly but surely declining. For her I only pray now for a bright and easy passage, for it is clear that prolonged life is more and more painful. Mr. Scott, too, has been in the school of affliction, and your dear daughter. May they abide under the shadow of the Cross!

The tomb had scarcely closed upon his wife before it opened again for that " beloved mother." She had never recovered the shock caused by her daughter-in-law's death. The elasticity of her mind relaxed; and her frame gradually decayed, like a noble branch of that old family tree, whose praise for so many years, has been in the Churches. A few particulars of her decline, written by her daughter, Mrs. Spragge, in the year 1842, in connection with what has gone before, will be interesting :—

August 29, 1842.

To-day she has been peculiarly lovely in her frame of

spirit, and requested us all to sing that magnificent doxology,

" Praise God, from whom all blessings flow,"

in the drawing-room, that she might hear it ; and then, the tune of the Old Hundredth Psalm, which she had asked for, disappointing her, from the smallness of our number and the incapacity of some of us to send out our voices with power, she took up the theme herself, and sang the verse most sweetly ; and then dwelt upon expressions in one of " Jenks' Prayers," of which she is very fond :— Behold His glory; enjoy His love; reflect His likeness; and sing His praise.

We had delightful sermons yesterday. That which I heard was on " The knowledge of Christ; what it is not, and what it is." And very sweet and touching was the manner in which my brother expressed his earnest desire that every one of his flock might indeed know Christ, and the power of His resurrection—know Him as their Friend, their Advocate, their Prophet, their High Priest, their King, and the Beloved of their soul.

He is tolerably well, but the sorrows of his heart are very deep; and I never go to his house without feeling that there is only one Comforter who can pour balm into his wounds.

October 31, 1842.

You are not forgotten, even in the absorbing interests of the scene which is passing before us. Sometimes its touching sweetness is beyond expression ; and, blessed be our gracious heavenly Father, never does our beloved sufferer utter one word that might not almost befit an angel's lips, in similar circumstances, were an angel capable of suffering. But, alas ! she does suffer very much, very increasingly ; yet many mitigations are vouchsafed, which she never fails to notice with tears of thankfulness. But the time of trial seems long; and now and then, with exquisite expressions, she breathes out those words again and again ; " Oh, blessed are the dead which die in the Lord ! When I get above, I shall be worthy to praise Him. Oh, I long to praise Him as He deserves to be praised, but I am altogether vile !

" ' Nothing in my hand I bring,
Simply to Thy cross I cling.' "

December 12, 1842.

The state of my beloved mother becomes continually more
and more distressing. Her weakness and her sufferings
increase, and the after-effects of sedatives occasion a
degree of mental aberration or excitement which is deeply
painful. Her patience is still unwearied, and still her
feeling seems to be, " though He slay me, yet will I trust
in Him."

Then cometh the end :—

" I write to request the prayers of your congregation for
my mother," writes Henry Elliott to Robert Anderson, " as
having been for some time a member of it. There is now
much more fear than hope. All is well with her soul:
sweet peace and beautiful patience. But her departure
will leave an inexpressible blank, and we dread a painful
and protracted issue. God may yet spare her to us, if it
is His holy will."

On Easter Day, April 16, 1843, she entered into rest; and
was interred in the family vault at Hove, with those she
loved so well.

Three months later, that same vault opened again for his
sister Mary. Her early life has already been referred to
in the beginning of this memoir. Her after-life reads like
a romance. She was a great favourite with her brother,
and justified his partiality. At the age of twenty-three,
her hand was sought by Captain Coote, R.N., a man of good
family : gallant, handsome, amiable, and pious. They were
engaged to be married, when, in 1813, Captain Coote was
directed to join an expedition to North America, in command
of H.M.'s ship *Peacock*. Captain Coote had endeared himself
to all with whom he came in contact; and Basil Elliott, a
midshipman, with other officers, had moved with him from
ship to ship, and now accompanied him to the American
coast. A long interval occurred without intelligence of any
kind. From the close of the year, and far into 1814, one
single note was struck by the trembling hand of his affianced
bride—" no news from America," " no news from America,"
—and when that sad note ceased, the silence of the grave
followed. Month after month went by; every vessel of the
squadron, but the *Peacock*, had communicated with the
Admiralty ; but no message had been received from her.

No rescued sailor ever appeared, no sealed missive ever reached the shore. One fragment of a boat, with some letters of the *Peacock's* name upon it, was after a long interval washed on shore, and that was all. It was supposed that the ship had struck on the shoals off the Carolinas, and that every soul on board had perished.

After a considerable interval her hand was again sought in marriage by a very distinguished scholar, an Oxford man, who had been tutor to Mr. Wilberforce's eldest son. But Mary Elliott refused the offer, was never married, and died three months after her mother.

Another sister, Mrs. Brasier, very dearly beloved, was laid by her side in January 1846.

Once more, alas! was that vault opened, a few years later, to admit Mr. Elliott's eldest son, that "bright one, that gladsome one, that sunny-hearted child," about whom at three years old his mother had sung so sweetly. His early childhood had been most hopeful. From a manuscript book of Mrs. Elliott's, called 'Records of the Children,' a few extracts may be made, interesting to parents, and lovers of children :—

1834.—Harry. I have always had a strong feeling of the precariousness of our precious infant's life, but it does not make me unhappy. He is God's gift, entrusted to us as long as God sees good ; and safe in His hands.

1836.—He certainly will have a love of humour not inherited from me. He is very good, but it is sometimes the most tedious process to get him to sleep, for he is so full of fun and drollery one does not know how to resist him.

1837.—Then he has so much of intellectual taste, his mind is opening so rapidly, and he has such a thirst for knowledge of some kind or other, that this gives a great influence over him.

1838.—He is indeed very dear, and perhaps it is the haunting sense of a something peculiarly fragile which so powerfully endears him : he is so very gentle, so docile, so clinging. I will send you some lines written on him. They are written with a mother's pen, so you must read them with a mother's, not a critic's, eye.

1838, *July 9.*—He loves to hear of Jesus Christ. His Sunday stories I generally keep for Sunday ; but he asked, "May I have something about Jesus Christ every day ?"

1840, *February* 9.—Harry was reading about the dedication of Solomon's temple, where Solomon says, "The Lord said He would dwell in thick darkness." Harry asked, "How can that be, mamma? Jesus Christ and the angels would make it light."

1841, *January* 3, *Sunday.*—His papa asked him one evening what the Lesson from the New Testament was about. (It was the visit of the Wise Men.) He could not remember anything about it. His papa said he must not go to church next Sunday. He felt this. He has begged to go on week-days, when we have service, but I have not thought it well to take him.

1841, *July* 15.—I think I mentioned the dear old blind woman: she is eighty-seven; but her faculties seem perfect, her mind stored with Scripture and hymns. It is a pleasure to see her and hear her talk. I took the children to see her, and to carry her a little bit of chicken. When I told Harry to wish her good-bye, he went up and kissed her. It was pretty to see his young soft cheek laid against her withered face! I should let him read to her, but I rather fear her injudicious praise.

These were childish days; but even then his intellect developed itself in the most striking manner. He carried off every prize that his age permitted him to contend for in the Brighton College, then, as now, in high repute for scholarship. The testimony of one of the masters under whom he was more immediately placed must not be omitted :—

Such brilliant talents, so well employed, and withal such an utter absence of all pride, such unaffected Christian humility, such childish simplicity and cheerfulness, such becoming reverence for his instructors, such affectionate gratitude, and, above all, such *guilelessness*, I never in all my experience met united in one boy.

In addition to this moral testimony, it may be mentioned as a proof of memory, that he knew all the Epistles in the New Testament by heart; and, as a proof of a precocious and well-furnished mind, that Mr. Elliott gave him once, as an experiment, a Cambridge classical examination paper to do, and said that he did it admirably.

He was now thirteen years of age, and was preparing for Harrow; and May 16, 1848, was the day fixed for h s departure. He was delighted at the prospect, and set to work settling his home affairs very methodically. His childish books were given to the little ones, and a present selected for every friend he knew. The gifts of his father were alone excepted. "Papa gave me that, and I cannot part with it," was constantly repeated.

On Saturday, May 13th, he ran in the evening to a house in Brunswick Square to pay one of his schoolfellows a sixpence that he owed him; and whilst playing together on the leads which cover the out-premises in the back yards of all the houses, some one dared him to a leap, which he attempted in ignorance of the deep gap beyond. He caught his foot at the parapet, and fell headlong into the flagged yard below. Mr. Elliott was instantly summoned, and helped to bring him home. He was rational, knew every one, felt no pain, and gave an intelligent account of the accident. No alarming symptoms at first appeared, but after a few days fever and delirium set in, and, after various alternations between hope and fear, at ten o'clock on June 2nd, three weeks after the accident, he breathed his last. There is not much to record of what passed during his illness, for conversation was impossible; and it was found after his death that there was a large quantity of extravasated blood at the crown of the head, and effusion of water on the brain.

The final change took place when the family were at prayers, but Mr. Elliott entered the room in time to receive the last breath of his darling child. He sank on his knees by the bedside, and said, "God's will be done. It is holy, just, and good: and I must bring my will into conformity with it!" Then, like himself, thoughtful of others even in his own deep grief, he separately thanked all those who had been in loving and unwearied attendance, and said, "Now leave me;"—and he remained alone with his dead child.

"I am sure," he writes the next day (June 3rd) to his half-sister, Mrs. Pearson, "I shall have your deep pity and your prayers, and those of your dear husband and son, when I tell you that it has pleased God in His inscrutable providence to take from me my dearest earthly treasure remaining. my darling first-born, a flower of the highest promise and beauty, just beginning to unfold his talents

and virtues. He met, this day three weeks ago, with
an awful accident, by a fall on his head down an unpro-
tected area. He sank last night about ten o'clock, and
so gently, that we scarcely knew when he drew his last
breath."

Some days after, he wrote at length to his two mourning
sisters, Charlotte and Eleanor; to the former of whom, as
his godmother, Harry had been inexpressibly dear. After
mentioning in the most affecting manner his many excellent
traits of character—his affection for himself, his good influence with his brother Alfred, his love for Julius, his
modest appreciation of his own powers, his conscientious
use of his allowances—and then the sad nature of the
accident, which prevented much converse on religious
subjects, he adds:—

Oh, my sisters! what a dream is life! How have I dis-
quieted myself in vain about many things in regard to
that darling. What fond hopes, what bright prospects
does the shadow of death now brood over! How mysterious are the Divine judgments! that I should for three
weeks have mourned my beloved first-born, in whom I
delighted, and yet be unable to mention the name of Jesus
by his dying bed except once. Yet all his delirium showed
the purity of his mind. " Blessed are the pure in heart,
for they shall see God."
God is also my witness that, so far as I know my own heart,
my most constant and earnest desire was to train him
for the heavenly kingdom. And having declined for
him a most likely career of great wealth, on the ground
that I preferred a curacy for him in the ministry of Christ,
I fondly anticipated that God would accept the offering,
and place my beloved first-born as an able minister of the
New Testament in His sanctuary. And when I foresaw
the high powers of his intellect, a gleam of joy came across
my mind, and I said, " I trust my Harry will be a defender
of the faith in his day and generation, with no ordinary
abilities and knowledge consecrated to the work of his
Redeemer." But God has declined my offering; or rather,
He has transplanted it before the time I had destined,
to serve in the Courts above, and to see the face of his
Saviour, which St. Paul declares to be "far better."
As for me I bow to that inscrutable and sovereign

will. . . . Again God has awfully and tragically snatched from me the dearest and brightest I had on earth. First, He took the incomparable mother, and now the darling and exquisite child—a child not unworthy of such a mother!
But in my time of anguish and desolation, prayer has been my unceasing refuge, and I can just reach the mark, THY WILL BE DONE, though not with the elasticity and decision of my Charlotte's beautiful hymn.
Many, many thanks do I owe you, my beloved sisters,—Charlotte, Eleanor, Ellen—for all your sympathy and intercession. Pray that I may know how "to be abased," and how to humble myself under "the mighty hand of God," that He may exalt me in due time. Dearest Eliza has been a most tender and comforting sister to me, and every day's post lets in upon me a flood of sympathy from my dear brethren in Christ Jesus.

These extracts show that Mr. Elliott felt his loss most deeply; he called it his "second great tribulation." The nurse has described one touching scene, when his deep-felt sorrow found expression :—

"Before dear Harry died, I met my master," she says, "going down stairs. He asked, 'How is he?' I said, 'Very ill.' He gave a deep sigh which pierced my heart. When God strikes, His strokes are dreadful. Nobody but those who saw Mr. Elliott daily could tell how this trial went to the core of his heart. How often have I heard him groaning under it! One day after Harry's death I had to go into his bedroom. Placed before him was the picture of the two so dear to him. He was gazing on it and crying sadly. 'Oh, what should I do now,' he said to me, 'if I had not God's word and promise to comfort me!' I shall never forget the scene."

Mr. Elliott's grief was shared by every member of his congregation, so that but one heart seemed to throb in every breast. His friends also deeply sympathised with one thus pressed with "sorrow upon sorrow." The Bishop of Oxford (now Winchester) thus beautifully expressed what many felt :—

June 8, 1848.

I cannot let this heavy affliction fall on you without begging you to believe how truly I have sympathised, and do sympathise, with you under its pressure. I can, I believe, enter into your sorrow more entirely than most people, for I know how all the unmeasured depths of affection which flowed beforetime towards the mother, circle round the motherless children. I know, too, from your introduction of your children to me, both your affection for them, and their (and I believe especially *his*) worthiness of that love. But I know, too, my dear friend (in some sort, I trust, from my own experience), in Whom you have believed, and that in this, as in so many other trials, He will be with you; and I know that He has said that His treatment of the branch *which beareth fruit* is that He purgeth it that it may bring forth more fruit." And so, whilst I feel the awfulness of being thus under His hand, and whilst my weak flesh trembles and shrinks from any fellowship in such sufferings, yet I do not doubt for you whilst I pray for you. May God bless and strengthen you!

On Thursday, June 5th, the body was interred, the Rev. C. D. Maitland reading the funeral service. All the mourners present descended into the vault together, and Mr. Elliott pointed out each of the coffins to his sister, saying, "This is my beloved's, and this is my precious boy's;" and kissed them both. After a pause he added, "'The Lord gave, and the Lord hath taken away; blessed be the name of the Lord.' Yes, blessed, for He doth not willingly afflict the children of men." Then, after another pause, he added, "Now, let us live for eternity."

[For a brief Memoir of the Rev. Julius Elliott, the circumstances attendant upon whose birth form one main feature of this chapter, and an account of the sad accident which terminated his life, see Appendix.]

CHAPTER VI.

HOME LIFE AND GENERAL CORRESPONDENCE.

A Stricken Man—Training of Children—Reverence for Holy Scripture—Truth—Anecdotes—Comments on Scripture—Prayers—Little Children—Studies—Hymns—Correspondence.

MR. ELLIOTT was now a stricken man. The charm of life was gone. He was "enduring affliction," feeling "loving-correction," and learning how to "comfort others with the comfort wherewith he himself was comforted of God." His submission was unfeigned, but his mind never regained its original buoyancy. All the bright colouring of life had disappeared; but there was tranquillity, resignation, acquiescence, duty—those grey tints that are so beautiful in the sight both of God and man.

The first part of his home life, as contained in this chapter, will be portrayed by the assistance of one who became the instructress and friend of his children after their mother's death; and then, stretching, as it will, over a period of ten years, will be supplemented by the reminiscences of those children themselves, and concluded by a wide and general correspondence on topics of the utmost importance, independent of dates, and running to the close of life.

The few years immediately following his wife's death were marked by abiding sorrow and deep depression; and the Scripture was fulfilled—"no chastening is for the present joyous, but grievous." Mr. Elliott saw very few friends; never went into society of any kind; and kept each anniversary as a period of the strictest seclusion. Still his heart was not closed to his children, and each day he would devise some means, as aforetime, for their amusement. But it was evidently "pain and grief" to him, and he never played with them himself after Harry's death, as in former times. He would make the attempt, and then cease and turn away, as if everything past came back to him. He often drew the little ones towards him, and would lay his hand on their heads with a look of unutterable grief, murmuring a prayer, or the words "My poor children! my poor children!" This was the inner life; but no home duty was neglected; and the training of the children in habits of early piety was conscientiously enforced and carried out. They were taught the usual forms of prayer, but were encouraged also to express their daily wants and confess their daily faults in their own simple way, assisted by the recollection of passages of Scripture which they had learnt.

Attendance at church was treated as a privilege, to be continued or withheld as something heard was remembered, or forgotten. This stimulated attention, banished weariness, and improved the memory. They were dealt with as "children of light and of the day." Mr. Elliott would ever press that character upon them: urge them never to do anything that would not bear the light of day, and especially of the judgment day. The punishments adopted were those of banishment from meals with the family, and dining in the nursery; and these were never suspended by the presence of visitors, so that relatives were apt to think the discipline too rigid.   There was in truth at this time something of austerity in the whole arrangements of the household; and in the general bearing of its head, something savouring of the character of Elijah—grave, stern, solitary.   This would naturally act also upon the children, and beget in them a species of fear and awe.

Children do not appreciate sorrow.   It repels rather than attracts.   They shrink from it.   But when time has mellowed it on one side and ripening intellect is able to appreciate it on the other, it then becomes, as in the present case, the strong cement of love.   If Mr. Elliott's sorrow at first inspired awe in his children's minds, it changed afterwards into the deepest affection, the highest reverence, the most intense and abiding love—of which this Memoir is a feeble expression.

Their Sunday evenings (so often mis-employed, and so difficult to be well employed) were periods of great enjoyment to the children.   In the articles of food Mr. Elliott always made Sunday a festival, and it was the same on Church Festivals.   On these occasions he always had tea with his children, lingering long over it, and not returning to his study.

Then followed simple questioning; then recollections of the sermon, or reading of the lessons.   All this was merged in conversation, and he would often run down to the study for some book, which he would read or translate, in elucidation of some difficult passage which had occurred in reading. The interest arose from his placing himself for a time on a level with the children, making himself a learner, feeling and showing interest in the matter in hand.   He never passed over difficulties, but met them fully, without dogmatizing.   The punishment of Moses and Aaron, the thorn in the flesh, and kindred topics. were all discussed.   On the other hand, he often admitted humbly that there were difficulties in the Bible which baffled him.   Ezekiel's Temple as seen in vision, he "gave up in this world;" and the Book of Revelation he considered extremely difficult.

He always inculcated great reverence in the perusal of Scripture; and one of his objections to certain novels arose from their lodging in the mind Scripture phrases in a ludicrous sense, or with a double meaning. Yet he did not carry this to an extreme, but, like Bishop Blomfield, would often quote Scripture expressions with a smile upon his lips. One morning, for example, he was inquiring how a guest had slept, and whether the bed was comfortable, and alluding to its unusual height, he added, "I think you will understand David's expression—'I will not *climb up* into my bed.'" On another occasion, a friend was dining with him, and expecting her husband who had been unexpectedly detained. He detected her wandering attention and wistful eye directed to the window. "Oh you remind, me," he said, "of the mother of Sisera, who looked out at a window and cried through the lattice—'Why is his chariot so long in coming! Why tarry the wheels of his chariot?'"

One day he was watching two canaries, one masterful and one peaceful. "Ah, yes," he said, "I see that one of you is Abraham and the other Lot. It is quite clear which of you it is that says, 'If thou wilt take the left hand, then I will go to the right: or if thou depart to the right, then I will go to the left.'"

When writing was becoming easy to the children, he would say: "I see you have the pen of a ready writer. You are an excellent little scribe; but don't become a Pharisee."

If some plan was submitted to him by his sick child, he would acquiesce with a smile, repeating the words: "Whatsoever the king did pleased all the people."

He liked, on principle, to leave a little cake on the plate for the servants, saying: "Thou shalt not wholly reap the corners of thy field."

To those who were unable to attend divine service in church, he would cheerfully say: "She that tarried at home divided the spoil."

Truth was a guiding principle with him. "If there is one point," he writes in later life, "more than another, in morality, concerning which I have been especially watchful in my own words, and earnest in teaching my children, it has been *strict truth*, even to the banishment of ordinary exaggerations."

If a child had made some trifling mistake, and said, "Oh, I am so *very* sorry;"—"Keep your sorrow, my child," he would say, "for a greater occasion." Even in writing notes of civility, and in making morning calls, he was urgent that politeness should not supersede truth.

One of his boys, when young, had contracted a habit of boasting, or what may be called in American phraseology, "tall talk." To cure him of it, his father often called upon him, sometimes effectually, sometimes ineffectually, to fulfil his boast. "I am sure," he once said, " that I could carry a pail of water from the kitchen to the attic without spilling a drop." " Let a pail of water be brought," said his father, "let him do it." The pail half empty and the water splashed upon almost every stair told their own tale, and taught the required lesson.

"I am sure I could eat six dozen eggs at breakfast," was one morning's assertion. But, like the " three crows," the boast was brought down by discussion to one dozen. Even this was too strong for a practical lesson. But the next morning *six* boiled eggs were set before him at breakfast. In this case, however, the lesson failed, for they were all eaten in triumph, and with no sort of inconvenience!

He was intolerant of excuses having a basis in untruthfulness. If any one in excuse for a breakage said: "I was holding it quite safely and it broke;"—"How very clever of it," he would say, "to fall down and break itself." So that "it broke," were words banished from the family.

He used to refer to Aaron's self-justification—"There came out this calf;" to Adam's—"The woman gave unto me;" to Saul's—"The people took of the spoil;" as compared with David's earnest, ingenuous, and pardon-getting expression—" I have sinned against the Lord."

He was glad himself to receive criticisms of all kinds, even from his children; and used often to mention his own past faults and errors, and say how he had benefited by advice. He would tell many stories of Mr. Simeon, and how he used to criticise his sermons. One day, after listening to a sermon Mr. Elliott had preached in his chapel at Brighton, Mr. Simeon said to him : " I see, my dear brother, that you have the attention of your flock, their undivided attention—but not their breathless attention."

· Having called upon him one day at Cambridge, and knocked at the inner door of his rooms at King's College, Mr. Simeon opened the door himself, and, as a preliminary, immediately and earnestly inquired: "My dear friend, I am delighted to see you ; but *have* you rubbed your shoes upon the mat?" "Yes," replied Mr. Elliott, with corresponding gravity, " upon all four." "Then," said Mr. Simeon," pray come in." ·

He discouraged his children from giving him presents,

saying: "The children ought not to lay up for the parents, but the parents for the children."

He did not usually say grace *after* meat, on the principle that it is not recorded that our Saviour ever did so.

His study of Holy Scripture and comments upon it, were very striking. There are in existence now, six or eight large folio volumes, down each page of which a strip of the sacred text is pasted; whilst all the rest is covered with extracts from the Fathers, eminent commentators, and distinguished divines. or with original remarks of his own. The volumes prove his reverence for Holy Scripture, and his studious habits. They form a treasury of learned research, pious reflection, and original thought.

A few of his thoughts and comments on Scripture may be inserted here briefly, with their references :—

Acts xxvii. 44. A plank of God's providence is better than a ship of man's building.

Isaiah vi. 4. What responses were these! They shook the building. The "posts of the doors" were moved.

Isaiah iii. 18—24. The Lord keeps an inventory of a lady's ornaments (the chains, the bracelets, the bonnets).

St. Luke viii. 2, 3. "Mary Magdalene, . . . Joanna, . . . Susanna, . . . and many others which ministered to Him of their substance." Here we have the first list of missionary subscribers, three by name, the rest anonymous.

Gen. xxviii. 22. The habit of accurate accounts is really a religious duty. How can the proportion of one-tenth ($\frac{1}{10}$) be kept (which is the least to be given in charity), unless we know the numerator as well as the denominator?

Numb. xvi. 6, 7. "To-morrow :"—a respite for repentance!

Deuteronomy i. 19. "That great and terrible wilderness" was the churchyard of three or four millions!

Job xiii. 4. God only, in deep sorrow, can heal the wounded heart. Men mistake the disease, or prescribe wrong remedies, or give it up in despair.

Ps. lxviii. 20. "Unto God the Lord belong the issues from death :"—as the Fifth of November.

Phil. i. 2. "Grace" precedes "peace."

1 Timothy i. 2. It is only in his Epistles to the clergy that St. Paul sends the salutation of grace, *mercy*, and peace.

Luke vii. 28. Nearness to Christ, and knowledge of Christ, it would seem mark the nobility of heaven.

A friend, in conversation, thought our Lord after His resurrection, kept His disciples at too great a distance. "How can you think so?" said he; "could Christ have addressed them in dearer or more familiar terms than when He said, 'Children, have ye any meat?'"

As his comments were often thus striking and original, so were his prayers. He was a man of prayer. He did nothing, and urged his family to do nothing, without prayer. A short journey to be made, a medical opinion to be taken, a trouble to be got rid of, all were made subjects, specially and directly, of prayer.

After reading St. Peter's enumeration of Christian graces —"add to your faith virtue," &c. (2 Peter i. 5)—his family prayer was that if we could not attain on earth to the fulness of such perfection, we might at least possess the *initials* of each Christian grace.

Another time he prayed that patience and grace might be apportioned to the length of the trial; that his children in the morning of life, and he in its last stage, might be more and more knit together in Christ.

Having commented on the pilgrim spirit, he prayed that in all our journeyings it might grow; that, like pilgrims, we might care little about our inns, or our roads, but that "onward" and "upward" might be our motto.

He often used Matthew Henry's petition, that "as we have brought much of the week-day into the sabbath, so we might be helped to bring much of the sabbath into the week."

He loved the motto " παθήματα μαθήματα."

He did not shrink, after a time, from speaking to his children of their departed mother. He told them that once a playful discussion arose as to the possibility of a quarrel and consequent separation, when she said, "Well, well, the division of goods would be easily made. I would take the children, and you should have all the rest."

The mass of papers accumulating ever more and more about him, and choking up the house, troubled her, and made her say mischievously to her sister-in-law, " I should not be very sorry if a fire, a *little* fire, broke out, and cleared the atmosphere."

His children were required, even when very young, to keep accounts, and, if correct at the year's end, they received a reward. "Stewards, not owners," they were taught to consider themselves. One day a sister very earnestly and elaborately gave an opinion on some point touching her elder sister's health. He took out his purse, and presented her with a doctor's fee. In the same playful spirit she was often, after some animated discussion, presented with a lawyer's fee.

If anything that was done for him was done imperfectly, he would have it done over again. "Now," he would say, "you understand the proverb—'Well done, twice done.'"

He delighted in watching little children at play: "Come here," he used to say, "and look at their little twinkling feet." Watching their movements in walking, he would say, "See how beautifully God has made the little pedestals to suit the figure of the child, and to grow with its growth." He liked a certain amount of gravity, even in a child, and said, with admiration. of a very little girl, that "no one could take a liberty with her." His inscriptions in books were very racy and apposite. A favourite inscription for a Bible was, "Speak, Lord! for Thy servant heareth." In giving a Bible, he wrote. "And he showed me a pure river of water of life, clear as crystal." In giving another to a Mary he wrote: "Mary kept all these sayings, and pondered them in her heart." In a very small New Testament he wrote: "A little and safe companion for time and eternity." For a sun-dial, his motto was, "My days are like a shadow that declineth."

He was very quick in detecting characteristic traits in young children. and often commended the prompt and avowed obedience of a little child:—"I can't allow you to throw that ball about any more; put it away directly." "*Yes, mamma.*" Again, on offering money to another, the boy drew back instantly, saying, "No, Mr. Elliott, mamma would not like me to receive money." And he was much struck with another who was taken to York Minster, at three years old. Awed by the majesty of the building, the little fellow exclaimed, "Take me away. take me away: the church is too great; and I am too little." Mr. Elliott used to say, "I wish that had been my child."

If letter reading. or interruptions, prolonged the breakfast hour, he liked his children to take up a piece of needlework. "It looks so respectable to be employed," he would say.

He joined personally in all the studies going on, and made one language a stepping-stone to another. One of his daughters. struck with the sound of Greek, which he often read aloud to illustrate its beauty, wished to learn it. "Not till you have learnt Latin," he said. It was the same with drawing: "Not till you can write fairly." Italian was learnt for the sake of knowing what was sung. When the children learnt French, all spoke it; and Mr. Elliott entered into it with such zest, that he often mentioned a fact which occasioned at the time both surprise and amusement:—He had rung for a servant, and desired him to bring some brown sugar. The man stared, and said, "Sir?" and at length Mr. Elliott found that he was asking him over and over again for "la cassonade."

He was very jealous of transgressing the boundary of facts, and took the 'Peep of Day' and 'Agathos' away from his children, because the one added to the history of Jonah, and the other spoke of beautiful carriages and horses, as exhibited by Satan at the third temptation. Of historical novels, such as 'The Talisman' or 'Ivanhoe,' he thought the perusal chiefly questionable as giving confused views of the facts of history, which, in after years, could hardly be erased.

He read beautifully himself, and would deeply interest his children, even to tears, by the pathos of his voice, as adapted to many of Shakespeare's characters, such as Desdemona, Ophelia, &c. He thought 'Hamlet' Shakespeare's finest play. He could never read 'King Lear' aloud; it overcame him. He so realized, often, the scenes in 'Macbeth,' as to start from his chair and partially act them. The older poets he loved most—Herbert, Cowper, Burns, and such like. The hymns of his childhood were generally preferred, with certain exceptions. Among the poems of the 'Christian Year,' he preferred, as chief of all, the 'Twentieth Sunday after Trinity;' then the Monday, Tuesday, and Wednesday before Easter, St. Matthias' Day, and the first Sunday after Christmas.

For his sister Charlotte he always felt the deepest affection; and shared with her his sorrows and his joys. The suffering and dependence of long-continued ill-health called forth his tenderest sympathy—and it was repaid by her with love and prayers. He rejoiced unfeignedly at the grace given to her and the benefits bestowed upon the whole Church by her sacred poetry, and especially the hymns already referred to. Of the two named he preferred for himself the hymn beginning "My God, my Father," to that beginning "Just as I am:" but he often said that he believed this last had done more good than he had in all his ministry.

He settled down into final admiration of the hymns, "Rock

of Ages," and "Jesu, Lover of my soul." They were his favourites above all. The latter, he said, was less poetical, but more clinging.

These records of intercourse with his children, and of home life at this period, will not be deemed trivial by any who desire to know Mr. Elliott. No one is known abroad; he must be followed and lived with at home.

His letters to his children in their early days might be added here, for they are very affectionate and wise. But they must give place to others of more importance, which will serve to show the power of his pen, the faithfulness of his reproofs, the wisdom of his counsels, and the tenderness of his sympathy. Most of the family or personal allusions, which give additional interest to the originals, are necessarily omitted. The reader will be contented with the jewel without the setting. The correspondence ranges over a period of about twenty years.

LETTERS ON BEREAVEMENT.
To Mrs. Carr. 1840.

While I feel that none but God can console you for such a
loss, I have the comfort of knowing that He will console
you. When He said to His poor trembling disciples, " I will
not leave you orphans," He seems to me, virtually, to have
said to the widow, " I will not leave you husbandless ;" and to
sisters, " I will not leave you brotherless;" and to friends, " I
will not leave you friendless." If, then, there be any consola-
·tion in Christ, may you, and may they, have it infused into
your bleeding hearts in a full measure. I cannot but believe
that God, when He says, " I am thy portion," will more than
fill up every chasm that death can make. In the midst of
tears, I trust you will call to mind God's great goodness to
him you have lost : how He entrusted to him a lovely spot
in his vineyard, and enabled him to cultivate it with no
little skill, and blessed his labours continually with the dews
of His Spirit, and gave him to see the fruit of his work,
and the beauty of the garden of the Lord, under his ministration. And, perhaps, though we see it not, there was
much mercy and an opportune time chosen for his departure.
I rejoice that he died in the midst of you and not at
Madeira. Heaven is, indeed, as near to Madeira as to
England, but still it is something to be in the bosom of so
tender and sympathising a family.

In afflictions there are two opposite dangers, the danger of taking them too despondingly and grievously, and the danger of making light of them by thinking we can bear up against them by our own strength. But you have learnt, my dear friend, that when God smites, He means the blow to be felt; and your danger would be rather, perhaps, to faint when "rebuked of the Lord." But after a while He revives the fainting heart; and, above all, He makes the softening influences of affliction the means by which He stamps on the soul His own likeness. At other times we are too hard to receive the impression; but under chastisement we become partakers of His holiness.

To the same. 1858.

I have been prevented from writing to you by my ignorance of your address. Nor should I have wished even now to have intruded on sorrow so deep and desolate, unless I had a sort of privilege, a *passe-partout*, into the houses of mourning. My own afflictions, which are still before me, embolden me to address the widow and the widower, and *the bereaved of children*, having suffered with them the like distress in its intensity; and even now I know not what is before me. Let me entreat you to avoid two things : first, the anxious anticipations of the future; its desolation to you by the loss of the beloved child ; the measuring the breadth and extent of the gap made in your innermost circle of domestic happiness ; and that you would keep in mind our Lord's command, "Take no thought for the morrow :"—and, secondly, the dwelling on second causes. It is the Lord that hath done this. It is the Lord who ordered your dear child's departure at the hotel, and its circumstances. It was out of the agony of my soul that, when my own precious firstborn died by an area-fall, after the buddings and blossoms of the most filial duty and the highest talent, the day before he was to have gone to Harrow, I preached on the text, "He hath done all things well." I stand to it still. I cannot trace that mystery, but I trust it was in love.

Accept my hearty sympathy, and the assurance that it is not without the prayer for you that you may be enabled, better than I have done, to glorify God in the fires.

To the late SIR PATRICK ROSS, *Governor of*
St. Helena. 1847.

A union of heart and life for so many years—a union too,
deeper and purer as it went on, and now resting on the
"Rock of Ages"—cannot be broken off, never to be renewed
in this life, without a severe shock to the whole of our
existence here. The shock will indeed, in its first con-
cussion and violence, pass away; but, like the earthquake
that is over, it leaves ruinous gaps and fissures that remain
in the edifice, and henceforth it can never again be what
once it was. None should know this better than I, who
have felt the shock in all its rudeness and suddenness. To
you it has come more gradually, and with notice and preparation, and at a later time of life, when the separation
cannot be very long.

But, dear Sir Patrick, I have to tell you of great mercies
mingled with this stroke of affliction. Your beloved
wife's death has been marked by visible tokens of the
Divine Presence. God was with her when she passed
through the last swelling waters; and God was, in her
whole passage "through the dark valley of the shadow of
death," from the beginning to the end, evidently with her.
I should use concerning her departure that glorious text
of St. Peter's that "an entrance was ministered to her
abundantly into the everlasting kingdom of our Lord and
Saviour Jesus Christ." On her birthday I administered
the Holy Sacrament to her, which she received with that
deep reverence, illuminated with a holy joy, that best befits
that sacred ordinance.

On the Tuesday morning she sent for me, and I was with
her for about half an hour, not much more than an hour
before her departure. I never saw so much life so near
to death. She always welcomed me with the kindest
affection; but on that day, when I came, she gave me her
hand, and, looking full at me, with a sweet smile, she said,
"I am going now very fast." "Yes," I said, "you are going
to Jesus." "I trust so," she replied. She asked me for the
Commendatory Prayer, which I offered up. She clasped
her hands, and fervently uttered the "Amen" at its conclusion. Then she turned to each of us, thanked us, and
blessed each of us individually, and prayed that God would
bless and reward us. Such collectedness, such sweetness,

such thoughtfulness for others, such tender gratitude for poor services, carried in the fulness and feeling of life to the very gate of death, I never saw.

When I left her I said, "Dear Lady Ross, is your soul at peace in Christ Jesus?" She answered without hesitation, "Yes; I am a brand plucked from the burning"—an expression I had often heard her use respecting herself before, and indicative of her habitual humility.

So she died, dear Sir Patrick, like the patriarchs, invoking blessings on all around her. What remains for you now is to follow her, as she followed Christ. Her humility, her spiritual appetite for the Word of God, her love to all around her, her patience and resignation, were most striking. These die not; these live with you, and are to be more than ever your companions till you find them perfected in life eternal, and associated with a body no more liable to pain and weariness and disease, but immortal and glorious, and like to the glorified body of our Lord and Saviour.

To the Rev. D. Barclay Bevan. 1855.

So it has pleased the Lord to put into your hands the bitter cup of bereavement, which, fourteen years ago, He gave me to drink, as a cup of astonishment and rebuke and trembling. I well know by my own experience how impotent and almost impertinent most letters are in such a tribulation. It is a time when the Lord speaks to us alone; and he will not allow His communion with us, and His closest interviews, to be intruded upon by those who cannot touch the case. "Cause all men to go out from me." He cries, as Joseph cried when he would be alone with those to whom he wished to speak. I will not therefore act in forgetfulness of my own observation.

May the Lord be very present with you; and give you the precious fruit of a sanctified affliction!

To the Rev. C. J. Bird. 1859.

In the ruinous gap which has been made in your domestic citadel, you know well, my friend, whither to flee as your refuge. To me it was a source of much instruction and consolation in that fearful November of 1841, and the following months, to make the Books of Job and Lamentations my study, with an interleaved Bible. God only

knows how often I reiterated before Him the prayer, " Oh
may much life come out of this death!" There is a double
danger of too much grief, and too little—and often, I
remember, I found myself oscillating between the two :
sometimes feeling the grief to be too strong, consuming
me; and sometimes relapsing into a diminution that
seemed to me like apathy, and presenting the accusation
that I was hard and insensible to a loss that could not well
be greater, and a memory that could not well be dearer.

My dear friend, you know well that (as I said in a sermon—
and I used the expression with a singular coincidence, just
before God took from me the desire of my eyes) " the word
irreparable is not in the vocabulary of our Faith in the
Lord Jesus." God can repair to you even your loss; and
He will repair it. " They that trust in the Lord," says the
34th Psalm, " shall not be desolate."

Ministers are not private persons. Among other uses, this
tribulation has fallen on you for the benefit of your flock ;
that you may be able, better able, to speak a word to him
that is weary, and comfort others with the comfort wherewith you yourself have been comforted of God.

To the Rev. J. Babington. 1858.

My dear sister communicated to me the startling intelligence
of the death of your dear sister, Lady Parker, which I
know must have been a sore trial to you, as one to whom
you were particularly attached. At our time of life, the
deaths of those dearest to us have one sensible mitigation—
that the reunion cannot be far off, and that the dreary
sense of their loss is only for a little while. And this
consolation is in addition to the greatest of all—that our
loss, which (to use a Scriptural phrase) " is but for a
moment," is their exceeding gain.

The deepest regret which one naturally feels is that such
a mother should not have been spared to so young a family,
just needing now, more than ever, the guiding eye and
tender love of her introduction of them into life. On
Sunday, I wrote and preached a new sermon on David's
decease, full of days and honour—I suppose because the
train of thought led that way. How wonderfully gracious
God was to him in raising him up, not only to His own
favour, and establishing him with His " free Spirit," as he

prayed in the 51st Psalm, but also in reinstating him in credit with His Church on earth. I do think that was in itself a species of miracle. "Let him hide his head, and go down to the grave in sackcloth and ashes," we should have said. "Let us not refuse him some pity and some hope: God will decide whether he is sincere; whether he is saved or lost, at the great day." But, no! wonderful to relate, he died full of days, riches, and honour; one of his latest acts a high dedication, and public thanksgiving, and benediction of the preparations he had made for the Temple that Solomon was to build: a splendid religious function in which he was chief.

As my pen ran on to you, the thought came into my mind, "the Archangel's voice!" Who is the Archangel? Is it Christ? as some contend,—or a created angel? Surely the Trump belongs not to the Chief in the procession; and yet we speak of the Trump of God, and the voice of *an* Archangel, or *the* Archangel. Are we right in calling it the Archangel's Trump? In 1 Thessalonians iv. it is the Archangel's "voice," not the Trump of God. Please to think these expressions over, and let us have a talk about them when we meet.

To Mrs. H——. 1859.

While the world's treatment of deep bereavement is mistaken and criminal, hurrying us into premature occupation and diversion; we may be more severe against ourselves than is right, and trespass by nursing and cherishing excessive grief. We may even make grief an idol. In your case God sends you to business; and it is your duty to attend to it. And God surrounds you with your garden, and assigns to your sorrow the sweet season of spring; and it is right you should hear Him speaking to you in the voices of the birds, and see His hand in the *resurrection* of the trees and flowers. But still there is an inner closet whither the chastened of the Lord should retire, and pour out their hearts before Him whose hand has chastened them. "Is any afflicted? let him pray." Now is the precious seed-time of earnest prayer. Now is the time to enter on the special study of God's Word. Now form the true estimate of the world.

Please to be very jealous of the world, and anything that may estrange you or yours from vital communion with God.

To a Lady. Easter, 1853.

If I have not written, I have not forgotten you. Full well I know the cheerless and awful silence and emptiness of the rooms which were so full of love, and all its busy offices; and which, by perpetual association, always presented a pleasant object for the eye to rest on, but are now suddenly and for ever, unpeopled. The charm is gone; the house is a kind of sepulchre. But so it is that God disenchants earth, and teaches us, reluctant as we are, to take up the words of the Psalmist, "I have said unto the Lord, Thou art my portion."

Happy are we if affliction has taught us thus to address our heavenly Father. It is a lesson of time so to learn it as to be able again "to rejoice in the Lord," and to resume our duties of daily life with interest and alacrity.

Wrapt up as you were in your beloved father, and utterly unnerved by his removal, I do not expect you to regain the equilibrium (if I may use the term) of true faith till after a season. The Apostle himself says of affliction, "*afterwards* it yieldeth the peaceable fruits of righteousness," not at first; and he does not define the length of the word "afterwards." I pray God that as your grief has been great, and your sense of the loss continual, so the fruits may correspond to the previous deep furrows ploughed up in your heart. You will not forget to make it a special time of prayer; for affliction is the harvest-time of prayer.

Most persons are not in danger of excessive sorrow, but I think you are; and therefore, my dear friend, I would ask you to remember the great resource for Christian grief as pointed out in 1 Corinthians xv. 58, " always abounding in the work of the Lord."

May the Lord, the risen Saviour, who has the keys of death and the grave hung at His girdle, speak peace to you— the peace that belongs to that cardinal fact, " the Lord is risen !"

ON THE PROPER FRUITS OF SICKNESS.
To Lord Haddo. 1854.

Mr. Elliott observes with reference to this illness :—

To me, the prospect is very afflictive, for in Lord Haddo (Lord Aberdeen's own son) I lose one of my kindest and most attached friends, whom I knew as a boy, who was my pupil in Cannon Place, and whom I have seen gradually for many years advancing in all that is holy, and settled in his choice of the service of God above all earthly distinctions.

I will confine myself to one point. I am persuaded that, however calmly you may be enabled to look the King of Terrors in the face (and it is a cause of thanksgiving to Him whose death hath taken away this fear), yet you will desire to bring forth the fruits of the dispensation of your heavenly Father to you in this sickness. God is to be glorified in every stage of life, in sickness as well as health, and he may be glorified more especially in the former.

In the glorious procession of the faithful in the Epistle to the Hebrews, in two examples the highest achievement of faith is reserved for the closing scene—Jacob and Joseph. Their dying graces were their brightest; their last faith was the most exemplary.

May I just put down for your remembrance and self-examination a few of the peculiar fruits of sickness, when improved by the teaching and influence of the Holy Ghost? They are these—resignation and patience. First, Resignation towards God, a conformity of our will to His will, till they are felt to be without contrariety. Second, Patience towards man, in rising superior to the little provocations and irritations which sickness brings with it, especially when it affects the nerves. But still, though physical excitement cannot be avoided, yet " My grace is sufficient for thee " applies to such " thorns in the flesh " as these; and it is equally desirable and necessary for one's own peace, and the edification of others, that we should show forth the power of God in us : " strengthened . . . . unto all patience," as the Apostle speaks (Colossians i. 11).

I like to look at the companions of a Christian grace. I find Patience in company with *Faith* (Hebrews vi. 12), if we would run with patience the race set before us. I find it in company also with *Love* and *Meekness* (1 Tim. vi. 11): walking, as it were, arm in-arm between those two, the one the flowing of the heart, the other its outward expression. " Love, patience, meekness." A sick man has but a small congregation, but they are very attentive; and he preaches with a double power from that affecting pulpit!

To a former Pupil, the MARQUIS (*now* DUKE) *of* ABERCORN, *on the death of his Stepfather, the* EARL *of* ABERDEEN, 1860.

I suppose no event has happened to you in your life, except the death of your dear mother, which can compare with Lord Aberdeen's decease, to cast a solemn shade over your feelings. I remember well your being with me on one sorrowful occasion when I was in Cannon Place. And now how swiftly have thirty years passed over us both, and how soon must we have to pass through the same dark "valley of the shadow of death!" Then little indeed will any earthly help avail us, and the one question will be, in what relation we stand to Christ. He alone can give us the sure hope, which will be a light in that dark valley. '*Sic transit gloria mundi,*' is the motto which belongs to the highest honours of rank or office, unless they be improved for Christ's kingdom. But what we do for Him, and out of love for His name, be it ever so little, will enjoy an undying reward. "Inasmuch as ye have done it unto one of the least of these My brethren, ye have done it unto me." Please to think of this.

I am sure it must have struck you as it struck me, how unwise it would be to put off the preparation for eternity till sickness shall claim all our attention for the poor body, and a few sentences from the Bible, and a few words of prayer, are all we can bear. Repentance, faith, and the service of our Redeemer, demand the energies of the best health and longest life; and to offer to Him only the dregs of life will cover us with confusion, and if deliberately designed, be, even in our own eyes, a base and unpardonable insult.

Never, dear Lord Abercorn, was there a time when the interests of religion invite and will repay so largely all the influence you, in your high place, can bring to her aid. Please to make this a time of more prayer, and special prayer. "Is any afflicted? let him pray." It is God's own prescription, you see. If I had less affection for you, I would not have written this homily. But believe me, when at such a grave as you have attended to-day, the lights of eternity stream in upon the conscience, and show the contrast between the things of God and the things of time and sense, it is a crisis which will leave us better or worse.

May God bless you! So prays your old friend and tutor.

LETTERS ON PERSONAL AFFLICTION.

To his Daughter. 1861.

When God in His great and undeserved mercy gave me my
child, how little did I know what a fountain of delight
He opened to me!

May the Lord, my darling, pour into your own bosom His
tenderest love and deepest compassion!

He appears to appoint to you the path of suffering as the
way in which He will be glorified by you. It was Christ's
own vocation, and He constitutes it yours. The text I
send you, my love, for the day, is from the lesson of last
Sunday evening, "My grace is sufficient for thee; for My
strength is made perfect in weakness." St. Paul prayed
fervently for the removal of the thorn in the flesh, and
the answer he *expected* was its removal. It was the
natural and direct answer; but the Lord had a better
answer—not so direct, nay, circuitous in its time and
manner; but it was altogether a higher discipline, a
discipline belonging to His highest school:—"My grace is
sufficient for thee, for My strength is made perfect in
weakness." It said, "Suffer on; think no evil of the
refusal of your petitions; accept your sufferings as the
field in which you must glorify Me." Then welcome was
the thorn in the flesh, and clear was the arena of the
conflict, and bright the victory through the aid that was
vouchsafed—the Saviour's aid. Fourteen years he kept
untold the secret of the promise, and the inward grace
which enabled him to glory in His infirmities, and at last
came to that height, viz., an earnest expectation and hope
that God should be glorified in his body, by sickness or
health, by life or death.

Adieu, my darling. All blessings be with you, and the
peace which only One can give. May you find shelter
under His soft wings, and His everlasting love! So prays
your earthly father with his fondest love.

To the Same. 1860.

What two precious letters have I received from you; one to
gladden Christmas day, the other to add peace and thankfulness to the New Year! What will it bring to us,
darling? What shall we ask that it may bring? Grace,
mercy, and peace from God our Father and the Lord Jesus

Christ? Yet the continual thought of your painful days and weary nights comes over me often as a dark cloud, though I know that the other side is light with the beams of Everlasting Love. And therefore I will resume the sentence which came into my mind, but which I was arrested in uttering, because to one so suffering, the words sound almost a mockery—"A happy, happy New Year to you!" If I were asked who were the happiest of the Lord's children, the afflicted or the unafflicted, I should say without hesitation, the afflicted; because God is a Father, and the tenderest looks, the sweetest smiles, the most watchful care of a father are always the portion of the child who is sick and suffering above the rest. Has He not said, "In all our afflictions He is afflicted?"

To the Same.

How severe is the frost! I have been compelled by it to issue another delivery of coals, which stands for to-morrow, so that I cannot come to you; nor on Thursday, till the afternoon, as a meeting engages me in the morning. Darling, I think of you, and the cold, and your eyes, day and night. The Lord be your strength and health!"

Tuesday.—I count the days when I shall come to you, and live a double life as to my sensation of cold and damp, and sun and wind—one for myself, which is hardy, and not much conversant with the barometer or thermometer; the other for you, darling, which is very acute and vigilant, watching the quarter, and measuring the cold. But what can I do for you, my precious children? Only pray.

Alas! my tender plant, how would I shield you, if I could, from the stormy wind and cold. And when it comes, as it came here this afternoon, with thunder, lightning, and rain, what a solace it is to recollect that you are enfolded in the everlasting arms of Infinite Pity and love! I shall be delighted to give you the Holy Communion on Wednesday.

I will bring you a few books. Bishop Daniel Wilson's Life will, I am sure, give you great satisfaction. But we must read it to you. I have pretty well got through my lectures, but not entirely. The schools could not all receive me at the times I offered; so I had none on Thursday, and three on Friday.

To the Same.

It is rather strange that the house, ever since you left it, though you never used to quit your rooms, seems un-peopled and lonely. Every time I go up and down stairs, there is the red door before the eye, but not now the consciousness how much is going on in that room—what a conflict of patience striving for its perfect work; and resignation aspiring to rise above every desire of ease and comfort, and to have no will of its own, but to say, simply and fervently, " Thy will be done :"—but on the contrary, there is no life there now; no morning or evening saluta-tions; no sweet and tender smile, in spite of suffering; no trust of little commissions to willing hands; no mutual communications of the events of the day, or the contents of the post, one to the other; no short words of prayer and benediction. But, in place of all this, there is a chilling silence and an absolute stillness. I have not been once into those rooms since they lost their jewel. I feel a strange repugnance to open the door; it reminds one of the great truth—" The place that knoweth us shall know us no more :" and then comes the great counterpart—" Lord, Thou hast been our dwelling-place in all generations."

May He be with my precious child where she is now, and " comfort her while she lieth sick ;"—no, the Bible transla-tion is more germane to the case—" The Lord strengthen her on the bed of languishing, and make all her bed in her sickness."

But I must come and see you, darling, with my own eyes, though an early afternoon train will bring me back to prepare for Holy Thursday.

To the Same.

As this is likely to be a ten-letter day, I must write fast, and short lines ; yet believe me that in the hasty current there is much love flowing underneath, although it may not rise to the surface.

I cannot tell you how dear and precious was your last letter but one ; balmy as the unguents in lachrymatories, and not to be read without some effusion of the eyes. I know what that meaneth—" Like as a father pitieth his own children," although these are the words of the Almighty, and my feelings are those of one who stands by and can do nothing.

Darling, how infinitely better it is that you should be in
His hands than in mine, even if I had some power
where I have none. For I should raise you up to gay
health, and sprightly days, and full occupation, and sound
and refreshing slumbers, and an appetite not satisfied
with minute morsels. But He who does all things well,
whether He heals or whether He afflicts with disease
or restlessness, keeps you still low and suffering, that
patience may have her perfect work, that you may be
perfect and entire, may want no purity or refinement
which the furnace alone can give. But still I cannot look
on unmoved.

From the preceding letters, which may tend to the
improvement or consolation of the sons and daughters of
affliction up and down the world, the attention of the
reader may now be turned to others, bearing more or less
on points of controversy agitated of late years. It seems
right that Mr. Elliott's opinion on these and kindred topics
should be known. He was never a party man. He desired
to avoid the bitterness and strife of theological differences,
whilst insisting in a spirit of kindness on the fundamental
points of the Gospel of Christ. He never framed his
system of doctrine or practice according to any party or set of
persons. He sought truth, and loved it wherever he found it.
Whilst deprecating neutrality, he recommended charity.

ON LEAVING A PROFESSION AND TAKING HOLY ORDERS.

In general you are aware that the apostle lays down this
rule against the change:—" Let every man abide in the
calling wherein he is called;" yet the general rule must
have had exceptions. For how could the Philippian
Church have got its bishops so soon, if certain adult and
converted laymen had not been raised to that responsible
office from their former trades or professions? I must refer
you, therefore, to 1 Tim. iii. and Titus i. &c. It will be
clear from thence :—

1. That the layman must examine himself as to his rule in his
   own family, whether he has been apt to teach his servants
   and to care for the salvation of those around him; and
   whether God has blessed such ministrations of his in the
   sphere of their exercise :—it is remarkable that the character
   of the wife enters into the qualifications of the husband.

2. He is not to be a novice; one recently converted to
the true faith: and is certainly to be above all secular
influences in the change, whether of money or reputation.

3. He must also be blameless, that is, he must not be liable
to the charge of unfitness in the eyes of men, much more
in the eyes of religious friends. "He is quite fit to be a
clergyman; what a pity he is not one!"—such was, I
remember, the impression that Mr. Maitland made on many
persons when he was as yet an Artillery officer; and
Mr. R. S—— made, in a less degree, the same impression.
On the other hand, I have heard said of a clergyman, a
clever man, well read, a graduate of the University, a
fellow of his college, of unexceptionable morals, sensible,
polite, agreeable:—"Mais c'est la profession manquée,"
"He has mistaken his calling."

I was recently requested to look, in manuscript, at the Life
of Bishop Daniel Wilson, which will soon be published;
and his transition from the silk warehouse to which he
was articled under his uncle, was most anxiously and carefully considered, submitted to Mr. Newton and Mr. Cecil,
and one or two others, and not determined upon till the
voice of Providence was so clear as to leave no doubt. I
should like you to read that chapter.[1] Slight circumstances
must not be taken as an indication that God wills a change:
He indicates His will by voices more loud, and more
articulate.

At the same time, I would express my satisfaction that you
are prayerfully committing your way to the Lord. Do not
be in a hurry. Do not make the decisive move till you
can hear the voice behind you saying, "This is the way,
walk ye in it."

I think it would be far better to go to Cambridge with
your mind not quite made up; as if "the great change
was settled." Why not go to the University, leaving the
matter open? A year or two of college life would be

---

[1] In July 1846, he had received Bishop Daniel Wilson, then home for
health, into his house, and entertained him joyfully. He opened his
chapel for appeals on behalf of the new cathedral, then contemplated, now
completed, in Calcutta; and the amount raised exceeded one hundred
pounds. At a breakfast party afterwards, a distinguished company of
clergy and laity assembled. The bishop addressed them on Indian subjects, and the discussion which followed was very interesting. Before the
Bishop left, Mr. Elliott brought all his children to receive his episcopal
benediction, with laying on of hands, as for the last time.

.profitable to any one as well as to a theological candidate.
And in earnest waiting upon the Lord there, you would get
more light, and be in the way of pious and judicious advisers.
It is not by a twilight gleam that your path should be traced.
God never meant such a conclusion as "His ministry" to
vibrate in doubtful scales. And as to the ultimate position
of a village curacy or rectory, believe me, it requires no
little portion of Divine grace for a man to keep his
head above water under the crass ignorance, the moral
obliquities, the painful obduracy of most villages which I
have seen and known and heard of, and one of which I
have myself tried. It requires a double portion of God's
Spirit to keep the heart tender and true under the suffocating
atmosphere of most village duties.

ON A UNIVERSITY LIFE. 1840.

At the kind request of your excellent father, whom I love in
the communion of saints, I would desire at your entrance
into the world to offer to you a few remarks, which by the
Divine blessing may be serviceable to your peace and usefulness.

1. Fortify yourself in the profession of the Gospel (of which,
I trust, you will not be ashamed) against the banter of the
worldly and licentious. To this end, study to possess your
mind with a deep sense of the dignity, responsiblity, and
the difficulty of the Christian character.

Hitherto you have been sailing about in a quiet and sheltered
port; now you are to launch into a wide and stormy sea.
Sail with your colours hoisted. This one rule will save you
from many perplexities and temptations. If men seek your
society, let them at once be aware on what terms you will
let them have it.

2. Let your society be select rather than large. A few
intimates are better than a host of acquaintances. You
must take courage to decline many advances; remembering
that you go to college to *learn* to play your part, and take
your station in life—not yet to take it. In after life, mental
occupation cuts off much lounging intercourse. In the
University there is the greatest market of idleness, I believe,
in the world, as well as of study; more idle men, I mean,
thickly crowded, and infecting others with their listless
habits, than can be found elsewhere.

truth in the world to come. Again, what means the
Apostle when he speaks of presenting his converts " faultless " or perfect in Christ Jesus, each individual of them ;
and that they will be " his joy and crown of rejoicing in
the presence of our Lord Jesus Christ at His coming?'
(1 Thess. ii. 19.) How can they possibly be to him his
crown of rejoicing at Christ's coming, unless he shall know
them, and know their spiritual victory over their ad-
versaries, and their salvation in Christ: that is, know
them, not only personally but internally; the secrets of
their lives and their religion; how they received and how
they obeyed the word preached to them; how they lived
and how they died ?

To the same purport, he speaks of the Lord's coming (1 Cor.
iv. 5), "who will bring to light the hidden things of
darkness, and will make manifest the counsels of the
hearts; and then shall every man have praise of God:"
that is, every man who deserves it. Why does he refer to
that full recollection which shall show up every man in
his true colours, unmask all hypocrisy, and clear up, and
shed light on all righteousness; so that no one shall doubt
of what character a man has been? He refers to it, as a
comfort to his soul, under the unkind and false interpre-
tations which the Christians had put upon his character;
that the true relative behaviour of himself to them, and
them to himself, would soon appear beyond possibility of
contradiction. But then they must know each other in
order to be able to understand this final judgment. Then,
again, the whole doctrine of a final judgment appears to
me necessarily to presuppose mutual recognition. For, if
all our relations of life—as parents, as children, as husband,
as wife, as friends—must come under a universal review,
then children will be confronted with parents, and parents
with children, just as Dives is represented as confronted
with Lazarus. But perhaps the argument which weighs
with me most of all is the complete union of believers in
Christ; union, not only with Him, but with one another;
by virtue of which, those who are converted from sin and
darkness are no more "strangers and foreigners" (Eph. ii.
19), but "fellow-citizens with the saints, and of the
household of God." But do not fellow-citizens and mem
bers of the same household know each other? Why is the
epithet or designation of "strangers and foreigners" re-

pudiated, except that in heaven every one will feel at home, knowing and loving every one? A family, the members of which do not "know" each other, is a misuse of the word. And in that most tender prayer of our Saviour's before His passion (St. John xvii.), so utterly abhorrent is strangeness and ignorance of each other from His purpose in redeeming His people, that He expressly prays for the most entire unity, not only between those who have known each other on earth, but between all His redeemed (ver. 21), "that they all may be one; as Thou, Father, art in me, and I in Thee, that they also may be one in us:" and then He goes on to say that for this end He gave to them the glory which He had received from the Father, "that they may be one, even as we are one." Now, my notion of unity is chiefly made up of *love*, founded on similarity of sentiments and opinions and tastes. Unity without love I cannot comprehend; and love without mutual knowledge is equally impossible. To touch that mysterious parallel which Christ Himself gives to us: "Does not the Father know the Son, and the Son the Father?" Now unity with each other in Them is to be of the same kind. For my own part, I go further still; for I find that the sinless Saviour had His natural tastes, which turned not wholly and entirely on piety, by virtue of which I conceive He loved St. John better than the other disciples; and when He beheld the young ruler, was attracted to him, and loved him; and as His humanity is the model of ours, so I am inclined to believe that in the world to come there will still exist an innocent diversity of tastes, in consequence of which some will be more drawn to some than to others; and perhaps those who have loved each other most here, will be permitted to exercise the same preference in the world where all will be high and holy, but not all equally high and holy.

ON THE COMPULSORY USE OF THE BURIAL SERVICE.

I return you your paper, which I have read with a full sympathy; for the dilemma is cruel which compels a conscientious minister to violate his conscience or else incur a legal penalty.

There are two evils in such a constraint which I should wish to see touched :—

1. That in these days of liberty it converts clergymen into reluctant automatons in the Services of the Church; and,
2. That it brings into palpable discredit our Church Services and her ministers.

For, if we consent to be the mere unintelligent or unconscious ministers of the canonical law, the whole parish regards it as a disgrace to a clergyman so to act, bound hand and foot to what he does not approve.

The remedy of Convocation I should greatly deprecate. If you recognise its power you strengthen it, and what it will grow to it is difficult to say.

ON SECESSION TO THE CHURCH OF ROME.

To VISCOUNTESS ——, *in answer to a letter received the evening before, announcing her secession to the Church of Rome.*

Last night, alas! the first communication of a religious kind that I have received from you since the death of that blessed and exquisite parent, whom God gave to you to be the guide of your youth, announced to me the sad tidings of your departure to the Church of Rome. It quite broke my sleep; and, waking, it is a weight on my heart. With a grief fed by the memories of a thousand hopes, and a thousand tender wishes and prayers for you, I cannot but deplore the painful fact that you never judged me worthy of being the depository of your doubts, whilst they were still doubts, and of your changing moods and convictions, whilst they were still soft and unset, but committed your fine understanding and young experience to the guidance of others, who imbued you with those fatal principles commonly called Tractarian, which, once admitted, I have from the first seen, naturally end in Rome. Much have they to answer for; for such is the mystery of the delusion, that, let the first errors enter, and settle in the mind without reclamation or suspicion, these fearful deductions become clear and easy. And then, if costly sacrifices attend them, such sacrifices lay the soul in an elysium of fancied truth and security, and are an opiate skilfully administered by the hand of the Evil One. Can your prayers be a finer test of truth than those of your blessed mother? But though I knew the peril you were in, I foolishly and fondly believed that the time would come when you would return to firmer and truer principles—

principles in which I saw you grow up to womanhood, and, as your sainted mother told me, to genuine faith in Christ, and holiness its constant fruit. You will not, therefore, wonder that, notwithstanding my preception of the tendency of the Tractarian doctrines which I had every reason to believe you had adopted, your letter was a great shock to me. It was an event in my ministry calling for self-examination and humiliation before God : and therefore I have been thinking over your early religious instruction ; your Confirmation preparation and vows; the sermons, as to their general style, which you used to hear, and which your dear mother used to read with approbation, and, as she said, with profit. On my knees I have solemnly implored the Divine forgiveness, if any fault or negligence of mine, any wrong spirit or want of judgment on my part, has in any manner prepared the way for your secession—the secession of one in whom I took, and must ever take, so deep an interest—from that which I believe to be the purest branch of Christ's Catholic Church, to a Church which the closest search only compels me to believe to be full of awful denials of Scriptural truth, and therefore of extreme peril.

I would ask you to forgive my plain and open speaking ; but you will not require an apology where a solemn duty only is discharged. If you are thus led to walk on giddy precipices, and to fall asleep on them, I pray you to cling to those Roman Catholic writers with whom my own soul ever finds, in spite of minor errors, a sweet and holy bond of unity. Be such a Roman Catholic as was Pascal, and Père Quesnel, and Nicole, and Arnaud ; and then we may yet meet on the great day when we shall find that unity is an idle figment (aye, and it may be a persecuting and destroying principle) unless it be based on truth, and be full of love. As for St. Mary's Hall, that is a mere feather in what you have written to me about. Your own recollection must tell you how I taught there. I thank God I have, to the best of my ability, taught there the Catholic faith. I thank God that He has not left me without evidence that He has taught with me and by me. To His Glory be it recorded; the testimony is very full.

But I never expected you, with your views, even before this last step, long to continue your countenance and support. I thought it was only your generous and kind feeling towards me, that made you unwilling to snap one of the few links that remained between us. Accept, however, my grateful thanks for what has been given. You only anticipate my wishes in regard to the future. You could not give, nor I receive, your patronage as a Roman Catholic. I write this letter as one that knows he must give an account for every immortal soul ever entrusted to his care. I write in deep sorrow, but with cordial affection.

In connection with the above melancholy perversion was the withholding a building, erected in the diocese of St. Asaph, for the service of the Church of England. The deceased parent had set her heart upon this, and, when on her dying bed, had committed the execution of her wishes to her daughter and her son-in-law. The bishop of the diocese, and a large body of clergy, had been present at the laying of the foundation-stone; and when the building was finished, the fulfilment of the pledge then virtually given was required. But in the meantime, both parties had joined the Church of Rome, and, on the plea of conscience, refused assent. Much might have been said for this had the idea *originated* with them, or had the money set apart for it been originally theirs. But the idea originated with the lady mother, and the money expended had been hers. They were but carrying out her intentions, with money which she had avowedly dedicated to the work. No plea of conscience, it is conceived, should have turned them aside. Their responsibility was that of obedience; and glanced altogether away from other points.

A FRAGMENT ON REVIVALISM AND REVIVAL HYMNS.

Do not imagine, I pray you, that I could possibly think that your most kind and Christian treatment of the subject we discussed required a word of apology from you. But I should not be quite at ease in my own conscience if I had kept back from you and those who introduced me to Mr. H——, the objections which I felt to his address at the Newburgh Rooms, and which I cannot regard as light matters, namely :—

1. An evident attempt at too much excitement—excitement which you may consider as a spiritual awakening, but which appeared to me to have too much of physical excite-

ment, and therefore requiring the same kind of food; and that failing, and the seed wanting deeper soil, in time of temptation the joy dies away.

2. Misinterpretations of God's Word (as I understand it), with fanciful allegories, and extreme stress laid on a single word or short phrase clearly not intended to bear that meaning, and contrary to the sobriety and sound sense of the Scriptures. Such a style of preaching would give a sad advantage, which I am sure Mr. —— and all of you would regret as much as I should do.

3. It appeared to me that the order of our Blessed Lord was inverted in that style of preaching. It was "believe and repent," rather than "repent and believe," which I need not tell you, was St. John the Baptist's method, our Lord's own order, and the Apostles' by His injunction. This inversion also, it seems to me, involves a disparagement of repentance. "Godly sorrow," St. Paul teaches, "worketh repentance unto salvation." Omit the "repentance" and come instantly to "salvation," and there, if I am not mistaken, is this new style of appeal, earnest, forcible, deeply interesting to many, but, as I should say, wanting the *proportion of faith*.

To my arguments you oppose facts. Forgive me if I desire to examine them a little more closely. I am sure Mr. —— would not wish to make any wilful misstatements. But such reports require to be tested by personal knowledge, and some period of probation. The accounts of the American revivals, and of the Irish revivals, and those of the Methodists in Wales, Cornwall, and Yorkshire, have all of them, if I am not misinformed, required some painful and large discounts. . . .

As to Revival hymns: One of my guests the other day sang some. I cannot think, however, that souls get to heaven by exciting or marching music. It is not with drum or fife that the battalions of the Captain of our salvation move. Excitement seems the great end of such spiritual songs.

NOTES ON THE PRESENCE OF CHRIST IN THE HOLY SACRAMENT:
FROM A CONFIRMATION LECTURE.

The partaking of the Body and Blood of Christ is called a sacrament. The word "sacrament," has two meanings:—

1. The Fathers used the word for any sacred transaction, and

especially for any mystery. Thus they speak of the Incarnation, the lifting up the brazen serpent, the giving of manna, and many other things, as sacraments.

It is expedient that we should be aware of this meaning, for thus all force is taken away from the passages quoted to prove that there are seven sacraments.

2. The true definition of a sacrament is admirably given in the Catechism: " an outward and visible sign of an inward and spiritual grace given unto us, ordained by Christ Himself, as a means whereby we receive the same, and a pledge to assure us thereof."

The Roman Catholics have tried in vain to bring all their seven sacraments to this definition, which definition they accept as true. . . . Our Church teaches that there are *two* only " generally necessary to salvation; that is to say, Baptism and the Supper of the Lord." By *generally* is meant whenever it is possible to receive them. Exceptional cases may occur when it is impossible; but for you they are *necessary* to salvation because you have the opportunity.

Now mark, to constitute a sacrament there must be an outward and visible *sign* (some matter, something tangible, material, an object of the senses), ordained by Christ himself as a *means of grace* (not merely a remembrance, but a *means* of grace), and a *pledge* to assure us thereof. God does not mean to tamper with us. The sacrament is a pledge that God means to work in us by His Spirit, so that in the Lord's Supper the bread which we break *is* a partaking of the Body of Christ, and likewise the cup of blessing *is* a partaking of the Blood of Christ.

Passing over the Sacrament of Baptism, we come to the Lord's Supper; . . . and to the question, " What is the inward part or thing signified?" Answer, " The Body and Blood of Christ, which are verily and indeed taken and received by the faithful in the Lord's Supper." Now, what is the meaning of " *verily and indeed taken and received?*" The Roman Catholics will say, " Does not your own Catechism teach you the doctrine of Transubstantiation?" You are probably aware that Transubstantiation means a change of substance. They contend that our Lord is *bodily* present whenever mass is celebrated; that the bread and wine undergo an absolute change of substance, although they still look like bread and wine, and that therefore a deception is practised upon the senses of sight, taste, feeling, and smell.

Now the truth of Christianity rests upon miracles, and miracles upon the evidence of the senses. Christ rested the truth of His mission and divinity on miracles. God Himself constituted the senses, the criterion of the truth of those miracles. If they had not been a sufficient and trustworthy criterion of His miracles and resurrection, He would have vouchsafed other proofs. If, therefore, you disbelieve your senses, you undermine the very foundation of Christianity.

The Roman Catholic may reply, "Do you not then limit God's power? *Can* He not change the substance of the bread and wine?" But the question is, not what God has *power* to do, but what He *does;* not whether He *can* turn the bread and wine into the Body and Blood of Christ, but whether He wishes you to believe that He does so turn it, *against* the evidence of your senses.

The Apostles were not surprised at the strong language, "This is My Body," for in the feast of the Passover the same form of speech is used when the Paschal lamb is eaten, "This is the Passover." But the disciples, being accustomed to figurative language, did not misunderstand Christ. They would, indeed, have been horrified had they understood literally the words, "This is My Blood," knowing, as they did, the express prohibitions on this point in the law of Moses. By a figure of speech, common to all languages, we say "this is," meaning "this represents so and so." Thus our Lord said, "I am the door," "I am the true Vine." And again, we read, "That rock was Christ."

In fact, it was not till twelve hundred years after Christ, that Transubstantiation became a doctrine of the Roman Catholic Church. Transubstantiation overthrows the very nature of a sacrament, for a sacrament is "an outward and visible sign of an inward and spiritual grace." The sign vanishes, and the mystery vanishes, if there is an absolute physical change in the elements.

We go deeper when we ask the meaning of "verily and indeed taken and received." There are two ways in which the Lord Jesus may be present in the Church : one in the body, the other in the spirit. When He says, "Lo, I am with you alway, even unto the end of the world," does He mean that He is bodily present in the assemblies of His people? No, His promise is fulfilled by His sending the Holy Spirit to convert, to heal, to refresh, to edify.

Did He ever intimate that He would be bodily present with us? Did he not say, "I go to my Father, *and ye see me no more?*"

There is a verse in 2 Cor. v. 16, which applies to this subject:—"Yea, though we have known Christ after the flesh, yet now henceforth know we him no more;" *i. e.* we know Him now only after a spiritual manner.

But it may be asked, if the soul is strengthened and refreshed by the Body and Blood of Christ is it not in some sense "verily and indeed taken and received?" Yes, truly. The Communion Service best answers this question. "We most heartily thank Thee for that thou dost vouchsafe to feed us . . . with the *spiritual* food of the most precious Body and Blood of Thy Son;" and in the exhortation, "He hath given His Son not only to die for us, but also to be our *spiritual* food and sustenance in that holy sacrament;" and again, "then we *spiritually* eat the flesh of Christ, and drink his Blood."

You see, therefore, that the Body and Blood of Christ are verily and indeed taken and received, but "only after *a heavenly and spiritual manner.*" "And the mean whereby the Body of Christ is received and eaten, is *faith.*" Whosoever draws near in faith, penitence, and love, receives Christ in a spiritual manner, believing that He is really and spiritually present to give efficacy to the sacrament which He Himself ordained.

ON THE RENUNCIATION OF THEATRICAL ENTERTAINMENTS PREVIOUS TO CONFIRMATION.

To a Clergyman.

I accept your kind expressions of thankfulness for the care bestowed on your daughter in preparing her for Confirmation, according to my best ability and conscientious opinions; and I am sorry that our opinions differ so widely, when they come to a practical test. To commit a child to the solemn words of renunciation used in Confirmation—to bring her to say, "I renounce the pomps and vanities of this wicked world," in a vague and general way, without any definite meaning, without any explanation or definition of what "the pomps and vanities" she solemnly renounces *are,*

without marks and tokens by which she may know them
when she sees and meets them, and so may avoid them,
is, in my view, to neglect the discharge of my duty to God,
and to the lambs of His fold. It would perhaps elucidate
your views to your child if you were to tell her what you
understand by the "pomps and vanities of the world," as
distinguished from the "works of the devil," and the "sinful lusts of the flesh." · Because I cannot but think it
highly offensive to God, and a profane mockery of the rite
of Confirmation, to bring a young person to renounce things
of which she has no specific idea; to vow to God, not knowing what she vows. This is what I deem to be presumption.
I have explained generally that they are to promise to give
up all amusements, however showy and gay in outward
attractions, in which

1. A morality is upheld and taught and applauded, contrary
to the Bible;—in which

2. God's name is taken in vain, and modesty and decency
offended;—in which

3. The amusements are furnished to the public with great
risk of the everlasting salvation of those who exhibit them
and without even the pretence of glorifying God in them
and by them.

I stated that theatrical exhibitions, so far as they were imita-
tions, were no more wrong than statues or pictures in
themselves; that the love of imitation is a principle inherent
in the nature of man for the wisest purposes, and therefore
that my objections to the Theatre and Opera were simply
as they are at present conducted. I taught that no Christian
living to, and following Christ (which is the baptismal
profession), would willingly encourage, much less take
delight in, public exhibitions contrary to His commandments and opposed to His example, taking His name and
His Father's constantly in vain; as for example, the Opera
abounds with "*O Dio;*" and the Ballet in an indecent ex-
posure of the person, which would not be tolerated in a
private room, or in any respectable society; which things,
I therefore said, must be most dangerous to the morals of
all who provide the amusements for the un-Christian taste
of *nominal* Christians—for *real* Christians would certainly
avoid them.

Dear Sir, pray consider what is the bearing of that commandment, "*Abstain from all appearance of evil.*" Is it

not generally considered a disgrace to any clergyman to
be seen at the theatre?   And can their wives and
daughters appear with propriety there, where no grave
and respectable man of their order is ever to be seen?—
especially if we recollect the admonitions to the Presby-
ters, who were not to be ordained to that holy office unless
they had "*faithful children*, not accused *of riot or unruly*,"
and who being ordained ought to be, every one of them,
" one that ruleth well his own house, having his children
in subjection with all gravity.   For if a man know not
how to rule his own house, how shall he take care of the
Church of God?"

I cannot reconcile it to my conscience to teach otherwise
than I do, and this not merely in my catechetical lectures,
but also in all my teaching at St. Mary's Hall.   At the
same time, I told all the catechumens that if parents,
guardians, husbands, or friends, in any authority over
them, insisted on their going, that they, not being at their
own disposal, are not to rebel against lawful authority,
but to go.   Filial obedience, I said, was a clear and
paramount duty; only I recommended them in such a
case to say humbly and dutifully, that, if they might be
allowed to choose, they should prefer not to go: and I
added, that there were few parents who, so addressed,
would not yield to the conscientious feelings and religious
tastes of a child.

I can only expostulate with you as the minister who must
give an account of his stewardship of this lamb of my
flock, committed to my pastoral care in the Lord for a
season.   If you doubt my views, take this letter to your
Bishop, or to our common friend the Archdeacon, and ask
them whether they are wrong.   Only please to understand
what these my views really are, for your letter gives no
very accurate account of them.   But on this point I decidedly differ from you (I would hope this difference may
not last), that it is my duty to give clear marks and tokens,
so far as I can do it, whereby these novices in the faith
may be better able to understand the meaning of every
part of their threefold renunciation, instead of wrapping
up the matter in vague generalities, and trusting that the
Holy Spirit will be given in their Confirmation to enable
them to discern and discharge their duties to God, their
neighbours, and themselves.

ON "PLAITING THE HAIR," "WEARING OF GOLD," AND
"PUTTING ON OF APPAREL."

My view of the Scriptural doctrine is, that it neither *enjoins* nor *condemns* the use of ornamental and costly dress : and that the two passages in the Epistles to Timothy and St. Peter are wrested to extract from them the prohibition. Like riches, ornamental dress may become the food of vanity and pride ; but the Word of God does not forbid riches, nor their use, but only their abuse. And I think it does not forbid the use of ornamental dress, provided, of course, it befit the station of life :—" they that wear gorgeous apparel are in kings' houses." But it also clearly supposes that there are rich men in the Christian Church who also wear costly apparel. The 2nd chapter of St. James speaks of a Christian with a gold ring, in goodly or *splendid* apparel (for "splendid," is nearer the original), coming into church ; and it does not condemn the ring or the apparel, but only the deference and respect paid to its wearer on account of it, to the neglect and contempt of a poor believer ; which was sinful regard to persons : and then the chapter sets forth, as the ground of its blame of such partiality, not the sin of the gold ring and splendid clothes—which would have settled the question, and established the reproof at once on an intelligible and easy ground, viz., " *Ye respect a man for his sin* "—but it takes a more circuitous way of censure, and shows how little riches, *as such*, deserve the veneration of the Church, since they were commonly perverted to oppress the Church, and were, for the most part, connected with wickedness ; whereas the poor believer was an heir of the kingdom of God.

Are we therefore to say that the possession of riches is sinful ? There were rich men, as Joseph of Arimathea, the Centurion, and others, who did not put their trust in uncertain riches, or make a bad use of them. Just as the Bible forbids the rich to have confidence in their riches, so it forbids the well-dressed to pride themselves on their dress. Their dress is not to be their ornament—then it would be external—but their ornament is to be a meek and quiet spirit, where the comparison is not between good dress and bad dress but between internal and external beauty of appearance ; and the one is exalted above the other by that common mode of Hebrew speech which seems to forbid or annihilate one affection when it only raises another far above it. As of the servant of two masters, "he will hate the one and love the other" (St. Matt. vi. 24)—meaning only a decided preference. And of the man who comes to Christ (St. Luke xiv. 26), and is required to hate father and mother, and wife and children, and brethren and sisters, and life itself—meaning only a decided preference when they come into competition. And that this is the true meaning of St. Peter is, I think, clear from his referring Christian women to the wives of the patriarchs (1 St. Peter iii. 5), who did indeed wear jewels and fine clothes, but had far better ornaments than such outward ones. If the Apostle had meant to forbid the jewels or elegant apparel altogether, would he have sent us to these women as our patterns?

My next argument is, that if St. Peter forbids any one of the three things which he mentions—first, plaiting of hair; secondly, wearing of gold; thirdly, putting on of apparel—he must forbid them all. But the putting on of *apparel*, in the Greek, is of any garments at all. The word translated "apparel" has nothing in it to designate any splendour *or cost*, but belongs to all clothes; and the word translated "putting on" is the simplest form of dressing, and has also nothing of care or refinement in it: it will equally forbid the Quakeress to put on her lavender gown and neckerchief, and the beggar *his rags*.

This argument, to my mind, is decisive against the use of this passage of Scripture, or that in 1 Tim. ii. 9, to prove any prohibition of gold or pearls, or elegance of dress, *so far as they are consistent with modesty and sobriety;* for in that passage the contrast is also between these things and good works—which cannot be substituted simply and literally for dress,—and not between elegant dress and humble dress. And I may remark, by the way, that the word translated "*modest* apparel" implies an attention to strict *order* and *propriety* or *decency*, if not elegance in dress; for it is the adjective ($\kappa o \sigma \mu \iota o s$) of the very verb used in the same verse, and translated *adorn* ($\kappa o \sigma \mu \epsilon \hat{\iota} \nu$). Indeed, it is an express command for a certain measure of attention to dress—that it be neat, and properly put together and arranged.

As to the passage in Isaiah (chap. iii. 16) which enumerates so many female ornaments, Vitringa considers that these were the purchases of the princes or great men of Jerusalem, out of money got by grinding the faces of the poor (ver. 15). However they adorned their daughters and wives with them, the curse of God rested on every part of their toilet, and these delicate females should be reduced from all their luxury of dress to the captives' lowest humiliations. The 16th verse certainly supposes that they indulged in an immodest exhibition of their fine dress ; but to say that these ornaments were in themselves sinful will make the use of the girdle sinful (ver. 24), and the bonnet, and the earrings which the Old Testament allowed, and which Rebekah wore.

My last argument is, that God takes, both in the Old and New Testaments, His similitudes of moral beauty from dress. Say that jewels in themselves are sinful, and what shall we think of the propriety of that passage: "They shall be mine in that day when I make up my jewels " (Mal. iii. 17)?

Are these in the Old Testament? The temptation to female vanity displaying itself in dress was probably as great in one dispensation as the other, and required as much watchfulness and self-denial. The Old Testament gave riches, and it gave the requisite warnings and cautions with them. The New Testament did not abolish riches, but made them still the gift of God ; and the New Testament enforced the cautions and warnings of the Old on riches. Why should we not put dress in the same position ? Why suppose elegant dress permitted in the Old Testament, but abolished in the New, while riches do not undergo the same change ?

But if they have become sinful, what shall we say to the angelic attire? They are described as clothed in pure and white (splendid) linen, and having their breasts girded with golden girdles (Rev. xv. 6). And to the Lamb's wife was granted that she should be arrayed in fine linen, clean and white ; and though it was added, " the fine linen is the righteousness of saints," would the *emblem* of what is lovely and beautiful in the eyes of the Lamb be that which the Gospel forbids as sinful? Or, rather, do we not find a uniform tenor in the Old and New Testaments on this subject?—the Book of Revelation only confirming

what the Prophets had previously represented; as when
Isaiah (chap. lii. 1) calls, "Awake! awake! put on thy
beautiful garments, O Jerusalem," he coincides with St.
John, who represents the armies of heaven as clothed in
fine linen, white and clean.   So also, I think, Solomon
speaks in accordance with St. Peter's and St. Paul's directions, when he says that "lips of knowledge are a
precious jewel."

Ezekiel has, perhaps, the strongest passage of all (chap.
xvi. 10), where God himself is represented as clothing
Jerusalem, His Bride, with broidered work, and fine
linen and silk, and bracelets and neck-chains, and jewels.
I cannot persuade myself that such imagery would have
been adopted if these things were sinful in themselves, or
hereafter to become so.

Is there, then, no limit to be put to dress and ornaments?
Yes, certainly.   Let all persons consider well the duty
of *self-denial*, and renunciation of the world, and alms-
giving, and the danger of personal vanity; and let them
act as seemeth to them right, remembering that they
are followers of a meek and lowly and suffering Saviour.
But let them not judge others.   One person wears jewels—
to the Lord she wears them; it may be, another wears
them not—to the Lord she wears them not.   Different
circumstances may require different styles of dress.   It
may be self-denial to some to dress well, and to others
to dress humbly.   None advocate, I believe, the same
dress for all ranks; and the degree of attention to be paid
to it may vary according to a parent's wishes, or the
feelings of a husband or other relatives and friends, or the
circumstances in which a woman is placed, and the company
she has to keep.   Let every one be thoroughly persuaded
in her own mind.   God gives great beauty to some, not
to others; and yet beauty is a greater occasion of vanity
than dress, which, I think, shows that we must seek for
the preservative within, not without.   If a woman adopts
that style of dress which, upon a full consideration of
Scripture, she believes to be right, she may be tempted to
self-complacency in her appearance if it is peculiarly clean
and neat, which we have seen it ought to be, as well as
when it is valuable and elegant.   God has given us
associations of ideas which make up taste and refinement,
and I am convinced He does not require us to excruciate

those sentiments, but only to watch and guard them, and bring them into subjection to the Gospel of Christ.

I do not find in my own mind (as I am sure you do not) any sympathy with that style of interpretation of Scripture which can denounce the plaiting of hair as a positive sin, but can tie it in a knot or twist it into curls without a ruffle on the smooth surface of the conscience. I am convinced that as women are to wear their hair long, they are perfectly justified in an ornamental disposition of it; for the Apostle himself says that it is their glory. But how can it be their glory if there is no elegance in the manner of dressing it?

Let every one be persuaded in her own mind, for " whatsoever is not of faith is sin."

AFTER THE INDIAN MUTINY.

To his Son Alfred.

May the Lord grant that the New Year may run to you in " green pastures " and by "still waters!" Such was not two years ago the stream of the Goomtee, or the meadows on its banks!

I read your 'Guide to Lucknow' after prayers last night, and thought it very creditable to you. From Gubbins' book (the third edition of which gives an extract from one of your letters to me), and from your photographs, I had a pretty good idea of the places. The ' Guide ' would have been more spicy, I think, if you had identified more places, or their sites, with certain stirring incidents of the siege; for example, the position of Johanni's house, where the fatal marksman used to pick off our men, and was at last picked off himself. It is curious how such little pieces of narrative kindle an interest well known to the great masters of history. For example, in the immortal history of the siege of Platæa by Thucydides, how admirably does he throw in the calculations of the besieged, as to the height of the Lacedæmonian circumvallations, by the counting of the layers of bricks by many persons, and taking the average several times to enable them to make the scaling ladders of the right height! There is a great Indian expected here next Saturday. Sir John Lawrence comes for the Sunday to pay a visit to Lord and Lady Shaftesbury. They were so good as to invite me this morning (Tuesday) to dine with them, and meet him on Saturday. But my Saturday's rule, and, besides, the necessity of going to town by the latest Saturday train, stood in the way; for next Sunday I preach at Lincoln's Inn another Warburtonian lecture. Perhaps I may be so happy as to meet him on Monday, if he stays. Lord Shaftesbury is also a man of men! He told me the other day, in answer to my question—" In which of your great works have you met with the greatest difficulty and opposition?" "I think in my Factory Bill. I expected to carry it in one year, and it cost me twenty-five years of hard fighting, with two Governments to beat, one of them Sir Robert Peel's. But the end was the strength of the cause, as it came to light; and the cry of the operatives carried me through." And how many, many myriads owe to him two hours per day for their wives and daughters, and children!

To the Same.

I write in haste, to save the mail, and to tell you that I was indeed every way delighted with the news of your unlooked-for promotion. *Every way* means that I rejoiced too in the amends it makes for the absence of your name from the Governor-General's list of civilians who perilled their lives and did good service in 1857-8.[1] Many others had, perhaps, more splendid single services and deeds of value to show; but your uninterrupted continuance in scenes of danger and responsibility, and the manner in which you acquitted yourself in them in Benares, Mirzapoor Gopeegunge, Fyzabad, Lucknow, and wherever you were placed (considering also that you had only begun your novitiate, and only touched Indian ground six months before, and had not passed your first examination), entitled you to a place in the Governor-General's list more than many that were there.

I rejoiced in your present promotion also, on account of the modesty and forbearance with which you spoke of your more favoured competitors, and above all, your recurrence, under a sense of your own insufficiency, to Him who is able to keep you from falling under temptation, and to give you, as He gave Solomon, wisdom for your high judicial

---

[1] This is not mere parental partiality; many Anglo-Indians, good judges, said the same.

and financial duties. He alone is safe who feels he is
not safe without God. Prayer conquers every difficulty;
for prayer calls in the Omnipotent to be on our side. In all
these things I rejoice. The additional rupees are the last
and least in the account in my eyes.

Lord M—— said to me when I read him your letter, "Tell
him that, in the way of promotion, the next thing to a good
claim is a good grievance."

To his Son Julius. 1859.

I cannot tell you, my dear Julius, what joy and thankfulness
the inclosed report, of which I send you the copy, has
given me. The Lord be praised! Have you any choice as
to the double of your prize? I should wish it to be a
double-double this time.

Now is your time to lay in a store of knowledge and education
which shall fit you to play your part diligently and efficiently
in your Lord's household. Pray that all may be consecrated.
The "singularly good" is the gem of your Report.

ON DISAPPOINTMENT AT A COLLEGE EXAMINATION.[1]

To his Son Julius.

I see by your letter that you have been disappointed in your
performance in the examination, and probably despair of
a place in the first class.

I therefore write this brief note to say that, if you do not get
the second even, I shall not be disappointed: for I am sure
you have done your duty in the preparation for it; and to
me, your conscientious improvement of your time is a
satisfaction, so far beyond the first place in the first class,
that, wherever you are, it will not be able to take away my
joy in you, and my comfort that you have been a witness
for Christ amongst your companions, and in the college,
during your first year.

Once I exaggerated sadly and sinfully the honours of the
University. But that time is long past, and I thank God
my first and most anxious inquiry is, "Has my son been
faithful to His Lord and Saviour?"—and if he has, all the
rest is as the dust in the balance.

---

[1] In earlier life Mr. Elliott had written to a favourite pupil : "Remember
that the failure of a friend, if he be very dear, only binds him, to the hearts
of those who love him, more closely."

ON THE CARE OF THE HEALTH AT COLLEGE.
To his Son Julius.

I am glad to hear that you found yourself so much better. You must not hesitate to give up your place in the college classes if you find that the effect of study entails a sacrifice of health. In such a case our heavenly Father indicates, too clearly to be mistaken, the necessity which I am sure you have not too hastily accepted. Only guard against the harm which any indulgence of a listless vacant employment of time is sure to foster. Let what you do read be, for the most part, such as will be of use to you in after life.

As to the "spurts" at last, just before the examination, I hold them in utter aversion. They injure the constitution, and, being generally an attempt to compensate for past indolence and misspent labour, they put a gloss and shine over former misdeeds; and, if successful, disturb the right and Scriptural estimate of an unworthy stewardship.

Last Sunday I preached my twelfth and last Warburtonian lecture at Lincoln's Inn, and I feel relieved at the conclusion of the task.

ON COMING OF AGE.
To his Son Julius.

This is the only letter I have time to write to-night; just to put on paper, my earnest expectation and hope that now you have reached the epoch of life which gives you legal privileges and responsibilities, you will not be an unfaithful steward of what God commits to your hand. I bless God that I have every reason to believe that you have passed "from death unto life," and that the great end is secured to which your incomparable mother's prayers were directed for you, on the first few days of your life which she was permitted to see.

Her prayers were registered in heaven. My prayers were a poor supplement to hers; yet have they been earnest and constant for you. On the day of her death, when the house was full of the alarm and grief of her decease on account of the scarlet fever, I baptized you in this very room in which I am now writing, in the presence of a few chosen and undaunted witnesses; and I again, on the twenty-first anniversary of your birth, shall take up those remembrances, and pray that the rest of your life may be answerable to those prayers and that beginning.

I hope to select some present for you as a memorial of your father's approbation, expectation, and love. I was rejoiced to find that your heart had been for some time turned to the ministry of the Gospel. May you be more and more the pupil of the Blessed and Holy Spirit, and be enriched by Him in all utterance, and in the deep sense of the inestimable redemption of Him who has bought you with His own blood, and given you to understand the value of 'His "unspeakable gift!" The Lord bless you with a larger blessing, year by year!

Turn your remaining studies into a preparation for your high calling, as a future minister of Christ Jesus.

THE THREE BIRTHDAYS.
To his Sister.

There are three birthdays. The first a subject of joy, yet joy with trembling; the entrance into a time of sojourning to be passed here in fear, the time of sojourning through a valley of tears; yet we thank God for that birthday, when we thank Him for " our creation." The second is far above the first, inasmuch as St. Paul teaches that to depart and be with Christ is " far better;" has more of instant enjoyment. This is the birthday achieved by death, where death is a conquered foe; and it admits into " Paradise," the place of the disembodied spirits of those who die in the Lord. This state of blessed existence lasts till Christ comes, and then is the third birthday. The living are changed " in a moment, in the twinkling of an eye, at the last trump," and the dead bodies rise from the grave to join the spirits to which they belong. Then they reappear in the likeness of Christ's glorified body, and with an inconceivable addition of glory, and therefore I presume of felicity.

My dearest sister, who now touches one of those epochs—a birthday of this life, another rounded period—has the unspeakable comfort to be looking forward to the second birthday, as surpassing, the first; and to the third as surpassing the second. An unchangeable God is the soul's Home; and each birthday draws us nearer and nearer to Him. May the new and fleeting period of another year, if it be allotted to you in its full dimensions, bring you many glimpses of the world to come, nay, foretastes of its blessedness, through the love of Him who purchased our eternal habitations for us!

ON CLEVER MEN AND BISHOP COLENSO.

To his Son Alfred. 1863.

As far as the experiences of my long life enable me to judge,
men fail more in their worldly career from rashness of temper,
and bitterness of censure of others, than any abilities can
ever compensate.   They grow up as stately thistles in the
field, with their motto underneath, " Nemo me impune
lacessit." So people acknowledge their tallness, but keep
their distance.   And then men of fine parts get soured, and
brood over their neglected merits till they become, if not
misanthrophic, yet exclusive and uncharitable; and the evil
done to themselves is far more, both in the impediment to
their promotion and in the deterioration of their general
benevolence, than that which they do to others.   The true
love and study of the eight beatitudes, or the example of
Christ, is the best corrective of this tone of mind; and the
thirteenth chapter of the First of Corinthians will prevent
a man making the error, not uncommon, that talents and
knowledge carry the day.

I   would   ask   you,   therefore,   to   believe   that   the   meek
(οἱ πραεῖς) inherit the earth and are *blessed*, both in this,
world and in the next.   The clever often inherit it, as far
as the acquisition and grasp of wealth and influence go;
but they are not *blessed* (happy) either in the acquisition
or the grasp.   Barry the painter, Clive and Hastings your
great Indian heroes, Savage the poet, and a thousand
others, are constantly recurring examples of this truth;
, while a little that the true disciple of Christ has, goes
.farther than the great riches of the clever and the worldly.
But enough of my homily, which I must ask you to take in
good part, as dictated only, and purely, by mere love to
you.
Now a few lines for other matters.
Colenso's two books, being from the pen of a bishop, have of
course stirred the very depths of ecclesiastical reproof.   I
have read a part of his first volume; none yet of his second;
though I have got both, and intend to read them through.
They are so full of palpable mistakes, that nothing but
his station would have procured audience for some of his
objections.   For example—his alleged impossibility of
finding lambs for three millions at twenty-four hours'
notice!   A very cursory examination shows that the

notice must have been of four days, to effect the separation of the lamb, to see that it was clean. The tenth day of Abib it was set apart: the fourteenth it was slain and eaten. But a very little more examination shows that the order was issued on the first of Abib—the sacred month in all probability: or else God made the whole of that month sacred, and first of months, when some nine days were passed. Hezron and Hamultha, grandsons of Judah:—the stupid idea of the parallelogram, eighteen in rank, before the tabernacle, instead of a fan-like spread :—the idea of the removal of all offensive matter to six miles' distance, when there were *four* camps, each containing three tribes : —such things as these show the Bishop to be very superficial in his objections. But, above all, they are popguns fired off against the Eternal Hills; and Christ's own saying, "If ye believe not Moses' writings, how shall ye believe My words?" and the rejoinder of the Bishop that Christ grew in wisdom—in this matter of Moses, the blasphemous inference being that He had clearly made a mistake—is sufficient to settle a mind not previously disposed to infidelity.

The Bishop of Oxford is reported to have said, " Ah, the arithmetical Bishop could not forgive Moses for writing the Book of Numbers!"

ON THE TWO ESSAYISTS, WILLIAMS AND WILSON.

To his Son Alfred.   1864.

You will hardly doubt my deep concern that the two Essayists, Rowland Williams and Wilson, have procured the final reversion of the mild and merciful sentence of Dr. Lushington. It is a heavy blow to our Church, and a triumph to the opinions of these two men; and will be a stumbling-block to many scrupulous and excellent men.

It is natural and easy to dislike anything like persecution and penalties for free thought and published opinions; and Wilson I should have pitied; but to read Rowland Williams is to dislike him. Even the author of the ' Edinburgh Review' apology for the Essayists lets fall some drops of gall and censure against the man. He evidently studies to enwrap his meanings in ambiguous phraseology, and to avow them without responsibility, under the shade of Bunsen. But still I think, in his whole tone and scope of reasoning, he disparaged the doctrine of our Church on " Justification by Faith," and " The Inspiration of the Scriptures." The second Collect in Advent was enough to condemn him. I have heard that he said, " I will defy them to define what is Bunsen's, and what is mine." About a week before the judgment of the Privy Council, I was at Fulham, on a short visit to the Bishop of London, and had some conversation with him on the subject. He was one of the judges in that tribunal; which consisted, as he said, of four Lords who were lawyers, and not theologians, and three Lords who were theologians, and not lawyers,—the four lawyers being the present Lord Chancellor Bethell, and three ex-Lord Chancellors; the three theologians, the two Archbishops and the Bishop of London. " Still," he said, " all we can do is to take ten or twelve short extracts, and pronounce our judgment whether those extracted sentences, or clauses of sentences, directly and absolutely contradict anything positively asserted on the subject in the Articles, Liturgy, or Homilies; giving the accused the advantage of a doubt, and requiring such contradiction to be explicit and palpable, as the consequences would be so penal."

Here I think they lost sight of what was due to the parishioners of the offenders. The clergy do not exist for their own benefit as a profession, but for the good of their flocks; and that they should be permitted in their parishes to preach and publish such errors is a grievous wrong. I told the Bishop that I was afraid the Homilies, though an acknowledged authority, had been little consulted. I had never seen them quoted in the argument. The Bishop allowed they had been little examined. I craved liberty to send him the result of my examination, if he could find time to read my statement. I sent him accordingly eight quarto pages of extracts from the Homilies, on the two cardinal points, the Inspiration of the Scriptures, and Justification by Faith. In answer, he thanked me, and said he would carefully look over what I had extracted, and my remarks.

From this correspondence, which might have been largely extended, Mr. Elliott's views may be learnt not only on matters of daily life and common sense, but on many of the " things which accompany salvation :"—on the lost estate of man, and the Law of God ; on the grace, efficacy, and limits of the Holy Sacraments ; on the doctrines of justification and sanctification by the SON and SPIRIT of God ; on separation from the world, and bearing of the cross ; on Irvingism, Revivalism, Rationalism, Romanism ; on the fitting qualifications, deep responsibility, and rightful claims of the sacred ministry ; on the uses of affliction, and on the faith and patience of the saints. It would have been the duty of a Biographer in any case to have unfolded Mr. Elliott's views on these and kindred topics ; but it is far better that they should be thus explained and enforced in his own words, and by his own pen. Let the reader look into the next chapter, as into a stereoscope, and he will see them all rounded into life, and carried into action.

CHAPTER VII.

LATER YEARS OF LIFE.

Various Institutions of Brighton—St. Mark's Church—Fracas at a Visitation—Select Preacher at Cambridge—Papal Aggression—Carus-Wilson—Lord Calthorpe—Ordination and Visitation Sermons—Newspaper Attack—Jerusalem Bishopric—Rich and Poor—Crimean War—Hurried Life—Archdeacon Hare—A Sunday and Week-day Scene—Indian Mutiny—Visit to Pau—Lord Bristol—Address at St. Mary's Hall—Bournemouth—Church Missionary Sermon at St. Bride's—Sir Herbert Edwardes—Lord Aberdeen's Death—Pecuniary Disinterestedness—Death of the Prince Consort—Missionary Reports—Lausanne and Rouen—The Night cometh.

IN his later years, Mr. Elliott, like " a tree planted by the waters," brought forth his fruit in due season ; and, like one over whom the " Refiner and Purifier " had sat, he offered unto the Lord an " offering in righteousness." Clear in his views of truth, he was active and earnest in their promulgation. He wrought not for Life, but from Life. Whilst stationary himself, his influence over others widened and deepened continually. This chapter—extending as it will, from 1849, the period assigned in this Memoir to his " married life," to 1865, the year of his last illness and death, and thrown latterly into the form of notes—will be fed from all sources, which, like little rivulets, will serve to supply the stream down which the reader may glide pleasantly and profitably, surveying at his leisure the multifarious and diversified opinions and engagements of this servant of God.

It will readily be supposed that Mr. Elliott took part in all the affairs of the diocese, and that he was actively engaged in upholding the many benevolent, charitable, and religious institutions of a large and important town like Brighton. Here, then, would seem to be the proper place for elaborate discussions on "Convocation" and the "Election of Proctors," on the "Grant to Maynooth," on "Sunday observance," on "Railway Excursion Trains," on "Training and Proprietary Schools," on "Dispensaries," "Missionary work," and "General Education." But what then would become of the pleasant floating down the stream just promised? These "vexed questions" are to the general flow of parochial or ministerial life, what rocks and snags, shallows and rapids, falling banks and fatal collisions, are to the American rivers. Such abstract discussions are not desired by readers of Biography, and Biographers are bound to consult their wishes. It will suffice therefore if, grouping these matters together, the opinions expressed by Mr. Elliott, and the part taken by him concerning them, are condensed and presented in one view. An occasional allusion afterwards, as the narrative proceeds, will be all that accuracy and fidelity require.

1. About the time at which we have arrived, Convocation, which had been long asleep, moved, stretched itself, and turned round. The election of Proctors, which had been a mere form, instantly became a reality; and those of the clergy who did not deem themselves likely to be properly represented, began, not always in the most open manner, to bestir themselves. Something of this sort occurred in the Archdeaconry of Lewes; and there was no small excitement in that quiet town when hotels were opened and conveyances provided, and the clergy came together to consider of this matter. Dr. Phillimore presided, and opened the proceedings in the church of St. Michael's. Mr. Elliott then rose and made an address, characterised by good temper and good sense. On the principle of "quieta non movere," he advised and proposed the re-election of the former Proctor, a highly respectable Vicar in the diocese. His nomination was seconded by the Rector of Woodmancote. Considerable discussion ensued; another candidate was proposed; and the proceedings were prolonged. But the effect of his address, and the confidence of the Clergy in him, were shown by a majority of forty-

five to twenty-six in favour of the candidate he had recommended.

2. On the question of the Grant to Maynooth, his opinion was very decided; and he withdrew his parliamentary vote from friends whom he highly esteemed, on that account alone. His opinion was made available, *pro* and *con*, in several contested elections at the time; and the documents remain in print, showing how averse he was to any compromise with Romanism.

3. On the Sunday Observance question he was clear, but not narrow or exclusive. He had preached before the University of Cambridge on the subject in the year 1832, and his views, as then propounded, were deemed lax, though in reality they were only moderate. In theory he held the Divine institution and perpetual obligation of the Lord's Day without reserve; but in practice he admitted of three exceptions:—"As I understand the law of the Sabbath," he was wont to say in public, as well as in private, "and as it is laid down by writers on theology, three kinds of work are allowable on the Sabbath—works of necessity, works of piety, and works of charity: the Sabbath being made for man, and not man for the Sabbath." He was accused at a public meeting at Brighton of inconsistency in that he drove to church on Sundays. He met the charge, by claiming for himself and all others the right to do so, under the plea of necessity. Neither he nor his children could attend church in any other way; much less could persons in the country, who had much further to go, and were in more infirm health. At the same time he limited the plea to an attendance at God's house, and stated the conditions always previously laid down in his own case, viz. that the horse should be fed at his expense, and the driver attend his church.

He would always quote in confirmation of his opinion how, under the far stricter letter of the Jewish dispensation, the laborious services of the priests, and the work necessary to be done for offering the sacrifices in the Temple service, were permitted. And, as an additional proof from usage, he was accustomed to quote the instance of the Shunammite woman, as recorded in 2 Kings iv. 23. Her husband asks, Why she wishes the ass saddled, seeing that "it is neither new moon nor sabbath;"—a proof that on new moons and sabbaths, when religious services had to be performed, it was customary to "saddle the ass."

In all attempts to prevent the desecration of the day by trading and by postal delivery, he took a prominent part; and in the year 1839 drew up an address to the shopkeepers, which was signed by the Vicar and fourteen of the Brighton clergy.   In his happiest manner he there touches briefly on *five certain losses* which would more than counterbalance their expected gains. (1) The loss of the rest and refreshment needful for body and soul. (2) The loss of a sweet family tie to bind a household together in all duty and affection. (3) The loss of the blessing of social religion. (4) The loss of golden opportunities for salvation. And (5) as the natural and almost necessary result of all the rest, the loss of the soul. "What shall it profit a man, if he gain the whole world, and lose his own soul?"

4. To Railway Excursion Trains on the Sunday Mr. Elliott strongly objected; and on the occasion of the terrible accident at the Clayton tunnel, on the Brighton line, he was roused, and roused others, to prompt and decided remonstrance with the Directors. "The dull heaving sentiment prevalent at Brighton"—thus he speaks—"was stirred." He preached a sermon to his own people on the Tower of Siloam, and at the request of the Vicar drew up a strong memorial. The Bishop put himself at the head of the movement. Eighty-three clergymen, resident at the time in Brighton, signed the memorial; and the names eventually of 5,000 of the laity were affixed to it. It was more than eighty feet long; and its prayer was "that the excursion trains might be transferred from the Sunday to the weekday." Mr. Elliott had scarcely a "scintilla of hope;" and the reply of the Directors was, as he expected, cool and discouraging. Good, however, was done, though not immediately apparent. "The Lord reigneth," was his reflection, "nor is the Board of Directors abstracted from His dominion."

Refusing to learn in one way, they have been deservedly taught in another!

5. The Brighton College had for many years in Mr. Elliott a staunch supporter; and he helped to pilot it amongst the rocks and shoals which threaten all such proprietary institutions, and wreck many of them. He was one of the vice-presidents, and, when in the year 1852 he resigned, he was waited on by a deputation requesting him to continue in office, as his withdrawal would be very injurious to the

institution. He consented to retain office for a time; but multiplied engagements supervened, and he eventually retired.[1]

6. To the Brighton and Hove Dispensary he was a constant, zealous, and liberal friend; and of its wide-spread and beneficial operations he was acutely sensible. His mind was ever young and fresh in such matters, and his pen ready. Let there be a candidate for any vacant office in the staff, and let his inquiries be answered satisfactorily, first as to the moral character, and next as to the surgical skill of the candidate, and at once the necessary notes were written, and the necessary calls made, and generally with good success; for to have Mr. Elliott as an ally was to win the battle. The contributions from St. Mary's to the funds for a series of years were nearly double those from any other church in Brighton, saving the Chapel Royal; and they had now risen to nearly 750*l.* Well might the Committee, when hearing of his death, adopt the following resolution, as copied from their Report for 1865 :—

The Committee feel assured that the Governors will sympathise with them in sincerely deploring the loss the charity has sustained in the decease of the Rev. H. V. Elliott, one of its vice-presidents, and oldest and most zealous friends, and from whose own purse as well as from his eloquent appeals from the pulpit, its funds so largely benefited.

7. The Blind Asylum also touched his heart; and the communication of the "Light of Truth" to the forty boys and twenty girls housed and sheltered there, was anxiously cared for. He proved his love by a grant of land for the erection of a new building, which the Committee entered in their balance-sheet as a gift equivalent to 500*l.* In the Report of 1860, this "special rule" finds place, that—

The Rev. Henry Venn Elliott, of Brighton, having presented the site for the new institution, the right of nomination from time to time of one boy or girl for the benefit of this charity shall always belong to him and his personal representatives and assigns.

---

[1] A gentle joke about the College was sometimes on his lips. Corporal punishment not being allowed as a matter of discipline, expulsion was of course sometimes necessary. "Ah," said Mr. Elliott, "like the French, they never flog, and therefore shoot."

8. The Local Associations of various religious societies were very near his heart, such as the Jews' Society, the Scripture Readers' (whose candidates he examined for some years), the Ladies' Female Hibernian Society,[1] and others; but especially the Auxiliary Church Missionary Society. Under his fostering care and stirring sermons the annual contributions from his church continually increased; till at length, in the last year of his life, they reached 750*l.* His most efficient services in this behalf are recognised by his relative and lifelong friend, the Rev. Henry Venn, Hon. Secretary of the Society, in a brief memoir written for the ' Christian Observer.' It is there said that " his zeal, like that of many others, did not flag after the Indian mutiny was over, but he sustained the collections then made in subsequent years, and placed his congregation at the head of the Society's List." . . . " His last secular arrangements, as death approached, comprised two legacies of 1000*l.* each to his two dearest institutions, St. Mary's Hall and the Church Missionary Society." . . . " I must give utterance," says Mr. Venn in his funeral sermon, after reciting these facts, " to my feelings as the official representative of that Society. His pecuniary remittances were munificent. But it was his deep sympathy, his warm encouragement, his sound advice, his earnest prayers on our behalf, in season and out of season, in times of difficulty which have assailed the Society, as well as on gala days of successful anniversaries, which constituted his most precious contributions to our cause." The autumnal Anniversaries of the Society at Brighton were a matter of deep and personal interest to Mr. Elliott. He always wrote the Report himself with great care ; and so graphic were his touches, that not only was the reading of it deemed the best part of the annual meeting, but copies were struck off at the request of the parent society for the use of other auxiliaries. On these occasions his house in Brunswick Square was full, and more than full, of friends assembled by his invitation to dinner, between the morning and evening meetings. The noble President was generally a guest; colonial Bishops,

---

[1] When in Ireland himself, he was much struck with the answer of a little Irish girl in one of the (then) Hibernian Society's Schools. A class of small and ragged children were before him, and he was questioning them on the parable of the talents, which they had just read. He said to a little girl, "My child, what talent have you to improve?" "*My poverty, Sir,*" was her reply.

with the dew of their dioceses upon them, were also present, together with a large number of clergy and laity. The board was plenteously supplied, but happy the guest who found a vacant seat at it! The conversation after dinner was never allowed to degenerate; but prominent and able men were called upon by the host, in his gentle and courteous manner, to open their treasures and enrich their brethren, and the discussion thus commenced was continued so long as time allowed. Very pleasant and profitable were these annual gatherings, and very spirit-stirring the public addresses.

9. The Diocesan Training School, and the Brighton National Schools, obtained a large share of his interest. The latter was a very important establishment, and flourished much under the fostering care of the Vicar. The funds were provided in part by contributions from the different churches and chapels in Brighton, and this gave the Clergy a *locus standi* with respect to these schools. About the time at which we have arrived, difficulties arose from the somewhat uncalled-for avowal of sentiments by the Master at a public meeting, of which some of the clergy did not approve. They drew up a memorial, and declined any longer to contribute to the support of the schools if such things were permitted. Mr. Elliott was amongst these memorialists, for he would never tolerate what he deemed error. But he was still the "peacemaker." In the present case, things soon righted themselves. The Master on obtaining a higher appointment resigned, harmony was restored, and the Vicar thanked Mr. Elliott for having "now, as always, poured some of the choicest oil upon the troubled waters."

By thus grouping these things together, and making Mr. Elliott the prominent figure in them, it is not meant to be implied that he never erred in judgment, or yielded to an undue bias; that he never spoke unadvisedly, or acted hastily; that he was uniformly right, and those who differed from him uniformly wrong; that his counsel was always followed, or his plans always adopted. In these particulars he shared the common lot of all men : nor did he ever profess to be a prophet, or a prophet's son.

Neither is it forgotten that he was but one of many like-minded with himself, fellow-workers in the vineyard, fellow-helpers to the truth, men of God and of great ability, feeding attached flocks, and adorning the doctrine they professed in all things. No pre-eminence is claimed for Mr. Elliott, however it may have been deserved, on this behalf.

But all will admit that he was a man who had no by-ends, and walked in no by-ways; a man whose scholarship was undoubted, whose experience was great, whose independence was assured; who affected no originality, ran to no extremes, rode no hobbies; but gave himself to God's work cheerfully, preached Christ's Gospel faithfully, used the machinery of the Church conscientiously, and inspired confidence everywhere by deserving it. Such a man could not but be a blessing to Brighton whilst he lived, and a great loss when he died.

These general remarks ended, matters of detail may follow; and the vessel, loosed from its moorings, may float, as promised, down the stream.

1849.

September.—On the 21st of this month the new church of St. Mark's, Brighton, was consecrated. Its erection had been a source of labour, embarrassment, and anxiety to Mr. Elliott for many years. So early as the year 1838 the Marquis of Bristol speaks of " the chapel which," he says, " I have so long and so earnestly wished to provide for St. Mary's Hall, and for the immediate vicinity of Kemp Town." The original proposal seems to have assumed form in 1837, and was received joyfully by Mr. Elliott, and communicated by him to the Bishop of the Diocese and the Vicar of Brighton.

To the latter he writes :—

If any good is to be expected to that part of your parish which is comprised in Kemp Town and its vicinity from the erection of St. Mark's (and I trust in God that the good will not be small), to St. Mary's Hall it will be mainly due ; not indeed as itself contributing any portion of its funds, but as suggesting the idea to that most noble-hearted Lord Bristol, and then as enlisting helpers for the completion of the work.

And in the Fourteenth Report of the Institution he says :—

And so it comes to pass in Christ's kingdom, that one good work is the parent of another, and institutions, which were originally raised by Christian benevolence, find themselves advanced to the rank of benefactors.

But a long struggle of ten years had to intervene before these results were obtained. Vested interests arose and strove; adverse sites were selected, rejected, changed, and again resumed. Church building was slow work in those days, and was encompassed with more difficulties than at present. Moreover, Church Commissioners interposed, misunderstandings appeared, the building was somewhat prematurely commenced, and, when roofed in, it stood for a long time unglazed and unfinished, as if "in Chancery;" whilst correspondence of all kinds accumulated on all hands. Mr. Elliott had made himself responsible for large sums of money which had been expended; and it seemed as if order would never come from this chaos. But through the good providence of God it did; and the steadfast perseverance of Mr. Elliott, aided by his co-trustees, and supported by episcopal influence, was at length crowned with success. Into all these details, filling huge packets of letters, which are still preserved, written by the Bishop, the Vicar, the Rev. James Anderson, the Church Commissioners, the lawyers, Lord Bristol, and Mr. Elliott, it would be a weary task to enter.

Results will suffice. The expenditure upon the Church, after it was erected and glazed, rose to nearly 4,800*l.*, of which Mr. Elliott contributed more than 1,500*l.* himself. The endowment money was invested in Queen Anne's Bounty; the patronage was assigned to the Bishop of Chichester and four trustees; the Rev. F. Reade was appointed first Incumbent; the Vicar of Brighton officiated at the consecration; and on September 21, 1849, the church, dedicated to St. Mark, was opened for Divine Service. "This was a great day in my life," says Mr. Elliott, "on which the Lord granted me to see the topstone thus put to St. Mary's Hall."

It is refreshing in the midst of the long and often painful controversy alluded to above, and henceforth to be forgotten, to turn to the sustaining affection and truthfulness of Lord Bristol. Baffled as he was, again and again, he never doubted that Mr. Elliott would finally succeed in obtaining the consecration of this church. "You," he writes in January 1849, "have done all in your power to give me this rich reward for all my zealous services to St. Mary's Hall; and to you personally I feel truly grateful, and shall do so as long as I breathe." To which Mr. Elliott responds at a later period :—

I cannot close the subject without giving expression to the deep feeling of gratitude which the re-perusal of all your lordship's letters to me, from 1839 to this time, has revived within me, or rather refreshed; letters written sometimes under the disappointment of our hopes in regard to St. Mark's, and the vexation of long delay, and the misunderstandings of parties who must now see how needless were their apprehensions and hindrances; yet always with a kindness and trust towards myself, so obliging, so invariable, and so condescending, that I could not read them as a series, without emotion which could only find one vent. May our gracious God reward your lordship in spiritual blessings, and in another world, for your dealings with me in this!

It was Lord Bristol's strong and frequently expressed wish, that Mr. Elliott should leave St. Mary's and take charge of St. Mark's. "It would be a great festival in my life," he says, "to hear you once in that pulpit." But this was felt to be impossible; as for other reasons so for this, that interested motives might have been imputed to him. He therefore declined, and remained unmoved in his present post. St. Mark's was given in the first instance to the Rev. F. Reade; and in 1853 to the Rev. E. B. Elliott, under whose faithful ministry it still remains.

1850.

February.—He now wrote the preface to 'Fox's Memoir.' It is interesting to know that this preface was the means of enlisting a fresh missionary for the work. He (the Rev. H. Andrews) was especially struck in the preface by the adaptation of Horace's Ode, "Quem tu, Melpomene, semel," &c.

"How little," writes Mr. Elliott, "did the Epicurean infidel imagine that an Ode of his would move a Christian missionary to go out and preach the everlasting Gospel of a crucified Jew on the shores of the Indian Ocean! The Lord be praised!"

April.—He visited Clifton for the Church Missionary Society, where he had to address fifty-eight clergy, to speak at three meetings, and to preach two sermons. Soon after he went to York and Leeds for the same Society.

" As. to clerical rest this summer," he says, " I had but little, preaching at Harrow and Clifton for Mr. Cunningham and Mr. Marshall ; and afterwards in the North."

Absence from home opens the door of his heart a little.

" It sometimes makes me sigh," he says to his sister Charlotte, " to think of the long distance between us, but I am too busy to sigh long for anything but that which pervades the whole scheme of my life, and tinges all the future with dark shades; and yet dark shades have a bright side."

September.—Sermons at visitations are gradually becoming things of the past. A. graphic account of one (like a relic disinterred) may be inserted here, notwithstanding its length :—

" The Bishop has just held his Triennial Visitation at Lewes," he says, " which was largely attended. Dr. Wellesley, Rector of Woodmancote, and Master of New Inn Hall, Oxford, was the person selected by the Bishop to preach the sermon. He preached a strong Protestant sermon on ' Ye are a royal priesthood,' showing that ' ye.' means all Christians, laity as well as clergy; and that while the Roman Church, standing between Christ and His people, refuses them access except by the intervention of the priesthood, Christ gave the liberty of free access and the communication of all truth to all of us who would draw near in His name.

" At the dinner which followed, the Bishop did not propose the Rector's health, but turned it over to the Archdeacon, who, instead of heartily praising the Protestant truth of the sermon, rather indicated defects in the composition. However, there were good men and true men there, and one of them rose to supply the omission, and to propose that the sermon should be printed. This was seconded; when up rose a clergyman and protested that he, for his part, would never consent to that sermon being printed, for that the whole length and breadth of Christianity lay between his doctrine and the sermon. Then up rose another, declaring that he had never heard a sermon at a Visitation which went more to the heart; and that he had six reasons, good and strong, for wishing to see the sermon in print, viz. six children, to every one of whom he wished to give a copy. Then men took sides; but 'Print it! print it!' resounded from a large majority. Whereupon the Bishop said, 'he, for his part, should be glad to read it in print; but it was obvious that the request to print did not come by the unanimous request of the clergy.' So the dinner broke up. I did not stay for it; but, foreseeing the storm, I got from seven of my brethren, with Lord Chichester and several of the churchwardens who attended the Visitation, authority to send their names, with my own, to Dr. Wellesley, as absentees from the dinner, with our request that he would 'print.' Meanwhile the men of caution and the Do-littles came about the Doctor, saying, 'You will bring a nest of hornets about you if you print.' So, as I wrote the letter, Dr. Wellesley called on me, having previously informed me by letter that he should only print, not *publish.* In this interview, after hearing all, I earnestly deprecated the *via media* of printing for private circulation, and told Dr. Wellesley, if I were he, the attack would only make me more resolute to publish. In the end, I undertook to look over and revise the sermon, leaving the controverted part as it was delivered; and now it is out. A reply has been written; but I hear the sermon stands its ground well. It was not vulnerable, in fact, where they would assault it. This was one of the matters that came to fill over the brim a full cup; for I had correspondence, interviews, and the corrections on passing through the press, to attend to."

November.—This month he was appointed by the Senior Proctor, Mr. Clement Middleton, to be Select Preacher again at Cambridge; and he chose for his four sermons the subjects of repentance and conversion, as illustrated in Zaccheus; the godly sorrow of the Corinthians; St. John the Baptist: and Cornelius. These four sermons appear first in a volume printed after his death. They are full of interest, and will repay an attentive perusal, besides affording insight into Mr. Elliott's sound doctrine and eloquent address. "It is an office," he says, "which I would not cross my threshold to

seek, on the one hand; while, on the other, I durst not refuse
it when it has been proposed to me."   This volume of Sermons
was very favourably reviewed and noticed in various publications.   The 'Guardian' spoke of the sermons as—

In the highest degree instructive and interesting, and full of
the light of the highest classical culture.

Other testimonies are to the same effect:—

What a calm, happy, wholesome atmosphere we breathe when
we turn to these beautiful sermons, in which love, and faith,
and peace are so deeply mirrored!

Before us lies a choice volume of sermons, abounding in fresh
thoughts, such as might have been expected from one
whose ministerial ability equalled his personal worth,
while both were the companions of a highly educated mind
and purified taste.

"I came here," he says, writing to Archdeacon Hare from
Addington Park, "on Monday, having accepted an invitation
from the Archbishop (Sumner) to spend a few days with
him at this beautiful place.   The Archbishop has received
an address from Oxford, signed by a thousand members of
Convocation, to press for an Ecclesiastical Synod to decide
on *doctrines*.   Ought not those of a contrary opinion now to
bestir themselves, and invalidate such a movement of the
belligerents, as I fear I must call them?"

"I almost broke down," he tells his sister Charlotte, "on
Sunday last; I was so exhausted and faint before I entered
the University pulpit, that I was obliged to lie down.   But
I had a strong confidence that God had sent me to Cambridge
and that I should get through, and so I did.   I preached on
Zaccheus' conversion.   I was listened to by a large Uni-
versity audience.   I go again on Saturday next.   The good
Lord enable me to speak in his name!"

December.—Controversy was very rife at this period, and
Mr. Elliott, meeting everything fairly in its season, preached
several sermons on Baptismal Regeneration, on Episcopacy, and
on the Scriptures as the sole rule of Faith.

1851.

January.—He took an active part in repelling the Papal
Aggression, which aroused all England at this time.

"I had the honour," he says, " to do my part in the great conflict now pending for Protestant truth. I moved the Brighton address to the Queen, and replied to the opponents who dwindled down from considerable uproar to twenty-five hands held up against the address. It took due notice of the Popery *within* the camp."

February.—He was called upon to mourn the loss of, and preach a funeral sermon for. his dear and valued friend Carus-Wilson, Esq., of Casterton Hall. He took for his text, Psalm xc. 1, "Lord, Thou hast been our dwelling-place," &c. Subject: "God the *only* home of the soul."

"The fairest earthly home," he says, " passes away, and does not answer the end. Even such a home as I knew Casterton Hall, thirty-four years ago—so fair, so bright, so glittering with all the dews of the morning, and the blossoms of the spring—what is it now? The second generation stranded on a distant shore, and incapacitated from paying the last tribute of respect here. The three daughters, whom I saw growing up in all loveliness, all sleeping in the grave! Such is now that fair earthly home, which Mr. Wilberforce said, ' he, having never before envied any man, felt disposed to envy.'"

In the afternoon he addressed the Clergy Daughters' School and Servants' School, with all the responsible authorities, urging them to " be strong in the Lord, and in the power of His might."

March.—Another member of St. Mary's congregation offered himself this month as a missionary. He was an usher in a school; sensible, and truly pious. His name was English.

"He came into the vestry yesterday," Mr. Elliott says, " to announce his decision, and he breakfasts with me to-morrow morning. So that, you see, I have my ' songs in the night;' sweet interruptions of my loneliness. I should feel very lonely, only I have too much to do to think about it."

April.—This year a legacy of 500*l.*, announced the year before, was paid to St. Mary's Hall. It was a great comfort to Mr. Elliott, and the more so because quite unexpected and unsought.

"I think it came," he says, "because our heavenly Father heard the note of distress uttered in the Thirteenth Report; and no sooner did that cry escape me than this large help came from one whom I never saw, nor even knew by name, and whose interest in St. Mary's Hall I have in vain attempted to trace."

September.—Hearing that Lord Calthorpe, his friend of many years, and who, he was wont to say, " quite spoiled him," was lying very ill in France, he made an effort, and travelled to Lyons this month in company with his lordship's brother. He sends his children an account of two sermons he heard on the 21st: one in the Protestant Church, and the other from a Roman Catholic preacher.

" There was no comparison between the two," he says, " in point of eloquence, talent, and delivery on the one hand, or sound doctrine on the other.   The Roman Catholic preacher gave us a sermon to incline us at all times and in all things to listen to, and cultivate, our 'Guardian Angel,' who was always watching over us, till we entered the theatre : and then, there were so many devils there, that he was obliged to stop outside and keep his distance.   The Protestant minister gave us an excellent sermon, on 'All things work together for good to them that love God.' "

Lord Calthorpe appeared to rally, and, with the consent of his physician, was about to travel southward.   But on the eve of his departure, and without a moment's warning, he expired. Mr. Elliott was glad to have been able to minister to him to the last : and, on his death, hastened back to his flock.

October.—He was appointed this month to preach the " Fox Memorial " sermon at Rugby.   Dr. Goulburn, then Head master of Rugby, now Dean of Norwich, recalls the circumstance, and says—

" On the day preceding, Mr. Cotton, one of the Masters (late Bishop of Calcutta), preached on the Beatitudes, and took them as representing the spiritual life in its successive stages.   Mr. Elliott expressed his dissent from this view privately, and gave forcible and interesting reasons for thinking that all the Beatitudes are present contemporaneously in each true believer.   Mr. Elliott left on my mind," adds Dr. Goulburn, " an impression of great argumentative ability united with great personal kindness and tenderness.   I am inclined to think that his speech must have been in a remarkable degree 'seasoned with salt;' for on this occasion, and when he preached a missionary sermon for me at Oxford he seemed always to say something interesting, or to put old truths in a new light."

Truly this is a glorious government, in which the reign is by
intellectual conviction and spiritual influences, in which
not only outward actions but every thought and feeling owns
its sway; and a man presents himself a "living sacrifice,
holy, acceptable unto God," his whole life being no longer
a conformity to the world, but a transcript of the good and
perfect and acceptable will of God.

Well might Jesus say to Pilate, "My kingdom is not of this
world." It is not framed of its coarse materials, nor will
it be satisfied with its scanty and external obedience.
Christ's kingdom rules over heart and mind and thought,
by a force which is like the great law of gravitation—
perpetually, universally, mightily acting, yet silent and
invisible. It is the wonderful power of Christ's love
manifested in the heart by the Holy Ghost that is the
central attraction of the system, and "we love him because
He first loved us."

August.—Mr. Elliott spent a few weeks of this summer
with his children in the country near Uckfield. The stillness
was delicious to him. He used to stand entranced by window
or door, looking out at the wide panoramic view of undulating
pasture and woodland, dotted here and there with cottages,
and bounded by a blue line of downs cleft by openings more
or less abrupt at Lewes, Glynde, and other Sussex towns and
villages. But we never hear now of romps with the children.
The merry heart is gone. He now looks ever to the resump-
tion of work. "May God bless this place," he says, "to
peace and the refreshment of spirit, in order to more vigorous
work when we return to Brighton!"

He came here for several consecutive years, and even
bought a piece of ground, with a view to building a house
which might serve as a sanatorium for St. Mary's Hall, or as
a summer residence for himself. This plan was not, however,
carried out.

Archdeacon Hare, who was engaged to preach the Consecration sermon at All Saints' Church, Brighton, having
been taken ill, the Vicar wrote to Mr. Elliott :

In case the Archdeacon should retrograde and be unable
to come, would you, the only one able to compensate for
the disappointment, most kindly help us in the hour
of extremity, by supplying the place of him whom you
once happily described as of European repute?

The necessity did arise, and Mr. Elliott preached and printed the Consecration sermon.

November.—He took his daughters to see the Duke of Wellington's funeral in this month, and often spoke afterwards of the impressiveness of the responses made on that occasion. He suggested to Bishop Blomfield for the epitaph, " The shields of the earth belong unto the Lord," but it was not adopted.

December.—He became, this month, an object of attack in a leading London journal, and was very much distressed under it. It appears, that at a meeting on the Lord's Day question, with especial reference to the opening of the Crystal Palace on that day, he had made some remarks which were interpreted as a charge of venality. He spoke on information privately conveyed to him, and named a large sum as given in payment for a leading article :—

" I meant," he says, " to make no charge of venality in this, any more than if I had spoken of a large sum given for a review in the 'Quarterly' or 'Edinburgh ;' and was only stating the highly remunerated talent and influence arrayed against us by the Press and the Crystal Palace, and the sums given for a first-rate advocacy."

But more was attributed to his words than he meant, and several crushing Articles were the result, whilst an explanation was tacitly refused. It wounded him deeply at the time ; and he left an unfinished account of the whole matter, from the beginning, amongst his papers, in order " that his children might know the truth after his death."

" I was, perhaps," he says, " too proud of my character, and knew not that the breath of calumny could assail it." " My own Diocesan and the Archbishop," he adds at a later date, " have only taken occasion to show me additional kindness, besides furnishing an ample acquittal."

Not only the Bishop and Archbishop, but friends from all quarters rallied round him, and rather wondered at a sensitiveness with which they still sympathised.

A letter from the Vicar on the first day of the opening year well expressed the general feeling :—

The first fruits, or well-nigh the first fruits of a New Year's morning I devote to you, with the sincere prayer that you may enjoy a portion (and the portion must needs be large)

of the happiness which you, during a long course of years
and faithful ministry in this parish, have imparted unto
others.

I marvel not that the diocesan meeting evinced a desire to
show you sympathy and respect—a respect which will
never be abated by the recent untoward event in connection
with the newspaper attack.

On the address (to you) published in the ' Brighton Gazette '
December 23, I set exceedingly little value as compared
with a higher testimony—the testimony of your own life
and conversation. You have, as our Bishop says, "made
too much of the thing." It would appear to me, dearest
Elliott, that you have been singularly blessed in having,
through the calm of a long life, exemplified the Italian
adage, " Non ha mai fatto dir di sè."

I gladly embrace this opportunity of acknowledging your
constant heartfelt co-operation in all that is good—a co-
operation which instead of abating has, at the close of
more than a quarter of a century, greatly increased; for
which I rest,

Ever yours affectionately,
H. M. WAGNER.

Referring to the subject a few years afterwards, he says :—

By the way, it is curious, as touching the newspaper attack
upon me, that I have had two proofs how little the writers
themselves believed what they wrote against my character.
The first was in the case of Mr. and Mrs.——(the former,
the chief proprietor), who, through a friend, proposed that
they should have a young person from St. Mary's Hall to
be a companion to their only daughter; saying that " they
should be glad of one who had been educated under
Mr. Elliott's influence." The second was some time after,
in the case of Mrs.——, the lady of the chief editor. She
was staying at Brighton, and being taken very ill, was, at
her special request, visited by me ministerially for some
time; for which she wrote and expressed herself afterwards as greatly indebted. *Thus I had my revenge.*

1853.

May.—During the Lent of this year he preached a course
of sermons on the Lord's Day, in his chapel; and was

appointed for the seventh time, by Dr. Jeremie, Select Preacher at Cambridge, taking for his subject the several appearances of our Lord after His resurrection. He writes on May 30th: "I have done my work here, on the whole, happily and successfully." These sermons will also be found in the printed volume before referred to.

July.—He went to Hereford this month, to attend the funeral and preach the funeral sermon for Mrs. Jane Venn, the last of her generation, his mother's favourite unmarried sister, and a most interesting person. She was ninety-five years of age, stooping a little, and her eyesight weak, but her hearing and her intellect perfect; and she was able to take an interest in all matters around her. She had been a most dutiful daughter herself, and God had given her "a soft and downy nest" for twenty years, and raised her up more than children, to watch her every look, and to minister to her every comfort, with the most dutiful love and reverence. Her last words were from the hymn beginning

"Hark! the voice of love and mercy," &c.

October.—He was invited by Archbishop Sumner to go to Addington Park, and meet Chevalier Bunsen. The question of the Jerusalem bishopric, and the conduct of Bishop Gobat, were fully discussed. Mr. Elliott says, in a letter to Archdeacon Hare :—

> It appeared clearly : 1. That the letter of introduction given to Bishop Alexander (the first bishop) by the Archbishop (Howley) was never accepted by those to whom it was addressed; and the real meaning of it was, kindly and without schism to enter into conference and amicable relations, and to lead the Greek Patriarchs to receive such help and light as might reform their Church from its abuses and errors.
>
> 2. Bishop Alexander is dead : and Bishop Gobat never came under that letter of introduction. Nor, when appointed by the King of Prussia, was it proposed to him to tie his hands by that document.
>
> 3. Bishop Gobat, finding that individual Greeks came to him with urgent appeals for light and reformation, has hitherto desired them to remain in their own Church and reform themselves, and has only assisted them with schools and advice.

4. These Greeks, violently persecuted by these Patriarchs, have, in considerable numbers, declared themselves no longer members of a Church that refuses the Scriptures and persecutes those that read them.

5. Subsequently to Bishop Alexander's appointment the Turkish Government have altered the law. All persons now changing their religion from one form of Christianity to another, are deemed independent of their former Church, and are not amenable to its officers or punishments. Formerly, the patriarchs and bishops were the judges and executioners of their own sentences. The reformed Greeks therefore stand in a new and separate status; and the only question is, whether they shall be refused admission into the Episcopal and Anglican Church, or by such refusal be driven, for the sake of spiritual life, to the American missionaries and their Independent or Baptist communities. They are already lost to the Greek unreformed Church. It may be said, "This is the consequence of your Bible distribution." It may be so. But the letter of Archbishop Howley was never meant to debar even Bishop Alexander from giving the Scriptures to the Greeks and Armenians. It is impossible to conceive such a dereliction of principle in the late Archbishop.

There was a Confirmation this month; and, writing on the subject, he says :—

Our lecture yesterday was on the blessing which attends making a voluntary and hearty covenant with God—an individual covenant for ourselves; as proved by the examples of Abraham, Jacob, Ruth, and David, the last of whom, in the darkening vale of declining years, comforted himself with the thought of the "everlasting covenant ordered in all things, and sure."

He expresses himself as charmed with the simplicity and unworldliness of two of his candidates, daughters of an English lady of high rank, who had sent them from France to attend his lectures.

This circumstance serves to prove the esteem in which Mr. Elliott was held by persons of rank; and gives an opportunity to remove the impression left upon some minds that he courted the great; whereas the real truth is, that they courted him. His position at Brighton, a place so frequented by the nobility, would be alone sufficient to account for much of his intercourse with them. But, in truth, a mind naturally delicate, enlarged by travel, refined by good society, and matured by experience, was appreciated by all; and no one who once knew Mr. Elliott would ever give him up. The Marchioness above mentioned, as just related, sent child after child to be under his instruction. When Lord Aberdeen's sons had left him, and their paths in life seemed naturally to diverge from his own, he intentionally ceased to visit and correspond with them, until their mother, Lady Aberdeen, wrote to him in the most solemn and pathetic manner, imploring him "not to withdraw his influence for good, which was stronger than that of any other person." What he did, was done in the most disinterested manner. He neither sought nor obtained advancement from any mortal man. Wherever he was confided in, and found an opportunity of doing good, he was ready; but where these were wanting, he withdrew, and dwelt happily amongst "his own people." He was indeed rather fastidious in such matters, and might have been accounted proud. Certainly no one could take a liberty with him. When, in one of his summer retirements, a lady of rank and high fashion sought friendship and intercourse with the ladies of his family, he withdrew from it; calling, and explaining with all courtesy, that, their paths in life being very different, it was expedient to check and restrict their intercourse.

It may also be mentioned, that if he took pains for the rich he did as much for the poor. He spared no pains for them (they themselves being witnesses); and he truly described the employment he loved best when, in a page of " Likes and Dislikes," he described his favourite occupation as "taking pains to do good."

1854.

In the beginning of this year much controversy arose in Brighton on questions raised by the Protestant Defence Committee, in all of which Mr. Elliott was of necessity mixed up; but though the papers are preserved, they require nothing more than this passing notice, as a record of his ministerial engagements.

March.—Many letters passed with Lady Haddo, then under deep affliction, owing to the dangerous illness of her husband, Lord Aberdeen's eldest son, whose " brief life" has lately been written by the Rev. E. B. Elliott. One

.of her children was delicate, and required sea-air, as the only hope of recovery. Mr. Elliott opened his house for the child, her baby sister, and their nurse. The change produced was marvellous, and the visit was prolonged to more than three months; and repeated in the autumn, at still greater length, when Lord and Lady Haddo went to Egypt.

April.—England was now drifting into the Crimean War, and a fast day was appointed "by authority." Mr. Elliott expressed his pleasure that it was appointed so early, "as a title-page to the war." "It will give us ministers," he says, "a great moral advantage in improving the occasion, and I am sure it must be no small satisfaction to Lord Aberdeen, that he has not drawn the sword till compelled to do so."

. A fast-day sermon was preached in St. Mary's, and the four points then pressed were :—

1. The duty of remembering the sovereignty of God.
2. The propriety of beginning such a war (so just and inevitable) with a national act of humiliation.
3. The duty of searching out our own individual guilt in the general amount: sins of omission, alas! how many, as well as sins of commission.
4. The fast that God accepts involves in it relief of the burdened, and alms for the destitute.

The collection amounted to more than 115*l*.

. *May.*—He again went to Cambridge as Select Preacher nominated by the Rev. J. Clark, and finished the course of sermons begun the year before, on our Lord's resurrection.

August.—Short were his holidays this summer, and little his rest. He was very much occupied with carrying sermons on "the War, the Harvest, and the Cholera," through the press; and in giving parting lectures to the Brighton schools, twelve of which were continually under his spiritual charge. The good results of these he called his "spiritual harvest." "How I wish they were once a fortnight, or once a week," exclaimed one of his young auditors, "for then I should be a better girl." As the year closed, he says, "he never remembered his chapel to be fuller. A great and open door seemed to be set before him; and he only wanted *Grace* to avail himself of it." His collections were proportionally increased, and on three nearly consecutive Sundays (Oct. 1st, Oct. 29th, and Nov. 17th) they amounted to 346*l*. Warm clothing, and comforts of every kind, were also gladly contributed for the Crimea, in answer to his appeals.

"The privations of our army call upon us with a trumpet tongue," he said, " to throw aside our selfishness. Such carnage, such disadvantages, such patience, such endurance ! If they do it to obtain a corruptible crown, what should we do to obtain an incorruptible one ?"

December.—He writes to Lady Haldo in Egypt after giving a report of her children :—

The anxiety has been intense here about the army at Sebastopol, ever since the battle of Balaclava. We required to be humbled, and God has humbled us. The tone of the newspapers has been awfully vain-glorious and self-confident. Think of one of them writing, " that with our steam navy we could defy the storms of the Black Sea!" If that sentiment was a true impression of the public mind, then the awful storm of the 14th was indeed needed. I think God will show the two mightiest nations of Europe to be like children grasped by His almighty arm, and brought low on their knees before Him; and then He will raise them up.

I heard yesterday, with great satisfaction, that Lord Aberdeen had offered the large and important parish of St. Mary-lebone, vacant by Dr. Spry's death, to Mr. Pelham, Lord Chichester's brother, a devoted and Evangelical minister. This appointment speaks well.

Thus unselfishly he speaks of the preferment of another to a post which might have been very naturally and very properly offered to himself. Many of his friends wondered that no preferment, even to the end, was conferred upon him, save that provided by his own family. The one or two small livings placed at his disposal in earlier life, though eligible and pleasant in themselves, could not be compared in interest or importance to the position he filled at Brighton. It is true that, in a pecuniary sense, he needed no preferment. He had enough and to spare. But there are posts of confidence and honour in the Church, which he would have highly appreciated, and to which he was justly entitled. As tutor to Lord Aberdeen's sons; as an influential clergyman in the Diocese of Chichester, and on friendly terms with his Bishop, he might naturally have expected some one or more of these. But he never sought them in word or deed, and never repined at the withholding of them. "God has kept me back from honour," he was wont to say, when his friends expressed their indignation or astonishment. Perhaps he was habitually too busy, and too hurried, to suggest the idea, or to invite the bestowal of any additional responsibility. And those who knew him best, might not have associated with his crowded desk and tumultuous papers the idea of a well-ordered Diocese or Archdeaconry. Even he himself used to call his study, "his Balaclava." But this was prejudging the case, and does not alter its general features. Nevertheless, God rules over all, and assigns to each servant his niche in the Church ; and perhaps, after all, Mr. Elliott filled that which conduced most to his usefulness and happiness. He was the proper man in the proper place. As Wilberforce amongst the Nobles, so was Elliott amongst the Dignitaries.

1855.

January.—At the beginning of this year, a district containing about 3,000 people was virtually assigned to St. Mary's, and Mr. Elliott was then enabled to construct the machinery necessary for ministering to the temporal wants of the people around his church. District visitors were at once appointed, and in due time all the parochial apparatus of clothing clubs, soup kitchens, coal distributions, Scripture readers, Bible women, and mothers' meetings were in operation. This was done gradually, and for the most part effectually.

His eldest son Alfred was now at college, and having *proprio motu*, chosen India for his destination, thought it well to avail himself of the first open competitive examination in the year 1856. On the public announcement being made, he went up to London without any special preparation, passed with great credit, and obtained an appointment in the Indian Civil Service. His eldest daughter also was leaving school, and "coming home," as he said, "to fill a niche which had long been vacant."

This proved in reality not a very easy task. Many years of a comparatively lonely life, with many engagements pressing upon one another, had produced an irregularity in domestic arrangements not easy to be overcome. There was in Mr. Elliott a pre-occupied, if not an absent mind. He was always inquiring, and laying up in store the information he

s

acquired, and he used often to tell a story of his earlier days :
—He was seated on the coachbox, and travelling on the Bath
road. As usual, he was questioning the coachman : " What
place is that ? " " To whom does this estate belong ? " " What
is the name of yonder village ? " To all such questions he
received the one invariable answer, " I do not know."
Vexed, as he always was when in contact with a man who
had " no eyes," he asked somewhat sarcastically, " What *do*
you know?" Without the movement of a muscle, the man
replied, " I know, sir, how to drive you from Bath to
Bristol."

Now, Mr. Elliott did not always know how to drive from
Bath to Bristol. His mind was too full, and all its cells were
overcrowded. Certain things he remembered, and certain
things he forgot. He persistently called sons by their fathers'.
names. He would, in his ministerial calls, be compelled to
ask if " the family was at home," because for the moment he
had forgotten their family name. He would enter a drawing-
room full of company, and greet each guest in succession,
though unknown, as if well known. Happily he was himself
well known, and his gentle smile and kindly word were fully
appreciated by all. Invited guests were also often forgotten,
and consequently unmentioned; and his daughter would be
startled by the entry of a stranger or two, who had evidently
come to dinner; and Mr. Elliott being often detained by
engagements, a feeble conversation had to be kept up for an
hour, perhaps, before matters were explained. In the same
way, guests would arrive in evening dress, of whose coming
the lady of the house had no idea. Mr. Elliott would laugh
heartily at the " tale of woe," as recounted afterwards—more
heartily than the young hostess at the time ! These matters,
however, were now set right, and for a time all things were
" done decently and in order." This was a pleasant episode
in his life. But it was short. The clouds gathered again.
Illness came, and necessary separations for a warmer climate
followed ; and the " Letters on Affliction," which have already
appeared (and many more), were written ; and whilst the
old hospitality continued, the old irregularities returned.
Many were the extempore dinners ; and happy the guests
who always found the bodily equal to the mental feast. In
his correspondence, the following words often find a place :
" We were rather short, but they were very kind, and did not
mind."

February.—His three sermons before referred to, on the Harvest, the Cholera, and the War, were now published; but he had to add a funeral sermon for Archdeacon Hare, who had died in the preceding month. He could not be said to agree with all the sentiments of that eminent man; but his friendship was based upon what was common to both—love to the Truth, and to Jesus Christ, who is " The Truth."

The death of the Archdeacon severed this friendship, after it had lasted for thirty years. It had begun when Mr. Elliott was resident at college; for he speaks then of a dinner-party which he had given to his friends Smyth, Whewell, Malden, *Hare*, Sedgwick, Venn; "and," he adds, "we had good talk." It was renewed when Mr. Hare was appointed to the living of Hurstmonceux, in Sussex, and nominated subsequently, by Bishop Otter, to the Archdeaconry of Lewes. They then often met at visitations, about diocesan business, and on the platform of the Church Missionary Society. On October 31, 1852, Mr. Elliott writes :—

I have a great hope that I shall be able to come over to you on Thursday. The opportunities we have of meeting now cannot be many: at all events they are diminishing, and I shall be sorry to lose one of them. The remembrance of my last visit to you is fragrant, and it bore fruit, thanks be to God.

And now, on January 30, 1855, he was one of many other friends who assembled to pay the last tribute of respect to his memory, and accompany his remains to the grave. Mr. Elliott himself describes the scene. He says :—

I followed his bier to the grave in Hurstmonceux churchyard, walking by the side of the Bishop of St. David's, his schoolfellow, his fellow-collegian, and his friend through life. It was a walking funeral, and three miles to the grave, and, as it fell out, with the snow thick upon the ground.

In response to a proposal that he should preach the funeral sermon, he received a message from the widowed Mrs. Hare, who was a " widow indeed," warmly thanking him for " his kind offer, which had only anticipated her great desire," and adding :—

That she knew of no one whom she would more desire to

speak to the people than himself; and that she knew also the deep affection the dear Archdeacon cherished towards him.

The sermon, therefore, was preached on the Sunday following; and, when printed, met with great and general commendation. The present Archbishop of Dublin said respecting it :—

I should receive with pleasure any sermon of yours, but more so if it came from your hand, and most of all when it turned on a subject so profoundly interesting to myself. I had not seen, but was very glad to see, so truthful a record of the many noble and generous qualities which adorned our dear departed friend, and of the grace of God by which they were all consecrated to the service of His Church.

Archdeacon Garbett says :—

I have read your sermon with great edification and delight. With great felicity and force you have seized upon such traits in his noble mind and its religious aspects, as should be most striking for commemoration of the departed and edification of the living.

A few extracts from the sermon will, however, speak best for themselves :—

Amongst the characteristics of his religion, Faith had a high place and a free scope: faith in the Lord Jesus Christ as the source of all light and life to man. His trust in God was remarkably firm and filial, breaking forth continually into thankfulness and thanksgivings. It was a living faith; a faith full of lively gratitude, very childlike, and marked by a beautiful simplicity. . . . Next to Luther, I hear that he prized Archbishop Leighton: a preference which none but a spiritual mind would have entertained. Such was his faith, simple and steadfast; and yet much I marvel that a mind so gifted with imagination, so familiar with German theology, so discursive in its appetite for every kind of literature, escaped untouched by the evil influences which such speculations usually leave behind them. Not a little, I think, he owed to a certain generosity and nobleness of nature, which grew up with him from childhood, before it came under the more decisive power of the grace of God. His love of truth, and his earnestness in the pursuit of it, were akin to that guileless simplicity which was felt by all who knew him to be one of the charms of his disposition, and which is a prime safeguard against scepticism. But still I must attribute it to the special guidance of a Divine hand, that so lively an imagination, and studies of so wide a range, should have been free from scepticism to the end. It was never one of his difficulties.

After speaking of his brilliant career and classical distinctions, his learning and wide-spread fame, and his tuition at Trinity College, conducted "with an ability not soon to be forgotten," Mr. Elliott continues :—

To his critical study of the Greek Testament for his lectures he always referred as letting in upon his soul much light from above. Religious difficulties and struggles indeed he had to encounter in this part of his history ; but he was never disturbed, he said, by any scepticism. After ten years spent in college, in 1833 he made the great change of coming to take the charge of this Living, which had been presented to him the year before by his brother. And this change was one which soon became fruitful in the Divine blessing to his soul. Here certainly the Lord met him. But He met him first in trials of heavy affliction. By the discipline of sorrows he grew, as Christians usually grow, in the knowledge and love of his Saviour. The branch was pruned that it might bring forth more fruit. The public fruit of that discipline was seen in the sermons on the " Victory of Faith " which, as Select Preacher, he delivered to the University ;—sermons which, I know, shed a new light on many an earnest and intellectual spirit, never so touched before, and kindled holy resolutions which are to this day animating public and important ministrations. After a time it pleased the Great Head of the Church again to subject him to the same school of affliction, and again the discipline brought forth both its private and public fruit—private, in his increased gentleness and love, and the genuine humility which characterised his demeanour in the diocese amongst us; public, in the second series of sermons, preached also before the University, and afterwards given to the Church and the world under the title, " The Mission of the Comforter."

It was in 1840 that he was appointed our Archdeacon by Bishop Otter. It would be difficult to surpass the interest and ability of his archidiaconal charges. They were

equally remarkable for their comprehensive grasp of their
subjects, and the stately and balanced march of his sentences in style and elocution. In them very conspicuous
was the genuine and outspoken love of what he held to be
truth and righteousness, accompanied by a largeness of
heart in seeking and discerning all the good that could
be found in all. Some of us were of opinion that his
generosity of praise sometimes precluded him from the
equal discernment of evil : and that his love of peace, which
had its roots in his heart, attempted unions which too
great difference of principles rendered impossible. But
his peace-loving spirit is gone to that kingdom where there
are no controversies, where the Gospel no more needs its
militant champions, and Paul and Barnabas have no dis-
sensions.

And now, dear friends, it remains that with more earnest
efforts and with fresh zeal and patience we set ourselves in
the strength of Christ to follow him. . . . Oh, that his words,
his prayers, his tears, may have a double emphasis, now
that he has been taken from us unto the rest that remaineth
to the people of God!

April.—Letters now begin between father and daughter,
when either were absent from home, extracts from which
will be given.

"We had a capital musical festival at St. Mary's Hall, on
Easter Tuesday," he writes ; " J. P—— sang 'Comfort ye
my people,' in a manner which surpassed all her former
doings. Mozart's 'Gloria in excelsis' was a capital chorus,
and the 'Requiem' displayed great accuracy and ability.
Yesterday I had my Quarterly Juvenile Church Missionary
Meeting, which was very full. Mr. Marsden (author of the
'History of the Puritans,' &c.) spoke for half an hour, and
I for another half. The collection was 27*l.* Next Sunday,
Mr. Marsden preaches for me.

"I have had another beautiful letter from Professor Sedgwick.
He liked my sermon on Archdeacon Hare very much.
There are eighty candidates for Confirmation this year.
The first lecture is over, and I am in the depths of my blue
bag full of papers. I am just going to begin a course of
lectures on the Ten Commandments in St. Mary's."

December.—His sister-in-law, Mrs. Whewell, died.

1856.

May.—During this month Mr. Elliott preached in the University pulpit at Cambridge, for the ninth and last time : that "awful pulpit," as he again and again calls it.

" The last sermon," he writes, " was to a very full University audience, and was heard with a striking attention. My earnest desire and prayer was that Christ might be glorified, and that I might preach that which should do most good, and not that which might be thought clever or bring me credit. So I took for my subject ' Christ our High Priest,' and, losing sight of self, behold, I found that it was as well received as any sermon I ever preached from that awful pulpit. Pray, my E——, that a blessing may go with it, and that I may have the strength and comfort of the ' Paraclete,' which means adviser, counsellor, bosom friend, to whom you reveal your perplexities or griefs, *whom you call in, in your need* (that last is the literal meaning), whether for advice or consolation.

" To the more select of the audience of Whit-Monday and Whit-Tuesday I find that my sermons gave satisfaction. Dr. Whewell, Mr. Hopkins, the great mathematical tutor, Mr. Clayton, and Mr. Methuen, have spoken to me to that effect. ' Hitherto the Lord hath helped.' May he be with me to the end ! Think of me as addressing a compact body of undergraduates at eight o'clock ; Clement Cobb (married in July to his niece, and now Vicar of St. George's, Barnsley) taking part with me."

July.—He paid a last visit to the Westmoreland lakes :—

" We entered by Patterdale," he says, " and were at Patterdale Hall by eleven o'clock. We went in the afternoon as far as Water Millock and the Knots, and it is impossible to describe the exquisite beauty or the indelible associations of the whole scene. Dr. and Mrs. Tait came over to call on Tuesday, and I had almost forty minutes with them —a solemn time." [1]

August.—His son Alfred now received his summons to India, to fill the appointment for which he had successfully contended. It came upon the family suddenly, and like a surprise :—

" What a sudden event," Mr. Elliott writes, " not unmixed

---

[1] Just after their touching bereavement of several children !

with many pangs, is Alfred's appointment and its speedy beginning. The days are numbered; but India now is not as India was twenty years ago. Railway and steam wonderfully shorten distance. Still a pain of heart comes over me, at the near prospect of long and wide separation; and I can only take my feelings and anxieties where a parent can best take them.

"I rose at 5.30 this morning, and have worked on without interruption (save breakfast) with the Divinity examination papers of St. Mary's Hall. Now it is two o'clock. The thirty-nine sets of papers are all done. Hurrah! I go to St. Mary's Hall to write their places in the class list."

1857.

This year he was much engaged, generally, in various plans for the benefit of Brighton, and specially, in getting up a memorial to the Rev. George Wagner, of St. Stephen's, who had finished his course of admirable usefulness, and died at Valetta. As a mark of regard for his memory, seventeen of the Brighton clergy agreed to have sermons simultaneously, to strengthen and enlarge the "Home" he had established in his lifetime.

January.—A Sunday evening and a week-day scene will be found interesting. Mr. Elliott himself shall open the drawing-room door in Brunswick Square:—

Last night, after tea, in our Sunday fashion, we took down Henry Martyn's Journals (two vols.), and Thomason's Memoirs, and intended to have examined Heber also, in order to compare together their first impressions of India; but the wonderful depth of Martyn's religion, and its beautiful genuineness, caught me and carried me away, so that I went on reading to the little home-party, and, seeing them interested, I indulged my own taste the more, and read on for the hour and half which brought on family prayers. But that book always charms me; and when the rest were gone to bed, I opened Thomason's Memoirs, and read about his ministry, so successful in the old church at Calcutta; and Martyn's sermons there, which gave such offence that another chaplain preached in direct condemnation of the doctrine and the man. Martyn's Journals have a deep tinge of melancholy; but that, perhaps, only fascinates me the more. May

Martyn's God be our God, and Martyn's religion our religion!"

So much for the Sunday; now for the week-day :—

Just now E—— is rather weaker than usual; perhaps because the weather has been uncertain, damp, and keen. A few evenings ago they exhibited two charades :—(K) Night-shade and Pyg-ma-lion—in a style of uncommon excellency. C. A—— was the statue which Pygmalion chiselled and addressed with passionate words of affection (his own words), and finally with an invocation to life; upon which the eyelids of the statue began to open, and the arms gradually moved to an embrace. Then, in that critical moment, the curtain dropped, and the transition from the statue to the living woman (too difficult to show) was left, just as it ought to have been, to the imagination.

April: Holy Week.—"This is a holy and blessed week," he says to his sister Charlotte; "I hope my congregation may take as deep an interest in hearing my investigation of the events of the week as I do in preaching them. This morning I preached on the triumphal entry into Jerusalem (John xii. 12). But it is hard work to study the subject and write a new sermon every day. I have written one daily these last five days except Saturday. My girls are at Hastings. E—— was much the same. The journey, though short, fatigued her a good deal. Her cough has never left her, and her appetite is a fragment of what it used to be. It is so mysterious to me, that of the two children who alone were like their blessed mother, one should have been taken away suddenly, and the other should be an invalid, with a dark shadow resting on the future. Thus, of my jewels, two are gone and one damaged; but, I thank God, all with tokens of a heavenly birth, the first pre-eminently and wonderfully holy and lovely. But 'it is the Lord; let Him do what seemeth Him good.'"

Nothing could surpass the affectionate sympathy and tender consideration of Mr. Elliott towards his dear and suffering child, thus referred to. No expense was spared, every kind of air was tried, and the tenderest nursing provided. Long sickness produced in him no weariness. To snatch every leisure minute and spend it in the sick-room, to tell every incident of the day, to consult upon each step to be taken, to hold converse upon the common salvation, to offer words of prayer, to give the daily blessing, to run upstairs with hasty steps, to come down slowly with tearful eyes: this was the course—varied, as we have said already, with frequent separations—for ten long years! And it will be seen hereafter that even a dying bed could not lessen the care and thoughtfulness of a loving father.

Easter Week.—It was a very interesting Easter to him this year, as any one may imagine when he knows that the communicants were more in number than ever they had been before; that the Offertory Collection exceeded 21*l.*; and that thirty widows and poor people sat down with him to a plenteous dinner. Labour leant on love; for on Easter Monday he left home at 10.30 A.M., and did not return till 8 P.M.

June.—The news of the Indian Mutiny now reached England: not realised in its full extent at first, but soon filling the public mind with consternation, and the hearts of friends and relatives with fearful apprehensions. It engrossed the attention of Mr. Elliott, more or less, for the whole of this year and the next. His son Alfred behaved with great bravery, and survived many imminent perils. "How remarkable it is," Mr. Elliott says, "that the Sepoys, with whom our Missionaries were not permitted to hold any intercourse, should have been the exhibitors of the true spirit of their religion and their character." Doubting whether there would be any national Form of Prayer, he called his congregation together for that purpose, privately, and met with a most earnest and encouraging response. Dr. Carr, successively Chaplain, Archdeacon, and Bishop of Bombay; the Rev. Francis Cunningham; the Rev. J. Babington, who had married Miss Eleanor Elliott, and now removed to Brighton; assisted him by their addresses and devotions.

"I have strong faith in prayer," he says, "far more than in armies or senates. The cause cannot be desperate which God accepts and aids, and He does not kindle in a thousand congregations such a spirit of prayer and mean it to fail."

But he was not content with private intercessory prayer. He thought the *Nation* ought to speak; and for this, as an individual clergyman, he strove with all his might. At the request of his brethren, he drew up a memorial, and obtained, by a week's incessant labour, the signatures of twenty-nine of the clergy in Brighton. It was sent through the Bishop to the Archbishop of Canterbury, who stated, in reply, that the same post that brought to him the memorial brought also a letter from Lord Palmerston, saying " that a day and a Form of Prayer was resolved on."

1858.

March.—The Archbishop offered him this year the Warburtonian Lectureship, and he was disposed to accept it, if he " found his prophetical knowledge could be brought up to the mark." His brother, Edward Elliott had held it four years before; and Mr. Goode's (late Dean of Ripon) course was just ended. Founded by Bishop Warburton, it required three lectures on Prophecy and Prophetical Subjects, to be preached each year in Lincoln's Inn. It was tenable for four years, and it provided an endowment little more than sufficient to cover the expense of travelling, and printing the twelve Lectures, which the Lecturer was supposed to do at the end of the course.[1] Mr. Elliott finally consented to accept the appointment, on condition that he should not be required to see Rome in the " Babylon " of the Apocalypse. He did not deny—perhaps he rather leaned towards that opinion ; but not sufficiently so as to enforce it. This liberty willingly conceded, he assumed the office and preached the sermons.

April.—Easter rapidly comes round :—

" Half hours," he says, " this Easter are very scarce. I have again preached a new sermon each day in Passion Week—three written and one extempore—and am none the worse in throat or strength."

June.—Speaking of his Confirmation class, and of one special candidate, he says :—

Sweetness of disposition makes the higher graces of the Holy Spirit more lovely in their manifestation, when they grow in such a soil. Adam of Wintringham said of himself, on the contrary :—" If ever the grace of God was grafted on a crab-stick, it was on me." But still, sweet and gentle as are some dispositions, they require to be remodelled and connected with their right centre, which is Christ.

November.—The Princess of Coorg (an Indian girl of seven-

---

[1] The supposition generally entertained, and sanctioned by usage for some time past, that the appointment belongs exclusively to the Archbishop of Canterbury, appears to be a mistake. It is vested in trustees, with a preference to the Preacher of Lincoln's Inn. See *Life of Bishop Lonsdale*, by E. B. Denison, Esq.

teen years) was entrusted to him to prepare for Confirmation.
She was pleasing and intelligent, and listened to his instructions with apparent interest. The hope was cherished
that she might grow up to consistency in Christianity, and
become a fitting wife for the Maharajah Dhuleep Sing ; but
the project fell through ; and in the end Mr. Elliott thought
she was not sufficiently instructed for confirmation, and had
better wait.

He paid a hurried visit this month to Pau, where he left his
daughters for the winter.

December.—On his return home, he writes :—

I cannot tell you, my precious children, how very near you
are to me, how my mind overleaps the eight hundred miles
between us, and comes into your room at Pau, and busies
itself with offices of love. How glad I am that I waited to
settle you, and know so well your "Flat" and its rooms,
and their aspects and their furniture. I have fixed to the
wall of my room the tender illuminated scroll, "The Lord
watch between me and thee," and it is just over the red
chair by which I kneel and pray in my bedroom, with your
sweet mamma's picture over it.

I have been making up my Church Missionary accounts. We
run very high this year, between 600*l.* and 700*l.*—the highest annual mark yet attained.

Christmas Eve.—May your hearts be visited with the anthem
joys of saints and angels to-morrow! I have been too much
oppressed by my week's work to have my heart open, as I
would desire, to the notes that sing of "Glory to God in
the highest, and on earth peace." The Lord look on my infirmity, and raise me above the depression of continual and
excessive demands!

1859.

January.—This year was opened by an attendance at the
Islington Clerical Meeting, and a visit to Fulham Palace. He
was received with the greatest kindness by the Bishop of
London, and " was beguiled into something like pleasure in
listening to the wonderful work of God wrought by the London
Missionary Society in Madagascar."

" I find here," he says, "rather a miscellaneous company, as
some would think. The person who has most interested me,
next to my host and hostess, is Mr. Ellis, a Dissenting

minister, who gave us this morning an account of the work of conversion carried on by the Spirit of God in Madagascar, after twenty martyrdoms and the banishment of every missionary from the island. They left two small bodies, who worshipped together, after baptism, fourteen and thirteen in number. Then, when they were left to themselves, they would dwindle of course to nothing? No; they grew and multiplied to eight thousand between 1836, the date of the missionaries' expulsion, and 1853, when Mr. Ellis visited the island. He read letters from the converts, chiefly from the martyrs; most Scriptural, most touching. All were deeply penetrated by the narrative, which was not at all formal, but interspersed conversationally with the questions of the hearers, chiefly the Bishop's. next frequently mine, &c. We listened from half-past eleven till two; then came luncheon, when, to complete the miscellany, who should call but Jenny Lind, who sat at the luncheon some little time."

February.—He went abroad for two months at this time, anxious to revisit his family at Pau. He found his invalid daughter somewhat better, but unable to return with him. He writes to Mr. Babington to thank him for his efficient services at St. Mary's during his absence, and says:—

Yesterday we left Pau at 10 A.M., and returned at 8 P.M., having gone into the gorge of one of the Pyrenean passes, and looked the Pic-du-midi, one of the sons of these mountain Anakim, in the face. It is ten thousand feet high; and there it stands, with its snow-capped satellites coming down in double ranks on the right and left, like rows of guards drawn up to dignify the throne of their monarch, as he bestrides the valley at the end. It was still fifteen miles from us, and. Saul-like, head and shoulders above the rest. So we did homage with our eyes to his royal *highness*, and with our mouths to a nice picnic dinner, in a beautiful upland by the side of the murmuring Gave, with a mill noiselessly striking the water with its floats, and within sight of a church, a ruined castle, and a modern dwelling-house, perched on a jutting promontory of the river on its other side—altogether a most picturesque spot. Some went in carriages and some on horseback. My chief object was to accompany my child, who requires a little variation of the monotony of her most affectionate attendance on her sister.

During his absence at Pau, Lord Bristol, the great bene-factor to St. Mary's Hall, died. In the Report for 1858-9 the following grateful recognition of his liberality appears, accompanied with details too long for insertion here :—

On Feb. 15th of this year, we lost our first and great patron, one who from the very beginning watched over the prosperity of St. Mary's Hall with a princely generosity, and a kindness almost paternal. It is right that his extraordinary benevolence should never be forgotten by the members. . . . Such a series of splendid donations no institution could ever have expected from one individual. Those who had the privilege to know Lord Bristol will remember well how the grace and amenity of his manner set off his noble acts. They were "apples of gold in pictures of silver." Often did they bring to mind that verse of Scripture: "All these, as a king, did Araunah give unto the king." So may we say, "All these, as a king, did Lord Bristol give to St. Mary's Hall."

April.—He was again in Brighton this month :—

Thankful to be permitted to preach in St. Mary's (that dear House of God!) and to receive the cordial welcome of so many on my return.

He arrived on Saturday night, and appeared in the pulpit somewhat unexpectedly on Sunday morning, preaching from —"the Lord was with Joseph :"—with him in his prosperity; with him in his adversity. Sixty candidates for Confirmation flocked round him, and his lectures at once began. The work was, as usual, laborious; but the results more than usually interesting and life-giving.

"Sometimes," he writes to Pau, "the overlooking the mass of papers reminds me of 'stitch, stitch, stitch,' paper after paper. Our gracious God has, however manifested His blessing on the work; and I feel confident that He is with us of a truth. I do not think my field is full of tares as well as wheat; but rather, it is an orchard of trees in full blossom. But there are east winds, exposed situations, and stems rather weak and sickly; and the fear is, that a good deal of this blossom will strew the ground before the fruit is set. The silence and stillness in the lecture-room is very expressive. Above half the candidates are, I am persuaded, in earnest. Two dear girls are as genuine, pellucid, and affectionate as any minister could desire; both decidedly religious. Then there is Lady ——, very interesting and hopeful. I invited a number of them to dinner last week, and the St. Mary's Hall candidates joined us at tea. We proposed games, but I got into the vein of telling them some of my adventures in early life, and showed them the Turkish dress I wore at Jerusalem. Then I retired to the back drawing-room, and dressed up Julius in full Turkish costume, and in all the wonderful amplitude of the Mameluke trousers. Then came the usual *petit souper*, and the evening was finished by my reading the first of my Palestine letters, written to my mother, forty years ago! That, they said, was the best of all the evening. Our usual family prayers closed the whole."

His 'Lent lectures this year were on the prophecies of the Patriarchal Age. It may be interesting to present in one view the series for fifteen years, from 1845 to 1859, inclusive, in their consecutive order. They were afterwards less connected.

1845. The Priesthood of Christ.
1846. Tradition.
1847. Malachi.
1848. The early Christian Church.
1849. St. Matthew xxv.
1850. St. John xvii. 1—24.
1851. St. Peter.
1852. Confession.
1853. The Sabbath.
1854. The Ten Commandments.
1855. The Growth of Moses' Faith.
1856. The first three Evangelists.
1857. The fourth Evangelist.
1858. The Temptation.
1859. The Prophecies of Patriarchal Times.

June.—The month of June found him again at Pau, wondering that a "person in my place at Brighton should ever get away from it;" and having parted from his flock at the service and Holy Communion of Ascension Day,

July,—he returned to Brighton with his family after a long and trying journey, aggravated by intense heat.

" *Dépéchez-vous, dépéchez-vous,*" he says, " are not soothing sounds to an invalid who cannot walk across the platform of the railway, but is obliged to be carried by strangers in a chair."

When settled at home, he opened his chapel for a third service, free to all comers. He began it himself by a sermon on the "Sower," and occasionally preached, though it fatigued him much, as an addition to the other services. He was delighted, however, at all times to minister to the poor, who flocked to the service; and glad to find that he could interest them, and that they understood him.

August.—A single copy of an address delivered this month at St Mary's Hall—being the anniversary of the opening day—and written out from memory, remains amongst Mr. Elliott's papers. Some extracts from it will be very pertinent, as supplying gaps left in the earlier account, and in the tribute to Lord Bristol; and containing many graphic touches. The arrangement was always the same. The lady superintendent, the sixteen governesses, the hundred pupils, the twenty servants, and generally some friends of the Institution, were gathered in the school-room, and, after the reading of Psalm cxxvii.: "Except the Lord build the house," &c., the address was delivered. On the present occasion it began as follows :—

My dear children, it has been my privilege and pleasure to read this Psalm here twenty-three times, and this will make the twenty-fourth time. Many and great have been the mercies which St. Mary's Hall has received from God, and I would desire most heartily to thank Him for them, and solicit a continuance of His gracious favour . . . You, the present generation, know nothing of the earlier trials and difficulties of St. Mary's Hall. You come and find a handsome house ready furnished to receive you, with a nice garden, and habitations surrounding you on all sides; but of the time when the spot on which the house now stands was considered one of the waste places of Brighton, you are quite in ignorance . . . . The idea of building St. Mary's Hall was suggested to my mind after visiting the Casterton Clergy Daughters' School, when I thought to myself that there was no place like it in the south of England where the daughters of clergymen with limited incomes could be educated; and it struck me that it was a long way to Casterton! So one day, while sitting in Lord Bristol's drawing-room, with Lord and Lady Bristol, after dining with them and giving his lordship an animated account of Casterton school, of which I spoke with much warmth and enthusiasm, I ended by saying: " I have some thoughts, my lord, of beginning some such institution at Brighton." Now, let those that love the Lord mark the openings of His providence. The next morning's post brought me a letter from Lord Bristol, saying briefly: "If you should follow up the project you mentioned last evening, *let me know.*" The question is, what was the value of those words, "let me know?" Some people would have considered them as good as a bank-note at once; yet there was no promise of help, merely the words, "let me know." I have the very letter in my possession now. . . .

The plan of the building was constantly in my mind. I thought of it, and dreamed of it. Soon afterwards, by mentioning it to my friends (for I had at that time large scope, and free access to many rich and influential persons,) I raised some subscriptions; not very large, it is true, but still pretty well for a beginning. My dear father, who, if he had lived, would have been a most worthy and liberal patron to St. Mary's Hall, was the first to promise me a hundred pounds, which however he did not live to pay; but I paid it for him, as his executor. Many, however, amongst even my own friends, looked with coldness on the scheme, and were not slow in expressing their disapprobation of the attempt. One clergyman in Brighton said to me: "Sir, it will prove a splendid failure." Certainly this was not very comforting. But I had collected some subscriptions, and was obliged to proceed.

Then I remembered Lord Bristol's letter; but I did not like to trouble him on the subject. However, I thought I owed it to the institution which was about to be born; so I put modesty in my pocket, and sat down to write to his lordship, enclosing a list of the subscriptions already received. In a day or two an answer came, saying he would give the land on which to build. This, then, was the value of the words, " *Let me know.*" Shortly afterwards his lordship took me himself to see the land which he proposed giving. It was situated in the open space where St. Mark's Church now stands, but which was then a field; he pointed it out to me, and said, "This is the land; it cost me twelve hundred pounds: but I will give it you." I noticed, however, that

T

there was a mews just in front; and I did not like the idea
of building St. Mary's Hall overlooking a mews.   So I
said, "I fear, my lord, you will think me very insensible of
your generosity, and ungrateful for your kindness, but I do
not like to build St. Mary's Hall close by a mews."   Instead
of being vexed or annoyed, or saying, "Well I have done
the best I can for you, and if you do not like this you must
manage for yourself," he brought me into the field where
this present house has since risen up, and said, "Do you
like this situation?   I answered, "Yes, my lord."   "It is
not mine," he replied, "but I know to whom it belongs,
and I will buy it for your Hall, but not the whole piece;
the frontage piece is too expensive, but I will give you
about thirty feet for an entrance."   Soon after there came a
cheque for 500*l.* from Lord Bristol, with which I bought
the land.   It was afterwards found necessary to buy the
frontage piece also, as well as the playground.   Lord
Bristol has been a most liberal patron to the Hall.   Besides
various other gifts, he gave the body of St. Mark's Church,
where many of you go on Sunday; when I am dead you
will probably all go there, but the Trustees, out of a kind
consideration for me, arranged that the first and second
classes should attend St. Mary's Chapel during my lifetime. . . .

The funds of St. Mary's Hall were not, however, at that time
sufficient to allow of our having a good architect; but let
us mark how Providence provided for that want.   One day,
whilst travelling outside the *Age* coach, a gentleman took
his seat beside me, whom I recognised to be Mr. Basevi,
whom I had met at Athens some years before, and whom I
had not seen since.   In the conversation which ensued
between us, I mentioned the project which was ever upper-
most in my mind, and he said, "I am not rich, but I will
do what I can; I will be your architect for nothing."   Accordingly he drew the most beautiful plans, worth about
500*l.* in all, which are now in the Trustees' room.

I then selected eight Trustees, men whom I believed to be
of firm Christian principles and blameless conduct; and it
is a remarkable fact that out of those eight, only one has
died during twenty-two years.   That one was the Rev. H.
Blunt, then a curate at Chelsea.   One day he sent me a
cheque for 50*l.*; I quarrelled with him about it, thinking it
too large; but the answer he returned me was, "I have

only given you out of what the Lord commands the ravens
to bring me." . . .

Many pupils, who have left us, have reached a high standard; and I am thankful to say that those who have
disappointed me have been the exceptions and not the
rule.

I have almost invariably found that my first class has been
my best class. Let me find it so still. You, now before
me, are a new first class, and have influence in the school-
room. Keep up the tone of your class, and endeavour to
use your influence aright. Think in the morning, " What
good can I do to such a person with whom I shall come in
contact to-day?" And in the evening, " What good have
I done to-day?"

All of you choose your companions from amongst those who
fear God. We know that all are not good here; the tares
must grow with the wheat; but you may be careful with
whom you associate yourselves. I wonder whether any of
those who have lately come to us have ever thought,
" Does the companion I have chosen fear God?"

Have true unity. Humility and love are necessary to produce it. Pray for me. St. Paul asks the prayers of his
youngest converts, and I will ask yours. Pray for your
superintendent: pray for the governesses. Remember that
without the blessing of God on their teaching it is labour
in vain; you learn music in vain; you learn drawing in
vain; you learn arithmetic in vain; you learn everything
in vain, if God is not with you, to bless both those who
teach and those who learn. . . .

Let none who are in authority be discouraged if trials come,
and you find your pupils do not improve and advance as
you wish. Do always your best, earnestly and prayerfully, and leave the rest with God, assured that He will
prosper you in the earth, if you only put your trust in
Him.

September.—On the 12th of this month he paid a curious
and interesting visit to Bournemouth.

" My call," he says, " was an urgent and a touching one.
An old lady of eighty-six, Lady Charlotte Hamilton, one
of the very earliest members of my congregation thirty
years ago, wrote to me to say, ' You must come and see me
before I die.' She was not ill; but she had a great desire

to see me. So I went; and never was a clergyman more
welcomed or more earnestly employed. Every day, in the
morning, I had to go to her bedroom before she was up, to
read and pray with her. Mrs. Denison, widow of the late
Bishop of Salisbury, and the Bishop's daughter by a former
marriage, were with her. It was strange to have my
ministrations so valued by one who was not sick, but only
very advanced in years."

October.—During this autumn he was much gratified by
the resolution of his Scripture Reader (Mr. Norton) to offer
himself as a missionary. The St. Mary's prayer-meetings
during the Indian Mutiny had awakened in him an inex-
tinguishable missionary zeal, which thus bore fruit. He
went out to South Africa under the auspices of the Society
for the Propagation of the Gospel, and still labours in the
Diocese of Grahamstown.

December.—The erection of a new and capital organ in
his chapel at this time, led to a great improvement in the
singing.

He was again alone; but good reports from his children
helped to surround him " with social and loving thoughts in
his solitude at this season." His Christmas morning congregation and Holy Communion were very large; but in the
evening very small. "But that," he says, "was not my
business, and the paucity was no disappointment. I preach
to whom the Lord sends me. "

1860.

February.—His health was very good this year, and his
labours consequently more abundant. "I preached three
times on Sunday" he says, "so that I did not get home the
whole day till ten o'clock at night, and yet I was not
overdone."

The Anniversary of the Jews' Society, to which he was the
local Secretary, was held early in the year. "It is good to
be reminded by these anniversaries," he says, "that our
hearts' desire and prayer to God for Israel's salvation should
not cease."

He was now also requested to preach two of the Oxford
Lenten Sermons.

April.—"The times are very uneasy," he tells his son in

India. " Government looks on war as impending with France; and then there is this Reform Bill! Lord Palmerston (they tell me) voted against it in the Cabinet, but was out-voted by Gladstone, Sidney Herbert, and Newcastle—the three Peelites. Meanwhile, ' God reigneth, be the earth never so unquiet.' I used to say that in the Indian Mutiny, and I say it now. Have you seen Munro's Life, or the Life of the late Bishop of Calcutta, Daniel Wilson? Bishop Wilson's has been read with intense interest by the religious public here. I preached on Sunday evening from the ' Burning of the Ephesian books to the value of 2,000*l*.' (Acts xix. 19.) If all the books which serve the cause of the Evil One in Brighton were to be laid on a similar bonfire in the market-place before the Town Hall, I fancy the flames would make a noble blaze! And I fancy there would also be some books thrown in, which their owners would be astonished to see so illuminated! "

May.—He was appointed this year to preach the annual sermon at St. Bride's, before the Church Missionary Society. He accepted the duty with many fears, but at the time of delivery was calm and self-possessed. The Archbishop of Canterbury and his chaplain, Dean Goode, Dr. Miller, Hoare, Auriol, C. Bridges, and five hundred more clergy, besides the laity, were present as usual. The Church was crowded and the collection large. He had long before selected a wide subject—" I, if I be lifted up, will draw all men unto me." But the time drew on, and he was not ready. On the Friday before, pressed by engagements, and hurried as usual, his sermon was not half done. He was obliged to throw the manuscript aside, and select and re-write one which he had preached before, on " The things which happened unto me have fallen out rather unto the furtherance of the Gospel." (Phil. i. 12.) The Indian Mutiny lent him some of the most effective passages. The sermon was printed as usual in the Society's report, and met generally with great acceptance; whilst the relief to his own mind, when it was over, was very great.

" It was an awful sight from the pulpit," he said afterwards, " when I ascended it. I have not recovered from the intense emotions of the sermon and yesterday's glorious meeting. The Report read there came like the tidings of another world, indicating that the time is hastening when the kingdoms of the world shall become the kingdoms of God's dear Son, and that peace on earth and glory in the highest is not an obsolete story."

But he was most struck with Sir Herbert Edwardes' speech, and sent an account of it to India, as follows :—

It was the most heart-stirring oration I ever heard; not so much from its intrinsic eloquence, though there was much of that, as from the electric sympathy of the minds of the four thousand who heard it, with his mind, and who, knowing him to be one of the bravest of the brave, were full of admiration of the hero who, after the perils of Peshawur and the Mutiny, was no less brave as the soldier of Christ, casting to the wind all ideas of pleasing men, or saying what was politic for himself, and thinking only of the "King of kings and Lord of lords." No one who was there will ever forget it. I had officially a ticket for a front seat on the platform, but being five minutes late through a slow cab, I lost my front seat, and could only get half a seat, which was kindly ceded to me. But it was a thrilling spectacle to see five or six hundred clergy and laity on the platform, losing the equilibrium of their gravity and dignity, and tumultuously rising up to cheer with hands, and feet, and voice; and when the cheer pealed itself out, reviving it till it rang again through the vast assembly up to its topmost pitch, and was only restrained from another reiteration by the hand of Edwardes, raised so as to intimate, "Hear me further." The two thousand ladies caught the enthusiasm. Their sex could not keep it down; and they, forgetting etiquette, stood on their feet, and numbers of them waved their handkerchiefs. Sir John Lawrence also, who came late, but got to a front seat by some one vacating it for him, took part in the tumult, but with a difference, by the heavy knock of his stick on the floor. The grandeur of the scene was far beyond admiration of eloquence as eloquence. It was the depth of the feeling, and its unanimity, rejoicing with exceeding joy that a great man had risen up amongst us, as a true exponent of its character and intensity. People shook hands and congratulated one another that they had heard it. Nobody thought much about what they did or said, but did or said what their excitement forced them to do or say. I spied, after a while, a front seat vacant by Sir H. Edwardes, and thinking it better than the uneasy half-seat I had so long occupied two rows behind, and having a right to it, I passed to it by the side of the chairman (Lord Chichester); and when I found myself by the man of men, I made bold to introduce myself to him, apologizing for the liberty by mentioning that I had lost the introduction at Lord Shaftesbury's table. I hope I shall know him better some day.

December.—He was called at this time to attend the last hours of Lord Aberdeen. He went in November, and again this month. His visit proved a great benefit to the dying nobleman. " Bring him again," he said, after the first visit. " The last was paid only five days before he ceased to be conscious. On both occasions he was much affected, and so was Mr. Elliott.

" Seeing before me," as he says, " in the house in Argyle Street, the ex-Prime Minister reduced to the weakness of an infant, understanding all I said, but unable to express himself articulately, I drew near to him, first spoke of Lord Haddo, and then took the Scriptures, selected a passage which spoke of Christ and His cross as our safety and our glory, and then prayed with him. I spoke to him, as I had often done before, of the salvation, so free, so glorious, of Christ the Mediator, who had said, ' Him that cometh unto me, I will in no wise cast out.' But ' sic transit gloria mundi.' Thus the scene spoke to me. Power and honour, and all the past, were now nothing to the dying Minister. The one question was of safety in Christ. When the hour comes to us, may we be safe in Him !"

Christmas.—" Yesterday," he writes to India, " we had our Christmas dinner, with loving remembrances of one so far away, in the midst of the heathen, who know not of the day in its true meaning, in its joy and glory as the angels knew it. The mystery of godliness contains four points :

" 1. A God incarnate.

" 2. That Lord and Saviour, that God incarnate, crucified.

" 3. The innocent afflicted, suffering, put to death, as a malefactor.

" 4. The guilty forgiven.

" These are its mysteries, and they are great. Great is the mystery of godliness."

1861.

January.—Towards the latter end of the year 1860, Lord Haddo had again been advised to try a winter in Egypt, and again much of the care and responsibility of his children, necessarily left behind, fell upon Mr. Elliott. "I do not shrink from it," he says; "and if it is any comfort to you that I should act for them, as I would for my own children, that is part of my reward. The higher part I seek from Him who blesses, as we cannot bless."

February.—He continued his Warburtonian Lectures. He had now reached the eighth, and the chapel in Lincoln's Inn had a full congregation of lawyers and proctors. He preached on Malachi's celebrated prophecy of Christ's Advent, "The Lord, whom ye seek, shall suddenly come to His temple." He refers to Bishop Horsley's four celebrated Sermons on the subject, and says that when the text is fully and carefully looked into, the prophecy comes out with curious accuracy and momentous truth :—

If it was *His* temple, then Jesus Christ was one with the Father, God as well as man. For the Temple, both the first and second, was called by the Jews, not Solomon's, nor Zerubbabel's, nor Herod's Temple, but always and in the Scriptures, Jehovah's Temple. Horsley with his Hebrew learning demonstrates this, and shows that the word " Lord," translated from the Septuagint κύριος, should be "Jehovah," the incommunicable name of God, given to the Messias in various prophecies of the Old Testament.

Whilst in London he called upon his friend, the late Sir James Wigram, who had but just rallied from an apoplectic seizure. He found him not much altered from his usual very pleasant style of conversation and kindness. He mentions that Sir James, very touchingly, said—" that as the stroke came upon him without an hour's notice, the next would probably come in the same way, and prove fatal; that he considered he was riding at single anchor, ready to slip his cable at an hour's notice." " Well," he said, " Sir James, I trust you are prepared, even if it should be so. You know it is a covenant ordered in all things and sure; and if in *all* things, then in the manner of our departure." The conversation then became deeply interesting and important, and entered upon the ground of the Christian's hope, and that " love of the brethren " which was one Scriptural test of its vitality and trustworthiness, " We know that we have passed from death unto life, because we love the brethren." He urged his hearer to grasp that promise.

Just then the Vice-Chancellor, Sir R. T. Kindersley, came in and exchanged greetings with Mr. Elliott, saying, " Though we have never met since our undergraduateship, I have frequently seen and heard you preach at Brighton." It may be remembered that they had been together at Trinity College, had attended the same lectures, and passed the same examinations.

March.—An attack of influenza this month brought on a fresh attack of deafness, which happily proved but temporary :—

"I trust," he says, " the deafness may pass away with the cold ; for as it is, if it became permanent, it would make a sad alteration in my state. It would shut up wide doors of usefulness, and the great joy and pleasantness of social intercourse. But in a temporary disability and infirmity of this kind, the test is presented—can I say of sight, of hearing, and of health, ' the Lord gave and the Lord hath taken away ; blessed be the name of the Lord ?'

" Sir Charles Locock told me, a month ago, that he went all the way to Berlin to be operated upon by the insertion of a tube in the ear, by a Prussian aurist. He refused in the morning an invitation to dine with the Ambassador, because, as a deaf man, he shrunk from society ; but having thoroughly and instantaneously recovered his hearing by the operation, he wrote to retract his refusal, and to the satisfaction of all the company, and most of all to his own, he sat down with the guests in high spirits, and enjoyed the dinner. Bishop Berkeley found out that the eye had no sense of comparative distance, the idea of distance being gathered by other senses, hearing being the chief, and by experience. So that a man blind from his birth, and suddenly cured by an operation, had no idea whether what he saw was within his reach, or a hundred yards off."

April.—He had this month recovered ; and as if he had not enough to occupy his time before, he says, " Julius has gone back to Cambridge. I read with him during the Easter vacation the Second Book of Herodotus ! "

May.—Of a friend who had become unsettled by the perusal of " Essays and Reviews," he writes:—" It is inexplicable to me how he can be so easily unsettled : for the ' Essays and Reviews,' though they may put difficulties in the way of the unwary and ignorant, yet are not formidable to one who has studied divinity. God knows, and God can help."

Of the musical performance at St. Mary's Hall this spring he says, " All was life and spirit to the end. Nothing was dull. M—— C—— was as calm and as cool as a little deep lake or ' tarn ; ' and has greatly improved."

In supplying the governesses for St. Mary's Hall, his time was greatly occupied, and his courtesy much tried. It was curiously tested once by his eldest daughter, then a merry-hearted girl, untouched and unsubdued by sickness. One dark winter afternoon she feigned to be a governess applying for a vacancy in the Hall, and disguised herself accordingly. She was shown into the dining-room, and in due time Mr. Elliott appeared. He was so polite, so kind, and so considerate in his inquiries, that for a time she thought she was discovered, and that he was only carrying on the play to please her. He shortly, however, left the room to seek his daughter, and ask her to come down and form a judgment herself of the young candidate ; but not finding her, he brought a visitor who happened to be present, and was much attached to the daughter of the house. But to the young applicant, the distant manner and formal questions showed that no inkling of the truth had been discovered : and at length, when courteously conducted into the hall, and the door closed upon her by her father, she was left standing on the door-step in the bitter wintry wind, full conviction was produced, that the courtesy and kindness had indeed been intended for the poor governess, though bestowed in reality on the disguised daughter.

June.—Various troubles arose this month of a minor kind, which he thus describes :—

I cannot join you at Ventnor till the twelve schools have had their lectures from me, and St. Mary's Hall has been put under its annual process, which leases describe as " painting, papering, cleansing, scouring, washing, whitewashing, &c. &c." But just now, in consequence of the death of Mr. Copp, the most faithful of clerks ; the resignation of

Mr. S——, my excellent curate; and the retirement of the superintendent of St. Mary's Hall, I have three difficult posts to fill at once, and meanwhile double work to do; for the three services of St. Mary's Chapel have now to be provided for, and the last three Sundays I have been obliged to preach three times, besides two sacramental services.

July.—He sends to his daughters an account of various matters of detail, and amongst them of the consecration of Bishop Gell to Madras, on St. Peter's Day, in the chapel at Lambeth:—

"I enjoyed it exceedingly," he says; "there was no intoning or choral service in the Archbishop's chapel, but it was quite full, with about three hundred devout worshippers, who gave the responses as I never heard them given except at St. Bride's, when I had to preach the Church Missionary sermon. The service was very well read. The Bishop of London, the Bishops of Durham (Villiers), of Carlisle (Waldegrave), of Chester (Graham), read their parts, all of them impressively and devoutly. Nicholson gave us an excellent sermon on 'Finally, brethren, pray for us;' but none the worse because it was short—not half an hour. The dear old Archbishop (Sumner) was not the less impressive because he alone was rather indistinct, and so reminded us of his recent stroke, and our frail tenure of such a head of the Church of England. The communicants were the great mass of the adults. The Bishop consecrated, went through his part very reverently and firmly, yet quietly and modestly. His family were all there: father, mother, brother (to whom there is a letter in Arnold's Life), and two sisters. How holy was the whole service, and how appropriate to St. Peter's Day! 'Feed my lambs,' 'feed my sheep.' I thought of my precious children on the same day receiving the Holy Communion. Never did I spend such a St. Peter's Day. After the ceremony, those who were invited went into the Archbishop's receiving-room for chocolate, sandwiches, and wine; and then I got a little talk, which was very pleasant, with the Archbishop, and with the Bishop of Durham, who spoke to me freely about his appointment of Mr. Cheese, and the storm which so unjustly fell upon him. I stayed a little after the rest to get a few more words with the dear Archbishop, who told me how suddenly his stroke had come upon him, the day after his going to the Church Missionary sermon, when he felt quite well. He also told me that Bishop Villiers, under the storm, had wished to give up his bishopric, but that Lord Clarendon (his brother) would not let him. I got back to Brighton at half-past seven. On Monday I was due at the Hall; but at four o'clock a telegraphic message carried me off to town on painful business, and I only returned last night."

August.—He had much of what he thus calls "painful business" this summer. It was not his own business; but almost every one who was in trouble, and was justified in doing so, sought to him for help and deliverance. A sense of repose and confidence followed the putting of anything into Mr. Elliott's hands. One of his sisters (Mrs. Babington) testifies that he was always the one they turned to in their troubles. Once in order to persuade him to interpose, she used the expression, "It is an emergency;" and often afterwards when appealed to, he would say playfully, "Well, dear, is it an emergency? These emergencies do come so very often!" If a case of conscience was in question, he must give an opinion; if a grievance existed, he must obtain redress; if a memorial was wanted, he must draw it up. He had also, of course, much secular business of his own to attend to; for his property was considerable, and not placed in what Lord Stowell used to call "the happy certainty of the Three per Cents." He had the portion, and perhaps more than the portion, of an "elder son." This was chiefly in houses, lands, and mortgages; but his whole income as derived therefrom was devoted to family expenses and charitable objects. He saved nothing. It may serve as an answer to all "evil surmisings" to say, that the fortune he left his children at his death was, as nearly as possible, of the same amount as that with which he had started in life. His own personal expenditure was trifling enough, for he had no expensive tastes. Early in life he had been fond of coins and medals, classical curiosities, and rare editions of books; but not then to any excess. His household was ordered like any other clergyman's in his position. He had his one-horse brougham, and that was kept rather for his family than for himself; and nothing more of externals. The truth is, that he took no thought for money, though he kept accounts, and especially Church accounts, most conscientiously. He abhorred waste, and held himself responsible to God for all. His charities were very extensive—far more extensive than was supposed, because he refused to let his right hand know what the left was doing.

A medical man in Brighton broke down from overwork. He sent him a cheque for 20*l.* to pay for flies whilst visiting the poor. Secrecy was enjoined at the time; and the matter was not known till after his death.

An author sojourning in Brighton for a time was straitened for means, and yet unwilling to receive pecuniary relief. Bank-notes which could not be returned, and told no tales, were sent to him anonymously from time to time.

The daughter of a clergyman had married foolishly and fallen into poverty. Her husband was indolent, and she herself improvident. Persuaded after a time that the constant money relief he had allowed her did harm, the stream was stayed. She called to importune him; and though steadfast in refusing money, he gave an order on his butcher.

He valued the principles of self-denial; and when he learned that ten guineas a year would educate two Irish girls, through the medium of the Ladies' Hibernian Society, he gave up being a member of the Athenæum, and devoted the ten guineas thus saved to this purpose.

A missionary's wife, delicate in feeling and in health, returned home with her children. He sent a 20*l.* cheque *for the children.*

Moved by the kindest motives towards a clergyman not in affluent circumstances, he offered to take upon himself the entire cost of sending a daughter of the family for a twelvemonth to one of the best schools in Brighton: and when this proposal, for certain valid reasons, was declined, he then promised 100*l.* towards the general education of all the children; and the second 50*l.* was paid after his death.

A relative died, upon whom he held a bond for 1,000*l.* He cancelled it, because he would not press upon the children.

A poor factory girl, during the distress amongst the Lancashire operatives (for the relief of which, as well as for the Irish famine, Mr. Elliott had made great and most successful exertions), came to Brighton to seek employment. She was in much temptation. Mr. Elliott heard of her, took her into his own home, had her taught the duties of a housemaid, instructed and baptized her, and at about the end of a year found her a good situation.

Not content with his avowed subscriptions to all public associations, and with his numberless private gifts of various kinds to St. Mary's Hall and its inmates, he gave much in secret. For many years one "Less than the least" subscribed 100*l.* per annum to the Church Missionary Society, and it was by pure accident that the banker's book, compared with the subscription-list, revealed the donor to be Mr. Elliott. In the same way, a donation of 300*l.* to St. Mary's Hall appeared to come from " A clergyman," that clergyman being himself.

" You must be laying by a good deal," a relative said to him one day. " I am laying by nothing," was the reply; and it was true.

" Your master is very rich, is he not ? " said an inquirer to one of his servants. " He had need to be," was the quick response, " from the quantity he gives away."

Property belonging to his children, or legacies bequeathed to them, he carefully invested in their names, receiving and handing over to them personally the resulting dividends.

One striking proof of his disinterestedness occurred at a somewhat later period. A Miss Bayley, who had been a member of his congregation, died at Guildford, on April 26th, 1862, and was interred by him in Hove churchyard. In her last will, after certain legacies, she directed that Mr. Elliott's four children should be her residuary legatees. This was entirely unknown to him. The will was dated June 23, 1852, when she was in Brighton, and nothing of the kind appeared on the face of it. But when the lawyers had done their part she sent for the will, and inserted this provision in her own handwriting, and had it legally attested. It was avowedly intended as a small token of gratitude for his unwearied kindness, and was accompanied by a legacy of 5,000*l.* to St. Mary's Hall. At the funeral, Mr. Elliott was casually informed by one of the executors that the deceased had intended, before her death, to reduce the legacy to St. Mary's Hall to 1,000*l.*, and to divide the 4,000*l.* thus left disposable, amongst a brother's children. The mention of this was quite enough for Mr. Elliott. He disapproved of clergymen receiving legacies for spiritual ministrations. Had he known of it, he would have objected at the time; and now he advised his children, so far as they were able, to carry out voluntarily the reported intentions of the testatrix. They were as willing as he was. In due course, therefore, when the exact amount had been ascertained and become disposable, 7,150*l.* was handed over by the executors to Mr. Elliott himself, as his children's representative. The very next day 5,000*l.* of this amount was transferred to Mrs. Bayley's brother, for his children; then the whole of the personalty (the law allowed no more), amounting to 1145*l.* 19*s.* 5*d.*, was assigned to St. Mary's Hall; and finally, Mr. Elliott, thinking that some deference was due to the wishes of the deceased, advised his children to receive 250*l.* each, or 1,000*l.* on the whole, which was accordingly done.

These are but specimens cropping out on the surface, and showing the rich vein of Christian charity and disinterestedness which lay beneath. Accident, or the grateful feeling of recipients, or the law, brought them to light. They serve to mark the general tenor of Mr. Elliott's life, and put to silence those who may have thought they saw in him some trace of the " love of money." The details given in the last case are long, but necessary; for the story, as now correctly given, was much distorted at the time, and the character of God's minister is precious to the Church.

With regard to the " painful business" which introduced this episode, he says :—

I concluded it with a success I did not venture to anticipate, and which I can only regard as a signal answer to prayer. I have received unbounded thanks from the four persons concerned, and I think they all ascribe it to God's most merciful overruling of circumstances. " He teacheth my hands to war and my fingers to fight," said David; and I daresay, when he said so, he thought of the smooth stones chosen out of the brook, and the well-balanced sling which carried as sure as a rifle, and with a force as deadly. What a strong arm and accurate eye were given to the stripling to make the stone strike the unguarded forehead, and actually sink into it, piercing the skull where it is the strongest!

December.—The death of the Prince Consort, on the 14th of this month, deeply affected him :—

" Heavy, heavy," he says, " were the tidings this day! I got the news as I was on my way to the church, and in consequence prefixed some remarks to my sermon. Many tears were shed, and some could not stay, but left the church from emotion. May the 'everlasting arms' be under our poor Queen—a widow in a palace!

"*December 21st.*—We shall have service on Monday, because of the funeral, and I must see to have pulpit and Communion-table hung in black for him whose decease has darkened the palace and the whole land.

"*Christmas.*—I think, of all the texts on Christmas Day, I would preach by preference from the angels' song. The division for the minister to handle, and the people to receive, is made by the text itself—

> 1. 'Glory to God in the highest.'
> 2. 'On earth peace; goodwill to man.'

But I do not take it to-day; my preparation was too hurried. It is very delightful to have Christmas love, even without Christmas joy. This is not a time of joy.

"Next week," he tells his daughters, now at Ventnor, "I go to William Henry Elliott's, at Lancaster Gate, Hyde Park, to meet Sir Herbert Edwardes, and a large gathering of friends; and then, in January, I propose to come to you.

"*Last Day of the Year.*—Time goes and goes! The forelock on his bald head I clutch, but often miss. The close of the year has its mournful memories, and its happy and unmerited mercies; its accusations many and great; its whispers of forgiveness melting the heart; some good done (to God be all the glory); much left undone that might have been done; but no year ever closed on me since I began to think aright, without shadow, and sadness, and shame brooding over my heart. Yet God has not discarded me. The district has been pretty well worked; several clear cases of conversion have occurred; I have had strength and animation given me for my increased duties and sermons; and last Sunday I again preached three times. Public affairs close with dark lowering clouds. The Prince Consort is the greatest public loss we have had since Sir R. Peel's death. The American war trembles in the balance. But 'the Lord reigneth!'"

1862.

January.—His visit to Ventnor was postponed by an event which, as recorded by his own pen, shows the tenderness of his spirit. A valued friend was suddenly taken to her rest, following her husband, and leaving eight children desolate! Everything fell on the eldest daughter :—

"I have always loved her," he says, "but this morning I admired her. She was so calm and collected; the little ones clinging and nestling to her, and she rising to her new responsibility as the head of the family. As I think little children should not be presented with gloomy views of death, I enlarged to the little ones on the felicity of the change, and the hope of an everlasting and glorious re-union. The bright face of their mother-sister made response to what I said, although her tears would mingle with that response. I told the little dears that 'sorrowful yet always rejoicing,' was no fiction and no impossibility. Now, my beloved daughters," he continues, " will see that if to visit 'the widow and the fatherless in their affliction' is a part of pure and undefiled religion—and in my case a claim also of official duty—it would be a very scanty performance of either of these responsibilities if I did not remain and see them daily till after the funeral. To visit the widow and the fatherless, when the widow too is taken away, and the fatherless are also motherless, and the eldest of the double orphans is only nineteen, seems a concentration of duty. So do not expect me, darlings, till next week.

"I reserve till then any detailed account of my Warburtonian Lecture, and of the quiet dinner at W. H. Elliott's, at which I met, and sat next to, and had a deal of talk with Sir Herbert Edwardes. 'We took to one another,' as they say. I wrote the lecture from beginning to end on Saturday, and preached it on a very dark morning in Lincoln's Inn, and with the disadvantage of my eyes close to the manuscript.

" To Him who sheltereth His own under His wings I commend you."

The "quiet dinner" at his nephew's, above referred to, was followed by a large and influential assemblage of Christian friends, to bid farewell, in the name of the Church Missionary Society, to Sir Herbert Edwardes, then on the eve of his return to India. The Hon. Secretary to the Society read a beautiful address, and Sir Herbert returned a most eloquent and touching answer. Mr. Elliott was wont to speak of it as a day much to be remembered.

February.—The measles broke out in the Hall, and he made daily journeys there, taking up the doctor on his way :—

"From the Hall," he says, "I have uniformly gone to your uncle Edward. who has been really very ill, but is now, I believe, slowly approaching to convalescence. He delights in my little visits, and they seem to be a comfort to the whole family.

"This envelope brings something to you very exquisite in Tennyson's verses on the death of the Prince Consort. He touches the chords with the hand of a master; but it is a pity that some of the verses want an Œdipus. Simplicity is a great charm both in poetry and prose, and the last part is beautifully simple. I heard in London, from what I deem good authority, that the Queen, at the first Cabinet, nerved herself to meet her Ministers with all calmness, despatched the papers, the signatures, the business, and then, when the whole official duty was over, bowed her head on the table and burst into tears and sobs. What prayer has been offered for her and for all the royal house!

"Yesterday I devoted a long morning to get my private affairs (which had become intricate, and required my solicitors' legal acumen to disentangle) put into a right position. I am happy to say we succeeded so far as we went; and some things, which, if I had been suddenly taken away, would have been a Cretan labyrinth to my successors, have got a *clew.* By the way, 'clew' comes from 'clavis,' a key; 'clew' was the old and proper way of spelling it; so I cling to it, and repudiate 'clue,' which obliterates the etymology. Tell E—— that I had not forgotten that she was to do the sacred monogram; there-fore a month ago, in calling for the Utrecht velvet patterns, I told them the monogram would not be wanted.

"We have got 43*l.* for the Jews' Society. Mr. Stern's foreign accent was against his being understood with ease in the pulpit, but on the platform his style is more familiar; and a more encouraging or picturesque appeal I never heard from the mouth of a Jew. He is a handsome man, with an extraordinary fluency of the English tongue. He had to give an account of his exploratory visit, first to the Jews of Arabia Felix in its capital, Saunah, where he was in extreme peril of life, and had to traverse the country absolutely barefoot; and secondly, in Abyssinia, near the Straits of Bab-el-mandel, where he discovered 250,000 Jews, all eager to hear the Gospel, and not indisposed to Christ."

March.—He met Sir John (now Lord) Lawrence and Lord Stratford de Redcliffe:—

"It is pleasant," he says, "to meet men of historic fame; the springs whom God uses to move the world, as he secretly ordains in His wise counsels. They may be the Cyruses of His purpose, or the Sennacheribs and Herods. I should have no ambition to see men of the latter class. The Emperor Napoleon!—I know not yet which class he belongs to. Upon Lord Stratford de Redcliffe devolved responsibility affecting the whole globe. That the Turkish Empire was not swallowed up by the Russian's greedy jaws was more owing to that nobleman than to any other man. To-day Captain and Mrs. P—— dined with me. What a different warfare did he describe when speaking of the Americans, whom he had recently left, and their strategy, as compared with the hand-to-hand and foot-to-foot struggle in the field and on the walls of Sebastopol!"

April.—I have again met that interesting man Lord Stratford de Redcliffe. He asked me to dine with him, and after dinner carried me to the back drawing-room away from the rest of the company, and let me into some of the secrets of the Crimean War, amongst which was this—that not being supported by the Ministry at home as he ought to have been, for three days he was in distressing anxiety, knowing that peace and war trembled in the balance which he held in his hands. At last, after a sleepless night, he arose early in the morning, and in his night-shirt, unable to resist the clear impulse which succeeded his agitation, wrote the note to Prince Menschikoff which decided the war."

April.—A warning voice spoke to Mr. Elliott this month—a warning voice against overwork. Would that he had listened to it!

"I got through Passion Week very well," he writes. "preaching ten sermons in eight days; I looked over six sets of Confirmation papers in the railway between Portsmouth and Brighton; wrote some urgent letters on my arrival;

and then posted off to the Sacramental Lecture which was going on. I sat it out; but it seems the hurry and the head-work brought on such a dizziness that when the lecture was over and the prayer prayed I could not stand. All things swam round me, and I was obliged to lie down flat on a form. I got home about 6 P.M., and went to bed. Yesterday I was better, and went up to St. Mary's Hall on urgent business; and to-day I am equal to perform the funeral service over a friend."

It is clear that no one should undertake more than he can properly accomplish. It is a fault, no doubt, on the right side, but a fault still. Mr. Elliott fell into it. He saw the error plainly enough, but failed in applying the remedy. No one ever sought counsel more readily or humbly than he did, even from juniors and inferiors. Amongst the many testimonials written by his brethren of the clergy, after his death, all depicting his character in the most glowing terms, there is scarcely one which does not describe some interview in which he sought to learn his own shortcomings, and what might to them seem defective in his pulpit or pastoral work, his temper or spirit, his walk or conversation, and that with an earnestness indicative of the deepest sincerity and truest humility. It was thus he once came to the writer of these lines, when resident at Brighton, and, seeking a private in-terview, asked for a candid and open opinion as to what faults in him had become apparent.

Considerably abashed at the inquiry, he was told, after some resistance and with much reluctance, that the only known fault was that he seemed always in a hurry, and vainly attempting to overtake his work; that he undertook too much; that, as a consequence, his people saw too little of him; that it would seem wise to do by others what the twelve hours of the day did not enable him to do himself; and that this would be but anticipating a time, which must come before long, when he would be called to lay down and others to take up.

To all this he seriously inclined his ear, and yielded his ready assent. But when details were entered upon, and the *practicability* of withdrawing somewhat from St. Mary's Hall, or of shifting upon others the management of some of the Societies, was suggested, it was declared to be "impossible." One thing would fail, and another would fall through, and a third could not be thought of! And at length the conviction was irresistible, that Mr. Elliott would certainly drive with loose reins even to the end; and so it came to pass. Would that all drove as well as he!

May.—The case of a young Jewish convert interested him much at this time, and subsequently he raised a subscription sufficient to educate and fit her for a governess. He refers to a party of eleven whom he gathered to bid her farewell. " I read," he says, " Acts iv., as suitable to the occasion. I trust that we had the Invisible Presence with us."

Ascension Day.—This morning, the glorious morning of the Ascension, he writes to his younger daughter, " I can only greet you, and tell you that I mean to preach on the 24th Psalm, which Lowth explains as a triumphal hymn, composed when the ark, containing the symbol of Christ's humanity, went up to Mount Zion. While it is in the ascent, a part of the chorus of Priests and Levites chants out verse 3. The full chorus replies in verses 4—6 inclusive. At verse 7 the ark comes to the Temple, and the attendant Priests, ministering and chanting, demand admission. From within is asked by another body of guardians, ' Who is this King of Glory?' The second clause of verse 8 answers.

" So Christ arises from Mount Olivet, with the clouds for his chariot. Angels join Him in His ascension. They find the gates of heaven barred against the race of Adam, and claim admittance. Angels within, astonished at the demand in the person of Man, ask, ' Who is this King?' Angels attendant answer, ' The Lord, strong and mighty.' Then angels within and angels without take up the song in full chorus (verse 9). The gates open, the triumphal procession enters, and through the long aisles of heaven the song echoes (as in verse 10). May the Lord give us clean hands and pure hearts, washed in the blood of the Lamb, that we may enter in on the great day, to be for ever with Him!"

June.—The reader will like to look at a missionary picture, such as follows:—

Yesterday I was to have preached twice (morning and evening), but Mr. Mason, a missionary for twenty-two years to the North Americans, came into my vestry, and, to do him honour, I asked him to take my place, which he did in the evening—the last time of his preaching in England. On Wednesday he is to dine with me, and to address our Juvenile Quarterly Meeting. On Saturday he sails for Hudson's Bay. He lost his wife early this year in England. He and his wife—the wife taking perhaps the stroke oar—have done a noble deed. They have translated the whole Bible into the Cree language. They have done it in the syllabic character, having for the language only four vowels and nine or ten consonants. A man learns to read it in a week. His wife laboured at it incessantly, and her prayer was, " O Lord, let me finish the translation of Thy Word." They had finished the New Testament before the Old. It is remarkable that she was just permitted before she died to finish Malachi. Then came the " Nunc Dimittis." These two have not lived in vain. Oh that, when we come to die, we may not have lived in vain !

Whitsuntide.—It would be worth your while to study my subject for Whitsunday morning—" the change made in the Apostles by the Day of Pentecost." Put down fairly the good traits of character and the bad ones, before the Resurrection; and which preponderate? I am afraid we must say that selfish eagerness for the highest place ; a defective love for one another ; self-confidence, and boastful protestations of inviolable devotion, which the first front of danger, and even the question of a maid-servant, put to flight, preponderate. But what a difference did the Pentecostal blessing make in these self-same men! His holy Inspiration will make the same difference in us, if we ask for it in penitential and faithful prayer.

Julius is this day demonstrating his manhood as a volunteer. As one of the Cambridge Corps, he is entering into certain bloodless lists of rivalry with certain London Corps.

July.—Dr. A. Roberts had left a legacy of one hundred pounds to St. Mary's Hall, contingent upon the death of his wife.

" I have just heard," says Mr. Elliott, " that it will be paid this week, free of legacy duty. So God takes care of that dear nursery of the daughters of His poor ministers !"

Bishop Gobat visited Brighton at this time and preached in St. Mary's Chapel for his Diocesan Fund.

" He is no polemic," Mr. Elliott says, " but of a sweet spirit, and true and simple evangelical faith and love. The collections amounted to above 70*l.*, with which the Bishop was well pleased, and so was I."

My sermon on St. Peter's Day, last month, turned on these points :—To-day is St. Peter's Day, celebrated at Rome with extraordinary external magnificence, all that can enchant the ear and the eye; especially with the wonderful illumination of St. Peter's dome—the finest illumination in the world.

We celebrate it in Protestant England with the recitation from the Scriptures of some of his great acts of faith, and the triumph of the Gospel by his means. What especially calls for attention is—

1. That St. Peter preached the first four sermons on behalf of Christianity. What was most remarkable in his sermons? They all began with " Repent ; " and all went on, the same day, to " Believe." Repentance first ; Faith and Remission of Sins next ; and then the gifts of the Spirit.

2. He did not rip up the general depravity of their lives, nor accuse them of the breach of the Commandments. He confined himself to one sin, in all the four discourses, which he charged home upon them—leaving out all others—" Ye have crucified the Lord of Glory." What is that to us? We, too, have crucified the Lord of Glory. Our sins were on Him on the Cross. He bore the iniquities of us all. He died for the sins of the whole world. Our guilt demanded that atonement. Get that view of sin at the foot of the Cross, and that is repentance. Pass on, and realize the fact that that blood was shed for us, and that is Faith ; and, involved in it, the Remission of Sins.

Send back, then, this Gospel to that land from whence it came. Send it by the Anglican Bishop to Jerusalem, whence it has spread, &c.

August.—I gave a half-year's parting lecture to one of my twelve schools this morning. Just opposite me was a young boy, sitting on a high stool, who thrice opened wide his little jaws, and gave a slow, deliberate yawn, evidently to his own satisfaction, though not to mine. I thought I was very impressive—rather unusually so ; till his little mandarin visage, by its profound insight into what was within his teeth and throat, compelled me to remember that God alone can prevent the best efforts of our speech from being as water spilt on the ground.

September.—He spent three hours this month with a friend in the Great Exhibition.

"It is decidedly superior to the last of 1851," he says, "and is a lofty monument to the greatness of England, the centre of the whole world in commerce and arts, round which revolve the other nations of the earth. I was struck with the greater decorum of the statues and pictures of this Exhibition as compared with those of the last. The Lord be praised!"

November.—Family details give interest to general narratives. Hence the following extracts from a letter written at the time to his son in India :—

Just now we have placed, as one of the most conspicuous ornaments of our drawing-room, your beautiful Delhi chessboard. I carried it to town myself, wrapped in a shawl, on my own lap, and deposited it in safe custody for carving and gilding a suitable pedestal for it. I have received also your book of legendary lore, and thank you for it. It reminded me of the mythological fictions of the gods and heroes of Greece and Rome. Your stories are told with a charming simplicity of style.[1]

Julius is now of age, and for the first time I asked him whether he had turned his mind to the choice of any future profession. He said that for two years he had earnestly desired to devote his future life to the ministry of the Gospel of Christ. I should not have dared to bias him; but it was a joy and delight to me to hear the choice he had made.

Christmas.—How grand and original was the idea of joy, *great joy to all people,* springing from the birth of the Babe of Bethlehem! And what an anniversary is that which is celebrated now throughout the world, if it were only celebrated in its true intention and blessing—" for unto you is born this day in the city of David a Saviour, which is Christ the Lord." God lengthens out most graciously my "twelve hours" of labour, but it is time to remember that "the night cometh when no man can work."

1863.

. In the beginning of this year he was still anxious about the

---

[1] 'Chronicles of Oonao'. By C. Alfred Elliott, Scholar of Trinity College, Cambridge.

health of his brother Edward. " This illness," he says, " so threatening, was the price paid for the fifth and last edition of the ' Horæ Apocalypticæ.' It is a work of immense research and the first of the kind. It is a work that will live."

March.—His own health also began to fail, and, in addition to the previous warnings, he fainted in church this month and was unable to perform his duty. " I must withdraw from some of the work," he says, " which I have hitherto, up to this time of life (71), gone through without distress."

The closing of St. Mary's for repairs for two months gave him some respite; yet it was not till after much suffering, terminating in an attack of jaundice, that he recovered tone and strength.

Whilst laid aside, he sends counsel to a friend who was leaning towards Dr. Colenso, which deserves to be well weighed :—

I gather that you rather open wide your doors to works of a sceptical, and, in my opinion, of a very unsound character; as, for example, Colenso's book, and Renan's ' Life of Jesus.' I have seen it remarked that a clever newspaper will materially change and mould a man's politics, if it be constantly read. And I have some fear lest some of your own religious opinions should run into a form of unbelief on various important subjects. We owe it to our own souls not to expose ourselves to the peril of what may lessen our reverence for God's Word, unless there be a necessity for it. And I observe with uneasiness that you seem to welcome the latitudinarian authors, and to turn a different countenance to those who are deemed orthodox. I do think we may do irreparable damage to our souls, unless we at all times approach Divine things in a spirit of candour and prayer for the light of God's Holy Spirit. But I pray to God to discipline your mind in His own holy school, giving you—what I constantly ask for myself—humility and contrition for our many wrong-doings; in short, that spirit in which the High and Holy One, who inhabiteth eternity, condescends to dwell. God bless you and keep you from all evil.

June.—In this month he began a prayer-meeting amongst his people for a more general effusion of the Holy Spirit on all his work and on all classes. He had held prayer-meetings on former occasions for the Lancashire distress, for India, &c.;

but " I ought to have begun this," he says, "thirty years ago; and now, when the evening shadows are falling, I begin."

August.—I had another night of pain, and have been good for little to-day. I am sure it is an easier path to glorify God in much activity than in much suffering; and if He appoints to us the more arduous path, shall we say that our life is useless, and, like Jonah or Elijah, be unwilling that it should be prolonged? " She hath done what she could " is no mean praise: and I am confident that many a sick-room, many a silent and unknown sufferer, will contribute largely to the praise of the ransomed ones; and though the praise be in the minor key, it will give the finest contrast, and the most thrilling harmony, as combined with the general anthem. God shall be admired in His suffering ones, and His hidden ones, whom He has allured into the wilderness to speak comfortably to them.

September.—He was much interested in Xavier's Life by the Rev. Henry Venn, the Hon. Secretary of the Church Missionary Society:—

" I am convinced," he says, " that the book is a death-blow to Xavier's exalted reputation. He was a great and a good man. But the Romish religion dwarfed all the proportions and symmetry of his natural magnanimity."

December.—I cannot but regret that a paper drawn up, and proposing a guinea subscription for a testimonial to the great merits of the late Archbishop Sumner, and circulated in merely the two dioceses of Chester and Canterbury, should not have met with a larger response. I send you some names. I used to make an annual visit of a few days at Addington Park, while the dear Archbishop was alive. It was always to me a great recreation; for he was so full of interest, and so kind to me, that I used to think a more truly humble man could not be found in the Church than the highest of its officers.

1864.

January.—Another year has been granted to me, after my illness last summer had brought before me the question, Is the Author of my life about to call me away, and to demand an account of my stewardship, that I may be no longer steward? May it bring to me and my children grace, mercy, and peace, through Jesus Christ our Lord.

. . . . The Bishop of London has been here for a week or so. He said the fifth volume of Colenso, just out, and which he was reading, only proved more strongly than the other volumes, the depth of his delusion. The controversy has now exhausted the patience of the public, and resulted in a very general condemnation of the Bishop and the authors of ' Essays and Reviews.'

February.—He glances at the Colonial Church, and at God's goodness in calling men so eminently qualified to take the oversight thereof, in spite of many discomforts and home-longings:—

" I met," he says " at my cousin Henry Venn's the other day, Perry, the Bishop of Melbourne, and his wife. Lord Chichester told me that no colonial bishop stood higher in the estimation of Government than Perry. He is a man of steady resolution and enlightened and holy principles. But Mrs. Perry says: ' Oh, how gladly would I give up the honours of my husband's episcopate, and take a small country living with him, if I consulted my own ease and comfort!' So thinks the lady of the Metropolitan of Sydney, Mrs. Barker; and so thinks Mrs. Thomas, the wife of the colonial Bishop of Goulburn, another and new episcopate bordering on the Sydney Diocese. The Bishop of Mauritius' lady, Mrs. Ryan, is just of the same mind. Yet I rejoiced, and take it as an augury of good for the propagation of Christ's blessed Gospel, that in the providence of God such excellent men have been sent out to be the fathers of new branches of our Church."

March.—This month he was saddened by the intelligence of the death of his former pupil, Lord Aberdeen :—better known in these pages as Lord Haddo. The sojourn in Egypt had been ineffectual for permanent recovery. He returned home, and after three years of gradual decline entered into his rest. As one endeared to him through life, Mr. Elliott was much affected. With the cognizance and grateful appreciation of his widowed lady, and as a tribute of personal affection, he wrote an obituary of the deceased nobleman, which appeared in the May number of the *Christian Observer.* Lady Aberdeen had requested him, and he had intended, to have enlarged this paper; but the end came, and the duty was performed subsequently by his brother.

Good Friday.—" Here we have," he says, " what seldom occurs —the Annunciation of the Blessed Virgin, and good Friday on the same day—a festival overshadowed by the fast, the promised life by the accomplished death. But they are really not incongruous. *Jesus* was to be the name of the Virgin's Son. He was to be great, and the Son of the Highest ; the throne of His ancestor David was to be His, and His kingdom was never to end. Philippians ii. gives the reconciliation and brings them together. In His humiliation to death, even the death of the cross, the foundations of His glorious and everlasting kingdom were laid strong and sure :—' I, if I be lifted up, will draw all men unto me.'   I think every Easter gathers more joy by the deaths of those who are summoned to Christ, and have light in the dark valley.   For was it not His pastoral crook that guided and comforted, His presence that illuminated the darkness and stilled the nervous terror? ' It is I ; be not afraid !' And the peaceful departure of those who have not occupied the first rank of the pilgrims to Zion, in one respect glorifies the care of the Good Shepherd more than that of the strongest and ripest for heaven.   For they are the witnesses that He has not forgotten His office, which pledged Him not to break the ' bruised reed ' nor quench the ' smoking flax,' but to bring even their trial to victory.   When our Passover comes, may we have confidence that there will be voices of hope and voices of welcome round the last scene ! "

April.—The question of the Annual Reports of the different Missionary Societies having been handled in the newspapers, and the decision pronounced *ex cathedrâ*, that " no one reads them," Mr. Elliott was led to consider the subject; and his remarks are well worthy of note :—

Whether it would be better, in Church Missionary Reports (in which there is very much to read, and very much to interest,) to curtail the mass of two hundred pages, and to omit much that is uninteresting, is a serious question.   If we consider merely the effect on the readers in England, the style's blunt end might be plentifully used ; but there are two hundred missionaries in India alone besides fifteen hundred catechists. No one of these European missionaries would like his work to be passed over in utter silence ; and if it were so consigned to oblivion, men of like passions with civilians in

India would miss the stimulus to exertion given by an annual mention of their labours; and if their employers held them not to be worth their notice, would perhaps shrink into the same opinion of themselves, and lose heart, and settle down into comparative idleness.   So that I give my vote in favour of Annual Reports.

May.—He refers incidentally to a curious instance of the force of imagination in a little child at St. Mary's Hall.   Some dissolving views with slides were being exhibited.   The figure of a Triton appeared—first without water flowing from his shell, and afterwards with silent streams flowing, gushing, falling so naturally, as to make their noiselessness a marvel. Mr. Elliott, who was present, said, "Now, dear children, hush! listen! Who hears the water fall?"   "I do," cried out one of the little ones; "I hear it."

June.—Visits to the sick, and the burial of the dead, were constant with him at that time.

"I have been this year," he says, "in death oft. One lady friend is in a dangerous state, nerves over-excited, unable to take anything, unfit to see any one but me.   By sympathy and prayer she was soothed somewhat, and said, 'God sent you to me to-day.'   The same afternoon I saw the Scripture Reader.   He is dying, but has no fear.   He counts on seeing me once a week.   So it is a comfort, if God makes me a comfort to any one.   Yesterday I attended the funeral in Hove churchyard of one who is now no more the harassed victim of disease, but with Him who is all truth, all light, all love.   Love, joy, and peace, set in the carved frame of tribulation, are as stars in a dark night."

Whitsunday.—"I have been preaching," he says, "upon the use we are to make of God's gifts in the Church.   It appears that we are to keep nothing to ourselves, but to impart largely and liberally to others.   This is our Whitsuntide lesson.   The gift of tongues, the original Pentecostal gift, was for that very purpose—to communicate far and wide the glad tidings of salvation.   I think St. Peter had this Pentecostal effusion in his mind when he wrote his Epistle, thirty years after.   It therefore may be regarded as his review of that wonderful day when three thousand souls were converted.   What judgment did he pass upon it after that long interval? Writing to the same class of persons as had received the original blessing, there is not in all the

Epistle one word about the 'gift of tongues,' nor of other 'miraculous gifts,' but much about fervent charity and unselfish large distributions."

His sister was ill, and he reports progress thus :—

" The doctor says your aunt has an uncommon disease, which she will carry to the grave, though, perhaps, it will not carry her there, viz., *enlargement of the heart.* Would that it were more infectious!

" The delight of receiving your letters " (from his daughter) "is great. But I entreat you not to write such costly epistles. The delight of receiving them has the pang of remembering what an expense of strength it was to the darling writer. If you had the pen of an angel, it ought to be an angel used to the speech of *Laconia.* I preached last Sunday on the 95th Psalm, and the distinction awarded it by the Church of always heading the Psalms for the day."

July.—A body and mind overtaxed, rendered some change absolutely necessary; and at the urgent request of his friends he set out on the 14th of this month to join his children, Blanche and Julius, at Lausanne. A fortnight's holiday, with a freedom from anxious thought and excessive business, sufficed to remove all unfavourable symptoms, and he returned at the end of July much recruited and strengthened for his work.

" We had a glorious passage," he writes, " over the Gemmi, and a fair familiarity with the clouds and the mist, sometimes below us, sometimes around us, or as usual, above us. If we lost the sunrise on the Righi we had at least a grand view of the Oberland Alps the evening before for half an hour, and the Lake of Lucerne (I should think without contradiction the most beautiful in the world) we saw in various moods, and to great perfection, during the five days we were there. It was worth all the journey to retrace in my memory all the impressions which forty-seven years ago were most vivid, but, as Locke says so beautifully of our ideas and of our knowledge, 'They still in their decay remind us of those tombs to which we are approaching, where, though the brass and marble remain, the imagery is effaced by time, and the inscriptions moulder away.' But, blessed be God, the memory of his loving-kindness and patient mercy, and the spectacle of that love unto death which draws all men to Him, knows not these obliterations—never dies—never decays."

From the Hôtel du Louvre, at Paris, he wrote to salute an old school friend, in words which tell of lengthening shadows and the sunset :—

July 29.

After a brief tour in Switzerland with two of my children, I am returning with them to Brighton; and bethinking myself that a Sunday spent at Rouen might give me the chance of seeing you and yours, I purpose to come by the afternoon's express train, and to put up at the hotel on the quay. On Monday morning we proceed to Dieppe, and hope to be at home in Brighton by the evening. But I should be thankful, if having begun early in life to seek the Lord together, we may have, now that we are old, the privilege to salute one another again in the name of the Lord before our pilgrimage ends, and to speak of His mercy and loving-kindness to each of us, to the glory of His great name. Let me have a line from you to-morrow on our arrival, if there is time.

August.—On his return to Brighton he plunged as usual into business, and especially into the business of St. Mary's Hall. Again, and for the last time, he looked over the examination papers, and admitted new pupils; again, and for the last time, he read the 127th Psalm. "I still suffered to remain," he says, with grateful wonder, "and so many taught by me gone! May I have a single eye to the glory of God, that for me to live may be Christ, and to die, gain!"

In the same letter he refers to Sir Peregrine Maitland, whose piety and decision he greatly admired :—

"Sir Peregrine," he adds, "ennobled himself, as worldly men say, at Waterloo; as *we* say, in Madras; where, rather than comply with the mandate of the Governor to order his men to do honour to the Hindoo festival Kalee, and to present arms and fire salutes for her idolatrous procession, he laid down his post of commander-in-chief, and resigned its salary of 10,000*l.* per annum. This Sir Peregrine I knew well, when he and Lady Sarah lived here. He is gone to that world in which the balances of the sanctuary are suspended, and 10,000*l.* a year does not outweigh the honour done to God by a conscientious refusal to worship idols or connive at it in others. The Governor of Madras, who issued the order,

I knew also pretty well; for I was his guest on board the *Fanny*, the Government yacht in the Ionian Isles, when returning from Greece to England, in the days of my youth."

October.—He printed a sermon which he had preached at Ickworth on the death of the second Marquis of Bristol, whom he had known as Lord Hervey in early life. The sermon is very striking, as containing something like a premonition of his own decease. He speaks of the conflict with the King of Terrors as a conflict which, a little sooner or a little later—" it may be very soon "—all will have to encounter. There were also peculiarities in this case which singularly resembled his own. Lord Bristol had to mourn the loss of a very dear wife and child. He had no fear of death before his eyes. He made a good confession of Christ. He was full of faith, patience, and resignation. Two favourite hymns comforted him. The prayers of the Church were preferred to all others. All these things found a curious and instructive counterpart, as will soon appear, in Mr. Elliott's own case. In describing them, and drawing from them a " sure and certain hope of everlasting life," he might be supposed to be preaching by anticipation his own funeral sermon. He asks Lord Arthur Hervey to send him some of the printed copies, for " many in Brighton would buy it as preached by their old minister, and, knowing your brother, would rejoice to find that he died in the Lord."

December.—He had two attacks of indisposition this month, but having rallied from them, he for the first time seemed to listen to the dictates of prudence. Being requested to give an address to the " penitents " in the late Rev. George Wagner's " Home," he declined, saying—

My first impulse was to accept your kind invitation; my subsequent reflection puts a stubborn and decisive veto on that first inclination. So please to make allowance for me and rest assured that when the pressure of this year's arrears is over, I shall be very glad to speak in your interesting house of mercy, as one who feels that he incessantly needs mercy.

1865.

Circumcision: January 1.—He preached twice at St. Mary's as usual, and administered Holy Communion on this day. His text in the morning was, "Occupy till I come;" and in the evening, "Grace be unto you, and peace."

> "Servant of God, well done!
>   Cease from thy loved employ :
> The battle fought, the victory won,
>   Enter thy Master's joy."

CHAPTER VIII.

LAST ILLNESS AND DEATH.

Sudden illness—Last visit to St. Mary's Hall—Epiphany of 1865—Flowers for his Coffin—Echo of his Words—Increasing illness—Fatal symptoms—Peaceful death—Funeral—Letters from Dr. Whewell and Rev. H. M. Wagner—Memorials—Tablet.

It is told of one of the Wesleys, or some other hard-working servant of God, that being asked by a friend what would be his course if warned that but one week of life remained, he took out his tablets covered with written engagements, and said, " I would fulfil all these."

What was thus proposed theoretically, Mr. Elliott performed practically. "He fulfilled all these." That which his hand found to do, he did it with his might. He worked while it was day. The night came :—and then God gave His beloved sleep.

The end was somewhat sudden, and must needs take the reader by surprise. It is true that there had been warnings ; but the vital energy continued unabated, and there was but little failure of the bodily powers. Throat and eyesight were weakened, and Mr. Elliott felt the pressure of over work. But his frame was well knit and firmly compacted together. He was still singularly active in his movements. He trod the Brighton pavements with almost the same quick and elastic tread as ever, returning, as always, with his kindly smile, the courteous salutations which greeted him from friends on every side. He mounted the stairs two or three at a bound, as had been his wont. The performance of his ministerial duties was as regular as ever. The portrait prefixed to this volume, enlarged from a photograph taken in his later life, shows a countenance marked indeed by time, but still full of intellect and vigour. He was in truth a fine representative, according to the grace given unto him, of an English clergyman and gentleman even to the end.

And now the end was come; and, thanks be to God, he ended well!

Let it be borne in mind, in considering his last illness and death, that three of his children were gathered round him; that his brother Edward and two of his sisters were resident in Brighton; and that his brother-in-law and friend of fifty years, whose kindness Mr. Elliott called "loving-kindness," was available for the supply of all Church duties. Surrounded thus, the inroads of sickness and the approach of death were attended with every possible alleviation and comfort.

On Tuesday evening, January 3, 1865, he paid a last visit to St. Mary's Hall. After some conversation on matters of business, he proposed commending everything to God in prayer for the year just opening All present knelt down with one accord in the general sitting-room—a room consecrated by many prayers: prayers for Confirmation candidates: prayers with pupils leaving school; prayers in time of trouble, perplexity, or deliverance. One of his concluding sentences was the following:—

We are commencing a new year, and know not, O Lord, what the issues of it may be; but we know that nothing can come amiss, if only it finds us safe in the covenant mercies of Christ Jesus.

Before leaving, he looked at a little present which had been selected as a gift from him to a former pupil who was about to sail for India; and then he spoke of his sister Kate, who had given him a similar present on his wedding-day, adding—

That sweet sainted sister said to us all on her dying bed, " I do not wish you to put on mourning for me; I should like you to dress in white. There is no need to mourn."

Accompanied to the front door, he left with his usual benediction, " The Lord be with you! " or " The Lord bless you!" and then the place that had so often seen him saw him no more. His last visit was an illustration of his constant aim in connexion with St. Mary's Hall—full of Love, Prayer, Blessing!

The Feast of the Epiphany dawned mild and beautiful, and conversation at the breakfast-table in Brunswick Square was long and animated. It was followed by Divine Service as usual in St. Mary's; by the last sermon Mr. Elliott ever preached, from 1 Tim. iii. 16, "Great is the mystery of godliness;" and by the last Holy Sacrament he ever administered. Almost immediately after service pain came on, and soon became so violent that he nearly fainted in the carriage which bore him home.

"Don't let Efie know," were his first words on entering the house.

In the evening he was better, and the next day was able to see Archdeacon Garbett, and to prepare for the press his annual abstract of the Church Missionary Society's Report.

On the Sunday he looked pale and worn, but spoke cheerfully, and inquired about the services and communicants. At night he looked at some flowers on the table in his daughter's room, and inquired the name. "Coronella! Little crown!" he repeated several times; and pondered on the words.

Some of these flowers were placed on his coffin!

The pain returning, he rose to leave, taking with him his interleaved copy of the book of the Prophet Isaiah. He had kissed his daughter and given her his blessing. But at the door he lingered, and turned, and very gently said, "God bless you, my love."

The words still echo in the room, and tell of "love!"

The next day he was worse. On the Tuesday, inflammation began; and then, probably, he realized for the first time the dangerous character of the illness, though he had before expressed an opinion that he should not recover. The pain became intense; but neither on that evening, nor on any other, did he fail to ask for the reading of the Second Lesson. It was now Romans viii.: "One of the most beautiful chapters," he said, "in the whole Bible." After it was finished, the opening words were repeated: "There is therefore now no condemnation to them which are in Christ Jesus." "Yes," he remarked, "but only to those who 'walk not after the flesh, but after the Spirit.'"

On Wednesday evening, favourable symptoms excited hope, and some flowers were given him. "I am past flowers now," was his remark.

Day after day passed on in great bodily distress. On Friday he asked for the Litany. "It is in illness," he said, as he had often said before, "that one learns the full value of the Liturgy."

When Mr. Babington paid him his daily visit on Sunday, and observed that the sick-room was sometimes a sanctuary where God's presence was even more vividly felt than in the house of prayer, he answered faintly: "Yes, sometimes; but not in paroxysms of pain. Then one can only pray for faith, patience, and resignation to what the Lord sends."

On that day he was prayed for in several churches in Brighton; and these prayers were followed by a mitigation of pain. On this being suggested to him, he fully assented, saying, "or else what would be the use of prayer?" He never once, from the beginning to the end of his illness, expressed the least wish with regard to the result. His word always was, "It is the Lord; let Him do what seemeth Him good."

He now began to set his house in order; and on being advised to delay a little in consequence of his extreme weakness, with an assurance that "these things do not press," he replied earnestly but calmly, "They do press; I know not what God may be preparing for me."

His mind was remarkably clear throughout, and he was able to take an interest in many minute details. He sent messages of love, and dictated letters to several dear friends. One of these letters was to the lately widowed Lady Aberdeen, and may be inserted here as the last which has been preserved. It is dated Jan. 16, 1865; and is, in part, as follows:—

I have been over-weighted all this autumn with extra demands upon my time and head, and I hope I may say in some degree, my heart; which took me down to Christmas week and the beginning of the new year, when we had a sort of Christian party with the Rev. J. Barton, a noble missionary of the Church Missionary Society, and the head of a Missionary College proposed to be founded at Calcutta.

On the Epiphany, Jan. 6th, I preached and administered the Holy Communion to those who sufficiently valued the festival to attend and be communicants. As soon as that was over, I hoped to begin your interesting packet, which reached me safely, but which I had not opened. But on Epiphany Day the hand of the Lord went out against me very heavily; though God forbid that I should complain of His sore correction! Why should a living man complain; a man for the punishment of his sins? If God recover me, I hope to revise your interesting manuscript, and to do what justice I can to it. If, on the other hand, it should please the Lord to remove an unworthy servant from a post of considerable importance in His vineyard, I ask your prayers, and the prayers of all my friends, that He would raise up a more holy, useful, self-denying pastor to St. Mary's flock and to St. Mary's Hall.

He sent his love to Mr. Maitland, his "dear aged Christian friend;" and to Lord Chichester, with thanks for his support in St. Mary's Hall, the Church Missionary Society, and every good work. It was wonderful that he could thus enter into details and despatch business, when the paroxysms of pain were terrible; and the intervals of ease were passed, for the most part, in troubled sleep. His kind medical attendant said that "it wrung his heart to witness such sufferings;" and he himself once said, "The Lord indeed has put me into the *furnace* of affliction." He would sometimes confess, "It was almost more than I could bear;" but generally he quieted himself with the oft-repeated words, "It is the Lord;" or with a prayer for "faith, patience, and resignation;" adding sometimes, "and self-control." More than once he desired the prayers of others, that his faith, patience, and resignation "might not swerve."

On one occasion, when he called for prayers, the question was asked, "What prayers?" "Always the Church prayers," was his reply. Again and again the service for the "Visitation of the Sick" was read, and he would join, saying Amen, not only at the close, but at each separate petition. "There is one little prayer in that service," he said, "I always like:—'O Saviour of the world, who by Thy Cross and precious Blood hast redeemed us, Save us, and help us, we humbly beseech Thee, O Lord.'"

Once, when the agony was intense, he asked eagerly for the text: "Fear not: for I have redeemed thee, I have called thee by thy name; thou art Mine. When thou passest through the waters, I will be with thee; and through the rivers, they shall not overflow thee: when thou walkest through the fire, thou shalt not be burned; neither shall the flame kindle upon thee." (Isa. xliii. 1, 2.)

It was thus his constant habit in severe pain to call for a text from God's most holy Word. It calmed the mind, and thus controlled the body. Occasionally he made a remark or two on what was read, but most frequently listened in silence.

One of the texts which seemed most to suit him was from Philippians i. 20, that "as always, so now also Christ shall be magnified in my body, whether it be by life or by death."

Sunday, January 21st, was an overpowering day. His irrepressible moaning was heart-rending; but no one thought how rapidly he was sinking. About this time he was trying with feeble hands to wind up his watch: "Ah!" he exclaimed, "man can wind up a watch, but he cannot wind up a life."

The three medical men in attendance still gave hope; and in the evening an operation was performed. It gave temporary, but only temporary relief. The illness assumed a still more serious aspect, and in the morning it was confessed that there was "no hope." The pain had ceased; but the end was near. Mr. Babington came in, and though prepared beforehand, he fairly broke down. The strong man sobbed like a child, exclaiming, "That love has been the love of my life."

He seemed sinking into insensibility, and prayer was made without ceasing that he might once more recognise and speak to his children. These prayers were heard and answered. He turned and recognised his sister Eleanor. "God bless you," he whispered. Then looking at his daughter Efie, he said, "My darling, kiss me: don't weep: don't grieve for me." His son Julius leant over him and said gently: "Dearest father, do you know that you may be with Jesus to-day?" He did not answer, and it was thought he had not heard; but in a few moments he slowly opened his eyes, and said, with a calm and joyful expression, "Is it so near? I did not think it would have been so soon!"

Almost immediately afterwards he said faintly, but distinctly, "I have some things to say to my children before I die. What a mercy it is that I am not afraid to die!"

He then spoke to his children about themselves and their friends, and sent texts to several of them. He signified his desire that, in choosing friends, they should fix on those who were decided for Christ, rather than on those who were naturally attractive. He sent his dear love and blessing to his eldest son in India. To his invalid sister, Charlotte, he sent a message, expressive of his undying affection. "Tell her," he said, "that I can never, never, requite her for all I owe her for her prayers." He sent other kindly messages, gave instructions concerning his burial, and made provision for those endeared to him by long and faithful service.

Presently he said, "One great fault of my ministry has been, not giving way when I felt my strength going:" adding, "I have to ask God's forgiveness for all my self-seeking, instead of seeking Christ only. I have been a most unprofitable servant." At another time he spoke of handing over St. Mary's to one less unworthy—adding, "Pray for me, that I may not perish at the last;" then, repeating, and dwelling on each word, "God so loved the world, that He gave His only begotten Son, that whosoever believeth in Him should not perish, but have everlasting life." (John iii. 16.)

Referring to his busy ministrations and their sudden ending: "Take notice," he said, "that after so long and active a ministry, the manner in which the Lord's termination of it came upon me was like a thunderbolt."

He then called Julius, and said, "The leading idea of my ministry has been the first revelation of Christ to his disciples, as 'the Lamb of God, which taketh away the sin of the world.'" (John i. 29.)

A little later he exclaimed, "Oh, the value of praying friends! I never before realized so fully that prayer of our Church, 'Suffer us not at our last hour for any pains of death to fall from Thee.' I lean only on Christ, the sure foundation. I should like," he added, "some of my sermons to be published, to show what doctrine I tried to teach." On being asked whether he referred to his University sermons, he said, "Yes, but not only those."

He expressed a wish to say farewell to his servants, and to thank them. When they were all assembled, and much overcome, he addressed them first collectively, and then gave to each his hand and his blessing separately, saying to one and another, "Live to Christ." "Live for Christ." "Follow Christ." "Work for Christ." "Give up all for Christ." "May you follow Christ here, and you will be happy eternally."

He then asked for the Litany, which was read. After the petition, "In all time of our tribulation; in all time of our wealth; in the hour of death, and in the day of judgment, Good Lord deliver us!" he stopped the reader—"Say that again;" and then fervently added, "Amen, Amen." Fearing he might be exhausted, the reader paused, but he said, "Go on." To the petition for "all sick persons," he added, "especially me."

As the Litany was being concluded his brother Edward came in; and when the dying sufferer asked for the "Commendatory Prayer," the book was passed to him. He tried to read it; but his voice failed, and the prayer was taken up by another. At the words, "With whom do live the spirits of just men made perfect," he said, "Not just in themselves." He then asked for the Confession in the Communion Service, and said afterwards, "I should have liked to have received the Holy Communion with you all, but I am too weak now."

He then bade farewell to his brother Edward, meekly asking his forgiveness for anything that might have appeared unbrotherly or unkind on his part; and John Babington having come forward and grasped his dying hand, he turned to his sister Eleanor, and said, "I don't think John has much to forgive." "Nothing," was the tearful response; "nothing but love for fifty years."

He inquired faintly what hour it was. His daughter Blanche told him it was two o'clock. Looking at Efie, he said, "Take care of her." He then kissed and blessed them both.

Before retiring, the text already quoted was repeated, "Fear thou not, for I am with thee." He responded, "I trust I may say, He *is* with me."

The hymn was repeated as often before :—

> "Jesu, lover of my soul," &c.

The last verse was given as in his own hymn-book,

> "Freely let me *take* of thee;"

he said, "I like better—

> 'Freely let me *drink* of thee;'

these are Christ's own words."

The next morning, Tuesday, January 24, he was much changed, but asked his younger daughter for the Second Lesson for the day (Matt. xxii.), exclaiming fervently, as the parable of the marriage of the King's son was read, "Oh, for that wedding garment!" He then asked for a paper he had to sign. He stretched out his feeble hand, but could scarcely hold the pen without help. It was a duty done mechanically; and, whilst doing it, he murmured, "To depart . . . to be with Christ . . . far better;" adding, "I have prayed all

through this illness that Christ may be magnified in my
body, whether it be by life or by death—by faith, patience,
resignation."

· About this time there came a holy calm and repose on his
countenance, and, seeing it, one of his children ventured to
say, " Christ is very near you, dear papa." With emphasis
he replied, "*Very near.*"

He slowly repeated a text and a prayer of wonderful
significance: "'I, if I be lifted up, will draw all men unto
me :'—Lord, draw me unto Thee."

The verse was quoted, " Thou, Lord, hast never failed them
that seek Thee." " NEVER!" was his fervent assent. His
favourite hymns—

> " Jesu, lover of my soul,"

and

> " My God, my Father, while I stray," &c.,

having been again repeated, he was asked if he desired
prayers. " Yes," he replied; " the prayers for the dying."
And when his children were leaving him for a little time, he
said, " Hold together, dear children, in the doctrine of Christ.
Nothing else will do."

His brother Edward, with his wife and daughters, now
came to receive his love and blessing; Mr. Babington also
bade him farewell with Aaron's blessing, " The Lord bless
thee and keep thee," &c. (Numb. vi. 24—26). Others also
were admitted; after which he was asked whether he wished
for prayer." " Yes," he replied, " a grand confessional
prayer!" " Do you mean the Confession in the Communion
Service ?" was asked. There was a momentary pause, and
then his lips moved—"O God the Father, of Heaven "—.
Thus the throne of the Most High God was his CONFESSIONAL
and the Litany his grand CONFESSION.

The day passed on, and the breathing became embarrassed.
There was now apparently no pain, but he was restless and
faint. Then came feebly-murmured words about "other
kingdoms," "nothing but light;" then a little wandering,
then renewed petitions for " faith, patience, and resignation;"
then the repetition of the comfortable words, " As thy day,
so shall thy strength be;" and then an earnest, humble, and
final prayer, " Suffer me not. . . for any pains of death . . .
to fall from Thee."

An expression of solemn calm amazement seemed then to

come over his face, reminding his attendants of Stephen looking up to heaven and seeing Jesus standing at the right hand of God; and while the Commendatory Prayer was being read he passed gently away.

Thus, "Blessed are the dead which die in the Lord : even so saith the Spirit; for they rest from their labours." His death was in entire harmony with his life. There was no excitement, no straining at effect on the one hand; but no doubts, fears, distrust, or repining on the other. Grace sufficient was vouchsafed. His departure was that of an earnest and true-hearted believer in Jesus Christ, who had meant what he said, and done what he professed. He was upon the Rock. The summons to him was very sudden, or, as he strikingly expressed it, "like a thunderbolt." It found him engaged in his Master's business, vainly endeavouring to overtake his work, and with little but his seventy-three years to forebode the end. But it found him prepared. The "Disce vivere" he had learnt; he had but to learn, as we all have, the "Disce mori." Pain was peculiarly distressing to his finely-strung nerves : but patience had her perfect work, grace triumphed, and he became finally "more than conqueror through Christ that had loved him."

A hearse with a train of mourning coaches slowly wending its way to Hove; a church draped in black, and filled with a sorrowing congregation; a coffin received by weeping relatives and officiating ministers, and followed by a long array of clergy and laity; a churchyard full of waiting friends; a little body of poor women standing apart, and making such great lamentations as to excite the inquiries, " Whence come you? and who are you ?" and to elicit the replies, " We come from St. Mary's," and " We are Mr. Elliott s widows;" the hand of the chief mourner grasped by many but unknown sympathisers; bells tolling, windows darkened, and shops shut :—all combined to show respect for the departed, love for his memory, and sorrow for his loss.

On the Sunday following, funeral sermons were preached in St. Mary's, St. Mark's, St. Peter's, Christ Church, the Chapel Royal, St. James's, Holy Trinity, All Souls, St. Andrew's, St. John the Baptist, and other churches. The congregation at St. Mary's were in deep mourning, and were addressed by the Rev. Henry Venn, the Ven. Archdeacon Garbett, and the Rev. Edward Hoare.

Many letters of condolence were naturally addressed to

the family on such an occasion. Two of them may be selected for insertion here—the one from their uncle, Dr. Whewell, Master of Trinity College, Cambridge; the other from the Rev. H. M. Wagner, Vicar of Brighton.

Dr. Whewell says :—

I was rejoiced to hear that there was so much that was consoling and cheering in the removal from this world of your dear father, my dear and valued friend for half a century. May we all follow where he is gone! He was a person whom I loved and honoured so much, that I must feel a deep interest about the last hours of his sojourn upon earth; and the account of his demeanour under the approach of death is deeply solemn, and yet encouraging to all of us. . . . Words so delivered must be to you an inalienable treasure, . . . a blessing through life, protecting you against temptation and mistrust of God.

The Vicar of Brighton says :—

Through a period of nearly forty years I have been connected with your beloved father by so many holy and endearing associations, that I hope you will allow me the privilege of a fellowship with you in the deep affliction which it has pleased God to lay upon you. Indeed, the whole body of our clergy would have desired to offer some general expression of their sympathy; but when I breathed this suggestion to a friend—one of the dearest friends of your father—he pointed out the very different relation wherein we, some of the oldest contemporaries of your father, stand, and the different degrees of sorrow, though all are mourners, which fill our hearts. Connected with your father for so many years, we have seen and appreciated the benevolence and consistency of his character, his great talents, his earnest desire to promote the interests of religion and charity, his devotedness to the congregation of St. Mary's, a congregation which will never find his equal. Indeed, there was nothing which he put his hand to which he did not adorn . . . . All in Brighton profoundly grieve, and tell, as with one voice, that we shall never have his equal.

The allusion in the Vicar's letter, and the general existence of such feelings bore their appropriate fruit. A Memorial to Mr. Elliott found in St. Mary's Hall its natural and fitting expression. In one week 1,100*l.* had been contributed; and when this had increased to 2,000*l.* two permanent scholarships were founded. Another Memorial Fund of 1,000*l.* was given by his children, to remunerate the examiners; and a festival was instituted, to be called "Founder's day." Five years later, the Institution was enlarged, by the erection of a new wing, as a Memorial to the Rev. Julius Elliott, by his brothers and sisters, and in fulfilment of one of his own latest wishes.

In due time a tablet was reared in the chancel of St. Mary's, the inscription on which, written chiefly by the trembling hand of one of those children whom, living and dying, he loved so well, tells that it is erected—

To the Memory of

THE REV. HENRY VENN ELLIOTT,

The First Minister of this Chapel,

BORN JANUARY 17, 1792; DIED JANUARY 24, 1865.

His varied intellectual gifts, his high University distinctions,
Were laid at the feet of HIM whom he loved and preached
As the Lamb of God which taketh away the sin of the world.
Esteemed by others a burning and shining light,
To himself he seemed " a most unprofitable servant."
The unremitting energy, the spirit of prayer,
The faithfulness and tenderness with which he laboured
To win and edify souls,
The Great Day alone will declare.
His wise judgment and administrative ability,
His unwearied sympathy and large charity,
Are best known to those who have reason to bless him
As the Founder and Father of St. Mary's Hall.
He began his ministry in this Chapel in January, 1827;
He closed it on the Festival of Epiphany, January, 1865.
From prayer and praise, and the Sacramental Feast,
He passed at once through the valley of the shadow of death,
Fearing no evil,
To HIM in whose presence is fulness of joy
And at whose right hand are pleasures for evermore.

CHAPTER IX.

SUMMARY OF CHARACTER.

The Archbishop of Canterbury—Bishop of Mauritius—Archdeacon Garbett —Professor Sedgwick—Archdeacon Ormerod—Dean Boyd—Rev. C. B. Elliott—Rev. A. Thorold—Rev. J. B. Marsden—Rev. T. Griffiths— Rev. James Vaughan—Lady Aberdeen—Mrs. Cameron—Poor Women —Pew-Openers—Servants—Conclusion.

WHEN an eminent servant of God departs hence and is no more seen, he leaves behind him a track of light, which survivors do well to observe and to record. This has been done in the present case; and hence this concluding chapter. The desultory character of some preceding ones enabled the writer to say all that he himself wished. Other pens more graphic, and other names more influential, may now be called upon to record the impressions made upon their minds by Mr. Elliott's "life and conversation." Some of the letters from which extracts will be made were sought for as reminiscences; others sprang spontaneously from hearts full of affectionate regret, and were addressed to different members of the family. If the interest of the reader does not flag, he will find much in the perusal which he would be sorry to leave unread.

The first extract is from a letter written by Dr. Tait, the present Archbishop of Canterbury:—

January 28, 1865.

I have seen the announcement of Mr. Elliott's death with the greatest regret, not for his own sake, but for the Church's loss, and the loss of all his many friends. His kindly Christian sympathy will be missed by many, and certainly will be missed by me. It was always a pleasure to see him, and to learn in seeing him what power there is in Christianity. He seemed to me to belong to that class, now becoming comparatively rare, to which my dear father-in-law, and Mr. Gerrard Noel, and Mr. Cunningham of Harrow belonged; and who in their old age shed a hallowing light on the generation that was coming after them. I trust it may please God to comfort you and your family under this trial.

The next letter is from Dr. Ryan, then Bishop of the Island of Mauritius :—

March 14, 1865.

The sad intelligence contained in the last newspaper which has reached us from England, has led me to sympathise very earnestly in the heavy loss you have sustained. Judging from my own experience of his warm kindness and intense sympathy with the work of the Gospel, I feel sure that a large circle of labourers in the cause of the Lord Jesus Christ will feel they have lost a devoted friend. No encouragement was more effectual to myself than that which I derived from my short stay with him, just before I left England in 1861: he entered so fully into the peculiar duties and trials of the work to which I was going. What a comfort it must be to you to know that so many have reason to bless his memory!

Extracts from the funeral sermon of Archdeacon Garbett follow :—

While I have been speaking of the glory which awaiteth the saints of God, your thoughts, brethren, like my own, have all along been dwelling on him whose place I am occupying, your Pastor, and my beloved friend. God has taken him. Our fleshly eyes behold him not, nor do our fleshly ears listen to him, but he lives in our hearts. Nay, he being dead still speaketh, and it is as though we still beheld him. It is so hard to feel and persuade ourselves that he is really gone. It seems a thing incredible, and beyond the realizing. Yet so it is. On earth we shall behold him no more.

Truly he had great talents to account for, before the judgment-seat of the great Task-master. What rare powers of prompt and decisive action, what discernment of spirits, and practical insight were in him! what indefatigable diligence! what force and clearness of thought! what a firm grasp of great principles, and their ultimate consequences! what a winning eloquence! what power to mould the minds of others! Whence came this power? From this :—there was a wonderful faculty of sympathy about him, an intuitive perception of the feelings of other hearts, and the thoughts of other minds. Thus he laid hold on the attention of the young, and fascinated them ; he touched the inner chords which the rude hand of natures less subtle fails to reach, but which vibrated instantly to him, by force of this intuition which was in him. There was frequently, too, an irresistible charm in the modulations of his voice, and in his earnest moments a pathos and tearful music, as some felt it, that went to the heart.

But it was not for this rare gift, nor as the scholar, nor the divine, nor the man of fertile brain, that I for one most admired him. Nor was it either for the singular and intense concentration of all his faculties at a moment's notice on anything on which he fastened as an end to be compassed, though all his friends remember how this characteristic power was stamped on countenance, and brow, and mouth, an image of the soul. No, what was most admirable was his single-mindedness, ever fixed on his Lord's glory, and on the lifting up, in season and out of season, of Christ Crucified. It was his faithfulness to his Lord. It was this which in his intercourse with statesmen and great men of the world, to whom his conversation and great abilities so often recommended him, never left unimproved any opening for declaring the truth and pleading for the dedication of all genius, wealth, and power to the glory of God. It was marvellous, the grace of God which had penetrated the whole man with one principle of thought and word, and action ; in him, and in all saints, the spring of Christian heroism.

The next letter is from Professor Sedgwick, and is given *in extenso.* Apart from its intrinsic excellencies, its exquisite simplicity and piety, it is full of the " old love " for his friend, and of sympathy with the children to whom it is addressed :—

March 2, 1865.

I have seen you in your days of childhood (by *you* I mean Efie and Blanche Elliott, who with affectionate regards sent me a copy of Archdeacon Garbett's funeral sermon, which I received last night), and I have seen you since your days of childhood. But some years have passed since I last saw your happy and cheerful faces.

A great sorrow has come to you ; but, thanks to your God and Redeemer, you have been taught by communion with His Comforter how to bear the sorrow. On this point I have nothing to tell you which you do not already know from a higher and far better teacher. I wish, however, to thank

you, and to tell you that I mourn with you (for I loved
your father), and to send you an old man's blessing.
May God for Jesu's sake bless you, and those whom you
best love; and He will bless you, because you have learnt
to turn your face to His with loving hearts.

Your late dear father was a true-hearted man; true in
principles, and in life true to the principles which he taught
—God working with him. He was an excellent scholar,
and in his own line of study a very learned man. But, far
better than any honours he gained on such ground, he was
a man of practical wisdom, of great benevolence, of never-
tiring zeal in carrying out the dictates of his enlightened
conscience. And so the grace was given him to be a bene-
factor to his fellow-creatures, and a bright example amongst
the loving servants of his God and Redeemer.

But, my dear young friends (surely I may so call you, for the
love and honour I felt for your father may be allowed to
pass onwards to his children), I am again only telling you
what you well know. Only my heart tells me to speak out
while I am writing to the children of one whom I loved,
and whom God has taken from us for a while.

If I live twenty more days I shall then have completed my
eightieth year. Your late father was just six years my
junior at Cambridge, but he was probably about seven
years younger than myself, for I was in my twentieth year
when I came to Cambridge a freshman. He had, therefore,
reached a good old age; and thankful you all should be that
he was so long spared for his duties and his friends. In
addition to the load of eighty years, I have many infirmities
which make the extension of my life extremely precarious.
I am striving to set my house in order, and—amidst some
great domestic sorrows—I am daily bound to thank God that
even now, in my old age, He is enabling me to be a comfort
and support to those whom He has placed near me and
taught me to love.

1 think I must give you joy that the Archdeacon, who loved
and knew your father so well, has been enabled to publish
such a warm-hearted and valuable tribute to the memory of
his honoured fellow-labourer and Christian friend.

Archdeacon Ormerod next bears short but valuable condensed testimony:—

Like my own dear master, Arnold, he wrought mainly for the

,world to come. If I may judge, Arnold's great and blessed usefulness was less in his books—good as they are—than in leavening those likely to leaven others. So Mr. Elliott, only with this difference—Arnold's influence was necessarily among future heads of families and those engaged in the hard, busy "give and take" of the world; Mr. Elliott's, if I mistake not, in the less hard, but, if possible, more solemn field—future mothers, future teachers, future home moulders of character. Intellect and scholarship of the highest class existed in both cases : and in both, the gift of winning souls. They both speak, being dead. May they be listened to !

The Rev. Canon Boyd, now dean of Exeter, says :—

There was in him a mixture of simplicity and penetration, of great attainments and an obvious unconsciousness of the extent of them, a geniality and gravity, which drew out in a very short space of acquaintance admiration, respect, and affection. One could hardly be a day in his society without feeling that very soon one must come to love him. I was surprised at the rich tokens of a well furnished mind which came to light without effort or pretension. We talked on many subjects—travels, the continent, the universities, literature, the Church—and all his remarks showed either much previous thought or wonderful immediate sagacity. With the sweetness of his manner and temper in the midst of a distracting pressure of duties I was particularly struck. I recollect his giving me a most graphic description of an ascent of Etna, made many years ago ; and it was done with all the ardour and freshness of a young Alpine tourist just returned from climbing the Scheideck or the Jungfrau ; and very shortly afterwards, some one mentioning the serious illness of one of his flock, of which he had not been before apprised, the whole manner of the man was changed, and the expression of distress which passed over his face, and the depth of grief with which he uttered the words, " She is worse, and no one told me," were enough to show how deeply the thought of others and a sense of duty could sink into his soul. It was a matter of surprise to me that a man of such gifts and attainments, such powers of usefulness and attraction, should have been so comparatively little known to the great world outside of Brighton (for there he was well known) as Henry Elliott.

Y

A very interesting home letter follows, from a nephew, the Rev. C. Boileau Elliott.   Space forbids a longer extract :—

May, 1866.

As to my recollections of him, he was a man whom it was impossible to have known in all the intimacy of brotherhood and ever to forget.   His intelligent countenance, his courteous manner, almost deferential, even to his juniors, and the harmonious modulations of his voice, combined to invest him with a rare charm, while his originality and intellectual superiority were universally recognised.   I have often told my children that I had no intimate friend or acquaintance in whose society I felt so strongly as in his that I was in the presence of a master-mind, to which my own bowed.

His knowledge and general information were not only varied, but always available and pleasantly communicated.   His conversation was original and sparkling.   This, added to habitual cheerfulness, made him in early life a charming companion.   He rose above what is commonly called humour, and was often witty in the highest sense of the term.   He played with ideas ever cropping up in his mind, rather than with words.   The commonest subjects would receive from him a touch that was uncommon ; and the simplest events would elicit from him au expression which, if heard second-hand, his intimate friends would recognise as his.

One day, speaking of a dog begging for a scrap, I remember his saying, that as the little animal's hopes were excited, the segments of a circle described by his tail increased in proportion.   Then playfully he added, " The arc of expectation, under such circumstances, grows larger and larger."

Yet, with a keen sense of the ridiculous, and a power of satire which, unrestrained, would have made him feared and disliked, he very rarely or never indulged it in a way to give pain.   He had early imbibed from his revered mother the spirit of wisdom and charity with which she was wont to enforce on the young the simple but impressive aphorism, " *That alone is sport which is sport to both parties.*

There was a combination of qualities in him not often met with, and very attractive when united.   The outside world of common acquaintances had little idea of the existence of some of those excellencies which lay beneath the surface. Amongst them was a tenderness which, exhibited to few, endeared him greatly to those who, in the inner circle of his family and nearest relatives, were the objects of it. It was the more striking because united to much manliness of character and firmness of purpose, not always exempt from a certain degree of sternness: especially when he was called on to rebuke sin, or to withstand what he deemed false reasoning ; and it was peculiarly drawn forth, together with a ready sympathy and gentleness of manner, in times of sickness and affliction. Not long ago I saw an unpublished memoir of a young lady, drawn up by her surviving sister. In this, speaking of the first visit he paid to the family, which was in the depth of their grief, she writes: " Mr. Elliott entered our house this morning a stranger to us all; he left it a friend for life."

Nor was he less remarkable for his *tact* in the sick-room. He knew the value of a *short* visit and a *few* words. I was present on one occasion when he came to see a suffering relative whom he found feeble and languid. Taking her hand, he said, " I see you are weak, and cannot bear much talking." She answered that it was so, and that she could not even pray. " On the morning of the battle of Blenheim, he replied, " a Christian soldier in the army of the Duke of Marlborough was overheard to offer up this short prayer: ' O Lord, think Thou of me this day; for Thou knowest I cannot think of Thee.' " With these words, uttered in his own soft melodious intonations, he gently pressed the hand he was holding, and with a look of affectionate sympathy quitted the room. More than ten years after, I heard our mutual relative advert to that visit, that manner, and those few words, as having proved a source of comfort of which time had not even dimmed the remembrance. He never forgot that he was God's minister. Every other relation was made subservient to that. He had the happy talent of leading, without forcing conversation, to what was profitable. Whether the general topic at the moment happened to be domestic, political, or literary, a word for his Master was sure to be spoken in due season, which would afterwards stand out prominently on the canvas of memory like " an apple of gold in a picture of silver."

He was a man of prayer. If he parted for a long period from any dear friend, if he was consulted in any difficulty, if he opened his own heart as to any domestic or personal trial, if he was brought into intimate communication with any one about to enter on some new and important phase of life, in each and all of such cases his habit was to propose a recurrence to God in social prayer. For him to omit to do so was the exception rather than the rule.

Men are often most esteemed by those who know them least. It was the reverse with him. He had his weak points, and they were on the surface. But the highest testimony to his worth is yielded by the fact that those who knew him best appreciated most the qualities of his heart and mind— qualities in which he rivalled the grandfather whose name he worthily bore, and that grandfather's daughter, his own incomparable mother, to whose early teaching and bright example, he was wont to say, he owed all he valued most for time and for eternity.

The Rev. Prebendary Thorold says:—

What I think most impressed me in Mr. Elliott was, first, that strong individuality which you generally see in marked men, and without which great enterprises never can be pushed to success.

Then his power of conversation was most remarkable. No pumping up of striking thoughts out of a deep well and with a long rope; no exaggeration or unreality. But it was the easy delightful flow of a silver stream through green meadows—genial, instructive, always kind, always large. In my own case I remember protracting the break-fast hour to a period which startled me at the moment, but which I could not repent.

What Tennyson calls

> "Heart affluence of discursive talk"

was eminently his; though we must add to it, "seasoned with salt," and "to the use of edifying."

The Rev. J. B. Marsden, late of Birmingham, says:—

Mr. Elliott's death is a great loss to the Church. One of our best teachers is taken from us.

I used to think, and I ventured to tell him so when I saw him last, that if I were laid up for life, I should, if possible, come to Brighton and live there for the pleasure and profit of his ministry.

But he has laid down his life and his charge together, and

has entered, without any of the distresses of extreme old age, into the joy of his Lord.

The Rev. Thomas Griffith, Prebendary of St. Paul's, says:—

Of the impressions he made upon me the deepest is that of the *completeness* of his mind. There were no extravagances, no overgrown and abnormal crotchets, no sharp cutting angularities of thought. His breadth of culture and fulness of scholarship forbade these. He was "totus teres atque rotundus;" and hence there was in him no dogmatism. What he held, he held as proportionate parts of a digested whole; and such a whole he could afford to hold with forbearance equal to his firmness. The very rotundity of his mind made it smooth.

Nor less did I appreciate the *devoutness* of his spirit. With nothing offensively demonstrative, nothing officious, still less of conventional cant, there was an everflowing undercurrent of devout emotion, which on occasion bubbled up in bright and fertilizing utterances; and at all times you could recognise the living stream beneath by the freshness and fragrance of the verdure above.

In some sketches of his early travels in Switzerland, his vigour of touch and richness of description revived in me what I had felt many years before when listening to some similar details of mountain scenery and adventure by that "old man eloquent," Mr. Coleridge.

I must be permitted to mention, as a final touch of character, the charm which he threw over whatever he said, by the polished *deference* which he exhibited towards those who conversed with him. It was with surprise that I felt him speaking to me as if on a level with himself.

In short, gentleness, urbanity, inexpressible refinement— these are the features which have printed themselves the most indelibly on my mind.

The Rev. James Vaughan, of Christ Church, Brighton, writing to Julius Elliott, says:—

Your beloved father, by the consecration of his high talents, and the beautiful union there was in him of rare intellect and a rarer simplicity of purpose, has left the stamp of his mind and heart as abiding monuments not only in the external Church, but in the affections and souls of very many who rise up on every side and call him blessed. To you—

brought by God's kind hand to an age when you can appreciate it all, before it passes out of your sight—his clear perception of truth, his exquisite acumen, his sensitive jealousy for God's Gospel, his well-filled relationships, his home fondnesses, and his exalted course—all crowned by the humility of his gentle, happy death—will be a very rule of life, and a possession for ever.

Reminiscences equally valuable and interesting might be inserted from the Bishop of Grahamstown (Dr. Cotterill), from the late R. Scott Moncrieff, Esq., the Rev. Wm. Garratt, Rev. A. Christopher, Rev. J. Spurrell, C. Eley, Esq , and from Mr. Elliott's curates, the Rev. F. Stapley, the Rev. C. H Oldfield, the Rev. M. Spencer, and others ; but for putting in the finer and the finishing touches, the remaining space must be allotted to the ladies and the poor.

And first to Lady Aberdeen, who says :—

My husband lived with him as a pupil for some years in Cannon Place, and liked to look back on those days. The work was hard and the hours early. They met in the morning at seven o'clock in the summer, and half-past seven in the winter. There was a fine for being late, and Mr. Elliott, always making himself one with his pupils, agreed to submit to the fine if he should be late. Once, and once only, they had the pleasure of imposing it upon him. My husband used to say, among other things, that he owed Mr. Elliott many thanks for having made him learn by heart a great deal of Milton and Cowper, and taken pains with his English composition; also, for having given him " Milner's Church History " to read on Sundays; and for having so impressed him with a sense of the evil of reading secular books on Sunday that he never gave way to the habit in after life.

When we lived in Regency Square, in 1843, he often spent the evening with us. It was almost the first break in his habit of entire seclusion, since the death of his wife two years before.

The effect of his intercourse was very beneficial on both our minds, and in the years following we used to say, " Let us go to Brighton to get a little *revived* "

Mr. Elliott was most kind to our children, and was a great favourite with them. He used to tell them stories to amuse them, and one especially about a great giant, who had lost his red night-cap—he acting the part of the giant with great humour.

His love for young people in general was very great. The labour he went through in preparing his candidates for Confirmation was *incredible;* and when, amongst the mountains of papers he read through at home, he found any which gave evidence of a mind taught of God, his joy was great, and he would speak of it with deep thankfulness. He remembered the young people whom he had prepared with affectionate interest ever after.

His conversation at meals was cheerful and interesting; but very often he became so engrossed with his subject, that he quite forgot the business in hand, and after talking a long while, when he found that every one else had finished breakfast or dinner, he would swallow his food with far too much haste. Sometimes he seemed quite unconscious that he was eating, and would make some curious absent remark about it.

The wonderful rapidity of his movements, even in his later years, was very characteristic. He ran upstairs like a boy; and to see him umbrella in hand, with his eye-glass on his breast beating quick time to his eager steps as he hurried along, no one could possibly have guessed his age.

His high Conservative view of the honour due to rank and station, made it all the more to *his* honour that he never shrank from giving the plainest expression to his sentiments, even where he thought they might give offence, when he felt it his duty to do so. His highly cultivated mind, and the elegance and charm of his language, gave him the opportunity of placing the truths of the Gospel before some men in high station who, perhaps, would not have listened to them from one less of a scholar and a gentleman than he was. But he took as much pains to bring home those same truths to the heart of the humblest maid-servant and the youngest child, and I have known him pray earnestly and by name for the conversion of some such as these.

Something of the grief I feel may be understood when it is known what a friend and almost father he was to me and my children, and I hope to thank him in the eternal world for all he was here to me and mine.

Mrs. Cameron writes:—

I should say that Mr. Elliott was peculiarly fitted for the

office of a comforter, from the power he had of feeling for
and with the sorrowful.   His very voice was an index of
this.   It had what the Germans call "a tear" in it, and,
like Mendelssohn's 'Songs without Words,' when he spoke
kind words the voice conveyed as much meaning as the
words themselves.

I wish I could say more; but all I have said is accompanied
with most grateful recollections of his extreme kindness to
myself at all times.   I think I was a little afraid of him; I
always thought him so very clever.

Many equally valuable and graphic reminiscences from
ladies might be added; but the conclusion must be reserved
for the simple and grateful records of the poor.

A poor woman remembers the first words her "dear
minister" ever spoke to her:—

Are you seeking after the Lord Jesus?   If you seek, you will
find Him precious to your soul.

When I and another wished to give a trifle to the Church
Missionary Society, for which he had great love; he shook
hands with us and said, "the Lord would make it doubly
blessed to us both."

Speaking on the subject of trouble, he said, "Don't be too
anxious to get rid of your trouble; let the affliction have its
perfect work."

I heard his last Sunday Sermon, "Grace be to you and peace."
"If you have grace," he said, "you will have peace."

I always used to think that his most solemn moments were
when he was preaching on the Bible, on Prayer, and on
reverence for the Sabbath.

The pen of another poor person runs on from a full heart,
as one who had known him from the time she was twelve
years of age, who had been educated in his school, been
present at the opening of St. Mary's Chapel, and had attended
there ever since:—

His kindness to me and my family is indescribable. Never
was Christmas allowed to pass without some treat being
provided for us. It was no uncommon thing for him to
pay for burying his poor people, and I have known him also
pay their debts. On one occasion I was in trouble because
a neighbour was going to set up a mangle in opposition to
me, which would have prevented my getting support for

my children. He inquired into the matter, and then said, "I cannot allow this to be done. This small street does not allow of more mangles than one, if people are to get their living." Thus he would enter into all our little difficulties, and settle them for us. He used to smile and joke with us also. "How old are you?" he once asked me, and when I told him, he said, "Why, you are nearly as old as I am; when one dies of old age, the other will begin to quake with fear." Once he was giving some presents to his widows, and offered them the choice of two things: "Which do you like?" he said to one of them. "Well, sir," she answered in fun, "I like both." "Then you shall have both." And he asked a number of us if we could tell him the greatest blessing God had ever given us. It went round. He asked us separately, but received no answer till he came to the last. "Now, Widow North," he said, "you have had many blessings. Has there been one more striking than another?" "Well sir," she replied, "my greatest blessing has been God's sending me His own dear Son." "Right," he said, "quite right; that is the very answer I have been waiting for."

Another poor woman says:—

One day he called when I was ill, and on taking leave asked if there was any earthly comfort I stood in need of. I told him he had been so kind I could not intrude further. He said, "I have my carriage, and if you can spare your little boy he shall go home with me and fetch something." So he went, and brought back a pound of tea.

Another says:—

I was one of his candidates for Confirmation, and at our last lecture he said to us, "As you pass up the aisle to the Communion-table I shall be standing by. Look at me, that I may distinguish my own candidates, and pray for them at the solemn moment when they kneel there."

Another relates, as an instance of his kindly sympathy and personal interest, the following fact:—Entering into conversation with a poor person to whom he had been very charitable, he found that she was much distressed by having her daughter and son-in-law to maintain, and that, in consequence, she had been obliged to pawn some of her things. Mr. Elliott listened to her story, and seeing the duplicates lying on the table, he took them unnoticed, and said nothing to the poor woman. When he was gone there was a great hunt for them, but they could not be found; nor was the matter explained till a person came in bringing all the missing things.

"To think," she said, "that he should not only have gone himself with the duplicates and done it, but even hired some one to bring them home!"

A poor woman living out of his district had a dying sister who wished to see Mr. Elliott. He wrote a note to the Rev. J. Vaughan, asking his consent, and then visited her till her death :—

He used to come in the evening when his day's work was done. The beautiful prayers he used to offer I shall never forget. They were times of great joy. Nor did he forget me. Three days after her death he sent his servant to me with two pounds, one to buy black, and one towards funeral expenses. "Take these," he said to her, "and cheer up Mrs. Ayton."

One person writes :—

He was the greatest earthly friend I ever had. He once advanced me 50*l.* when there was great need. Not very long after that was arranged, I called at his house. I was in great want of 10*l.*, but Mr. Elliott having been so kind previously, my mouth was stopped. But I asked the Lord to put it into his heart to offer it. When I was about to leave his presence he said, "I can let you have 10*l.* if it will be of any service to you." I remember also a poor woman in distress who applied to him one Sunday for relief. No shops were open, and he had no money with him; but he went into the house of a person he knew, borrowed a large loaf of bread, and gave it her.

Another poor person tells of a " word in season : "—

Mr. Elliott came to see my mother on a Sunday evening, and said, "Have you been to church to day?" Well, no, sir; I have had so much to attend to, I could not get out." He looked earnestly in her face, and asked again, "Have you had your dinner to-day?" "Yes, sir." "Well, then," he replied, "your soul needs food and nourishment as well as your body." I often think of his words and look, when I feel careless and indifferent about church; and then I put on my things and go.

A poor widow went to him in great sorrow, owing to the then recent loss of her husband. He asked what she needed. She said, " A little money to bury my husband." He took her into his room, talked with her, and prayed with her. She then, at his request, repeated the hymn beginning—

> " When I can read my title clear," &c.

" We then both sang it together," she said, " and when it was done he gave me one pound from his own purse, and another pound from the Offertory Fund. At the time of one plentiful harvest he gave to each of his widows ten shillings."

One of the pew-openers of his chapel says :—

I feel as though all my love is buried with him. Many a Sunday have I entered the church with an aching heart, owing to a great trial which befel me, and saying to myself—

> " A broken heart, my God, my King,
> Is all the sacrifice I bring."

But I always returned comforted by Mr. Elliott's sermons; they were so appropriate to my case.

It was his custom, after the Sunday evening service was over, to have the pew-openers wait till he came out of the vestry, that he might shake hands with them all, and bid them good-night. " I like to see you all at the last," he would say.

" It did us good to hear his voice," says another pew-opener. " One Sunday he called me into the vestry, and saying he was sorry to hear I had been poorly, offered me some little nicety. " Well, sir,' I said, ' if you will excuse me, I will take part of it home to my children.' 'Ah,' he said, 'that's like the mother; always thinking of the little ones.'"

One of his house servants says :—

I can never forget the impression made by the first interview I had with him. He hoped that, by my entering his service I should not only strive to serve him, but also to serve my heavenly Master. In my first year it pleased God to lay me aside by an accident I met with. On that very night he came to me with great kindness, and wished me to see the doctor, but thinking the accident slight, I did not care to do so. He wished me good-night; and 1 thought he had retired for the night, when shortly after he returned to me with the doctor, he himself having been for him. I felt that I could do or suffer anything for one who had done so much for me.

His nurse remembers, when she was first engaged, how anxious he was to have a person about his children who truly feared God; and how earnestly he said, "I trust the blessing of the Lord will rest upon our engagement."

"When we were staying in the country," she goes on to say, "he took the greatest interest in the poor. They were far from the church, and were like sheep without a shepherd. He obtained leave from the clergyman to preach in a barn, both on Sunday and week-day evenings. Many attended; and I saw three or four reckless youths listening outside the barn after their day's work was done. An old Wesleyan said, 'He is one of the right sort!'

"Sometimes I used to think he was too strict in certain things about governing his house; but, perceiving this, he would repeat the text: 'If a man know not how to rule his own house, how shall he take care of the Church of God?'

"I remember a young nursery-maid saying, 'I really like my master better after he has scolded me.'

"One morning there were six poor persons waiting to see him in the hall. One looked like a tramp, but he was indeed a clever man. The Bishop of Oxford had taken great interest in him. Mr. Elliott used to have conversations with him. I heard him once talking to him very earnestly about his soul. He gave him soap and clothes, and tried all he could to raise him, but never succeeded. Mr. Elliott saw five of the persons that morning, but as he had a clergyman with him and an appointment elsewhere, he said he could not see the sixth. The poor woman, when the door was opened, pressed into the room, when Mr. Elliott placed his hand upon her shoulder, and said, 'I cannot hear what you have to say; it is past the time.' The poor woman said to me, in an angry voice, 'Why, Mr. Elliott took me by the shoulder and put me out of the room.' To which I said, 'Well Mrs. ——, if one of his own children had gone into the room as you did, he would have acted just the same.'

" He was very firm.   Twice I have known him to put a stop to men fighting in the street.   I perhaps should not have known it, but he came home with a spot of blood on his shirt.   He went between the men and said, 'If you want to fight, fight me.'   The police commended him for the way in which he did it.   I cannot remember what they said, but I know he rebuked the whole assembled crowd for encouraging the fight: 'You call yourselves Christians,' he said, 'and yet delight to see your fellow-creatures fighting like wild beasts.   Do you not know that your bodies were made for God's service?'   The mob at once dispersed.   I wish I could tell the whole story as it happened.   He always did things so heartily."

Yes.   *He always did things so heartily!*   This witness is true.   Poor and rich, learned and unlearned, alike bear testimony to Henry Venn Elliott; and his own works do follow him!   Surely a place amongst the worthies of the Church may be assigned to one so learned, so good, so kind, so faithful, so free from extremes, so true to the Master whom he loved, so humble in his walk with God.   The niche is ready.   May this story of his " Life " be instrumental in raising him to it!

APPENDIX.

Containing a brief Memoir of the REV. JULIUS M. ELLIOTT, *with an Account of his Ascent of the Matterhorn in* 1868, *and of his fatal Slip and Death on the Schreckhorn in* 1869.

No one will have read the fifth chapter of this Life of Mr. Elliott without a feeling of deep sympathy. All that preceded was descriptive of a happy home, a loving circle, a buoyant mind, and an active life; —all that followed was, in sad contrast, descriptive of a house of mourning, and a chastened man, bereft at once of mother, sisters, first-born child, and much-loved wife.

The little INFANT left to him as a sad legacy, and baptized in tears, survived. He was named Julius Marshall; and scattered notices of his early life, and of his education in the Brighton College, have been already given. In due time he was entered at Trinity College, Cambridge; and his course as an undergraduate, though not distinguished like his father's, was most exemplary and of high promise. There was in his character a peculiar mingling of gentleness and firmness—gentleness in manner, firmness in purpose. You thought he would yield at once to your persuasions; but if principle was at stake or pledges had been given, nothing could move him. Towards the close of his College course, his expressed desire to take Holy Orders delighted his father; at whose death-bed, however, he was first called to minister, and from it to learn deep lessons for future life. Shortly after that event—that is, in March 1865—he was ordained by Archbishop Longley to the Curacy of Pluckley, in Kent, upon a title given by the Rev. Canon Oxenden, now Metropolitan of Canada; and in August 1866 he became, in succession to his father, and with the concurrence of the Vicar, Incumbent of St. Mary's Chapel, Brighton. There he commenced a course, short indeed, but marked by abundant labours, encouraging success, and a singular accumulation of personal influence. It was a trying position for so young a man; for he had to do at twenty-five years of age what his father had found difficult at seventy-three! But he did it well. All marked his rapid maturity, and his growth in grace, holiness, and usefulness. The church continued full, and the congregation remained steadfast—"contented, pleased, and profited" by his ministry.

"He was one," says Archdeacon Garbett, "in whom God does not work the spiritual life by fire and stormy conflicts, but by imperceptible growths, as of the spring flowers, or the tender morning dew. Thus the sweet tempers of nature are sanctified into graces; and they were so in him. But, as he grew from childhood to manhood, certain periods of spiritual growth, and the quickening of spiritual consciousness, were, I am told, vividly marked in him. Such was the period of Confirmation, his entry into Holy Orders, and that most Christian death-bed of his father, at which, with such filial tenderness and holy faithfulness, he ministered with his sisters. Those who saw his daily life were conscious of an ever-mellowing and deepening spirituality of soul in him. There was, doubtless a gift of grace too a singular truthfulness and conscientiousness in the smallest matters. He had been ill, and unable to prepare his morning sermon. He took one of his father's; but before he began he said, 'Illness has prevented me from preparing my discourse ; I am going to read you one of my father's." So, on another occasion, when Mr. Babington had been too ill to preach, and Julius was applied to at the last moment, he took Mr. Babington's prepared discourse, and said, 'Now, dear friends, I am going to preach to you, not my own composition, but Mr. Babington's.' In this transparency and absolute truthfulness he bore all his faculties, one fair and perfect chrysolite. Year after year there was more and more devotion to God. There was an evermore vivid consciousness of the Divine presence in his heart; there was a more vigorous appropriation, through personal faith, of the Redeemer's sacrifice; there was an ever deeper and deeper union and communion with Him, as the way, the truth, and the life. His life was a life both for and in Christ."

" If I had been asked," says Dr. Griffith, the Principal of Brighton College, who knew him well, "for an opinion as to whose life, as a young minister, was most valuable, my first thought, unless I am extremely mistaken, would have been of Julius Elliott. But God sees not as man sees; God can spare his servants, and still have His work done. But if you wanted a man whose whole soul was pervaded by the spirit of his work—who made his work a matter of the most earnest prayer—who made his work his daily, hourly study—who, by the study of God's Holy Word—who, by devoting himself to prayer and good works—who, in all simplicity, embracing the truth of the Gospel, in faith tried to do the work of an Evangelist—I think it was he. He was not negligent; he did not find fault with others; but he worked himself. Instead of objecting so much to the errors of others, though he could see them, what he did was to try to ' build you up in your most holy faith.' He set before you Christ, and Christ's work. He set before you Christ, that you might have the power to work. He set before you work, that you might give the proof of being in Christ."

But this was accomplished by a lavish expenditure of bodily and mental vigour. Julius Elliott allowed himself but little respite. As in the case of his father, engagements were too numerous, and days too short. Though his frame was well knit and full of activity, yet he suffered from this early strain; and each year showed in succession a gradual descent from perfect health at the beginning to great prostration at the end.

Snow and ice were his great restoratives. At Brighton, he was the overworked clergyman; in Switzerland, he was the unwearied mountaineer. His own words to a friend describe graphically the effect this change of life produced in him :—

The air on the tops and slopes of the great snow mountains is to me more than anything the restorer of health and strength, the dispenser of enjoyment, the inspirer of hope. Their solitudes counteract the worries of incessant occupation in town life, their icy streams repair the shattered nerves, their glorious views minister ceaseless pleasures, and it is my own fault if their wondrous beauties do not raise my heart in deeper thankfulness, and truer affection, and more real comprehension to the great and loving Father whose hand is so visible everywhere.

Thus the Alps, which caused his death, enabled him to live. His death was occasioned by a slip in ascending the Schreckhorn, on July 27, 1869; and the general interest excited by that event, when made public, combined with the desire of bearing testimony to one so much and so deservedly beloved, has called for this Appendix. It is compiled chiefly from the letters of Captain Phipps, R.A., published in the *Times* and *Daily News*, combined with additional information supplied by a relative, and by the Rev. P. W. Phipps, his friend and fellow-traveller. Many of the incidents thus communicated were summed up in two valuable funeral sermons, from which extracts have been already made, preached by the Ven. Archdeacon Garbett and Dr. Griffith, which have been printed and placed at the disposal of the family. The narrative of the ascent of the Matterhorn, which properly precedes the fatal ascent and accident on the Schreckhorn, was written by Julius Elliott himself, and parts of it have appeared in the *Brighton College Magazine.* It is as follows :—

If ever it is true of anything, that it inspires different people with different emotions, it is true of the Alps; for to some they are objects of aversion and even terror, while to others they are objects of greatest delight and intensest longings. And if this be true of any one mountain more than another, that mountain is the Matterhorn.

I have heard it described as "black and awful, forbidding and ghastly;" and I have myself thought it the most graceful and fascinating mountain I have ever seen. Certainly, no mountain in the European Alps can boast of such rare curves of snow and rock, such overhanging precipices, such incessant and terrific avalanches, and such an appearance of inaccessibility, which, even now that its virginity has for ever gone, will isolate it to the last.

It will be remembered how, in 1865, the mountain was climbed for the first time, and how that brilliant success was turned into a most awful failure by the slip of one of the party, and the consequent destruction of four of them; an accident that not only restored to the mountain its former reputation, but invested it with a superstitious dread it had not possessed before.

It was climbed again the same year, but from the opposite or southern side; and in 1867, I believe, it was ascended three different times from the south side (once by guides, another time by an Englishman with those guides, another time by an Italian): but the several attempts made on the north side all, from one cause or other, failed. And so the superstition gathered strength, that every one who was rash enough to assail the Matterhorn from the north side would never get down alive. It was useless to represent that the accident was the result of the inexperience of one member of that first party, and that the northern slopes were more gentle than the southern, and therefore must be easier. With the tenacity of uneducated minds, the guides of Zermatt clung to their prejudice, and refused to make the attempt. Others, however, who perhaps from their inexperience might justly have entertained these fears, took truer views. Biner, I knew, was disinclined to make the attempt, even were his feelings no stronger : and I could hardly venture, I thought, without him, with a strange guide, whom I should not trust, and who would not trust me. I reached Zermatt over the Alphubel and Alphubel-Joch, and on Monday did the Dom; and then, thinking I was up to the work, I sounded Biner on the subject of the Matterhorn. His answer was very touching to me. As far as I can recollect, it was this :—" Dear sir, I love you well. I know you are strong, and sure of foot, and I should like to go with you everywhere. But my mother—if we should slip and fall, it would be sad for me, and sad for her." It was unanswerable. I turned the subject, and said, " Well, will you try the Weisshorn? Do you think it can be done now? and do you think I am up to it?" " *Ja wohl, Herr*," sounded out with a full and round voice, very different from the previous words. So off we went, and did the Weisshorn. This settled the question in my mind, that, come what might, I would try the Matterhorn, weather being good. The work on the Weisshorn is spoken of as so hard, and I found the ascent so easy, though the descent was very difficult, that I got a higher, perhaps vainer, idea of my powers. The east side also of the Matterhorn was almost wholly free from snow. Certainly there was snow on the top, and plenty of it; but I thought, as the wish will direct the thoughts, perhaps the new snow may make the final peak of the Matterhorn easier, as it made the Wetterhorn and the Mönch. So I tried again at Biner, after doing the Weisshorn, and said to him, " Biner, will you go with me to the shoulder of the mountain ?" (where you are obliged to change sides). "I know there is no danger as far as that, and I won't ask you to go a step further." A shrug of his shoulders was at first his only answer : a reluctant look was in his face. Perhaps I ought not to have asked him again. Presently he said, " I will speak again to my mother." In the afternoon he returned with a sad and wistful look, and said, " No, sir; I cannot go. My mother cried much when I spoke of it, and said, ' Do not go, Franz, I entreat thee. Do not go.' " I at once responded, " That settles the question ; don't go, on any account; you have done quite right to make that resolve." And so it happened that I found myself, on July 24, 1868, without my own trusty guide, making arrangements with two men who knew nothing, and of whom I knew nothing, who had not been up the Matterhorn or any really dangerous mountain, and of whose capacity to render help when wanted my opinion did not increase upon experience. One great difficulty presented by the mountain was the length of the climb from Zermatt, nine or ten hours' good walking. This had been remedied by the praiseworthy enterprise of M. Seiler, the landlord at Zermatt, who was then building a hut about seven hours up the mountain. This hut was to be my sleeping-place the first night ; and it offered this double advantage, that so I might pass and repass the dangerous spot where the accident happened, before I had a chance of being tired, and before the snow at the top had had a chance of being melted by the mid-day heat. But the great difficulty, compared with which all the rest were as nothing, was the mental struggle with the ghosts of old fears, which would not be laid, but returned with increased force the night before I left Zermatt, and made that night memorable in my life. To one in such a state of excitement, action was the best remedy. I dozed on till nearly 5 A.M.; then had my breakfast, ordered a porter and provisions, and started at six. The work of breasting the steep slopes of the Hörnli was an indescribable relief; the weariness of the restless night was soon forgotten, and not another apprehension crossed my mind.

The way up to the hut was not difficult, though difficult enough in places to warn inexperienced men off; but the view at my back was marvellously grand all the way, and a sunset seen from a height of between twelve and thirteen thousand feet is not soon to be forgotten! I reached the hut at 1 P.M., and spent the afternoon in clambering up and about the mountain, reconnoitring the route of the morrow, and enjoying the view.

Sunsets and sunrises are impossible to describe, but as Nature speaks to the vexed spirit in her own calm tones, and as it realizes that the heavens are declaring the glory of God, there are surely few that have not felt something like a nobler thought or a deeper peace than common. And so the peace came to me, as the sun shone upon glorious mountains of cloud, piled like Ossa on Pelion, dwarfing the greatest giants of mountains, till they were resplendent in light of gold and silver, and then of tenderest crimson. And as I saw the tender colours, and experience suggested that they were too tender to augur well for the morrow, the morrow seemed insignificant, and I lived only in the present.

We turned in early, for at that height it soon gets cold. I slept well, and at 4.15 A.M., after a hurried breakfast, I was off with two of the men who had been building the hut and were now to act as guides. They had made an ineffectual attempt the previous year, and they had no expectation that we should get to the top, and took little trouble to conceal their thoughts. The weather was bright, but an ominous cloud—ominous yet lovely as the loveliest, appeared in the east, piled far away above Monte Rosa. It seemed like a great flat roofed temple on many pillars, with a huge pile above, and from its depths came forth ever and anon flashes of lightning. Was it the anger of the clouds at our audacity? Were they about to sweep us from the mountains? Or was it only the playfulness of summer? A few hours would decide. The sun rose, and as its beams smote upon the pillars, the cloud waned and died. Of that sunrise and that sunset I think with as much real pleasure as of anything in the expedition.

At first our work was easy enough; a few corners to turn and ledges on which to balance oneself, all at an easy slope; then a few steps to cut in the ice; and in two hours we were at the foot of the final peak. Two objects of interest there were, however, in this part; one the wonderful *arête* or ridge, that runs down to the Hörnli, one of the most striking ridges I have ever seen. It is broken into the most wild and fantastic forms, sometimes solid as massive buttresses, at others wild and pinnacled, and shattered into fragments tottering to their fall. The other object of interest was the perpetual fall of stone avalanches, which, when on a large scale, are some of the grandest and most terrible things in nature. I saw many of them that day, and they made the very mountain tremble. This is one great danger of the east side of the mountain. That smooth slope which seems so easy to ascend is like a glacis perpetually swept up by the enemy's shot. It surprised me much that I had never heard of this, and also that I saw so little of the glaze of ice on rock, which was supposed to be the chief danger. But in this respect, of course, the mountain varies from year to year. On account of the avalanches, we kept always as near the ridge as possible, till we come to the shoulder. From this point we turned over to the northern side for the rest of the ascent, working round two or three steep crags by easy slopes of hard snow, intermingled with projecting rock, till we came to a more formidable barrier of steep rock, which runs right across the face of the mountain. This is undoubtedly the chief difficulty on this side, but I cannot say that it struck me as anything remarkable. The handhold and foothold were fair, and I fancy I have climbed as bad cliffs alone in Cumberland. Beyond this the slope grew less steep, rocks gradually disappeared, and at last an unbroken snow-slope led us to the top at 8.45 A.M. The top was a ridge of frozen snow, narrowed to a knife-edge in parts, and in places formed into a lovely cornice overhanging the southern side. Two eminences on this ridge vie with each other for the credit of being the true summit.

I turned to enjoy the view, and really I know of no view at all its equal. I had had ample opportunity to enjoy it as we came up, for the men moved very slowly; but those times were rich to me in enjoyment. And now as we were on the top, and the whole scene burst upon us in the early morning light, it was almost more than my capacity of enjoyment was equal to. Mont Blanc, with his attendant *aiguilles*, ever magnificent; some way to the left the Grivola and grand · Paradis—the Grivola as marked as ever by the curved *arête* which had moved my ambition last year; the Grand Combin between us and the Mont Blanc range; all the Zermatt mountains clear and cloudless, and Monte Rosa trying its best to look respectable on this side. But beyond, towards Italy, cloud; and towards the Tyrol, cloud. The glorious peaks of the Mischabel-hörner were striking as ever; and then, most lovely of lovely things, the whole Bernese Oberland, from the Jungfrau to the Galenstock, and I think the Tödi, set as in a picture between the Mischabel and the Weisshorn, and covered with that exquisite blue atmosphere of distance which gives so incalculable a pleasure. The Weisshorn was there, far grander than from the Riffel and its neighbourhood, with a great rocky buttress running down to Zinal, which gives an amazing force to it. The most astonishing of all astonishing peaks, the Rothhorn, looked marvellous and unearthly. And beyond and over these the mass of the Blümlis Alp and Altels, and more to the west the great masses of glacier from the Wildstrubel, Wildhorn, and Diablerets. But most striking to me of all the peaks was the Dent Blanche close by, a peak almost as grand and as white as the Weisshorn seen from the Aeggischhorn. At our feet lay Zermatt, its hotels and church plainly visible.

I think my first impressions, after the first wild delight of finding myself at the top, were those of caution and doubt, whispered, as by an enemy, "Yes: but you are not down safe yet." But never came there a moment's apprehension. A passing shudder there was as I saw the place where "they" fell, and the hopelessness of arresting such a fall.

But my guides were impatient to descend. They had insisted on our leaving our ice-axes below the final peak, and I think they now began to realize their mistake. For we had to descend a slope of snow lying 1½ feet thick upon rock at an angle of about 45°, increasing in steepness till it ended in an absolute precipice, and we had but one axe to stop the fall of all three, if any one should slip; while full upon our recollection flashed the memory of what happened on the first descent. Well for us was it that it was early in the day, and we ourselves fresh and strong and in capital condition. There are some positions in which the sense of danger is the best security against it. And I never wish for a stronger stimulant than the certainty that my guide will not hold me if I slip. I had this full certainty on the present occasion; for the slope is in parts so smooth that it is very difficult for the most prehensile feet to gain a good grip, and prehensile power was not one of the few accomplishments of my guides. However, the crust of frozen snow (still frozen at that early hour) gave something of the hold to the hands which the feet wanted. And at length, after many delays and many ridiculous exhibitions of incapacity, we stood at the foot of the peak, and all danger might be said to be at an end.

Then we discarded the rope, ran down the sides as best we might, bringing small avalanches of stones in our train, stopped to take a last meal at the hut, and then started off again in our descent. Most inferior guides have a great notion of frequent eating and drinking, and as two hours was the very outside that my companions could exist without recruiting famished nature, I soon grew wearied of them, and, breaking from them, reached Zermatt by 4.30 P.M., long before I was expected, and in twelve hours from the start in the morning. There I learnt that all Zermatt had discovered us that morning at the top, and turned out to look at us. At dinner that evening a most tasteful bouquet was sent to me by Madame Seiler, and a bottle of champagne from M. Seiler, while a discharge of improvised cannon completed the commemoration.

One of the most astonishing, and, I must add, humiliating, things that happen to the climber is the nature of the remarks that are made to him upon climbing. A gentleman said to me that afternoon, "Have you been up the Matterhorn? Well then, I suppose you will try Mont Blanc." So marvellously does the belief cling to many Englishmen that Mont Blanc is the hardest, instead of one of the easiest of mountains. I hope no one who reads these pages will follow this gentleman's advice, and take his preliminary training for Mont Blanc by ascending the Matterhorn. If it be attempted, it should be attempted by men who have won their experience and proved their powers on many a crag and many an ice-slope. For them there is, I believe, no great danger; and there is an irresistible attraction.

So long as the Matterhorn retains its marvellous outline, and those subtle curves which made Ruskin call it 'a rearing horse of rock,' so long will men love it, and yearn after it, and count it the king of mountains.

Thus Julius Elliott concludes his modest and graphic account of the ascent of the Matterhorn.

He returned to Brighton, and in the summer of 1869 the rest and refreshment which had again become necessary, were again sought in Switzerland. He had it in contemplation then to ascend the Schreckhorn, usually considered the second most difficult mountain in Switzerland; and with this object in view he started from Grindelwald on July 26th. He had with him a porter from Zermatt, and Biner, his own guide, who had accompanied him in almost all his ascents. In this guide, Biner, Mr. Elliott had the greatest and most well-deserved confidence. The party were to pass the night in the cave at Kastenstein. They were accompanied by the Rev. P. W. Phipps, who had with him Baumann, the Grindelwald guide, and who had intended to leave them next morning, and to cross the Strahleck. The morning of the 27th, however, was so fine, that both parties determined to attempt the Schreckhorn; Mr. Phipps going separately with his guide, so as to leave Mr. Elliott free to ascend at his own rapid rate.

The two parties did not follow precisely the same route; but at nine o'clock they were within hailing distance, although separated by about a quarter of an hour's climb. The first party (Mr. Elliott's) had at this moment reached the end of the snow, and only had before them half an hour's climb to ascend the last rocks. The second party was roped; Mr. Elliott's was not. All the difficulties had been apparently overcome; the parties *jodelled* to each other in congratulation; and the first party prepared to pass from the snow to the rocks. The porter, who had been leading, and cutting the steps, now passed on to the rocks, but called out that he was not firm. At that moment Mr. Elliott, who was next him, sprang on to the rocks, and, falling backwards, began to glide down the long snow slope that falls, at a tremendous depth below, on to the Lauter-Aar glacier. Biner succeeded in catching Mr. Elliott by the arm, but it slipped through his grasp; and so he swiftly glided away far from all human help. It was difficult to believe that that swift and unbroken sweep down the snow was death; but it was death; and without a cry or sound he passed away!

The guides declared, with truth, that it was impossible to descend the slope, and that nothing remained but to return to Grindelwald, and to send a party round by another route to the spot on the glacier where the body was presumed to be lying. Before leaving the place Baumann was lowered as far as the ropes of the party would allow, to shout and see if he could obtain either an answer or a view of the body, if it had lodged anywhere. The attempt was useless. It appeared that this slope is specially mentioned in Ball's "Alpine Guide" as dangerous; and as sending down avalanches on the least disturbance—a character, it will be seen by what occurred later, it fully deserved. The descent was difficult from the state of the snow, and it took nearly nine hours for the two parties, now joined, to reach Grindelwald. Herr Bohren, of the Adler Hotel, at once sent off six of the best guides, with three days' provisions, to cross by the Upper Grindelwald glacier to the Lauter-Aar glacier, and to recover the body. Early the next morning another party of four, including the guides present at the accident, followed in their traces. In eighteen hours this last party returned, having reached the spot where the body must have fallen, as marked by the furrow made in the slope above; but as they found no trace on the glacier, or the cave, of the guides, it was evident that the first expedition had succeeded in recovering the body, and were engaged in bringing it by some easier route to Grindelwald. At last, fifty-four hours after the party of six guides had started, late at night, their lights were seen coming down the rocks by the side of the lower glacier. They had succeeded in finding the body at once. It had sustained little injury, but it was evident that death must have been instantaneous. The spot where it had fallen had been quickly found; but the ice there was deeply crevassed, and it had been difficult to remove it. No sooner had the party withdrawn it to a more secure place, than an avalanche of rocks and snow came down the slope, covering the very spot on which it had lain!

"From Tuesday evening," says a friend, writing from Grindelwald, "till Thursday at midnight these men had been constantly in motion; they had to use the greatest caution in approaching the place where he lay, and it was at the risk of their lives that they removed him. Then they had to carry him back over glacier after glacier, winding among the solitary places, four of them carrying him, two cutting steps in the ice. Throughout all this journey their care of the body was wonderful. Men who had not known and cared for Julius would have refused—would have said it was simply impossible to carry the body uninjured over such places. Several times their provisions ran short; and when at last they arrived at midnight on Thursday, utterly worn out, and Bohren was sending them straight to bed, they said, 'No, we have found him, we have brought him here; we will not leave him till we have done *all* for him that the hands of men can do.' So they went straight to the *pasteur's* house, and there these rough and weary men laid out and tended the body of their friend with a woman's gentleness and care before they suffered their eyes to sleep, or the temples of their head to take any rest. That was love. Indeed, under no circumstances, not if he had died at home in his bed, could the last offices have been performed for him with a more tender and reverential care than by these honest-hearted men, to whom his courage, his manliness, and his goodness had made him so dear. I saw all the guides, and Bohren translated to them the few words I said. I told them how Julius had always accounted the Swiss guides as amongst his truest friends. And now, I added, it has fallen to the lot of those guides to perform the last offices of friendship which any friend can render to him here. They showed great feeling, and said they wished themselves to lay the stone upon his grave. They did so: and pieces of Grindelwald marble were arranged around it by Herr Bohren, in order, as he said, that Mr. Elliott might have all that Grindelwald could give him."

Before concluding the narrative, a few questions of interest will naturally arise in the mind of the reader. They have been asked in anticipation, and been answered by him who is most competent to do so. They concern the ice-axe and the roping :—

" There are two things," he says, " on which every climber more or less depends for safety—the ice-axe and the rope; yet in this fatal instance both were wanting. How came it that Julius Elliott lost his axe? How came it that he was not roped?

" The first question may be answered with comparative certainty. The violence of the unexpected fall jerked it from his hand. It was seen gliding after him down the slope, a few feet behind, but it was never found.

" It is not so easy to account satisfactorily for the absence of the rope. It will suffice to say that it was no chance omission, but his own deliberate decision, in answer to the suggestion of the guides. A rope is a great hindrance to rapid climbing upon rocks, by the delays and entanglements it involves. The safety it gives is at the cost of only one man moving at a time ; even then, if the rocks are rotten, or the snow-incline too steep, the fall of one may imperil the lives of all. It becomes a temptation, therefore, to an active and experienced climber, to dispense with it upon occasions ; and in this case, no doubt, the temptation was doubly strong from the individual excellence of each member of the party. Had one of them been wanting in experience or power, the rest would have sacrificed their own convenience and speed to afford confidence and security to him. But Julius Elliott was on a footing of equality with his guides, and was rather accepted by them as a leader than as one needing help. These were Biner's words a few days before the accident :—' M. Elliott, c'est un des premiers *guides*. Il a la tête d'un chamois, et surtout sur les rochers.'

" Most cautious and considerate where the safety of others was in question, there must have seemed to him no need for special precaution in this instance for himself. Moreover, he declared, again and again, that he had never been in such peril as in the ascent of the Weisshorn, from being roped to an incompetent porter.

"In addition, it may reasonably be doubted whether even the rope would have saved him on the spot. Imagine three men in the act of ascending a very steep stair of steps cut in the snow. The first is Lauber, the second Julius Elliott, the third Biner. They have reached the base of the rocks, which run down to their left. The leading man, Lauber, by Julius's direction, gets on to the rocks. He finds them rotten, as the rocks of the Schreckhorn in so many places are, and he exclaims that he is insecure. On hearing this, the second man, Julius, turns aside, and springs to the rocks upon his left, hoping, no doubt, to obtain a better landing-place. He slips, and falls!

"The first intimation of the accident received by Biner, the third and lowest, is the rushing sound of the fall above him; and, looking up, he grasps at the arm nearest him, with his left hand, as it passes. But Julius has already acquired too great velocity from the exceeding steepness of the incline, and he slips through Biner's grasp.

"'Had I been able to hold him,' were Biner's words, 'I should have gone too.'

"Consider, therefore, what the chance would have been of Lauber's ability to support such a fall in his insecure position, had he been roped to him. And consider what the chance would have been of Biner's holding, had the weight of two men, roped together, fallen on him?

"And whilst with aching hearts we bow our heads, and avert our eyes from what is needless pain to dwell upon, may we not now think of him only, as ever affectionately, generously brave, so in the last act of life, in his unselfishness, saving others?"

Dr. Griffith truly says:—

He was no mere citizen of a city, who had ventured his life among the mountains in order to acquire a name. He had been used to the wild scenes of Cumberland, where there is as real danger as elsewhere.

In speaking of the steep ridge of the Matterhorn, he said, "I fancy I have climbed as bad cliffs alone in Cumberland." No one finds fault with a guide because he climbs about the Alps. I have never yet found any one to say a word against the chamois-hunter, who leaps from crag to crag. And he who from his boyhood had thus been brought up; he who in his iron frame was as strong or stronger than his guides; he who in his prac-tised step could balance himself as few others could; he who with his short sight, but keen eye, could discern the safest path upon an unknown mountain, and at times advise better than his guides; he who felt that unroped he was as safe as if he were roped, and that if anything did happen he would not be accessory to the death of another—he was permitted to slip. . . . God shows His will through the will of His people at times, and we must acknowledge the will of God not unfrequently in the will of His servants. I know the strong prejudice that exists in some men's minds on this subject; but I will only say, "Let each man be persuaded in his own mind." The man who has been accustomed to such scenes is in no more danger there than the person who has not been used to them is in various other circumstances. Julius Elliott has not described to any one his feelings as he ascended the mountain that day. But I know that he was worshipping God in his spirit, and not only preparing for more active discharge of his duties, but preparing his spirit for deeper, holier, more real communion with his Saviour, on the steep side and in the pure air of those Alpine heights. With the weight of his great work for a time removed, with his Prayer-book over his heart, and prayer in his heart, I doubt not he was meet for any change, as I know he was meet in another ascent. I have met him here in the streets of Brighton—he was ready then. God met him in the height of the Alps, and we doubt not, we have no reason to doubt, his heart was ready then.

The interment took place at 4 P.M. on Friday, July 30th. Owing to the kindness of Herr Bohren, the chief man of the place, and of the Swiss *pasteur*, the service and all the arrangements were admirably conducted. The coffin was carried by six guides, followed by his friend the Rev. P. W. Phipps and by Biner,— mourners themselves, indeed, yet conscious representatives of other mourners, still nearer and dearer, though far away! Other guides followed, and in this order all entered the church. A large bunch of Alpine roses was picked by the Grand Duchess of Baden, and laid on the coffin by her wish, to be afterwards reserved, and sent to his sisters. The service was read as in England, by the English chaplain, the Swiss *pasteur* walking by his side, and reading the sentences in German alternately with him. There was a fairly large congregation of English and Swiss. Before leaving the church, an address was made by the Swiss *pasteur* to the guides, and he held up to them the Prayer-book which had been found in Julius's pocket, showed them how it was underlined, told them how good he was, and how prepared to die, and how worthy of his well-known father. They then proceeded to the grave, which is close by the church door, and there the service was concluded by the chaplain. It was a most impressive scene.

The eloquent words of Archdeacon Garbett will form a fitting conclusion to this touching narrative:—

The whole form and countenance of Julius Elliott bore the impress of the inner man. There was a singular breadth and muscularity of chest and shoulder, with arms of unwonted development and power. It was a frame fitted for athletic feats and a mastery of the arts of the cragsman and mountaineer. To this, like his father, he added a light and bounding step, elastic with vigour and joyousness. The countenance was very attractive; a broad and open forehead, with clear bright eyes, and a mouth full of a certain sweet resolution and a gentle manliness. The chin and lower jaw manifested resolution and firmness of purpose, like his father's. He who had it could not fear. The expression showed both power of thought and action, and ever beamed with an innocent and boyish radiancy, which went straight to one's heart. Nobody could gaze on that face and figure without spontaneous trust and love.

Wherever he went there was an atmosphere of goodness and manifest holiness about him. All men loved him. The very guests at the *table d'hôte* at Grindelwald were heard to say that, if any were ready for a sudden call, and death without warning, it was Julius Elliott. Think for a moment of the many ways men die in, and then say if Julius Elliott's was not a happy one. Look at him a minute before his end. He is full of happiness and joy in the midst of God's grandest works, almost in those spirits which Scottish superstition thinks an augury of death. The foot slips! He falls! There comes a descent down the steep, ever faster and faster; a consciousness of coming death, a committing of the soul to God through the blood of Him that died, a sudden vision of all his past life, a moment's pang, and then the pure spirit stands with the eye of God lovingly on him, on the ever-lasting shore. O stainless Christian life! O happy death! Even the heathen poet pronounced that they whom the gods love die young: how much more they whose souls are washed in the blood of Christ, and cradled in the Everlasting Arms! Nay, we may go further, and even consider it an answer to his desires. He had often said that he would choose, if it pleased God, a sudden death: and so in the fulness of health, strength, and Christian cheerfulness, he was, so to say, taken and *rapt* away with a tender violence into the world of glory. He was fond of thinking of the sweetness of peace and the eternal quiet, and so he sleeps early " where the wicked cease from troubling, and the weary are at rest."

THE END.

LONDON:
PRINTED BY WILLIAM CLOWES AND SONS,
STAMFORD STREET AND CHARING CROSS.

www.ingramcontent.com/pod-product-compliance
Lightning Source LLC
Chambersburg PA
CBHW031132120726
47905CB00006B/1668